REMEMBER. . .

These Men:
CROCKETT, a man's man of paradoxical inconsistencies, whose driving restlessness will challenge his own legendary greatness.
BOWIE, slave trader, philanderer, fighter, an adventurer of bottomless courage who will fight his last bloody battle in bed.
TRAVIS, hot-headed, impatient, a maverick with the blood of his wife's lovers on his hands, anxious for revenge.
SANTA ANNA, the enemy, tyrannical, obsessive, perverse, feared.

These Women:
KATE, a homely widow whose passion smoulders daringly beneath a homespun dress.
PAULA, a half-breed who sells her body to lavish men but saves her love for the one man who cannot possess her.
POLLY, a beautiful young virgin whose fate will be a monumental and heartbreaking marriage.
LEOTO, the child concubine who awaits the evil abuses of her infamous keeper.

These Men and these Women: Entwined by history. . . caught up in one unforgettable moment in time. . . joined forever at. . . THE ALAMO.

THE
BLAZING
DAWN

James Wakefield Burke

PYRAMID BOOKS   ▲   NEW YORK

THE BLAZING DAWN

A PYRAMID BOOK

Copyright © 1975 by James Burke

Pyramid edition published December 1975

ISBN 0-515-03903-9

Library of Congress Catalog Card Number: 75-29854

Printed in the United States of America

Pyramid Books are published by Pyramid Communications, Inc. Its trademarks, consisting of the word "Pyramid" and the portrayal of a pyramid, are registered in the United States Patent Office.

Pyramid Communications, Inc., 919 Third Avenue, New York, N.Y. 10022

To:

JAMES RICHARD BURKE
A son who is beautifully tolerant of his father's grumblings, profanities, foibles, bad advice—and evils. A young man to whom Fate has attached the blue thread of nobleness and devotion. Pray God his spindle be full.

The boast of heraldry, the pomp of power,
  And all that beauty, all that wealth e'er gave,
Awaits alike the inevitable hour.
  The paths of glory lead but to the grave.

Thomas Gray
(1751—Stokes Poges churchyard)

THE ALAMO

Trailing the threads of their lives behind them over half a hemisphere, four men as dissimilar as the far corners of the universe congress at the old Mission San Antonio de Valero, called Alamo. For three of the men it is the emptying of the spool—the end of the thread. But for the fourth man, his spool is prodigal; he will continue to trail his sheen for a full forty years hence, a black thread that like the spoor of the fitchew will foul and poison all it touches.

Fate, perhaps quixotically, had chosen for the life cord of each man a different color—black, red, white, and purple.

The man trailing the black thread is General Antonio Lopez de Santa Anna, president of the Republic of Mexico. He is on this day forty-two years and thirteen days old. His color tells that he craves power, demands to be recognized; that his sanguine temperament must prevail, his opinion dominate; it has to be his will against all opposition. The black tint of his thread warns that he is capable of negating everything else to achieve these things.

To James Bowie, the knife fighter, Fate had at birth attached a red thread, perhaps because of the trail of blood he was destined to leave in his wake during his forty years on this earth. But the red cord foretokened more. It meant vital force, the positive impact of will, the righteous faith behind the determination to win; it declared a great courage, and hunger for that which offers the most intensity of living—the present.

To the oldest of the four men, David Crockett, the frontiersman who brought cheer to any crowd he joined, Fate had fifty years before tied a white thread, perhaps to match the white hat he never in all his life had on his head but which for millions of David Crockett followers would symbolically be his. That color—or absence of color—revealed the man to be light-hearted, expansive, uninhibited; a happy cheerful spirit, full of hope and vitality. It signified that he liked to be free from burdens and restrictions, that he welcomed the warmth of sunlight—a man who loved change for the sake of change.

But for William Barret Travis, the Alabama gallant, whose spindle is about to wind empty when he has tagged a mere twenty-six years, four months and twenty-five days of life behind him, there could be none but the purple thread that signifies the timelessness of eternity. His color revealed a man of fretful and inconsistent behavior, one constantly in need of emotional and biological stimulation, and who, whenever rejected, experienced mental agitation; it is a color that tattles of femininity and sensitivity, boasts of devotion and bluffness, reveals arrogance and impetuousness. Purple meant for Travis that he not only craved to be associated with glamor, but at the same time wanted to charm and delight others—to exert a degree of fascination over them.

Fate. What is the image of Fate? What does the face of Fate look like? In the imagination of myth Fate is materialized as a woman—or rather, three women. Fate! *Moirai*. The *Moirai* are given names—Clotho, Lachesis, and Atropos. These ladies are always present at our births and there they determine the course of our lives. Each has a different task. Clotho, the Spinner, holds the distaff; Lachesis, the Alloter, controls the spindle; Atropos, the Inflexible, cuts the thread.

In the circumstance of our story, is it not possible to conceive of Fate as being other than these three women? Why not accept the *Devil* as Fate? There he is, big as life, Mephisto in person, sitting smugly upon the wall of the Alamo attired in nineteenth-century elegance, glowing with supreme exultation. For today he will gather to himself a basketful of empty spools. He is about to enjoy the feast of his lifetime,—violence, barbarity, savagery, inhumanity—the beefsteak of his existence. And looking back into the lives of our four leading men, he can rejoice in the human foibles he most cherishes: envy, pride, anger, vanity, covetousness, greed, and gluttony in the pursuit sex. Assuredly on this day the Devil is a most pleased and joyful fellow.

It is Sunday. The year is 1836. The date: March 6th. The drama is to be enacted within the two-and-one-half acre area of the old mission-fortress Alamo. Time has already wheeled away the first one hundred and twelve minutes of this bloody Sunday.

A man, naked to the waist, lies in his marquee some four hundred yards outside the walls of the Alamo. He is drowsing in the euphoric half-sleep of one well-dosed with opiate. His head rests on the thigh of a girl scarcely fourteen years old. She languidly fans away huge mosquitoes from the man's handsome, heavy-featured face; now and then she bends over his chest to interrupt the landing of one of the slow-moving parasites, and in so doing her young peach-like breasts brush his cheek. Soon the man will awake from his self-induced doze. Soon the fierce and blood-soaked Sunday will begin. The man is Mexico's General Santa Anna. This girl mistress in his service is not the first in his life. She is only one of a long list of unripe maidens that this remarkable Creole-Mexican will acquire in his long and stormy life, as he desperately tries to emulate Napoleon Bonaparte in the western half of the world.

The furnishings of the marquee are elegant: silver teapots and cream pitchers imported from England, Meissen china from Germany, crystal tumblers and de-

11

canters with gold stoppers—such magnificent things as the child *amante* had never dreamed of before. She sits beside the reclining president-general on his Empire bed, her legs like a child's drawn up under her. She is completely nude, and with the innocent decorum of the very young, unashamed and unabashed. In Santa Anna's presence she has learned to disrobe casually. It is his desire to gaze upon her nude body with an inspired look in his dark eyes. And whenever he comes to her he expects to find her awaiting his pleasure.

His pleasures are erotic, and erratic. At the most unexpected moments he will throw himself upon her and proceed to make violent love. Again he will approach her and sink his fingers hard into her flesh, and when her eyes brim with tears he will turn away with a beatific smile on his lips. And yet he can, too, be very loving and gentle. Sometimes, softly, he will run his dark hands over her smooth belly and small, firm breasts. He will drop to his knees beside the bed, draw her to the edge, open her limbs and implant kisses on the nubile flesh of her inner thighs, culminating in the kiss that seals all kisses. Lowering his mouth to that succulent pericarp, he will feast upon it like it was an everlastingly tender flower. All this the child tolerates with a vague, sweet devotion, always submissive and with complete complaisance. Whatever his desires and his demands of her, his beseeching eyes constantly seek assurance from her face that she is responsive and impassioned by his sado-masochistic lovemaking.

Whenever her lord is not present she quickly slips into one of the silken robes or costumes which the great man has showered upon his new toy. Whenever his voice rises, in the forepart of the marquee, she lifts her big soft eyes and glances tenderly in his direction.

A fortnight ago this girl was a child playing in her mother's patio. Then a "god" bedecked in glittering gold braid swept into the town amid waving banners and the trumpeting of lively airs and the stirring *Te Deum*. Never had anyone in San Antonio seen such splendid uniforms: the dragoons in their red short coats

12

and vivid blue trousers, their high black helmets decorated with horsehair, the men armed with lances and pennons, with sabers, with carbines, and holster pistols. But this stately god riding in the fore of the column was the most elegant of all. With his indigo blue jacket and his slashed trousers disappearing into the silver guards of his stirrups, Supreme General Antonio Lopez de Santa Anna Perez de Lebron, Emperor-Dictator of all of Mexico, waved his sword like a lord as he rode. In golden epaulets and red frogging, and a high-peaked hat with black plumes that undulated softly with his horse's every stride, he surveyed the crowd with sensuous eyes. And then these eyes glimpsed—and held—the girl as he passed.

Santa Anna could not put the vision of the young beauty out of his mind. When his marquee was set up with its elegant trappings, and his royal bed arranged, it seemed a lonely and empty place. The Emperor-Dictator called General Manuel Fernandez Castrillon, one of his most trusted aides, and ordered him to conduct a search for the nubile girl. The next day Castrillon brought to the *generalissimo's* marquee a dozen young maidens but all were sent away with scathing denouncements; none of them was the girl that had stirred Santa Anna so deeply.

Searching for houses of occupation for the officers, General Castrillon entered the dwelling of a middle-aged lady and her daughter, the latter strikingly beautiful. Her name was Melchora Iniega Barrea. The mother and daughter, well-bred and intelligent, seemed panic-stricken at having to give up their home. Castrillon knew he had found the girl his president-general coveted. He put Santa Anna's lecherous proposition up to them. The mother felt indignantly insulted, saying that her deceased husband had been an officer in the Mexican army; and finally, to put the discussion on a somewhat more moral basis, agreed that Santa Anna could have her daughter provided he was prepared to marry her. On that decision she stood firm.

General Castrillon bore the disappointing news to

13

Santa Anna but suggested a stratagem. Colonel Jose Minon, he said, always aspired to be an actor, and was a man who would do anything to please his commanding general. Colonel Minon was sent for, given his orders. Necessary vestments were acquired from the San Fernando church, and in the *generalissimo's* marquee the fake marriage took place. Santa Anna at once renamed Melchora Iniega. Leota was a name his hero Napoleon had been particularly fond of and Santa Anna favored it himself. "It seems so perfect for this little flower," he proclaimed after the bogus wedding.

Leota's mother happily went back to her home in full possession of her dwelling. Santa Anna, too, is happy; by no means a mystic, he nevertheless believes, as did his historical hero Napoleon Bonaparte, that a successful military campaign is not quite possible without the blessing of the love of a young maiden for the commanding general.

From the shadows of his marquee Leota looks with adoration—or is it gratitude?—upon her lord's expressive countenance, his dark, fine eyes, his rampant black pompadour, his thick, almost negroid lips, his sallow pallor, his melancholy air—"placid sadness," Leota's mother had called it with her own simple admiration.

When the massacre of the Alamo is over, this child will be sent in Santa Anna's private coach, alone and lonely, to Mexico to be ensconced in a house on one of the president-general's estates near the city of Jalapa, to be ever at his beck and call. How many others before and after her Leota will never know. But her life will be quite content, far away from San Antonio and her mother, in a strange land.

Lieutenant Colonel William Barret Travis crouches atop the three-foot wide stone and adobe wall of the old mission. The near-full moon, partially obscured by scuds of cold clouds, lights the plain around the Alamo and a chill north wind is blowing over the sixteen-foot wall. Below, the languid river, flowing to its confines

14

from the early rains, reaches toward the mission like a huge shimmering bolo blade. Santa Anna's soldiers had days before cleared the space between the river and the mission's walls of brush trees, live oak, cacti, and mesquite; and sadly cut and burned have been the padres' beloved *alamos*—cottonwood trees—among which the mission had stood nearly a century and a half and for which the Texan settlers had nicknamed the old mission.

Alamos: The Alamo. Santa Anna has made sure there will be no *impedimenta* in the path of his engineers and soldiers who must command and mount the walls. Out there, Colonel Travis estimates, are five thousand Mexican troops. Inside the Alamo are one hundred and eighty-three Americans. Beyond the farthermost bend of the San Antonio River, a good six hundred yards distant, he can see the Mexican army headquarters. General Santa Anna's marquee is darkened while the president-general sleeps before the battle. But outside, all around the headquarters, there is feverish activity.

Two flags are pulsating in the night breeze above the supreme general's headquarters. One of the flags is of the new Republic of Mexico, designated by President-General Santa Anna himself for the nation whose government he has usurped. It embodies Santa Anna's cynical hypocrisy, the big lie without which no dictator can succeed in his megalomaniacal schemes. The flag flaunts the tricolor of white, green, and red in vertical stripes: white denoting the purity of the Catholic religion, green boasting independence, red for the union of the Spanish element with the Mexican: and in one corner is the national coat of arms, an eagle perched on a cactus holding a snake in his beak, the famous Eagle and Serpent of Aztec mythology. The other flag, truly representative of Santa Anna the man himself, is the blood red "no quarter" flag, the twin of another which the Mexican general ordered raised above the bell tower of San Fernando church ten days ago, when Colonel Travis answered with a cannon shot his demand for the unconditional surrender of the Alamo fort, its men and works. The blood red flag means that when the assault upon the Alamo comes it will be inspired by the sounding of the *deguello*, whose musical equivalent of no mercy, whose not-unpleasant bloodthirsty cry, a dark, modulated succession of low C notes, has become Santa Anna's personal battle signature since it had first blown fortune to him at the battle of Medina twenty-three years ago, starting him on his climb to the "benevolent" dictatorship of all of Mexico.

Associated with the most terrible of blood baths, the *deguello* had for centuries been the signal for beheading and throat-cutting, the fire and death call, exhorting soldiers to extreme mercilessness. It was an alien cry when the Moors first sounded it in Spain long ago and the Spanish had named it after the verb that means "to slit the throat"—*degollar*. Spain in turn used the call in her long war with the Moors, sparing neither age nor sex nor holy man; and it had meant the wanton destruction of not only lives but property.

Santa Anna has vowed to exterminate the Texan forces, to make an example of them, and to frighten the Americans into submission and open the way for Mexican domination all the way to the Pacific coast. Upon crossing the Rio Grande at Laredo, where he had been a guest at a fancy ball staged in his honor, he had issued decrees about the punishment in store for the Texans. He would execute, he said, all leaders of the revolution, confiscate Texas property to pay for the expense of the war, drive all participants in the uprising from the province, remove all non-participants into the interior of Mexico, treat as pirates and execute any Americans who had come into Texas as part of the volunteer armed forces, and, finally, liberate all slaves while forbidding future settlement to all Anglo-Americans.

As Colonel Travis watches from his perch upon the Alamo wall it becomes clear that the all-out assault upon the fort is being set for early morning. He raises himself cautiously. For long minutes he listens. In the darkness he can hear the shuffling of hundreds of feet, sandals clopping on the damp ground—the rain has ceased barely an hour since—as the various battalions are forming into columns of attack. About two hundred yards beyond the wall, arrayed in a semicircle, is the Mexican artillery, consisting mainly of two- and four-pounders, with several heavier pieces and two howitzers, which Travis judges to be eight- or twelve-pounders. According to the commitment of the enemy cannon, the main assault will be concentrated upon the northeast wall. This section, at its south ending, connects the chapel with the two-story barracks and is only half as high as the rest of the wall. It was here that four days ago the Mexicans had placed a huge charge of powder and blown an opening. Colonel David Crockett and his volunteers, however, had quickly closed the breach and thrown up a lunette of earthen breastwork, upon which they mounted two four-pounders. Inside the crescent of Mexican cannon and about a hundred yards from the wall, Santa Anna's cavalry is being drawn up. In front of the cavalry and almost directly under the wall, *los zapadores,* the Mexican engineers, together with the infantry, are forming. In the semi-darkness Travis is able to count eighteen scaling ladders, five elevator platforms, several large crowbars, numerous axes and mauls.

Santa Anna's strategy brings into focus the savagery that lurks in the mind of that self-styled "Napoleon of the West." This ingenious assault plan will make it mandatory that his own men cut down any of their comrades who falter or retreat. If the *zapadores* are repulsed, the cavalry will turn them back upon the wall or cut them to pieces. Should the cavalry become disorganized by fire from the bastion wall and fail in their barbarous duty, the artillery will train its cannon upon the combined units. It is to be a do-or-die attack.

There is little doubt in Colonel Travis' mind as to the outcome of this battle. One hundred and eighty-three Americans inside the mission walls—many sick, all fatigued and hungry, their outside water supply cut off—cannot by the most optimistic reasoning withstand Santa Anna's cannon and gun and bayonet and sword for long. A well has been dug in the courtyard of the mission, but its clouded water is suspected by Dr. Amos Pollard of being the cause of the wave of dysentery that has for days plagued the men.

For a week now Travis and his staff have known that no relief can be expected from General Sam Houston at Washington-on-the-Brazos or from Colonel James W. Fannin at Goliad. It was that many days since General Houston had sent final clear and precise orders, both to Travis as commander of the regulars and cavalry and to Jim Bowie, in command of the Volunteers Aid, to abandon the Alamo, blow up its works, and march the men to Goliad, ninety miles southeast: there to join with Fannin's force of approximately four hundred and await the arrival of the new army being formed under command of himself. Led by Travis, the little force behind the walls of the Alamo bastion had held a consultation and elected to remain in the mission and fight, in defiant contradition of Houston's orders. "Victory or death!" was their cry.

As Travis is about to lower himself from the wall, the grating of a ladder against the masonry freezes his attention. A Mexican scout on the wall? As stealthily as an alert cat, Travis moves toward the noise, his hand closing around the black leather grips of his *Kavallerie* sword. Excitement flushes his cheeks. Since leaving his wife and son in Alabama this youthful lawyer-soldier has learned to relish the taste of danger. He has vowed never to leave Texas. Here he has found the excitement of venture in a brazen new world, where a man must be bold and sure of himself to stay alive. Throwing himself flat on the top of the wall, he waits. He listens. But his excitement betrays him; he coughs. The Mexican, incautious, unwisely leaps in the direction of human sound. Travis lifts himself, sword extended. The intruder in mid-air does not feel the long blade as it passes neatly through his breast, impaling him. He ex-

18

periences only a sudden vast emptying of strength as Travis draws the sword from his body, allowing blood to spurt as if from a fountain directly from his heart. The dying Mexican gives a groan, not of pain but rather of surprise. How quick and quiet and painless death can be. *"Dios! Dios! Dios! . . ."*

Travis ejects the soldier's body from the wall. It falls to the ground with the sound of a wet sack of wheat. He wipes the blood from the blade of his Prussian sword, sheathes it and lets himself down into the courtyard. That will put an end to the Mexican reconnaissance. What intelligence did Santa Anna seek? The three Mexican traitors who went over to the enemy last week surely told all there was to know. Now he must alert the men of the Alamo, tell them their thirteen day wait is over. The assault is about to begin.

But first, he must see Jim Bowie.

Bowie! Jim Bowie, the fighting man! What a loss, Travis thinks, as he considers the imminent battle. Misfortune had dealt Bowie a double blow. First he had dislocated a hip in a fall from a scaffolding while helping the men position one of the big cannons on the roof of the chapel; then, lying helplessly on his cot, he had developed a typhoid-pneumonia. Unable to stand on his feet, he had called Travis to his cot and turned over command of his volunteers to the cavalry officer fourteen years his junior.

As the youthful Colonel Travis crosses the yard he glances toward the sky. If overwhelming the Texans numerically were not enough, the weather, too, is with the Mexicans. The freezing northern wind has carried away the clouds, and there will be no morning fog to foul the Mexican guns. The Mexican armament consists mostly of flint fire-lock pieces requiring the use of exposed powder; rain or damp weather, even heavy fog, would cause them to misfire. The infantry is equipped with *escopetas*, short carbine-type rifles with flintlock plates, and .69 caliber flint muskets and a small number of old-fashioned *misquelets*, whose mainspring is on the outside of the lock plate and exposed—all subject to

19

bad-weather fouling. There are a few muzzle loaders and a scattering of pistols, mainly in the hands of the officers. The *escopetas* and pistols are short range weapons, and inaccurate. Once fired, they require an inordinate lapse of time for reloading. At close quarters the Mexicans are prone to abandon them in preference for bayonets and sabers, with which they are far more accurate. The Americans also have flintlocks; but many are in possession of converted cap-and-ball rifles and percussion pistols, which they have brought with them from the east. And the Americans, they are deadly marksmen—all.

Travis cannot help but admire his adversary. Santa Anna is determined to destroy him. What would be his own bent of mind, were he in the Mexican commandant's boots? Victory would be uppermost in his mind, of course. But would victory gain for Santa Anna immortality? *Immortality. That's the thing.*

How cunning the mind! As William Barret Travis strides across the yard of the Alamo, his thoughts are swept far away from killing, imminent death, weapons of destruction, and battle. He sees himself in time past, back in Alabama. He sees his angular six-foot frame bent over law books in Judge James Dellett's law offices; he sees himself standing before his teen-age pupils, where he teaches in an exlusive girls' school while studying law at night. A quick grimace crosses his face as he thinks of Rosana Cato, one of his pupils whom he seduced in his quarters during a thunderstorm; he thinks of his marriage to her. He sees frame after frame of his life, like quick vivid portraits in flashes of lightning: Rosana's jealous fits because of his promiscuity; Rosana threatening "to do likewise;" the birth of their son. . . . And there are other frames, dark haunting frames: the infidelity of Rosana; his abusing her in the futile hope of assuaging his wounded pride; the midnight bark of a cap-and-ball pistol; a young man lying on the plantation lawn with a hole in his head; a young lawyer swimming his horse across the Alabama

River by starlight, setting out for Texas. Had he come to Texas seeking a rendezvous with death, plagued by doubt and guilt? Had Rosana really been unfaithful? He will never know.

Then there are pleasanter scenes; a quick pain crosses his heart as he thinks of San Felipe, his new home in Texas—and Rebecca Cummings, his fiancée. There's a woman he could be happy with; woman enough for any man. He glances at the cat's eye ring on his finger, her gift to him at their last meeting—her token of everlasting love. His heart warms. Texas! By God! What a place! A man can find glory here!

The blood of the slain Mexican is in Travis' nostrils. A surge of the wild recklessness with which he has consumed his life rises within him. The Alamo and immortality! His frame trembles with exhilaration. Upborne by a sense of supremacy, he is impatient for the battle to begin.

"I shall never surrender or retreat ... I am determined to sustain myself as long as possible and die like a soldier who never forgets what is due his own honor and that of his country. Victory or death!" Why had he replied with those words to General Houston's orders to abandon the Alamo? Now, here in a land far removed from his native Alabama, he, Bill Travis, the youthful *lothario* who was adored by all the young girls and rebuked by their mothers, is about to breathe life into those heroic words—*his* life. He grins as he recalls some candid words flung at him by his friend and mentor, Judge James Dellett, in a rare moment of exasperation: "William Barret Travis, you're a goddamned Southern purist—a philandering, perfumed, silken-underclothed, womanizing dandy!" Well, after this battle they can all take another look at Bill Travis. . .

Suddenly a form slips off the wall, blocking Travis' path. Travis' hand grips his sword. "Crockett!" Travis is surprised and relieved.

His heart warms at the sight of David Crockett. If Jim Bowie is a man, David Crockett is a man's man. Travis suddenly feels pride and renewed strength in thinking of Crockett and Bowie. With men like these at his side, perhaps victory is not so impossible?

"Colonel," David Crockett says, "I've got my men positioned on the wall. I figure old Santa Anna's gonna hit us by dawn."

"I'm afraid you're right, Crockett. I'm on my way to inform Bowie. Want to come along?"

"Naw. Reckon I'll get back up on the wall with my men. My Tennesseans want the first crack at the Mexicans when they charge. I'd sure love to get that strutting dictator in the sights of old Betsy." He lovingly pats his long rifle. "He'd wish by the horns of the Devil he'd never come into Texas."

From his cot in the chapel of the Alamo Jim Bowie raises himself on an elbow. He studies Travis' face. At the foot of Bowie's cot sits Sam, Bowie's faithful slave, and in a remote part of the room, resting on a pallet of Indian blankets, is a young woman. In her arms she enfolds her child Angelina Arabella. Sam and the woman look anxiously at Travis. Nobody speaks.

Finally, from Travis: "Jim, you all right? No pain?"

Jim Bowie ignores the solicitude. "When, Bill?" He fixes the young officer with his steady slate-grey eyes.

"About daybreak, I figure."

The woman gives a little gasp. Bowie and Travis turn to face her. Her eyes are like a frightened doe's. She raises her face to them, imploring. In a kindly voice Travis speaks to her. "Mrs. Dickinson, Sam here will take you and the child to the sacristy. You'll be safer there. Would you like me to send your husband to you?"

The woman chokes on words but nods her approval. Colonel Bowie to his servant: "Sam, find Lieutenant Dickinson and tell him where his wife and child are."

Travis approaches the woman and child, bends his tall frame, and drops on one knee. He holds the child's cheek in his hand a moment, then pulls from his small finger a gold ring, looks tenderly at the black cat's eye stone mounted in it. He takes off his *kepis* and works a

22

thread out of the gold trim on its visor, slips it through the ring and loops it around the child's neck. "I won't have any use for this now. Maybe one day *you* will —when you get married."

Alone, Travis and Jim Bowie drop formalities. "Santa Anna will hit us with all he's got," Travis murmurs. "And, as you well know, it will be to the tune of the *deguello*. But by God, Jim, it'll cost him!"

"Any regrets, Bill?"

"For myself, no."

"I mean for not pulling out and blowing up the place."

"Why do you say that, Jim?"

"You know damn well why. Thrice General Sam Houston has ordered us to pull out. The General knows only too well we can't hold the Alamo."

"Jim, I joined the Texas revolution to fight. Not to run. Dying is part of it."

Jim Bowie fixes the young zealot with a hard stare. "But will dying help General Houston win Texas?"

Travis' eyes are burning. "My mind's been made up for days. We stay in the Alamo."

Jim falls silent. When he speaks his voice is charged with irony. "Bill, if we don't die here every goddamn one of us will and ought to be court-martialed."

Travis grins savagely. "If General Houston wants to go by the book, yes. And I cannot say he would be wrong. But there are times, Jim, when an officer *should* ignore his superiors, and I feel this is my time." A strange light comes into his eyes. "Sometimes, Jim, a man is stronger by insubordination."

Jim shifts his six-foot-two frame on the narrow cot, tries to sit up, grimaces in pain and leans back against the wall at the head of the bed. "This is not a time to become philosophical. Santa Anna's got cannon, musket and bayonet out there. General Houston needs all the men he can muster, just to hold Texas territory. And to win he's got to destroy Santa Anna's forces."

"Maybe our dying here is the best way to destroy Santa Anna."

"That's just so much cow shit! Dead men don't fight." Jim Bowie looks hard at Travis. "You're crazy, Bill. And I'm hurt beyond getting on my feet. I don't know which is worse for Texas." He catches a glimpse of the little taunting curve of Travis' lips. "Bill, goddamn you! I'm no more afraid of death than you are!"

"I'm sure you're not afraid of death, Jim. You've proved that all your life." Travis leans down until he is eye-level with the fever-ridden invalid on the cot. "But you mightily hate the thought of dying."

"Goddamn you, Bill! You keep talking about dying. Like you're looking forward to it. Tell me, by what warrant do we stay here and die?"

"No warrant, Jim. But a *cause*."

"And what would that be?"

"Overwhelming opposition will make our glory. The greatest people of a nation are those whom it puts to death. Socrates was the glory of the Athenians, who would not suffer him to live among them. Napoleon was twice expelled from France with ignominy. But Santa Anna is an unlearned butcher. He little knows that by putting us to death here in the Alamo he will make us the glory of Texas. You ask what is my cause. It is liberty—freedom."

"Which is it? Liberty or freedom? There's a difference."

"How so?" The remark puzzles Travis.

Jim Bowie reflects for a time. Then, fixing Travis with a hard stare and carefully choosing his words, he speaks. "A man may have the liberty of a dungeon but not his freedom. I can set my slave, Sam, at liberty, but will the poor devil have his freedom? Not by a damn sight. I can only give him the liberty to find his freedom, and a license to take that liberty. You say we must fight and die here that Texans may have their liberty. Liberty to do what? Liberty to name their own leaders, make their own laws, levy their own taxes, encumber themselves with governmental shackles? Make their own wars? Sure, the liberty to erode away the

24

people's freedom. Remember what Stephen Austin said. " 'Liberty taken to excess always becomes license in the eyes of those in power. Freedom is something that must be gained day by day, even as one must fight for his daily bread. Liberty is only the right to carry on the fight for freedom. When you cease the fight you lose your freedom.' " Jim unlocks Travis' eyes and looks fondly upon Sam. "And one day, Bill, to the horror of Southern sentiment and convictions, Sam's progeny may be given that liberty."

"Never!" Travis enjoins. "It would mean the end of our society's culture. Jim, the world has always been divided into masters and slaves. I believe, as my good uncle the Reverend Alexander Travis taught, that the Creator *intended* the black man to be the servant of the white man. Our Negroes, Jim, need—indeed they beg!—our gentle and civilized hand of guidance. But I do not deny a man the liberty to give his slave freedom when he determines that that slave has earned it. Like the Romans did with their Greek slaves."

Jim Bowie laughs. "You would die in the Alamo for what you conceive as 'liberty.' Liberty to set Sam free but to enslave him in a thousand ways other than personal servitude. Liberty, you say? Freedom? Freedom will not be enough. There must accompany freedom a matching quotient of brotherhood. My good mother Elve used to tell us children a story from the Bible about the Apostle Paul returning to his master a runaway slave whom he had converted to Christianity. Saint Paul made the essential distinction between equality and brotherhood; the former being a fraudulent political concept, the other a free and equal relationship between man and man based on a sense of belonging to one human family whose father is God. You preach liberty and freedom. But you haven't given equality a thought. Bill, you're a goddamn bigot and a hypocrite. All you want is glory. Travis glory."

"My concern here is with victory and liberty. Liberty is my *cause*."

Jim falls silent: a little ironical smile creeps over his

25

fevered face. "With a good cause you can sanctify war and hallow all the killings."

Travis takes a moment to digest this barb, then his eyes light up. "I'll make it the other way around. We'll give Santa Anna such a good fight that the battle itself will sanctify our cause!"

Jim laughs. He painfully pulls himself to the side of the cot and, elbows on his knees, continues to laugh. Travis paces the floor, plainly out of patience with his rival's inability to comprehend his complex mind; if Bowie cannot fathom him, he in turn cannot fathom Bowie, this rough plainsman-knifeman who can think like a killer and still think. He turns abruptly upon Bowie.

"Jim, are you here because you believe in Texans' liberty? Or are you here, really, to protect all that land you've bought at two cents an acre? How many millions of acres have you got deed to? Santa Anna can disenfranchise you on a moment's notice, you know. This *is* Mexican territory—Mexican land—and you, like the rest of us, are insurgent. You quite well know how Santa Anna deals with insurgents. The firing squad—quick and neat." Travis swings a foot onto Jim's cot as a gesture of contempt; the smile on his face becomes sly. "Then you'll never be able to take away all that silver from the lost San Saba mines, would you?"

Jim's anger rises. Here was a revelation—and a mystery. How did Travis, a Johnny-come-lately to Texas, know about his discovery of the San Saba silver?

"Bill Travis, you're taking advantage of me. That kind of contempt triggered one hell of a fight between you and me in the Bexar Tavern a fortnight ago, as you damn well remember. If I were on my feet I'd whip hell out of you—here and now!"

"I'm sure you'd try, Jim Bowie. It would have been a fine fight if Colonel Crockett hadn't ended it. I'm sorry we won't have a chance to finish it one day."

"In that case I'll promise you one thing, Travis! I'll waylay you in some dark corner of hell and give you the whipping you never had—and badly needed—in this life!"

"We've got a date, Jim Bowie. Now, down to the business. What about the men? I want to give Santa Anna one hell of a fight. Who can we count on to fight to the last?"

"David Crockett—for sure."

"I'm glad he's here. Crockett and his long rifle are worth fifty men. I wonder what brought him to Texas?"

Jim laughs. "A two-barrel dream. He wants to become a war hero, like General Jackson. And he wants to kick Old Hickory in the ass. That is, when he becomes President of the United States. You know, don't you, that he was a magistrate in west Tennessee, before he was a Congressman? He kept no records of his court at all, being hardly able to read or write. When the legislature required him by law to keep written records of the actions and judgements of his court, he gave up his judgeship and ran for Congress, where lack of such refinements would be no handicap.

David Crockett possessed the essential attributes of an adventurer: the talent for falling in with strangers, a memory for names and faces, a gift of storytelling, inexhaustible invention, an indomitable valiancy, a remark-

27

able ability for sharp-shooting, and that freedom from conscience that springs from a contempt for pettiness and bureaucracy. He placed great store on "liberty" and "personal rights." When he arrived in Texas to join the Texans in their fight for freedom from Mexico and was about to enroll as a volunteer, he noticed that he would be obliged to uphold "any future government"

"That could be a dictatorship!" he exclaimed. "Liberty! Rights of the individual man! That's what I that might be established.
came to Texas to fight for."

When Judge John Forbes of Nacogdoches administered the oath of allegiance, Crockett outdid them all. He dramatically stopped the proceedings and refused to sign until the wording was changed to "any future *Republican* government."

In whatever group David Crockett appeared he brought the flavor of frontier life. He was a free soul and he sought only the company of those of like temperment. There seemed to have been graven into this liberated man from the canebrake of Tennessee a reluctance to be tied down, to be obligated for long to any engagement, to own anything save his long rifle. He once sold a female slave for four hundred dollars and three hundred acres of good bottom land in Madison County for one hundred dollars to settle a debt so he could "pull up stakes and move on."

In his autobiographical *A Narrative of the Life of David Crockett* he tried to draw a portrait of a casual man, a man who had set himself free. He was a man who could shoulder his rifle, turn his back on his weeping wife and sad-eyed children and trek off into the wilderness, giving no promise of when he would return or if indeed he would return. He explained to a lady in Nacogdoches who inquired about his family: "I have set them free—set them free—they must shift for themselves."

Crockett had been called "The Indian Fighter." But in truth he was a sincere friend of the Indians. Hadn't he led the fight in Congress against President Jackson on behalf of the uprooted Indians? And in doing so he invited a direct challenge from President Jackson—a man whose will few dared oppose.

The rough-hewn rifleman from the Reelfoot Lake country in Tennessee had proved in his three terms in Congress to be a man with a high degree of solemnity. Natural ability had supplied what he lacked in education and welded of him a man of glory and virtue. If Bowie was popular in the southwest as a knife fighter and leader of men, Crockett was reknowned throughout the whole country as a rifle marksman and a shrewd politician. As a Congressman he became the idol of the young rebels of the nation, the students and young people who believed they were misunderstood and were about to be disenfranchized by their elders and betrayed by the politicians who had made a shambles of their society. Crockett suddenly became their man on horseback. He was of just the right mixture—adventurer, hero, and politician—to ride the next political crest in young America. Was he sincere? The world will never know. Jackson, whose keen political acumen told him immediately who were his threats, was quick to sledgehammer Crockett.

David Crockett always carried with him a foretaste of the future, of lands beyond, of realms not yet experienced. And he was a man in a hurry. He drove himself further and further forward toward those glimmering distant frontiers with the haste of one pursued by the hangman. And indeed he might. One of his dreadful lurking fears was to be realized. He often told his friends that he had to achieve all his new experiences before the age of fifty, "because," he said with self-conviction, "I'm tagged never to hit the half century mark." He once proclaimed to a fellow congressman: "Either we live by accident and die by accident, or we live by plan and die by plan. I live by accident and I expect to die by accident."

"Make way for Colonel Crockett!" cried an usher at the President's house one evening, when the famous congressman from the backwoods of Tennessee presented himself with a number of other callers.

"Colonel Crockett makes room for himself!" was the exclamation of David as he strode into the room.

Until manhood David Crockett lived by his wits. He barely could read and write. His syntax jolted people even in an era that cared little about spelling and grammar. His rifle was his substitute for learning. It brought him political success and national fame. He was the man who shot forty-seven bears in one month, who grinned a bear into retreat, who pointed his rifle into a tree and a coon came down to surrender. "When a man can grin and fight, flag a steamboat, or whip his weight in wildcats, what's the use in reading and writing?" he wrote in his autobiography.

David Crockett was the enucleation of a man who became a legend in his own time.

Jim Bowie's slave Sam comes into the room where Jim and Travis are talking. "Marse Jim, I done took Missy Dickinson and her young'un to de sacristy, and I tole de lieutenant where she is. De Lieutenant, he was up on top of de chapel wid de cannon." Delivering himself of this message, Sam goes and takes his place at the foot of Bowie's cot.

"That girl, Lieutenant Dickinson's wife, is hardly eighteen," Travis remarks.

There is more to be said between the two men but each finds it hard to speak his mind. Jim reaches for a jug underneath his cot, takes a long pull, hands the jug to Travis who refuses it. Jim takes another pull. "Bill," he says, "would you like to know what's going to happen to us here in the Alamo? Sam here, he's got a private Zuk that visits him in his sleep and tells him things."

"A Zuk?"

"Yes—you know—like a witchdoc or something. He comes to Sam in his dreams."

Travis steps to the foot of the cot, looks down upon Sam. "Well, Sam, how 'bout it? What does your Mr. Zuk say as to our fate?"

Sam looks questioningly to his master, then slowly turns his brim-white eyes up to Travis.

"Massa William," he says hesitatingly, "I don't know nothin'. Honest I don't."

"Come on, Sam," Jim urges. "Tell the colonel what you told me this morning. Maybe he can make some sense out of it. I sure as hell can't."

Sam lowers his eyes. He looks from Travis to Bowie. His voice drops an octave. "Marse Jim, you don't want me to say what my Zuk tole me."

"Sure, Sam. Tell the colonel."

Sam, speaking from deep within his throat, begins slowly. "My Zuk, he come last night, and he say, 'Everythin' dat's gonna be always wuz, and everthin' dat always wuz is gonna be.'" He casts a furtive glance at Colonel Travis, lowers his brow and mumbles some more. "My Zuk he say, 'You can tell folks dere's a billion stars out dere in de sky and dey believes you. But you tell dem de wall's just been painted and dey has to touch it. Nobody can tell you nothin' dat ain't half asleep in yo' haid already. Sam, you wanna know de secret of death,' he say, 'but you ain't gonna know it 'til you first know de secret of life. Yo' star goes down only to rise and shine on some other mountain.'"

31

"But what did your Zuk tell you of us—and the Alamo?"

Sam continues as if Travis hadn't spoken. "My Zuk, he say, 'Ain't no death. De sun, he shines upon you for a little moment, den you just melts into de wind.' " Sam looks up to Travis. "Zuk say, Massa William, you been goin' up de mountain all yo life—and you gonna git to de top, all right. But, he say, only den will you begin to climb."

Travis walks in thought from the foot of the cot to the thick rock-and-mortar wall; he turns and places his hand gently on Sam's head. "But what of the Alamo, Sam?"

" 'Bout de Alamo? My Zuk he say, 'bout de Alamo, he say tain't gonna fall in Massa William's lifetime."

Travis smiles. "Thanks, Sam. Your Zuk's a reassuring fellow."

Jim takes another pull from his jug. The liquor glows inside his skull, and in sheer desperation of his helplessness, he lashes out at Travis, at his impotence with it all. "What are we!" he explodes. "Rebels? Adventurers? Pirates, as Santa Anna labels us?"

"Let's say we are patriots, Jim," Travis answers quietly.

"Patriots—doomed to die. And you, Bill Travis—damn you!—you're enjoying it immensely." He peers at the tall, younger man. "You're a strange bastard. You're carrying around in that heroic chest of yours something that's eating you up. I'll bet if I'd open you up with my blade here I'd find a little defeated man inside your rib cage, hiding from the world. Is that why you have to take every lady you meet to bed—to prove you're a man on the outside? That long sword continually swinging from your waist—do you fancy it as an extension of your peter?" He lets out a ribald laugh.

Travis' face flushes. Jim's words had slashed to the quick. Travis sucks in his breath angrily, on the verge of retorting with a ringing challenge of Bowie's credentials. But he takes control of himself. He hears Jim's voice, harsh, goading. "Of the whole lot of us I wonder how many real patriots there are out there. There are some, of course. There always are. But most are thieves, renegades, murderers—looking for something or running from something. Me? I've killed—sure. With my knife." He looks accusingly at Travis. "You, Bill, you've killed with that trigger-happy fowling piece between your legs. Just what are we, anyway?"

"I'll tell you what we are!" Travis shouts. "We're fighters. And those men out there, they're fighters, too. Every one—to the last man of them!"

"Yes, Bill, they are fighters. They'll fight for you. And they'll die for you. Oh, you'll take them to hell in a blaze of glory. And if General Houston wins out—in spite of our damn foolishness here—one day monuments will be raised bearing your name. Won't that be the goddamndest joke on the politicians and school teachers and all the little children of Texas!"

Jim lays back on his cot and enjoys a good laugh. Then his voice changes. "I guess what I'm trying to say, Travis," Jim resumes, "is—are you sure you want to take all those men out there with you?"

"They made their choice three days ago."

On the night of March third Travis had called together the men of the Alamo and told them there would be no relief for the besieged fortress; it was the night he drew the line in the dirt of the patio with his sword. Over a week had passed since he had dispatched James Butler Bonham, his oldest friend whom he had persuaded to give up his law practice in Alabama and come to Texas and join the revolution, with a last urgent appeal to Colonel James W. Fannin at Goliad to send men and supplies without further delay. Now Bonham was back in the Alamo after a do-or-die horseback dash through the ever-tightening enemy lines around the fort. Bonham brought the depressing news that no relief could be expected. Hesitancy, indecisiveness, procrastination, poor judgement, and lack of imagination plagued the West Point trainee. It would be senseless, Fannin told Bonham, to waste the only Texas army in the field on such a foolish mission. For Travis,

33

Fannin's decision not to send help meant but one thing. Colonel Fannin, as well as Houston, thought the Alamo had no chance of survival, with or without reinforcements.

Throughout two and a half decades of living, nothing had come easy for Travis or seemed to run smoothly. Fate had shadowed his life in tragedy. Starting at the top in the law profession under Judge Dellett in Claiborne, he had abandoned career, family, and left by stealth of night. Upon his arrival in Texas he had been imprisoned for fifty days for challenging a despotic customs official at Anahuac, near Galveston. And now, again, as he stood at the very edge of the world, Fate threatened to deny him that which he craved most—victory in battle against despotism.

Across Travis' mind flashes a story related to him long ago by Judge Dellett. The judge told him about a friend who craved to achieve a measure of fame in life that would cause him to be remembered beyond the grave. While on the "Grand Tour" of Europe he had stood for three hours in the campanile of the Leaning Tower of Pisa, waiting for the structure to fall. The fame-seeker had read in a tourist brochure that the famous old tower, built in 1174, leaned more and more every year and would one day surely fall. Returning home, the judge's friend complained that Fate had denied him fame and immortality. The tower hadn't toppled while he was in it. Would Fate smile more kindly upon William Barret Travis?

If Travis was indignant, it was not at Fate, but at all the self-seeking stupidly circumspect people who, lacking vision and courage, would not lend a hand to make his life glorious at the respectable age of twenty-six. Always, it seemed, he had been hemmed in by gradualists and dullards, people who calculate probabilities and weigh one side against the other. For Travis there was never but one side.

The night of March third, when he had had time to digest what he had learned from Bonham, Travis stood before his men, who were assembled in the courtyard-

34

plaza. The yellow moon cast a murky light over the scene. The men faced their youthful commandant in various postures and wearing all manner of nondescript attire. There were buckskin breeches and jackets, wool and fur and buffalo hide mackinaws, "beegum" hats and other headpieces of various description. Their commander, however, was dressed in a style worthy of his position: grey swallow-tail coat with red facings, bright blue pantaloons with red stripes and a forage *kepis* with braid of gold. He always wore his sword at his side. Some of the men were resting on their muskets, while others fingered their pistols or ran their thumbs along the edge of their Bowie blades. Jim Bowie had asked some of his volunteers to lug him on his cot outside with the others.

Foregoing the formality of calling the men to attention, Travis said what he had to say and got it over with. He told them without apology or excuses there would be no relief forthcoming from Colonel Fannin's forces or from any other quarter. On the other hand he gave them all the reasons why he thought it was imperative for them to continue to defend the fort.

He concluded his speech with these solemn words: "Men"—the level and tone of his voice was friendly but authoritative—"when Santa Anna attacks these works it will be a total commitment, no quarter assault. We stand less than two hundred men against five thousand. Only a fool would promise you victory. I will promise but one thing—and that to Santa Anna. A dear price for the Alamo! My resolution is taken. It is to remain in this fort until victory or die fighting. This I shall do, even if left alone." He then drew his sword and traced a long line from right to left. "I call upon every man who is determined to stay here with me to come across this line."

Above the rising murmur, Jim Bowie's booming voice: "Boys, set my cot across that line!"

But David Crockett was ahead of him. The fifty-year-old ex-congressman had already leaped across and his Tennessee volunteers were scrambling after him.

Jim Bowie's volunteers to the man followed his cot. For the remainder there were minutes of indecision, scraping of feet and mumbling of voices. Then, led by Jim Bonham, one by one and two by two the others crossed the line. Until but a single individual remained, his feet unable to carry him across the death trace.

Louis Moses Rose stood in fur cap, mackinaw and grey cloth trousers, his face working and unable to give expression to the words that stuck in his throat.

"Colonel," he finally began, as a silence fell over the assembly, "I am not a soldier of Texas. Nor am I a member of Colonel Bowie's Volunteer Aid. But I was once a soldier. I marched with Bonaparte's army all the way to Moscow. It took me two years to get back to Paris. When the Emperor fell I emigrated to New Orleans. I am not a coward. I consider myself brave enough—when there is a reason to be. I am a businessman, a French trader. I was caught here when the Mexicans marched into San Antonio de Bexar . . ."

Travis spared him further humiliation. "Several couriers in the last days have succeeded in penetrating the enemy's lines. It is your privilege to try, Monsieur Rose. You will receive every assistance from this fort."

When Crockett crossed the line drawn by Travis in the dirt of the Alamo courtyard, it was far more than a short step of bravery. It was a leap into legendary glory of fantastic dimensions. That step omitted, David Crockett would have become a rather insignificant encyclopedic footnote: Crockett, David (1786-1836), Tennessee congressman; three terms.

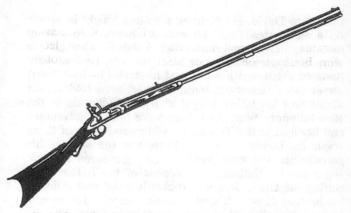

Antonine de Crocketagne. David Crockett rolled the
name over his tongue, trying to fix in his child's mind
an image of what a man with such a name would look
like.

He was laying on his side, his head propped up with
an arm, looking across the bosom of his sister Lovey
into the dying embers of the fireplace. It was late into
the night, and since his Uncle Robert with his wife and
their two children were visiting the family and all the
beds abovestairs were occupied, his mother had thrown
a cornshuk pallet before the big fireplace of the tavern
downstairs and put David and Lovey to bed there. The
two children had talked for a long time about the conversation they had listened to all evening, concerning
the Crockett family history. They had learned that An-
toine de Crocketagne was an illustrious fore-bear of the
Crocketts of Tennessee; that he was a Norman Huguenot who fled to England over a hundred years ago and
settled in the Batony Bay area (wherever that was) of
Ireland. Young David knew where Ireland was all right,
and England, too. His mother Rebecca had pointed out
these places to him and his brothers and sisters on an
old map she had brought from North Carolina. "A
gift," she said, "from your grandmother Hawkins."

This fellow Antonine de Crocketagne sounded romantic to David. He pictured a gallant knight in armor on a white steed; and he saw the brave hero slaying dragons and conquering other knights, who always wore black armor and rode black mounts. Undoubtedly these fancies owed a great deal to stories he had heard about more recent relatives. He had been told stories about how his father fought at Kings Mountain in the Revolutionary War. And there were tales of adventure and heroism in the Tennessee wilderness, some of them tragic for David's relatives. There was the story of his grandfather and grandmother being murdered in their log cabin by Indians; the account of the Indian chief cutting off Uncle Joseph Crockett's hand and holding his brother James, "Dumb Jimmie," captive for twenty years and finally releasing him when they decided he really was a deaf mute. There were nine children to hear these stories, three girls and six boys, of whom David was the fifth.

"Lovey," David said, "you reckon it's true—about Uncle Jimmie?"

Lovey too had been facing the fire. She turned on her back and gazed into the dim shadows of the high ceiling. "I reckon 'tis. Uncle Robert sure knows a lot about our folks, don't he? You like Uncle Robert, David?"

"Yeah, I suppose so. I ain't so taken with his woman, though."

"Aunt Bess? Why, David?"

"Aw, I don't know. She's too chunky I guess."

"What do you mean—too chunky?"

"You know . . . big in the behind. Big in the bosom. Betcha she couldn't get a gun to her shoulder fast enough to shoot a deer on the run. For sure she couldn't run fast enough to keep up with one if she shot and only wounded it."

"Suppose I should get chunky like Aunt Bess. Would you still like me?"

"Lovey, you ain't ever gonna look like *her*. You're built like a boy."

"Is that why you like me, David? Because I'm built like a boy? I ain't exactly, you know."

38

"Yeah, I know. You're a girl all right."

They got back to the conversation they had been exposed to during the evening. They had learned that life on the frontier in eastern Tennessee was hard and their father, always a man of impatience and discontent, sought to improve on a miserable existence by moving to the little settlement called Cove Creek, where in partnership with Mr. Galbreath, he erected a water mill to grind corn into grits and meal.

David and Lovey giggled as they relived the day the mill was swept away after a severe downpour and nearly drowned David and two of his sisters. "You sure did learn to swim fast after that," Lovey said, still giggling.

"Yeah, in the river alongside the water moccasins and beavers."

They talked about the move to Jefferson County, after the loss of the mill. There David's father opened a tavern, called in those days an "ordinary," which was a resting, eating, and sleeping facility mainly patronized by waggoners who plied the frontier roads with their cargoes. Taverns and ordinaries sprang up all along the frontier roads to accommodate the spread of civilization into the wilderness. They fulfilled a social as well as a practical need. The Crockett tavern was on the road from Knoxville to Abbingdon, Virginia.

David turned on his back, resting the back of his head in the palms of his hands. Lovey turned on her side, snuggled closer to her brother. "David. . . . If I should get chunky when I grow older—and I don't always look like a boy—will you still like me?"

"Sure, Lovey. You're my sister, ain't you?"

"Yes . . . but I don't mean it that way, David."

They remained silent for a while, David gazing into the dark of the ceiling, Lovey looking fondly at David. It was Lovey who spoke first.

"David," she said softly, "do you want to do it to me?"

"Aw. Lovey. . . . You know what Pa said when he caught us doing it in the peach grove. He said we gotta stop doing it. Pretty soon it would be dangerous for you—when you start having your days, like your sisters Maude and Dolly."

"I ain't had them yet."

"It's about time, ain't it? You're almost thirteen."

"Come on, David. Let's do it!"

"Suppose Pa comes down the stairs and catches us. You ain't forgot the bad whipping he gave us with the ramrod of his musket, have you?"

Lovey's hand was exploring; it found David and he became quickly aroused. "Ooo David! Such a fine ramrod *you* got. You *do* want to do it!"

"Lovey! Lovey . . . Stop it!"

Lovey moved her hand away. "You ain't mad, are you?" she pouted.

"Naw, Lovely. I ain't mad. You . . . You—shucks, Lovey. You get me crazy."

She moved close again, her hand renewing its work. "Then why don't you do it to me?"

"Aw, Lovey . . . I don't know why . . ."

"I bet you don't say that to Becky Jones."

David turned to face Lovey. "What you know about Becky Jones and me?"

Lovey giggled. "I saw you doing it to her—down on the bank of the creek."

"You watched us?"

Lovey giggled some more. "You was sure doing it to her—hard and fast. I was at the creek, looking for you. And there you was on top of her. I squatted in the willows and watched and listened. Becky sure was taking on. I got goose-pimply all over. And when I put my fingers in me down there, I was all wet and real hot. Tell me, David—" She snuggled closer. "Do you like doing it with Becky better than with me?"

"Naw, Lovey . . . I mean—aw, Lovey—such a question!"

Lovey's hand stroked him gently, lovingly. "Am I prettier, David?"

"Sure, Lovey. Becky's kind of dumpy—and soft. You're slim and firm."

"And pretty?"

"Sure."

David did not see the pleased look on Lovey's face nor the sparkle in her dark eyes. He only felt her pressing warmly against him. Her breath came hot against his cheek as she cooed. "Come on, David. Get on top of me. Do it to me!"

"Oh, Lovey . . . you always have your way with me . . ."

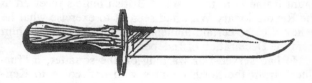

Elve Bowie snapped the book shut. She couldn't keep her mind on what she was reading: not while that obstinate sheriff kept Reason locked up in the Logan County jail. Her hand passed over the mound of her belly and she felt the child move. She lay George Augustus Moore's "Hail and Farewell" on the table beside the family Bible and Thomas Gray's "Elegy Written in a Country Churchyard," arose from the rawhide chair that she favored both for reading and treadling her spinning wheel, and went looking for Zeb. She found the number one household slave lounging in the breezeway, cooling his face with a cardboard fan.

"Zeb, I want you to hitch the two bays to the buckboard and bring it around to the front porch. We're going into town."

Elve then went to Reason's accounting room, selected two lightweight flintlock pistols from the gun rack, saw that they were primed and loaded, and concealed them in the folds of her voluminous linsey-woolsey dress. Hearing Zeb pull up in front of the house, she strode confidently out, climbed onto the buckboard and told him to drive to the county jail. She had no intention of having her sixth child while its father languished in jail.

The sheriff had been reluctant to make the arrest in the first place. For in all that section of Kentucky no family was more respected than that of Reason Pleasants Bowie and Elve, the good and sensible woman who was his wife; the woman who ran the plantation household, made her husband content and raised his children, read Irish authors and quoted English poets in church meetings.

The trouble had come about because Reason, whose gaunt frame bore the scars of British bullets received in the Revolutionary War, had seen fit to exercise what he believed to be certain inalienable rights accruing to him from the Declaration of Independence.

He had served fair warning on the squatter, a "furriner" from the north country who had come to Kentucky to settle on a rich section of land which was part of the Bowie plantation, but the arrogant stranger had chosen to ignore the warning. Either by foolhardiness or complete ignorance of the temper of the owner of the land, the man had continued to trespass, thereby committing an error not only unfortunate, but fatal.

Reason Bowie wasted no more words. He simply took down his fowling piece from its pegs, walked over to the squatter's clearing, and let him have both barrels. It was not a pleasant sight when the sheriff rode out to conduct an investigation. The man's head was blown completely to shreds.

The Revolutionary War was less than a score of years in the past and any veteran of that war was looked upon with high esteem, a man who almost could dictate his own laws. Besides, under the code of the day there was strong justification in killing any intruder who dared encroach upon another's domain. But the sheriff felt that the dignity of his office demanded at least the formality of an arrest. He was entirely civil and pleasant when he explained that, so as not to undermine the very office which Reason himself had supported, Reason ought peacefully to come along to the county jail and take up residence, while he, the sheriff, arranged procedures to squash the whole affair. "Meanwhile," the sheriff said, "talk of the mess will die away."

Reason Bowie was a reasonable man, and he felt that he certainly was a law abiding citizen. Without any protest, he kissed Elve, patted his five small children on their heads, charging Reason Jr. with certain instructions for making the others mind their mother during his absence, and departed with the sheriff.

Three days without Reason was quite enough, Elve decided; and she was determined to have her husband beside her bed when the new baby came as he had been when all the others were born. She reined up the two horses in front of the log jail. A plump little woman, but quite active and sure of herself, her keen eyes swept the almost empty street and the general store down in the next block as Zeb gently handed her down from the buckboard seat. Elve took care that the generous dress she wore did not betray the pistols concealed within its folds. Her oval face appeared pale under the hood of her blue calico sunbonnet that nearly matched the color of her eyes. With the sureness of a Scottish woman going to work, she pulled her white knitted shawl closer about her shoulders and started for the jail entrance.

"Mr. Watson," she said as she entered the small anteroom that served as the sheriff's office, "I've come for my husband."

"You mean, Miss Elve, you want me to unlock his cell and turn him loose—right now?"

"Yes, Mr. Watson. Right now. This foolishness has gone far enough."

"But Miss Elve, I gotta wait for the judge. I'll admit I ain't wanting the trouble and expense of collecting a

43

jury and all that. I just gotta explain to the judge and keep my own skirts clean. You understand, don't you, Miss Elve?"

"No, I don't, sheriff. Now please take your keys and unlock Reason's cell."

"I'm sorry," the sheriff said firmly and, having spent his modicum of courtesy, reverted abruptly to the commonweal official. "He'll stay until the judge gets here."

"I'm sorry, too," Elve said just as firmly, and the sheriff suddenly found himself looking into the large bores of two flintlock pistols, his eyes bulging. "I told you I've come for my husband. Right now!"

Mr. Watson took up the key ring that rested on his desk, led the way to the cell where Reason sat and unlocked the door. Reason stepped out, needing no explanation. He knew his Elve. He took one of the pistols from her.

"Thanks, Elve," he said, pushing her bonnet back and kissing her. To the sheriff: "Silas, when that judge comes you tell him to forget the whole business. Tell him you locked me up for three days and I ain't serving no more time for killing a goddamn squatter."

Reason and Elve walked the sheriff to the front of the jail. "No hard feelings, Silas," Reason said.

"Sure, Reason. You ain't gonna hear another word about it. I promise you. I reckon the judge ought to know it's justifiable to kill anybody and everybody that ought to be killed. And I'll tell him that durn squatter ought to been killed." He made a little bow to Elve. "I didn't know you was so determined to have Reason back home, Miss Elve."

Reason Bowie was duly at his wife's bedside when the child came. He was a strapping boy of eleven and one half pounds. He seldom cried, but you knew he was there. And so it was to be throughout his life. There was something about him that drew people to his cradle. He grew up to become a powerful man who did not need to say much, his presence was felt, and he felt that it was felt. People sought him, he didn't seek them.

44

Elve had to "push like the almighty," Reason told Zeb when he showed him the healthy baby.

"Dat sho is a biggun. I'll bet he'll grow up to be a fine farmer. He'll be stout enough to clear a lot of land. What yo'all gonna call him, Massa Bowie?"

"Elve gave him a good Scots name—James."

Farming was not what that fellow sitting on the wall of the Alamo had in store for James Bowie. Before drawing him to an invalid's cot in the Alamo, where the thread ended, he would lead him through the splendid salons of New Orleans and other grand old cities of the fledgling continent, to the great mansions of the opulent South, and through the bloody dives of Natchez-under-the-hill, among other dangerous and adventurous climes.

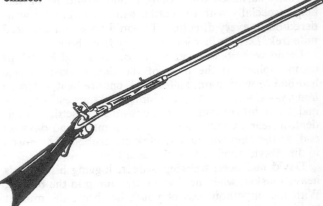

It was at John Crockett's tavern on the road from Knoxville to Abbingdon, Virginia, that Jacob Siler, an old Dutchman, saw and came to admire young David. Jacob Siler was a sandy-haired, portly, solemn man of powerful stature and few words. While he rested and tarried at the wayside tavern, he studied the quick-eyed, energetic David. "Like a boy from the old country," he told David's father. "Mindful of his elders and obedi-ant."

Before the old Dutchman departed on his journey, he

45

talked David's father into allowing the boy to leave with him as a herder and helper. Siler had come to Tennessee five years earlier from Pennsylvania to clear and settle a two hundred acre stretch of land near Kingsport. He became discontent with the wilderness country, never being able to throw off his longing for the rolling fields of Pennsylvania, which reminded him so much of the undulating countryside of his native Germany. Now he was on his way back north where he would join his son-in-law, who had a large spread of farmland a few miles south of York. He was hauling his life's possessions in a sturdy Conestoga wagon drawn by four horses, and trying to herd eight head of cattle at the same time. He sorely needed an extra hand. He correctly surmised that young David would be of vast help, especially with the cattle, which continually wandered off in every direction. It would be a four hundred mile trek, David's first journey away from home.

David was no stranger to the dangers and hardships commonplace to the lives of the backwoodsmen. He had had to work hard, suffer cold, endure heat, often go hungry—always shifting for himself. At an early age he had been introduced to a harrowing, unsettling accident, a near tragedy. He had shot a man: and days on end, as the man waned and sank but stubbornly refused to die, David agonized for the man's life.

David had been tracking a deer, lugging his father's heavy musket, when he saw a dark clump in the bushes. With the impetuousness of youth he thrust the musket to his shoulders and fired. The ball made a great, ugly hole through the body of a neighbor who was out gathering blackberries. He carried the wounded man to his house and stood nervously by as his father drew a silk handkerchief through the victim's lung and out his back. Miraculously the man recovered.

They traveled, day after day, old man and boy, the man reliving memories of the old world he would never again see, memories which each time he relived them became more and more refined of all discontent, and the boy thinking only of adventure and dreaming of experiences that lay ahead in his shining future. Behind them towered the Great Smokeys and before them the long wall of the Blue Ridge Mountains, with a riot of peaks farther northward. They kept to the valley, moving the Conestoga and small herd ever northeast toward the gentle rolling plains of Pennsylvania.

By diligent attention to his chores and the loving care he took of the cattle and horses, and especially by his prudence of speaking only when spoken to, David quickly won the old Dutchman's warm approbation. And Jacob Siler won David's undying admiration and envy through the excellence of his marksmanship that he demonstrated with the German rifle that never parted from his hands during the day and which rested in the crook of his arms at night. The handsome gun and the old man's sureness of shot kept the travelers bountifully stocked with fresh deer meat, wild fowl, and small furred game.

One day, noticing David's eyes as he avidly admired the rifle, Siler asked the young enthusiast if he had ever fired a gun.

"My father used to let me take his old smoothbore out hunting now and then. I'll bet that ain't no smoothbore you've got, Mr. Siler."

"No, boy, tain't." He handed the gun to David. "Dot's a Prussian rifle, made in Leipzig. My *vater* gave it to me ven I left the Old Country. It's got spiral grooves cut in the inside of the barrel. I seen you vatching me ven I reload, and I see the question on your face ven I hammer the ball down the barrel mit a ramrod and mallet. You vant know vhy? In dot vay, boy, the ball is threaded to the grooves. It has to follow the spiral ven the explosion drives it out through the bore. It comes out spinning. Dot keeps it on the track to its target. It von't bounce around in the air as a musket ball does."

David fondled the Dutchman's rifle lovingly. For days he had longed to lay his hands on this beautiful weapon. He ran his fingers over its smooth metal, he

47

drank in its polished brass fittings with shining eyes, he rested its butt against his shoulder and sighted down its long barrel.

In the early nineteenth century when settlers from the Continent began to arrive in the colonies, they brought their weapons with them. They had wheel locks, snaphances, and flintlocks. Most of these guns were smoothbore muskets. But not all. The Germans had been experimenting with rifled barrels for more than a hundred years; and when they came to Pennsylvania they brought a perfection of this art with them. Life in America was not easy. Their families had to eat. There was game aplenty. But it had to be shot to be eaten. Lead and powder was scarce and it was necessary for the hunter to be in possession of an accurately-firing rifle. The spiralled-barrel German rifles were avidly sought for this purpose.

David turned the German rifle in his hands, admiring it, summing it up. He examined it not as a curious teen-ager fascinated by a toy but as a young backwoodsman appraising a weapon necessary to his very existence. The barrel was browned; the stock was of walnut and ran almost to the muzzle, and it had been made dark by rubbing the wood with soot and oil. It felt smooth as ivory under his fingers. The butt, where the gun is likely to be set on the ground, was protected with a brass plate. There were other brass mountings inlaid in the wood. There was a German formé cross on the left side where the marksman's cheek rested against the stock. Directly opposite this, on the right side, was the lock plate on which the visible mechanism of the lock was mounted; also on the right side, near the butt, was the brass cover of the patch box, embellished and gleaming. The box itself was hollowed out of the walnut. The entire length of the gun was almost five feet. He rested it on the ground and measured its length against his height. It came up above his shoulder. He balanced it in his hands, seemed quite pleased with its equiponderance. David Crockett was looking at the forerunner of the famous "Kentucky" rifle.

Among the early settlers in Pennsylvania were skilled gunsmiths. Undoubtedly some ingenious woodsman from the "wilderness" or "Kaintuck," as the Kentucky territory was called, had traveled into Hickory Town, whose name was later changed to Lancaster, and had got one of the German gunsmiths to fashion a rifle to his own ideas. The Kentucky rifle had a much smaller bore, generally .44 or .45 caliber against as much as .75 for the German rifle. And the Kentucky rifle had a longer barrel, as long as six feet. The longer barrel and smaller bore gave the Kentucky weapon the same accuracy and carrying power with the use of less powder and lead, items not always plentiful in those days.

David's alert mind saw what he considered to be a flaw in the German rifle. "But, Mr. Siler," he said, "it may be just fine for squirrels and other game, but I'd sure hate that reloading with a mallet when a passel of Indians was coming down on me."

"Ain't no denying the truth in vat you say, boy. But there's a vay to get around dot. Venever it's necessary to reload fast, and there's no time to swedge a ball down the barrel, ve use a different ball, one three hundreth of an inch smaller than the bore. Dot size bullet vill roll down the barrel. To give it a grip on the rifling and make it spin, dot ball is loaded mit a greased leather patch wrapped around it, a little patch about twice the size of my thumb nail." The old Dutchman unsnapped the ornamented cover of the patch box, produced one of the "Indian killer" balls with grease patch and pressed it into David's hand.

David looked up into the old man's eyes. "Mr. Siler, will you teach me to shoot your rifle?"

Siler studied the youngster's face for a time. "Ve'll see, boy. Ve'll see."

When Mr. Siler and David arrived at their destination, the old Dutchman handed David six silver dollars as wages; then he took him aside, looked down upon the boy for a while with his serious, brown eyes. "Boy, you've been a fine helper," he said judiciously. "You

49

know the meaning of vork, like a good German *Kind*. I vant dot you stay mit me here. If you stay I vill teach you to shoot my rifle. And I vill make you a fine sharpshooter, the best in the land."

David's mind had been on returning home. Now that his job had ended, he'd allowed his thoughts of home and family to stir him deeply. In his youthful fancies he envisioned his homecoming as a triumphant affair, a gala occasion, a joyous reunion with his brothers and sisters and his mother and father. Home. How many times during the long trek had he turned the word over on his tongue. Home. *Home*! It tasted sweet. It was music to his ears. He had been prepared all along to start for Tennessee immediately after the journey was completed. But Mr. Siler had dangled a powerful and dazzling arabesque before him.

"You'll really allow me to shoot your rifle, Mr. Siler?"

"Boy, I'll teach you to shoot like nobody in Tennessee ever dreamed of shooting."

The days that followed were exciting times for David Crockett, and he pushed back in his mind all thoughts of family and home. First, Siler, taught him the proper care of the rifle. Oil—a good grade of thin oil—not too much, not too little, at the right places and at proper intervals, just a smidge here, a drop there; at some delicate points he showed David how to carefully apply a tiny dab with the point of a toothpick. After each series of firings, when the hunter was safely home, he should clean the riflings with a flannel swab, slightly moist with oil. And the walnut of the stock had to be rubbed every so often with soot sifted onto a soft oiled cloth. "Never treat a rifle unkindly," the old Dutchman told David. "Think of your rifle as a part of you. Look upon your gun as your pet dog. Don't abuse it no more than you vould the dog dot you love."

Out in the field the real business came to hand. "Fast and accurate shooting depends on vat you do before the gun hits your shoulder," Siler told David. "Always see dot your left foot is in command of your body. Don't stand mit your feet too vide apart. Remember, the gun at your shoulder is heavy. *Heavy.* And if your left foot is not in the right place ven you fire, the recoil vill throw your entire body off balance. On your other foot there should be no veight, but just the same it should be on the ground."

The old Dutchman showed David how to execute what he called the *easy swing.* Siler's principle was "start the swing slow, even it out, and always follow through with the swing after pulling the trigger." The old mentor saw that the boy grasped these fundamentals quickly. Then he drilled him in the meaning of *lead.* "A ball charge takes a fraction of a second to go from gun to muzzle to bird." The Dutchman always referred to the target as "bird." "And by the time your eye tells your brain to tell your finger to pull the trigger, another fraction of a second is used. In addition, it takes time for the hammer to fall. And dot's not all . . ."

Siler took a stick and drew a diagram in the dirt in the shape of a triangle, with its apex pointing toward David. He then divided the triangle into four sections of varying sizes. The smallest section, at the left of the triangle, he labeled *time of hammer fall*; the next largest, *ignition time*; the next, *travel of shot*; the last the largest section he labeled *personal reaction time.*

"Now, boy," he lectured, using the stick as a kind of *Kapelmeister's* baton, "you've got to learn to coordinate these four elements into distance, capabilities of your gun, and your own reaction control. These factors, plus the movement of the bird, create enough time lag so dot you shoot vere the bird is going to be ven the ball reaches it."

He made David practice the swing half a hundred times, interrupting his pupil again and again to correct irregularities of stance, movement, and poise. "On the end of the sving, slow down. Dot is, in the last fourth of the sving, before you have to stop to begin the sving in the other direction. But in the middle, keep the same

51

rhythm. Dot's vat ve Germans call the *leicht schwingen Gebiet*—the easy sving area."

The Dutchman saw that David's arms were getting weary. The rifle began to sway and his movements were uneven. Abruptly he put an end to the exercise.

"Tomorrow ve shoot," he said.

David awakened early the next morning. This was to be the big day. He'd show the old Dtuchman a thing or two about shooting.

Siler first made him practice shooting at stationary targets—a fence post, an old clay jug, a piece of broken cast iron skillet. As David aimed, Siler eyed him closely, taking in all his movements, never concerned greatly whether he hit the target or missed it. "Never lift your head ven you shoot," he cautioned. "If you raise your *kopf* from the shooting position the gun vill shoot in one direction vhile you look in another. Keep your line of sight alvays the same as the barrel. Remember, boy, always *look mit the barrel*."

David fired thirty rounds the first day. The last twenty-one were on target.

The next time out the Dutchman drilled him in shooting at moving targets. Standing behind David he threw horse apples (the large green seed fruit, about the size of a falconet cannon ball, of the bois d'arc tree, common to mid-America) in a great arc over his head, cautioning David to fire only when the "bird" reached the apogee of its parabola. After a while Siler took a position in front of David and made him shoot at in-coming targets. In this manner he kept the boy working on outgoing and incoming "birds" for a few days; then he shifted the procedure to crossing targets. "How much you should lead the bird," he said, "depends on the speed, distance from you, and the angle of flight. Of course, I'm counting on you remembering vat I told you about *time of firing*, so you can also take into account, before you pull the trigger, dot kind of time lag as vell."

"I haven't forgot, Mr. Siler."

"Vell, then, ve vill see if you can hit a crossing bird."

The Dutchman threw a horse apple. David fired and missed.

The old Dutchman yelled at David. "Everything vas sving in time, your feet vere wrong." Siler walked around in a circle, calming himself. "Now, ve try again. Remember, boy, you shoot mit the *entire* body. Think of your arms as spokes of a veel, mit energy flowing from hub to rim. And don't forget—look at the bird mit the barrel of the rifle."

During the days that followed the old Dutchman permitted David almost complete freedom with his rifle. David wandered into the woods, shooting wild fowl on the wing and rabbits on the run and squirrels scooting up tall trees. He tried hard to remember everything that Mr. Siler had told him. He improved and refined his posture, stance, and swing. He corrected for tilting and canting by learning to position the rifle properly on his shoulder. He watched for little mistakes and errors; he caught himself pushing his left hip forward sometimes when firing. "Like a goddamn girl!" the Dutchman had screamed at him for doing this. He discovered for himself that this error restricted his swing area and caused bad recoil trouble. By learning what not to do he learned what caused most misses.

What the old Dutchman had given him—the supreme confidence that he could survive in the wilderness and prevail against his enemies with the long rifle—he would carry with him for the remainder of his life. He had found and become one with and master of the long rifle.

David's yearning for his family again possessed him, and this time he could not overcome his nostalgia. As he wandered in the Pennsylvania fields and hunted in the woods—even as he tended the chores of the farm and barn—he languished for his native Tennessee surroundings. Images of his brothers and sisters and his mother and father kept creeping up in his mind; he continually tried to recall their voices, to capture the scenes and smells of his home.

53

One day while he was walking along the road a little distance from the farmhouse of Mr. Siler's son-in-law, there came along a wagon train of three Conestogas. The lead waggoner stopped and inquired of David how far it was to the nearest tavern. It was growing dark and he and his two sons, who were driving the other wagon, were weary and in need of a good night's rest. The tavern was about seven miles down the road, David told him. The waggoner said his name was Amos Dunn, and that they were hauling household furnishings and farm equipment to Knoxville. David's heart leapt at the sound of Knoxville. That was near his home! As they talked David learned that the Dunns, on previous hauls, had stopped at his father's tavern, and he lost no time in asking Mr. Dunn if he needed another hand for the trip to Tennessee. He was mighty anxious to go home. He was told that if he appeared, free and clear of his present guardian, at the tavern at daylight on the morrow, he might join the wagon train.

David did not tell Mr. Siler of his plans. He feared that the stern old Dutchman, now that he had invested so much time and patience in teaching him to shoot, would not hear of his leaving. He went to bed early that night but the anticipation of the trip home would not allow him to sleep. Lest he be apprehended when he left the farm, he got up about three hours before daylight, while everybody else in the house was soundly sleeping, recovered his six silver dollars from underneath the mattress where he had stored them for safekeeping, bundled his belongings and silently slipped away.

When he arrived at the tavern the Dunns were already astir, making preparations to pull out. He assured Mr. Dunn that he was "free and clear," and was greatly relieved when the waggoner told him to climb aboard.

David's father once told him that home is a place where, when you go there, you are always let in. David found, upon returning, that home was little more than such a place. He also learned that the dream of returning home had been sweeter than the actual event. There was no celebration, no fatted calf killed in his honor.

His mother kissed him on the forehead and told him to go chop some wood for the kitchen stove. His brothers and sisters asked a lot of silly questions about towns and people he hadn't seen or didn't know about. The six silver dollars interested his father mightily; and he tried to hire him out to a number of waggoners who passed by, but with no success.

Since waggonage was a thriving industry of the time, in the fall David took to the high roads hoping to hire himself out to a waggoner bound north. His first bit of luck was with a wagon-master by the name of Thomas Cheek, who took him as far as Fort Royal, Virginia. At Fort Royal, Mr. Cheek paid him off with eight silver dollars; and for a time he drifted about, shifting as best he could, working for a meal here and there, sleeping in barns and behind bars in taverns. Eventually he joined another wagon train, this time bound for faraway Baltimore.

The waggoner was named Soloman Horn, a lean man with a leathery face and shifty eyes. David turned over for safekeeping to Mr. Horn the eight silver dollars he had received from Mr. Cheek, which was not uncommon; the wagon-master was a sort of combination banker-counsellor-father of the cargo trains of the day. When the wagons arrived in Baltimore, Mr. Horn announced that everybody would have three days to enjoy the city; but he warned them to be back on board promptly, as he would be loaded by then for a trip south into the Florida territory. Meanwhile everyone could indulge himself as he wished.

David found the city of Baltimore exciting, fascinating. It was, in his eyes, a great and glorious place. Indeed, it was the young nation's third largest city, with a population of nearly fifty thousand. He marveled at the great buildings, wonderful houses, and the hurry and bustle common to any city but alien to a boy from the wilderness. He walked along the streets straining his neck at the rows of neat brick houses of two and three stories with sharply angled roofs. He stopped to gaze and marvel at some of the larger dwellings with white upper stories, set back in immense yards of watered-green grass and manicured hedges, with their great sweep of the roofs, which rose steeply from low eaves to a lofty ridge running a full hundred feet from one gable to another, some covered with red tiles, some with yellow tiles. What in the world, he wondered, does anybody want with such a big house!

He walked for hours, looking and admiring. Eventually he came into the city proper. Why were people in such a hurry? It seemed that everybody was playing some kind of game, all trying to get to some place before the next fellow. Ah, the smells! He drew them in deeply. There was the aroma of bread baking in Dutch ovens, the brown scent of fish frying in deep fat, the manly redolence of a leather shop, the faint perfume wafting from some unseen candy factory.

There were splendid carriages to be seen, spick and span and drawn by fine horses in brass-studded harness and driven by Negro reinsmen wearing black coats and top hats. And the elegant passengers! Powdered ladies in high-waisted dresses with puffed sleeves of silk, satin, and silk muslin. Some carried little white parasols against the spring sun, others wore poke bonnets in colors of mustard, green, or yellow. The men riding in carriages and coming and going from buildings and in the street looked important and handsome in their beavers and top hats, polka-dotted stokes, green and blue Spencer jackets, cutaway coats of different hues, bright-colored breeches, riding boots and short boots and pumps. This was elegance! Wait till he got back home! Nobody would believe him. He walked and walked, all over the city, the wonders to see, finally coming to the waterfront.

Baltimore, lying at the head of a deepwater estuary of the Chesapeake Bay, had been established by the family of the Barons Baltimore as an outlet for tobacco grown locally, and was still a tobacco port. But now there was other merchandise for shipping as well. Merchants from Germany, France, and England had come looking for iron and copper products, flour and grain. And there were others who had come, bringing in the hulls of their ships cargoes of Negroes for the slave market, and who sought exports of timber, wheat, salted pork, corn, rice, cotton, indigo, and tobacco. Lying at anchor in the bay, David saw schooners, great square rigged ships, brigs, barks, sloops.

Eventually David felt he must escape the patronage of Mr. Horn and explore this exciting world on his own. In the morning of the third day out from Baltimore, David effected his escape—but without his eight dollars and his belongings. On the same day he was lucky enough to land a job with another waggoner. His new master was a kindly Pennsylvania German by the name of Henry Myers, an honest man. Mr. Myers owned two good rifles and three hand guns, of which he allowed David free use. David became the chief game procurer for the train. This gave him ample opportunity to practice his marksmanship; and he found that many of the fine points of shooting he had learned under the tutelage of the old Dutchman were easily applicable to hand-gun shooting.

David remained with Mr. Myers for three years. During that period he visited many of the young nation's cities. He acquired knowledge of woodcraft, gained maturity and sagacity and judgement. He saw many new and strange places, met many and varied people, heard many stories; he saw evil and good in men; he witnessed many forms of cruelty and saw little evidence of honest regeneration in mankind. Yet he liked all men, simply because they were people. Before his trip to Baltimore, other than his short sojourn with the old Dutchman, Siler, he had never known any country but the environs of eastern Tennessee and he assumed that all its corruptions were the normal state of things. Now he learned that the evils of the world were the product of mankind.

One day Mr. Myers informed David that he had a wagon train going south to Knoxville. Would he like to visit his home? David had not been troubled with nostalgia of late, but with Mr. Myers' words came new thoughts of family and home, and he felt pangs of homesickness. But he told himself that it was merely curiosity. He'd like to see his family again, certainly, see how they had changed after these years. He was aware of the changes in himself. He was quite sure of the restraint and confidence he had gained out in the world on his own.

When the Myers wagons arrived within about three miles of his father's tavern, David left the train and went the rest of the way on foot. He would slip in unnoticed. He wanted no welcome, no embraces. When he arrived things were astir at the tavern. It was nightfall and nobody paid him any attention. He mingled with the men and kept out of sight of his family. When everyone was seated at the table for supper, he still was not noticed by any member of his family. Soon this began to annoy him, and he reached underneath the table and pinched Lovey, his favorite sister—the one who could always have her way with him—on the leg. At first she ignored the intrusion and he wondered if she was inviting an improper advance from a total "stranger." Then he turned his broad grin on her and she recognized him as her long absent younger brother.

First love can be a powerful force in any young man's life; it often is painful. It was almost devastating for seventeen-year-old David Crockett. Linda Kennedy was an attractive teenager with apricot skin, a small Irish nose, and a smile that was made bright by sparkling white teeth. Her waist was small, her legs smooth and slender, her breasts like ripening pomegranates. Her father was a well-to-do planter in North Carolina, and she was the niece of a Mr. John Kennedy, a Quaker friend of David's father, who had a farm where Linda was visiting about twelve miles distant. At first sight of her David was overwhelmed by her amazing wide blue eyes. It was the first time he had ever been really fascinated by a girl. Several young maidens whom he had

met in his travels had submitted to his impetuous puer-
ility, but only casually. This was the first time his will
and imagination had been overwhelmed. He found that
he had now lost that privilege of simple nature, that
dissociation of love and pleasure. Pleasure henceforth,
he devoutly thought, could no longer occur as simply as
tumbling a farm girl in the glade or on the bank of the
creek. A new awareness was working inside him. All his
feelings were being complicated by love. Now was beginning that exotic loss of one's self, that dramatic
neglect of everything but one's histrionic thoughts about
the beloved, that feverish inner life all turning upon this
exquisite creature suddenly before him. That first sight
of Linda Kennedy made an etching in his mind that remained tender for the rest of his life. Years later in his
autobiography he would write: "I found myself head
over heels in love with that girl; and if all the hills
about there were of pure gold, and all belonged to me, I
would give them all if I could just talk to her."

David was a son of the backwoods, where love was
looked upon as a devotion; and the tavern songs he
might have heard reflected the romantic cult of ideal-
ized womanhood. He was a son of the wilderness with
only four days of schooling behind him and when he
said over and over to himself that she was beautiful and
refined and educated, none of these attributes that
made her less obtainable had the power to quench his
impetuous and tender exhaltation. He showered all this
adulation upon her from afar, glimpsing her from his
work in the field as she appeared briefly on the porch or
in the backyard. He urgently had to find a way to get
her alone and press his suit.

His opportunity came on a Sunday when Mr. Kennedy asked him to hitch up the sorrel to the buckboard
and drive Linda to church. As he went about this chore
he regretted that the buckboard was old and shabby,
and swung in the old-fashioned way on leather braces.
The elliptical steel springs, invented by Obadiah Elliott
a dozen years earlier that he had seen on the fancy car-

riages in the cities, had not yet made their way into the wilderness of Tennessee. He was full of excitement. For the first time he would be alone with Linda. He would declare his love for her, tell her how he had adored her from afar. He simply could not live without her. He would marry her immediately.

Barely were they out of sight of the Kennedy farm before he halted the buckboard.

"Linda," he burst out, "you're bound to know how I feel about you. I want to marry you. I'll speak to Mr. Kennedy right away. We'll go back right now and tell him."

With half closed eyes and an air of authority she brought out these words. "David, you poor boy. I am aware that you are attracted to me. But it is an impossible situation. I am engaged to my cousin Edward. And, even if I loved you, you'd have to attend school at least two years before I could even consider marrying you. Why, you can't even write your own name."

He seemed to sink away into space, infinitely tiny, infinitely unwanted. He took one more look at that embodiment encompassing all that he loved, all that he craved, all that paradise denied him, handed his lady the reins, climbed out of the buckboard and walked away. He did not dare look back. Straight ahead he walked—across the field, into the woods, through a thicket, over a creek, unmindful of the cold muddy water.

He came to a black stump and sat down, put his elbows on his knees, his hands over his ears. He worshipped Linda. He reminded himself over and over again that he worshipped her, making the sound a sort of incantation, which became the catalyst for a profound resolution: he would, somehow, in spite of all else, get an education. She knows me and has rejected me, he said to himself. Years later, after two wives and a houseful of children, and when he had learned that all progress, all climbing, was to be gained in the world of contest—among men—and women were but leaden shackles upon his ankles which handicapped him in his struggles, he stated to a fellow Congressman: "People would never fall in love if they had not heard about it."

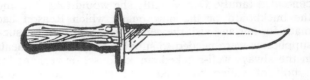

The indefatigible woman who brought James Bowie into the world was indeed remarkable. Aside from presenting her husband with a child at least every two years, she managed not only to rear a happy, carefree flock, but to give each of the children sound academic and religious training. Before Elve delivered her husband Reason from the Logan County calaboose so he could be at her bedside for the birth of their son James, there had been David, then Sarah, Mary, John, and Reason Pleasants, Jr. All the children were fair and grey-eyed, but James' hair gave promise to being almost golden.

The new arrival was fortunate in his family. The Bowies were not wealthy folks, but they did come of good, thrifty Scottish Presbyterian stock and were moderately prosperous—according to the standards of that part of Kentucky. The plantation, covering approximately five hundred acres of good black land, was given to cotton, sugar cane, and tobacco; and its cultivated acres were tilled by half a dozen slaves and their families. Elve's husband, being of a mechanical bent, established on the place a lumber mill, which supplied most of the material that went into the building of the Bowie home, a rambling log and plank structure to which Reason made additions as the family grew. The slave quarters, small log cabins, stood in the rear.

Elve never complained about the furnishings, although before her marriage she had been accustomed to better; now she made do with homemade chairs, tables, cabinets, except for her fine spinning wheel and some expensive rugs which her family had given her before they left Savannah. Elve knew how to raise a healthy, contented family. Occasionally she would take Zeb and the buckboard or the new buggy which Reason had made for her and visit the general store in town for such supplies as were needed to supplement the cured meats in the always well-stocked smokehouse, or perhaps for a bolt of calico to make into shirts, dresses, and drawers for the little ones.

Early in their marriage, Elve served notice on her husband that the children would "get plenty of schooling." But since there were no schools in that section of the wilderness, Elve, who had received her education in a Savannah academy for young ladies, became both teacher and spiritual instructor to her children. She was aided in this by a small library she had brought from Georgia, a selection of books which included an arithmetic, a Latin Primer, several readers, and a number of the classics. She took great pride in her thick volume of Shakespeare's plays and poems and in Alexander Pope's volume containing "The Rape of the Lock." Recently she had received from Savannah a copy of "Sayings of Benjamin Franklin" and some of Thomas Paine's fiery articles. But she also taught her brood things beyond the knowledge found between the covers of books—such things as independence, thrift, truth, and courage.

Reason Bowie contributed to the boys' education in a different but important way. He took them, when they were old enough, on hunting expeditions and taught them how to stalk game and to handle a rifle. He brought them into the fields to teach them the mysteries of planting and harvesting crops and let them help with the cutting and sawing of the logs at the mill. He taught them outdoor games and played with them the war game of "Rebel and Redcoat" along the banks of the creek. Afterwards they would sit around him begging to hear again the stories they had heard over and over: stories of how he had harried the British as a member of the band led by General Marion, the "Swamp Fox." And he told them how, after he had been captured and imprisoned by the British, he'd met and married their mother. The Savannah prisoners were often visited by their sympathizers, women bringing them clothing and delicacies; Elve Jones, of a prominent Georgia family, was one such young lady so engaged in ministering to the prisoners' needs ... Prisoner Reason Bowie fell in love with her, and when he was released in 1782, they were married.

When Reason sold his Kentucky holdings to try their fortune in the more productive soil of Louisiana, ten-year-old James already was looking upon himself as something of a *bravo*. He was a husky, energetic lad with hair that had become golden-taffy, almost red.

Here was a beautiful and verdant country—the rich bottom land of Opelousas in the old Parish of Imperial St. Landry. It was a land of palmettos and moss-hung oaks, where half the populace spoke the French of the Arcadians and where rusty-back alligators flounced in the dark lagoons of the swamps and in the hyacinth-choked streams that filtered into the bayous. Great fields of sugar cane stretched for leagues across the lowlands; while along the bayous sawmills whirred, supplying the boatmen with timbers and plank lumber to float down to New Orleans.

Here Elve Bowie was happier. Here was civilization reminiscent of her native eastern Georgia. She could buy a variety of goods in the stores of Opelousas. She took pride in her family and saw that they made a fine showing at church on Sundays: the girls in their tight-bodiced, full-skirted dresses; the young gentlemen in

63

their snug, blue pantaloons, their broadcloth coats, silk vests, and high socks. All the children, through contact with neighboring "Cajun" families, soon acquired a sound knowledge of French and a little Spanish, and the older boys became almost as conversant in those two languages as in their own.

James, more than any of his brothers, learned to love the bayou country, because he possessed, at least in Elve's estimation, the most imaginative mind, the most romantic inclinations. However, she credited John with being the most practical, and young Reason as being the most likely to make a name for himself in the ordinary pursuits of business. The three were firebrands, never happier than when galloping horseback around the countryside or engaging with other young men of the community in wrestling matches and other rough games, like riding alligators with ropes knotted surchigle-fashion about the bellies of the reptiles.

Sundays in Arcadia country was a day of repose for the elders, but for the young it was a day for sports. Sunday after Sunday young Jim Bowie had noticed the girl, for it was him she always watched during the wrestling matches or alligator sports. It was an April Sunday and the day for the big alligator riding contest, without a rope. The winner would be the contestant who stayed on the reptile the longest, bare-handed. Jim looked for the girl among the crowds along the bank. Could it be that this Sunday, of all times, she would stay away? At last he saw her, hanging back in the crowd and wearing her buckskin breeches and calico shirt, as always. Jim hadn't intended to show off, but today he wanted to make the girl especially proud of him, for he had made up his mind, at last, to talk to her. He had thought a lot about her, and he wanted to find out who she was—and maybe walk her home, after he had won the contest.

Jim expected to win without much difficulty. He often practiced staying on the reptile's back in private. Once on the alligator's back, the trick was to grasp the upper jaw firmly and gouge the thumbs into the eyes. Then the big beast couldn't see to do much and the leverage on his jaws would keep him from ducking under water with the rider. The rider then only had to avoid the gaitor's flailing tail, hang on until one of them was willing to give up.

Easily the winner, Jim climbed out of the bayou and went looking for the girl, his leather breeches squashing water, his pulse racing pleasantly. Adventure always stirred him so.

He found her walking away from the crowd, going toward the canebrake. "Wait!" he called.

She stopped, glanced back at him and, appearing frightened, started again to run away. "Wait, please!" He ran after her, catching her at the canebrake. "I only wanted to walk you home."

"You can't do that."

"Why not?"

" 'Cause." She started to move away.

"Stay," he begged.

"What do you want?"

"I just want to talk to you."

"Why?"

"I—don't know. I've seen you in the crowd. You're always looking right at me, and I wanted to walk you home."

"Well, I'm going that-a-way." She thrust her arm out in the direction of a distant plantation. "You can talk as we walk along."

Her awkwardness left her as they strolled along together, and he could not help but notice the gladness in her eyes at having him at her side.

"Where do you live?" he asked.

"Over yonder." She pointed where she had already indicated and, giving him a sidewise glance, asked, "You don't mind the others seeing you with me? . . ."

"Why? Because of your breeches?"

"You don't know?" She stopped and faced him, her dark eyes searching his. "You haven't noticed? . . ." Her voice was laden with gratitude. "It really doesn't show?"

65

"What?" He was genuinely puzzled.

She sat down on the log of a long-fallen oak, and motioned him to do likewise. She allowed herself a long silence. "You're James Bowie," she said holding him with her wide, searching eyes. "You go to church and everybody speaks to you. People go places with you, they talk with you. I'm Paula. I don't even have a last name of my own. I can't go to church, nobody ever takes me anywhere. Can't you see, Jim Bowie, I'm a Negro—"

Jim studied her face. If she was a Negro it certainly didn't show. Her skin, true, was less fair than his own, dark really, but it might have been made golden by long hours in the sun. Her eyes were a dark brown. Strikingly, her nose was straight, high and Romanesque. And her mouth—nothing Negroid there: small with a short upper lip, the lower full but not fleshy.

"Paula, it doesn't show—really."

She stood up. "Now you don't want to talk to me anymore, do you?"

"Sit down, Paula," he commanded gently. "I do want to talk with you. Do you know that you're a pretty girl?"

This pleased her and she smiled a little grudging smile. She sat down on the log beside him, looking at him, waiting for him to speak again.

Nothing else came to Jim's mind, so he said, "You're not all black, are you?"

"My mammy says I'm a quadroon. My mammy's pappy was a white man. My pappy is, too."

"Do you know who your pa is?"

She didn't answer immediately, her eyes gave him a glancing search, then became fastened on a knot in the log. After a time she lifted her face, having made up her mind to give him an answer. "Yes—I know who my pappy is. But I'm not going to tell you. I'm not going to tell anybody. I'm going to run away to New Orleans and find me a way to live like white folks."

Jim couldn't think of anything to say for a long time. They sat there, his eyes moving from her face to her

66

buckskin breeches to the cane in the field. She held her head slightly bent but raised her eyes now and then to him.

At length he reached out and cupped her chin in his hand. "You sure are a pretty girl," he said with complete conviction. "Nobody in New Orleans will ever take you for a Negro. You could even marry a white man and he'd never know the difference."

"Mammy says I can't do that."

"Why not?"

"She says since I came out whiter than she is, my children will likely be as black as my grandmother."

"How black is that?"

Paula gave a little huff. "You might say she's so black a piece of charcoal would make a white mark on her."

Again silence fell between the two young people, each in his own world, searching his young mind for some kind of answer to her dilemma. Finally Jim said, "Tell you what, Paula. I'll talk to you—anytime you want. Let's meet again, huh?"

She turned grateful eyes on him. "When do you want to see me again?"

"Next Sunday. Let's meet next Sunday."

"Where?"

"Right here. At this old log. I'll meet you here next Sunday, Paula, right after dinner."

The quadroon girl's eyes shone. She had, at last, found a friend.

David could not bear to go back to Mr. Kennedy's. Remembering that the Quaker had a married son on another farm about fifteen miles away from that dreaded place, and on whose farm there was a school, he went at once and succeeded in hiring himself to the son, making arrangements to go to school four days a week and work for the Quaker's son the other three days. In this manner David Crockett managed to obtain six months of formal schooling—all he ever had.

But love had smitten and scorned him, and in the process had left him a determination to obtain a wife. In the daytime at his work he thought about girls; at night he dreamed about them. He had worked a year for the Quaker's son and earned enough to buy for himself a rifle and a horse. Whenever there was a shooting match, a dance, a gathering of any sort, David showed up. Girls were always there and he danced with them, courted them, and went home and dreamed about them. He admitted to Lovey that often after these dreams he had awakened to find that "I had wetted myself with love juice." But like the child whose fingers had got burned, he did not dare venture too close to the fires of matrimony—not yet, anyway.

One day the Quaker's son told him about a Scottish widow who lived about twenty miles northeast of the

Quaker's farm. She might be the right one. After all, she'd had a husband. There shouldn't be a necessity for all those delicate preliminaries. She just might be in need of a strapping young fellow; and not being young and virgin, he felt sure he could talk with her and not be hurt or rebuked in return, as he had been with Linda Kennedy. He took his rifle, mounted his horse Jeb, and set out to call on the widow McCrory.

Night was gathering when David arrived at widow McCrory's farm. He was not entirely a stranger to her; she had seen the young marksman at some of the shooting matches. When she told him that she knew him, he tried hard to recall having seen her. He was certain he would have remembered her, for, as he later wrote in his autobiography, she was "ugly as a stone fence." If it weren't for the loose-fitting homespun dress she wore, he thought, she'd easily pass for a male farm hand. Her chin was broad, she had a large flared nose, and she had trimmed her hair short, further diminishing her feminity. Notwithstanding, David was glad he had come.

Kate McCrory proved to be a warm and lonely woman. She welcomed David informally and jovially, and cooked him a late evening meal of fried salt pork, green beans, hominy, and apple pie. He helped her in the kitchen while she washed the dishes and cleaned up after the supper. The widow went to the cellar and came up with a bottle of wine that she said her deceased husband had brought from faraway Pittsburgh. They drank wine and the widow McCrory talked in a most friendly and effusive manner, and it became obvious to David that all her cordiality was nothing less than an invitation for him to sleep with her. But the more wine he drank and the longer she talked, the stronger became the vision of his lost Linda. Finally he arose and excused himself, saying that it was time to go to bed and if she didn't mind he'd like to sleep in her barn. Kate—she had insisted that he call her Kate—took this rebuff in the most gracious manner.

"Certainly, David," she cooed. "If that is where you

want to sleep. But I can fix you a pallet here on the floor. Wouldn't you rather sleep here in the house?"

"No, ma'am," he said. "I'd rather stay the night out in the barn."

Kate McCrory produced a quilt and two blankets, took her oil lamp, and led the way to the barn. She made him a bed on some straw in the loft.

David dreamed that night, under a deep wine-sedated sleep. He dreamed of Linda. He visioned her coming to him out of a brilliant sun—or was it a soft mist?—draped in a transparent gown of blue silk, her white out-thrust breasts protruding against the gauze-like garment. She approached slowly, arm outstretched toward him, and as she moved he could see the dark triangle of her womanhood. He felt a stirring in his breast and hot passionate sensations in his groin. His eyes sought Linda's face, even veiled from him in the translucent mist. Then he saw her face, suddenly appearing out of the nimbus. There was that mocking, condescending smile upon her lips. His mouth opened to cry out against her but no words came forth. He tried to scream—No! Go away from me! But it was words only in his dreams—silent noise. Then as suddenly as it had appeared, the vision was gone; but he did not re-enter that soft veil of black nothingness. Slowly he came awake. And just as slowly he became aware of a warm, soft body lying beside him, voluptuous thighs pressed against his bottomside; an arm extended over his body, and a hand gently fondled his private parts. He lay still for a moment, while awareness crept over him fully; moreover, the sensation he was experiencing was so pleasant.

Slowly he turned on his back. Kate's voice was warm in his ear. "David, I couldn't sleep. Please don't send me away."

His body felt stiff and unyielding as he lay beside her; like a plank, he thought, that would break and splinter if she did not let go of his penis. When she moved he felt the warmth of her great breasts against

70

his side. She took her hand away and began to stroke his chest, his belly, his thighs. And after a while, because she did nothing else, he began to relax. And then her arms went around him and she held him quietly, his chin proped upon one of her enormous breasts. Bemused as he was, he found no words to say. He was enjoying the situation immensely. He was glad she had come to him, and he realized with an urgency growing within him how mistaken he had been about the body concealed underneath that linsey dress. It was a body of voluptuous contour, and full of pulsating desire.

"David," she said, "would you like to kiss me?"

Her mouth was on his; her lips came down over his, mercilessly and somehow possessively. He felt her tongue probing his mouth, now virtually pillaging it; all the while her hand was fondling, squeezing his upreared, iron-stiff manhood. Suddenly she threw off the coverings and her mouth went to his neck, his chest; and he felt her tongue teasing his muscle-hard belly. Then gently, lovingly her lips found their ultimate target. He felt her tongue exploring its cloven, heart-shaped head. In a moment her mouth encompassed it entirely.

Eventually the sensation of pain-pleasure became so intense that he stiffened, and she raised her head and lay on her back beside him. She reached out, found his hand and drew it to her warm, melon-like breasts. He felt her nipples harden under the palm of his hand as he stroked them, first one, then the other.

"David," she whispered, "I ain't had a man since Angus died. That's nigh onto four years. Don't you want to fuck me?"

Without further ado he climbed over her and, opening her limbs, he postured his body over hers and she guided him inside herself. At first entrance he experienced no sensation. She felt enormously large and loose. He stayed inside her without moving, embedded in that wet, fecund cavity, and then in another minute she began to move, inexorably and steadily, her body straining against his. When she sensed he was not pick-

71

ing up her rhythm, she ceased momentarily. "What's wrong, David? Ain't it good?"

"Kate, you're too big. I don't feel a goddamn thing."

"Wait a minute, hon . . ."

She uncoupled, reached out, found the flannel night-gown she had stripped off when she came into the barn loft, twisted a portion of it around her two forefingers and, using this as a kind of swabbing ramrod, swiped out the vault of her vagina. "Hon, there was just too much love juice. I ain't had none for so long."

This time around David felt everything. Gradually he picked up the rhythm of her movements and his strokes became long and probing, allowing him exquisite knowledge of her contour and depth. There was a growing enlarging of himself, there was a feeling of what a marvelous old girl Kate was, how delicious and voluptuous she was! Transported violently, he became completely lost in her. All his being knew her, loved her—even if for the moment. There was a great rushing, a terrific urge for speed. Then when speed became all but blinding, she like a wild mare on a rein, and he the rider to hold her in lest she destroy herself, running wild and free. A huge cry came from her, and all of her moved, quivered prolongingly.

If David had not acquired complete status of manhood that first night with Kate McCrory, he clearly earned his golden seal in the months that followed. There were pleasant Sundays at Kate's, eating baked possum, roasted deer and bear that he had shot, and in-season melons and fruit from Kate's garden and little orchard. They hunted together, (Kate was a pretty good shot, but David improved her marksmanship by teaching her some of the old Dutchman's refinements), went to church together, slept together, made enormous love; and he helped her in her garden and with her plowing. She taught him simple computation, othography, and gave him an appreciation of books. She had a dozen books that Angus had brought with him from Pittsburgh. David read John Hammond's *The Two*

72

Truthful Sisters—Virginia and Maryland, Thomas
Ashe's *Carolina,* Thomas Paine's *Common Sense* and
The Wild Honey Suckle and *To a Caty-did* by the
Huguenot from Princeton University, Philip Freneau.
During the long still evenings, when only the chirping
of the crickets broke the quiet of the fields outside and
the bassoon voices of the bullfrogs complained to the
moonbeams bouncing off the surface of the pond, Kate
read to David from these books.

But David was not entirely devoted to Kate. He
would in later life come to realize that Kate McCrory
taught him a lesson that no youth dares to confront:
that in the most perfect union of love one person loves
less profoundly than the other. Never had he given up
the thought of finding another Linda and "taking myself
a wife." It was the thing to do. Wasn't that the course
of all the backwoods folks? Take a wife, raise kids to
help with the land and crops. Sure, Kate would make
some man a fine wife. But a man like he ought to have
a young wife, a wife with many years less than her husband. That was the way of the frontier people.

Nevertheless Kate McCrory's love for David was that
rare kind of love that it is said only mothers and prosti-
tutes are capable of, the all-embracing, overpowering
love that continually demands of the lover some sacrifice to be made for the loved. And Kate realized she
was not sufficiently attractive to bind some man to her
maintenance. She long since had sensed David's restlessness. Instinctively she knew when he had longed for
a young pretty girl or had seduced a farm wench, yet
she made no form of jealousy or gave no sign, electing
to suffer the pangs of discontenance in silence—and, as
the nature of some sensual women, enjoying the pains
of her heart.

One day she told David that she knew of a girl who
would be "just right for him." She was the daughter of
an Irish woman Kate knew. David pretended little interest and refused to allow her to take him to the Irish
woman's house. But one day when he and Kate attended the festivities of a shooting match, she led him to a

house where a number of young girls were being prepared for the dance that afternoon. Mary Finley was one of those young girls. And when David laid his eyes upon her something inside him reached out for her, something awakened within him. Was it her wide slate-blue eyes, her small Irish nose, her warm smile that aroused the sentiments once stirred so powerfully by his lost Linda? Her Irish mother, having listened to Kate's glowing recommendations of David, immediately pressed the case with him on behalf of her daughter, whom she, for reasons known only to herself, called Polly.

They came from far and wide for the shooting match. There were young men and old men, fathers and sons, farmers, hunters, riverboatmen, merchants. They brought rifles and muskets, muzzle-loading and breech-loading, matchlock and flintlock. Among ordinary guns of the day David saw several interesting and rare guns. There was an early Kentucky long rifle made in 1810, one of the first of these rifles, an experimental prototype; there was a flintlock musket, 1795 model, with French hand engraved brass mountings; and there was a breech-loading, action-barrel rifle made in Britain only recently. David's own gun was a modified Kentucky rifle with four spiralled rifles accommodating a .45 caliber ball. Some marksmen brought their own resting stands or forks for stationary shooting. There were to be two classes of competition, one for the musket shooters, another for the rifle shooters; a rifle being designated as a firearm with a rifled bore, the musket, of course, being smooth bore. Everyone brought his own target. This consisted of a board or slab of wood with a white paper facing. Three concentric circles were drawn on the paper, in either black or red ink; both colors being permissible. The inner circle was one half of an inch in diameter, the next or middle circle one inch, and the outer circle three inches in diameter. The target was placed at forty yards for firing free and sixty yards for firing with a rest or stand.

The womenfolk and non-shooters supplied the prizes. This was a "merchandise shoot;" no money was offered. The prizes consisted of everything from homemade plows to wagon and buggy wheels to sacks of flour and grain to paint and white-wash to household utensils such as iron pots and skillets, oaken buckets and galvanized pails. And there were fancy things handmade by the women: quilts, tablecloths, bedspreads, dresses, and underthings. The prizes were displayed at one of the designated houses and the contestants were allowed to view them and specify which items they would shoot for. There were no contests of shooter against shooter. Some prizes required only one shot to be placed on target, while others, depending on the value the donor had placed on his item, required two or all three shots to be placed within the three concentric circles.

The shooting began around ten o'clock in the morning and lasted until late in the night. When it grew dark, a lighted candle was placed on either side of the target. The dancing began in the afternoon and continued, intermittently, along with the shooting and feasting and other festivities, as long as there were fiddlers to play and dancers to dance.

David went to the house where the prizes were on display and put his name on two sacks of flour and a sack of rice, an iron pot for boiling clothes and a crocheted bedspread—all for Kate. Then he surreptitiously placed his name on a long white wedding gown with gold spangles and fancy lace. "I figured it would just about fit Polly," he told her mother when he handed it over to her after the shooting.

David was the favorite shooter. Always when he stepped up to the range with his rifle everyone ceased what he was doing and came to watch the famed marksman. To the delight of the spectators he scorned the shooting rest and placed his shots, one after the other, always right on target. The crowd cheered and Kate was filled with practical delight, for her little house would be enriched because of David's expert marksmanship. But then he neatly placed three bullets on a target and won the wedding gown, and she shed silent tears.

In the days that followed David saw a great deal of Polly, but seldom without her possessive mother constantly hovering in the background. One day while riding his horse through the woods on the way to Kate's farm, he came across Polly who said she had lost her way in the woods. He dismounted and they sat on a green patch of grass and, as he told her mother later, "without kisses or passion" they came to a decision to get married.

The wedding was set for a Thursday of the following month. David arranged to have the wedding party at his father's tavern. On the morning of the wedding he arrived at Polly's house with an extra horse. His bride-to-be was dressed, packed and ready, thrilled to be rid of her bossy mother. The old woman was quite distraught at the thought of losing her daughter, and an argument arose between David and the Irish parent, with the result that David stormed out and mounted his horse and told the mother that there were plenty of other birds in the forest. Polly came running after him, begging him to take her away. She'd go with him and stay with him whether they ever got married or not, she declared. Having asserted herself so clearly, she boldly mounted the horse David had brought for her. The old lady grabbed the horse's reins and demanded that Polly "get down off that horse before this young hellion makes a scarlet woman of you!"

David assured Polly's mother that he'd marry her before he bedded her.

"Then do both in my house!" her mother demanded.

David struck a compromise with the Irish mother. He agreed to get married in her house provided she promised to keep her blabbing mouth shut, but be damned if he would frig any girl under the old biddy's nose. The wedding party would be at his father's tavern, as was planned.

David's folks laid on elaborate plans for the wedding celebration. The large table in the tavern, hewn from a slab of timber and supported by eight stakes driven in auger holes, was laid with pork, poultry, wild turkeys, venison, and bear meat; and there was the accompaniment of cornbread, potatoes, and other vegetables. Pewter spoons, somewhat battered about the edges, and others of horn, were laid out in a neat row. The guests were expected to cut their meat with their hunting knives, always worn in leather sheathes hung from their belts. And there was the family whiskey jug labelled "Black Betty."

When David arrived with his bride, the guests had already assembled from far and wide. The men came dressed in dearskin moccasins, leather or coarse spun cloth, leggins, heavy hunting shirts of all conceivable styles of material, and all homemade. The women wore gowns of homespun and home-woven cloth, composed of linen and wool, called linsey-woolsey. Those who were not barefoot wore very coarse shoes, and some sported buckskin gloves of their own design. David wore a bright green calico hunting shirt, a bell-crowned hat, black cloth breeches over his buckskin leggins, and moccasins. Polly, as was to be expected, was the prettiest, dressed in the gown that David had won in the shoot.

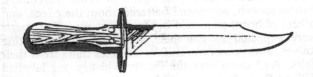

Young Jim Bowie, more than his brothers, learned to love the bayou country. Elve Bowie began to see in three of her sons, James and Reason and John, a characteristic she secretly admired. They did things together, in concert; they relied upon each other, consulted one another. Yes, these three would one day become a credit to their old Revolutionary "Swamp Rat" father. Elve's prophecy was already coming true. People often spoke of "the Bowie brothers." From their father they had learned woodcraft well, and he had taught them their lessons in survival. They became clever at stalking a trail. Each became a deadly marksman and proved it in Sunday shooting matches. While John adhered close to the land and business, Jim and Reason were more adventuresome.

The three brothers hoarded their money. In many ways they were niggardly. But not in all things. They would spend freely to develop the land they were acquiring, and on trips to the city they bought books. Reason laughed at Jim when he brought home a Spanish grammar. Jim, not given to taking the butt of any derision, turned the laugh on Reason by chiding him in perfect Spanish about the prematurely thinning of his hair.

Along about that time Reason decided on a change in the spelling of his name. Reason was the thinker of the three. A lot more went on in his head than in an ordinary man's, or so Jim thought. He was the best educated, too. He could read Ovid and Suetonius in the Latin and quote Gray's "Elegy Written in a Country Churchyard" from beginning to end without missing a line. One day, refering to Alexander Pope, Reason told Jim that the simplest way of spelling a word was the best way; therefore, since everybody pronounced his name Rezin, the only sensible way to spell it was the way it sounded, and so for the remainder of his life he wrote Rezin for his signature.

Elve saw something else in Jim and Rezin. They were rebels, of a special sort. They were perfectionists, rebelling against a half-a-load that life offers those who dream best. Both were fortunate and successful in material things. But Jim wondered if that was enough.

After that first day, when Jim and Paula became friends, they met regularly on Sundays. It became a ritual with them; it was not easy for Paula but she always showed up. Sometimes she had to lie a little and sometimes she had to "slip off." But as surely as the sun rose on a Sunday morning, Jim could depend on seeing Paula at the appointed place and time that afternoon. For her, Jim was everything. She felt close to no one else. He had surprised her with understanding when she had expected derision. It became a bond between them, that understanding.

Often Paula imagined conversations with Jim, continued in her mind from the brief words they had passed the previous Sunday. Everything grew from that. She lived on it until their next meeting. Their slow-ripening understanding had reached beyond a consciousness of others. He was not bothered by the half-hostile, half-sly glances that followed them into the woods.

Between Paula and Jim was a secret compatibility they shared and it shut out the rest of the world. She had long ago taken the last veil of mystery away between them. She told him all. Her father was Jonathon Halley, her owner, who also owned over one hundred other Negroes to work his vast lands. Mr. Halley had never spoken to her about her parentage, but silently they both knew and each respected the other's dignity. Mr. Halley was known throughout the country as a humanitarian slave owner. He maintained a school on his plantation and saw to it that the Negroes at least learned to read and write and that they got a Christian background. For Paula, he did much more. He assigned her to his daughter Theola as her personal maid, and directed that she attend school with his daughter. Paula quickly became companion as well as handmaid for Theola.

Paula no longer met Jim in leather breeches and calico shirts. She owned a sizeable wardrobe of fine but slightly worn dresses, shoes, and underthings, Theola's castoffs.

Paula took pride in Jim's success. Sometimes she would wander over a new piece of land the brothers bought, revelling in its vastness and richness. She admired the sawmill that Jim, Rezin, and John had established two miles down the bayou. Sometimes she walked that way, finding a strange vanity in the whirring of the huge circular blade as it cut through the long cypress logs. The green smell of the great mound of sawdust gave her a quaint exhilaration; and if she got a glimpse of Jim working around the mill, she thrilled at the way his hair turned from taffy to gold in the sun.

That she had developed into a beautiful woman, Paula was fully aware. But how different was she from her half-sister Theola? Did the Negro blood in her make any differences in their bodies, she wanted to know. One day when Theola was away, Paula stood naked before the big full-view mirror and appraised her ripening body. She saw that she had grown tall and slender but rounded in the right places. Her breasts were firm, large and upcupped. But their points were dark, almost black. This annoyed her. Why couldn't hers be pink like Theola's? But hadn't her mother warned her that the last drop of Negro blood would always be seen in the nipples? Standing there admiring her body, she cupped her breasts in her hands and

80

stroked their points, causing a sensuous feeling to arise in her pelvis. She passed a hand over her smooth abdomen, turned this way and that in order to appraise the rest of her body. She saw that her waist was small, her hips symmetrically curved, and her alabaster thighs were lovely frames for the elongated patch of hair that partially revealed the pouting lips of her sex. She was glad that her fleece was short, curly, and lay close to her body. She reflected that Theola's was thick, bushy, and protruded like a mop down there.

She stood long before the mirror, adoring herself and caressing her body with her hands. Strangely all the while no thoughts of Jim entered her mind. She revelled in her loveliness, enjoying a vague, luxurious sensation, enraptured only with her own body. There was a difference between hers and Theola's; hers, though slightly darker, was much lovelier.

Paula was grateful to her secret father, grateful that he had seen to it that she was as well educated as his recognized daughter. She certainly did not talk like the other slaves; her diction was as precise and cultivated as Theola's, and her choice of words just as refined. Her mother, on the other hand, had drilled into her mind and her heart and her soul the clear understanding of what it meant to be a quadroon in the world of slave society. Slave women toiled, her mother told her, but they were also expected to bring forth children, as many as they were able, to increase the slave population. These were not children of love, but of necessity. To be a slave woman was not easy. To be a quadroon was hard. But to be a beautiful quadroon woman was a lifelong of negation. Her body did not ever and could not ever belong to her, but to some man—some white man. Otherwise its beauty and wonder were worthless. The beautiful quadroon woman, her mother advised, found a haven with some wealthy planter or merchant who would keep her in luxury as a *placée* in the little colony of establishments on the Rue de Palisades in New Orleans. At worst, that would happen to Paula, as she had planned; at best, because of her lighter than saffron skin and nordic features, she might, if she was

81

lucky and if she wished, "cross the line." But Jim Bowie kept getting in the way in her mind, putting her plans all awry.

Sitting under a low-spreading oak on the banks of a lily-covered stream, she tried to tell Jim that. She found the oft-repeated words: she would run away to New Orleans; she would find a life of her own in the city where a great many Negroes managed to live their own lives, something she could never do here in the upper country on a plantation. She saw the comprehension in his eyes and she saw something more—compassion and love. She quit fumbling for expression and went into his arms.

"Your body is unbelievably soft," he said into her hair.

She wanted to tell him how firm and iron-hard his arms felt and how broad and powerful his shoulders were. Instead she opened her lips and received his kiss.

"Why do you close your eyes when I kiss you?" he asked.

"I don't know—" and then with sorrow in her voice —"maybe I don't want you to see what's in them."

He tilted her head back, trying to read her face. He could see only the shadow of dark lashes against her cheeks and he felt as though she had shut him out.

"Why won't you look at me?"

She let him kiss her, then her cheek burrowed against his, her eyes still guarded against his.

"Jim—Jim, my only friend. It makes me feel so— bad, so sad."

"I—I make you feel sad?"

"Oh, can't you see? . . ." There were tears in her voice. "It's all so hopeless—so impossible."

"I want you, Paula. We'll be married."

She moved out of his arms, hurt in her eyes. "Never! Jim, I must find my own life. You have yours and there is no place in it for me."

He reached out for her. "I'll make a place. My brothers will listen to me, my mother will understand."

Again she drew away. "The law, Jim. You can't.

82

You can buy me. You can sell me. You can whip me. You can take me at your pleasure. You can do anything with me—except marry me."

He found himself sharing her humiliation. He bent his head, trying to think of something to say to her, seeking the words to tell her how he felt. Finally he said, "All I know, Paula, is I want you. I—I guess I've loved you from that first day I walked you home."

She was calm and she spoke with pain in her voice. "There are but two ways you can have me. You can purchase me—and be sure of getting your money's worth. But the other way is the simplest and is not at all involved or complicated."

"And how is that?"

She stood up, quickly undid her clothes and slipped out of them and, naked, lay down on the green grass beside him.

"You won't be sorry, Jim—ever."

David's father, as master of the house, was standing at his door with Black Betty in his hand. Each guest was expected to have a long pull at the jug as he entered. The young women were not excused from this ritual, although some of them gagged and made faces upon swallowing the fiery liquid. When David and Polly entered amid shouts of joy and congratulations, his father

83

handed him Black Betty. He took a long pull and put it to the lips of his bride, who drank joyously. He then, as was the custom, handed it to his next of kin, and so the jug passed through the whole company.

Negro slaves made the music, one strumming a banjo, another playing a fiddle, and a third shaking the bones. A fourth called the tunes and the changes of step. The bones sounded a quick rat-tat-tat that set the party in motion. Meal had been strewn over the floor to make the rough timbers smooth for dancing. Everyone danced as if none would ever tire. Songs like "Sell the Thimble" and "Grind the Bottle" and "We're on the Way to Baltimore" were sung and danced. David knew the way to Baltimore well, but this was a pleasanter journey than the one he had taken. He knew the verses of the song, too. Hoisting his pretty, redheaded bride upon the table and climbing up beside her, he sang it lustily, to the cheers and shouts of everyone present.

> *We're on our way to Baltimore,*
> *With two behind and two before,*
> *Around, around, around we go,*
> *Where oats, peas, beans, and barley grow,*
> *In   waiting   for   somebody.*

> *'Tis thus the farmer sows his seed,*
> *Folds his arms and takes his ease,*
> *Stamps his feet, and claps his hands,*
> *Wheel around, thus he stands,*
> *In   waiting   for   somebody.*

With his young bride David was quick at the lively steps. The pair was readiest when the turns were called, loudest in the singing. They danced and feasted and revelled until long after midnight. Then, David leading her by the hand, they stole away in the midst of the uproar, climbed the ladder into the garret above, where David's mother had prepared the nuptial chamber. There was the feather bed set in a bedstead of oak, a large crockery bowl beside a pewter pitcher filled with fresh spring water on a dresser nearby; beside these were towels and a bar of homemade yellow soap.

A faint streak of moonlight came through the window and fell across the foot of the bed, splashing itself against the wall. David sat on the side of the bed and silently undressed. Polly retired to a remote part of the room, where David's mother had placed her carpetbag, and prepared herself for the nuptial rites. When she came to David, he was already under the covers. She slipped in beside him. They lay there, David in the nude, only Polly's homespun nightgown separating their bodies. Neither reached out for the other. The quiet of the room was broken only by an occasional shout from the revellers below that echoed in the high attic.

After a while, David said, "Well, Polly, we're married."

"Yes, David."

"How does it feel?"

"I don't know yet."

David turned on his side and tugged her gown up. It caught between her middle and the mattress. "Take it off, Polly."

She sat on the side of the bed, took the gown by its hem and peeled it over her head and let it fall on the floor. David gathered her in his arms. His lips found hers, pressed hard over her mouth. She opened her lips a little and began kissing him back. His body was molded against hers now. By God, he thought, by God she was his—he could take her as he pleased. But he hesitated; as his hands moved down her smooth back, he felt her tremble and there was a slight quiver passing through her whole body.

"Polly, are you cold?"

"No, David."

"You're shivering."

"I guess I'm a little frightened."

"You needn't be. I'll go easy."

He held her tight and kissed her, she kissing him back, until she became calm. Then he moved over her, his knees between her legs, spreading them apart. His

85

hands went between her thighs, and quickly moved away.

"What the devil is that?"

"Oh, David, I'm sorry. It's ... it's just some grease—lard. Mama said it would help—the first time."

He gave a little laugh. "That damn Irish mother of yours! She even found a way to get into bed with us."

"Isn't it all right?" Polly asked, embarrassed.

"Sure, hon. Sure. Everything's fine."

He realized he had called her hon; that was what Kate always called him. He felt a little squirlish.

He was gentle at first, as he promised—lulling her into an almost-security—until that final, terrible thrust. Her body heaved upward in agony, as if a knife had been plunged inside her. But her scream was lost and muffled against his encroaching lips. When he felt some of the tension go out of her, he began to move a little, slowly at first, then steadily, ignoring her flinching, which gave way gradually as the pain lessened. He felt her trying to respond with a kind of stunned compliance. But there was no cadence in her movements. He was not sure whether she was trying to dislodge him or clumsily trying to assist.

"Do you want me to stop?"

"No, no. Do it. Whatever you have to do."

"Why don't you move a little—go with me?"

"You—but you hurt me."

"I'll never hurt you again, hon. It'll only get better."

If he had to do it all himself, he'd do it like a journeyman. He placed his hands on the bed beside her shoulders, raised himself free of her bosom, and began to thrust and thrust and thrust, reaching for the very depths of her.

"Oh, David! David!" she cried, but he did not let up.

He was lost in a rhapsody of fancies and emotions. Across his mind flittered many visions which he later shamefully regretted, when he had come to love her deeply and truly. But he could not proscribe them. He was doing all the loving, all the taking, she submissive and terrified. As he worked at his task, hurrying now to

86

get it over with, visions of other girls he had made love with arose in his mind. He saw Kate's great melon-like breasts, and sensed that her soft hungry mouth was over him down there; he felt the fat thighs of Becky Jones straining up to meet him, her tongue searing the inside of his mouth; there was his devoted sister Lovey, her lean belly and hard mons beneath him, her long, lovely legs interlocked behind his back. And there came and went a montage of others, stretching from the cotton patch to the peach orchard to the creek to the Shenandoah Valley. Then it was over. Tenderly he lay away from Polly, his hand covering one of her round, firm breasts.

After a while she asked, "Is that all there is to it?"

"I told you, hon. It'll get better."

"I don't know why mama made such a to-do about it."

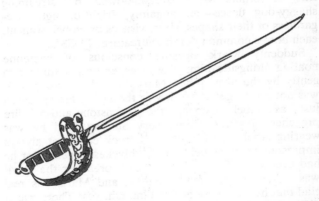

Two hundred and fifty miles southeast, in a little town called Red Bank Church, South Carolina, at the same hour that David Crockett was performing nuptial rites with his bride Polly in the attic of his father's tavern, Mark Travis, sleeping alongside his wife Jemima, was having a most perturbing, if not frightening, dream. He could not come awake, nor prevent the nightmare as it happened. But since he was dreaming of his favorite subject, an unconscious smile crept across his lips and he went on dreaming.

He was dreaming of pussy. Pussies were chasing him. He was running, running, running—in a white mist—he didn't know where—with the pussies at his heels—pussies of all sizes and shapes and of all demeanors. There were great pussies and small pussies; pussies with elevated airy legs and melon-like tits for bodies, pussies on short spidery legs and big, flat duck feet, pussies with phalli as legs and testes as heads; pussies with smooth, neat orifices, pussies with droopy lips; chocolate- and saffron-colored pussies with rose-hued mouths, and coralline and flesh-red and sanguine and blowsy and candy-pink ones that reminded Mark of the all-day suckers he used to lick as a child. Some attractive little pussies were adorned with tenuous curls of blonde or light red hair, while the huge ugly eliptical slits of others were overshadowed by streaming shaggy-dog fleece—an ungainly, frightful sight. Regardless of their shapes, sizes, visages or embellishment, each bore a common dominant feature: PUSSY.

Suddenly Mark became conscious of someone floating alongside him. The stranger was holding him gently by the arm. When Mark looked he saw that it was not a stranger at all; it was the Devil. He appeared just as Abel Gooch, the brimstone-and-hell-fire preacher, described him every Sunday, and he was wearing Abel Gooch's split tail frock coat that always impressed Mark as being of the blackest black color he had ever seen. But unlike the fiery preacher the Devil was a handsome, friendly fellow, and Mark was real glad that he was there beside him. Oh, yes! There was a difference: Old Scratch's hands were not hands at all but red claws, and his feet were of red brimstone and cloven, and curling up from the vent of his frock was a long red tail whose tip-end was a little spearhead of fire. Mark felt that—somehow—his friend would save him from the pursuing pussies.

A heavier mist came down and enveloped Mark and Old Scratch, and the running and fleeing was all over.

After a time the enshrouding nimbus disappeared and the Devil was gone. Mark found that he was lying at full length on a cooling board in the large parlor of his house—dead. But he was not dead, really; everybody just thought he was. He could hear the rasp of carpenter Ebenezer Jones' saw and the rat-tapping of his hammer as he labored just outside the window building Mark's coffin. They had laid him out on the cooling board so his body would not begin to putrefy and start smelling up the place before Ebenezer Jones finished his coffin and they could bury him in the family plot of the churchyard cemetery.

Mark could hear the low rumble of voices in the room. He listened a long while, trying to recognize the voices. Finally he sneaked a look, being careful that nobody in the room would see that he was not really dead. There were four men present. Although they were not exactly family friends, he recognized them instantly from accounts he had read about them in newspapers and journals and in history books.

There was Benjamin Franklin adjusting his square-cut spectacles; and Thomas Jefferson, his long, angular body bent slightly toward Napoleon Bonaparte, trying to catch the general's broken English. And there was Herr Professor Arthur Schopenhauer, the misanthropic German philosopher, looking on with a vinegar-face.

Mark heard Benjamin Franklin ask, "What did he die of?"

"Eating pussy," Thomas Jefferson replied.

"Monsieur! I beg of you!" Napoleon protested. "Mon Dieu!—one does not die from eating the pussee."

Arthur Schopenhauer gave Napoleon a cynical glance. "Begging your pardon, Herr General, I emphatically disagree with you. Women are poison. Their bodies are saturated with deadly venom."

Jefferson stood by listening with interest to the conversation. "There must be some danger in it," he offered. "But I wouldn't know, really. You see, I've never eaten any pussy."

Napoleon was astonished. "My dear Tom!" he ex-

claimed. "Surely you jest. A man of your exquisite refinements—never, *nevair* have you eaten pussy?"

"I'm afraid I haven't."

"What a pity." He looked at Jefferson with sorrowful
eyes. "You poor man."

"I've long felt it wrong—somehow. The thought of
doing it always made me unconsciously compare myself
with a pig. And besides, we do have laws against humans eating humans. I presume pussies are included."

"And a mighty good thing, too," put in Franklin.
"Where would we be without laws preventing cannibal-
ism? The human race would soon gobble itself up. Consider the millions who eat pussy already."

"You don't need laws to restrain me," Schopenhauer
said. "I heartily agree with Herr Jefferson. Have you
gentlemen ever looked at a woman closely, eyeball-to-
crotch? The pussy is indeed a most unattractive
Schale—ugly and highly unappetizing. I once threw a
Berlin *Strassenmadschen* out of my apartment and
down the stairs for coming to me with a smelly pussy.
The ungrateful creature brought a legal process against
me and I was forced to pay her a monthly redress for
the remainder of her life. And since then I have come
to detest all women—that narrow-shouldered, broad-
hipped, short-legged, undersized, inferior race. I hate
the sight of them. I abhor to listen to their gabble. I do
not like the touch of them. I am repelled horribly by
the scent of them. And I certainly have no desire to
taste them."

"One does not eat pussy for the taste," Franklin rejoined. "As a matter of fact, it has no flavor at all. It's
done purely for the aesthetic satisfaction one receives
from it. And, of course, for the gratification he derives
from his ability to send the eatee into such heavenly
bliss during the feast."

"Quite true," Napoleon agreed. "But monsieurs,
you're not taking into account the exquisite fragrance of
pussy." He paused while he lightly kissed the tips of his
fingers and rolled his eyes heavenward. "Ah! How I enjoy the aroma of woman in her full exhudation."

"Humph!" Franklin sniffed. "I prefer my women after a hot tub."

"Mon Dieu!" Napoleon protested. "You cheat yourself! When coming home from a campaign I always sent a courier ahead with a message for Josephine: 'Don't wash. I'm on my way.'"

Schopenhauer gazed at his French neighbor with a look of disgust. Franklin shook his head slowly. Jefferson permitted a little smile to crinkle his lean face. "When I get back to Monticello," he said judiciously, "I shall sample my girl Sally." Then, glancing at Napoleon, he added a qualification. "If you will pardon, Sir—after she takes a hot tub."

All this Mark Travis heard while lying stretched out on the cooling board waiting for Ebenezer Jones to complete the construction of his coffin. He wanted to rise up and proclaim in the name of honest fucking the joys of old-fashioned, every-night lovemaking. But he was dead . . .

He needn't have bothered. For there came a crashing thud in the room, and near Mark. He sat bolt upright. The connoisseurs of pussy-eating stared at the Red Bank Church Lazarus in utter amazement. But before any one of them could speak they all disappeared in a great puff of smoke; and when the smoke cleared there stood, in their stead, Old Scratch himself. Mark saw that the crashing thud had come when the Devil had driven his pitchfork into the floor. Little whisps of smoke were curling up from the plank where the red-hot prongs were embedded.

The next thing Mark knew he was again in the sky, sailing along with Old Scratch at his side. On and on they soared, up and up. Presently Mark grew a little panicky. He wanted to tell his companion they were headed in the wrong direction. But he supposed the Devil was master of his craft and certainly knew which way he wanted to go.

Directly ahead Mark saw a frightening thing—a great elliptical crevasse overhung with masses of black hair. He was flying straight into it. He looked toward the Devil for reassurance but Old Scratch merely smiled a gleeful smile and let him go sailing ahead toward the awful hairy slit. On he sped, unable to check his speed or alter his course, right into that frightful crevasse. Close now, he recognized where he was. It was his wife Jemima's great pussy into which he was flying. He struggled and struggled but he was sucked inside— and all was darkness . . .

Mark came slowly awake. His hand was clutching his testes and his hard joint was nudging his sleeping wife's thigh. He lay quietly, trying to retain all the images of his dream and at the same time make up his mind about the fine hard-on he was nursing. Or, indeed, whether he should do anything about it. But he ought to do something. It would be a shame and a crime against the flesh to go back to sleep and waste such a lovely stiff. He could close his eyes and think of Lucy and run it off by hand. Better still he might slip out of bed and go across the back lawn to Lucy's hut. But it was a frosty night and already he had the sniffles. Besides, the last couple of times he had done it with Lucy he sensed that on her part it was only an accommodation, to keep the good will of her owner so that she might not be ousted as housemaid to Mrs. Travis and be sent back to the cotton field. He strongly suspected that Big Buckeye, the stable Negro, had long-dicked him with Lucy.

After a time he moved his leg over Jemima's thigh, turned her on her back and climbed atop her. As his fingers sought the puffy lips of her sex he wondered why some women had to have so much goddamn hair down there, and why some pussies were so ugly and some so ravishingly lovely. That girl Lucy—now there was a pussy! Hardly any fleece on it at all, just a small triangle of tight black curls; and what a snug little box it was! He parted the labial cleft of his wife's soggy olla and went inside her. Jemima grunted and awakened.

"Mark, what's got into you? It's the middle of the night."

He did not deem a reply necessary. He merely went

about performing a loveless, lackluster function of nature in a perfunctory manner, trying not to notice his wife's mushy breasts drooping off toward her armpits. A half dozen strokes and it was over. The fluid went out of him, his staff quickly softened, retracted, and slipped out of that massive wet cavity. Jemima turned on her side and went back to sleep.

Mark Travis, relieved but far from satisfied and completely disgusted with both himself and Jemima, moved away from her, drew up his knees and told himself, as he had a hundred times before, that he'd be goddamned if he'd ever fuck that lard-assed wife of his again. When he finally went to sleep his mind was made up: he'd not haggle over the price anymore, he'd buy that fourteen-year-old mulatto girl from Colonel Harrell tomorrow. He reckoned she was big enough now.

In her sleep Jemima moved over and snuggled her large buttocks against Mark. Little did she dream that the seed which Mark had planted in her would burgeon and grow into a child they would name William Barret Travis, and that at the Alamo he would unwind, finally, his spindle of purple thread that The *Morari*, who are everpresent at births, tied to him, and gain that which all men crave and few ever achieve—lasting memory in the minds of other men.

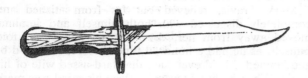

Jim had not loved before, and he had no way of knowing that it would be many years before he learned that few women were capable of giving him the deep, overpowering and all-encompassing love that Paula showered upon him. There was no stopping after the first time. Each new caress was a part of the miracle of discovery. Their couch was the grassy bank or a moss-covered spot underneath a cypress. Nights, after their lovemaking, he would wander back to the spot where they had lain. Here he lived their happiness again. She had whispered her ecstasy and now he remembered every word, every sound. He would touch his cheek: the feel of her lips was still there. Her tenderness humbled him. In his ordered mind the future baffled him. She would, he knew, one day leave him. There had to be an end to their love. He struggled to condition himself for its happening, but the struggle was painful and frustrating.

And Paula, lying on her pallet at the foot of Theola's big canopied feather bed, her eyes wide and troubled, would remember how the red dusk bronzed Jim's hair, how deep and powerful were his thrusts when he made love to her. She would go over and over in her memory all the movements, all the little nuances of rhythm, searching for ways to improve her responses to him, make it more enjoyable, more beautiful for him.

Night was always kind. Its shadows shut out the disorders of her world—a world she never made, one from which she must flee. She tried to imagine what it would be like in New Orleans. She had heard stories about that place and they frightened her, but only for a little while. Her thoughts wandered their circle and returned to Jim, and to the memory of his strength and tenderness. She felt suddenly weak, drained of all force, as if any resolution were beyond her power.

Paula knew the time had come to leave the Cajun country the morning she got up and became sick to her stomach. Fortunately Theola was downstairs having an early breakfast with her parents, and there was no one to witness the retching, which left her weak and frightened. She knew exactly what it meant. It was the certain thing her mother had cautioned her about and schooled her against. But, having only the open woods for a love-chamber, she had no opportunity to practice the arts the old mulatto had passed on to her. Now she had to leave; it was the forced beginning of her life's dream.

Little by little she took the gowns, blouses, shoes, and underthings that Theola had from time to time given her out into the barn and hid them until she was ready. Meanwhile she found an old carpetbag that Mr. Halley had discarded, scrubbed and polished it, and packed all her things in it. Having long planned her escape, it proved not to be difficult. Rafts and barges, loaded with lumber, sugar cane, molasses, cotton, corn, cattle, and tobacco daily drifted down the streams and into the Mississippi and thence to New Orleans. Before anyone else was up and awake, Paula left the Halley plantation. With her precious carpetbag, under the cover of darkness, she stowed away among stacks of sawed planks and lumber with a jug of fresh water and enough fried salted meat to last for the four days journey.

By daylight the unwieldy craft was being poled through the placid bayou waters. By nightfall the barge was approaching the Mississippi, and the men tied it up and camped along the bank. The next day, when the large craft reached the broad stream of the river, she felt safe. Here the current caught it up and carried it smoothly along. The pole men kept the barge close inshore to lessen their labors. The nights were warm, their only annoyance swarming insects against which Paula drew her shawl snugly over her exposed skin. Twice steamships passed, pouring smoke from their twin stacks. She had never seen a steamboat before. They seemed marvelous symbols of the scene in which she would seek her new life.

When Paula did not meet him the next Sunday, Jim knew it was the end of what they had together. Although knowing the hopelessness of it, he went to their trysting place three more Sundays, then set about finding something else to put his mind to. He found it quickly: getting money. Embittered, he directed all his thoughts and energy to becoming rich. The sawmill was making a handsome profit; now to put more of the land they had bought under cultivation. His father loaned him two Negroes and together they began clearing out the stumps and trees, getting more land ready for planting. He'd put it in cotton and sugar cane; those were the products that were bringing the best prices.

About that time an old friend of the family came along. Tex Delacey was a tall, balding, wiry man with skin the color of an unripe pumpkin and one eyelid that drooped. "Tex, you old buzzard!" John exploded, being the first of the brothers to see him approaching. "We'd begun to think the Karankawas had captured and eaten you up!"

"Naw, but I had plenty of narrow getaways in that Texas country."

Tex looked over the sawmill briefly, glanced from one brother to the other. "Looks like you boys got something good going here."

96

"Just a starter," Jim said. "You looking for work, Tex?"

"Well, I reckon after my wandering around I'll put in with you boys for a spell. If you want me."

"Very well," John said, glad to have a strong hand such as he knew Tex was. "You work with us and we'll all get rich, Tex, old fellow, if it's money you're after."

"Not so much money, boys. I found that beyond just enough not to be a burden to anybody, money gets to distorting things. People treat you different if they think you've got money. You can't ever tell who's your friend."

"Later I want to hear all about that Texas country. But right now let me show you what we're doing, what we got . . ."

By the time a month passed, Jim knew Tex Delacey's coming along at this time was a lucky turn. Tex was a powerful man, although a thin one in body. He never seemed to tire and he never seemed to have enough work to do, always finding something else that needed doing. He taught Jim many things. He always carried two knives, one in a scabbard inside his shirt at the back of his neck and the other slung on his belt. The one at his neck had a fourteen-inch blade, double-edged and tapered to a "toothpick" point. He used this as a throwing knife; told Jim he had killed two men with it—in self defense.

"It's called an Arkansas Toothpick, and you carry it behind your neck so if somebody commands you to 'stick 'em up' you can slip it out and whang it at him. The sonuvabitch won't ever get a chance to pull the trigger. The thing's real deadly."

He demonstrated his accuracy with it, showing Jim how he could whip it into a four inch target at thirty feet. When Jim examined it, he said thoughtfully, "This knife has only one purpose. You can't skin an animal with it and it's hardly fit for quartering meat. It's only to kill with. You'll teach me to throw it, won't you, Tex?"

"Yes, and I'll teach you how to fight with this here

97

hunting knife. You can protect yourself better with the right knife than with a pistol once you know how to use it on a man. The basic thing to remember is never handle a knife like you're going to chop. And never go for the head. That's the mistake the Indians make, using a knife like a tomahawk. You hold it with your thumb next to the parrying guard, like so—" Tex handled the hunting knife, holding it at waist height, its blade straight forward. "When the sonuvabitch raises his arm, you go for the belly and the lower rib case. That's the spot—if you want to kill him."

As time went by Jim Bowie worked hard, always with a coldness inside him. Over the years, working side by side, he and Tex Delacey became fast friends. There always seemed to be a silent bond of competitiveness existing between them that bound them ever closer. Whatever one of them did ,the other felt he had to better. But Tex had long ago conceded that Jim was a better man with a knife. "You just got a natural knack for the blade," he told him.

In the meantime, with Tex to supervise the Negroes, Jim had erected a home in Bayou Boeuf. He and Tex lived there, enjoying what seemed an idyllic life for two men who liked to spend days in the woods hunting and fishing. During long nights by the log fire Jim listened to many wonderful and adventuresome stories about Texas. Rezin thought Jim was more at peace with himself than he had been in a long time.

Rezin and John both had taken wives, but Jim preferred the solitude of the woods and the enjoyment of his work. He showed little interest in acquiring a wife and family. But all the while, secretly, he was haunted by the memory of Paula. There were days when he convinced himself he hated her; when he felt the hurt of betrayal by a friend rather than that of being jilted by a lover. Deep down he had a feeling of seeing her again—someplace, sometime. And when that time came, by God! he would be rich enough to buy a dozen Paula's.

Another year went by and Jim began to [grow] restless. Maybe he'd like to see some of the places that Tex always talked about: Little Rock, Memphis, Nacogdoches, Anahuac, San Felipe, Washington-on-the-Brazos, San Antonio. "With a little cash stake," Tex told him, "a man can become land rich in Arkansas and Texas in no time."

Then out of the blue Jim received a letter from Paula. It came like a voice from the grave, for that's just about where Jim had put her in his mind after so long a time. How long had it been, he asked himself. God! Nearly six years. The note, written on a fine quality paper with an engraved Gothic P at the top, read:

Jim,
You used to speak of making a business trip to New Orleans one day. I wonder if you've been here during the past years. In case you do come here and care to see me, I have a house in Rue Conte. Number 5.

Paula

It was a fact that Rezin and John had thought of sending someone to New Orleans to see if a better deal could be made for their mill output. It was believed that by barging their lumber to New Orleans themselves and selling it direct, on the wharves, they could increase their profits. Now the notion suddenly came alive again, and Jim offered to go. A barge was leased, with Negro polers, and Jim and Tex set out with a capacity load of pine and cypress lumber.

Jim's first glimpse of New Orleans was disappointing. Upon approaching, the winding river flowed eastward but before reaching the city looped south in a big horseshoe turn of about five miles across and three miles deep. New Orleans stood at the very apex of this loop. First they saw the new part of the city called the American Colony, sprawled into the outlying fields. In the bend of the river were many ships: schooners, their tall masts against the sky, brigs, barques, rafts and barges, and a few steamboats.

They worked their barge ashore among half a dozen other craft, where willing frontiersmen lent help in making it fast. Jim waited with the cargo while Tex went to find a buyer. Jim didn't need to wait long. Lumber was needed in the spreading town, and the several dealers Tex brought back with him were soon bidding for the merchandise. Jim sold to a man named Pierre DeFarge, who agreed to accompany the barge on its return journey and consult with John and Rezin about the purchase of future shipments. The price Jim got was handsome, and he was paid in gold.

Tex led the way into town from the wharf. He had been to New Orleans before, many times. Besides the docks and warehouses, he knew the taverns, hotels, gambling establishments, and he knew just the right hotel for them. They kept to the waterfront following the Rue de Levee, passed the old Fort St. Louis whose abandoned fortifications had been robbed by builders, and found themselves on a wide, cobbled street, the river on their right, and the old town on their left. Indeed, no city in the New World seemed so heavy with the futility of the past as New Orleans, with a whiff of the river drifting through its narrow, quaint streets. They passed some taller buildings of stone and mortar, two and three stories high, then they reached the Common. Across the Common, facing the river, Jim saw the Cathedral of St. Louis with its twin bell towers.

In the open space were Creole gentlemen in bottle-green frock coats craftily cut and padded instead of merely being stretched to the point of bursting as Jim's shoulders stretched his own garment. Most wore bell-crown beaver hats, many wore cravats instead of stocks. There were nankeen breeches and colorful pantaloons, Hessian boots and buckled slippers and stockings. Some barefoot Negroes wandered about. There were a few ladies in light dresses that foamed above their feet, the tips of tiny satin slippers just peeping from beneath their hems. The sky was feckless, a blue vault—a lovely May afternoon. The ladies seemed anxious to preserve their magnolia complexions. Some carried parasols slanted against the sun's rays, some were trailed by young Negro girls holding parasols over their heads, others wore sunbonnets of pink, blue, and white.

Two young ladies went by, chatting lightly in French. Jim found it difficult to make out what they were saying. Very cultivated French, he assumed, different from his Cajun *patois*. A faint subtlety of fragrance was left on the air by their passing. His eyes followed them. How tiny they seemed, their waists of a stemlike slenderness.

Side by side Jim and Tex walked along, still on the Rue de Levee; they crossed the Rue Charteris and Jim gaped at the stately Ursuline Convent with its many brick chimneys and its dormered roof. Across the street raked the iron pickets of the Place d'Armes, a grassy oblong flanked by flower beds and chinaberry trees. A block further lay their destination, the Hotel de la Marine.

Jim's thoughts turned to Paula. During the trip down the river she had been on his mind constantly, his breast warming at the prospect of being in the same city with her. Now that he was here, near her, he was overtaken by a strange perversity. Maybe he'd not even bother to look her up. Hadn't she left him without even a goodbye? Hadn't she told him that she was schooled to love on command? If so, by the same token she could cease to love on command? He was plagued by a long festering scorn for her, and goaded by an intense curiosity to see her again. What should he do?

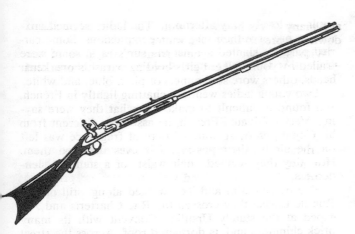

Polly's mother saw that the newlyweds got a spinning wheel, a plow, a horse, two cows, and a calf as Polly's dowry; and she arranged for David to rent a small farm near her own. David pushed his dreams of the world beyond the wilderness back in his mind and struggled valiantly with the soil, while Polly sat in the little cabin treadlling her spinning wheel, taking time out to give birth to three children—two boys, John Wesley and William, and a daughter, Margaret. John Wesley grew up to follow in his father's footsteps and was elected to Congress.

David's spirit of wanderlust never died, and as he wrote in his autobiography, "I found that it was therefore the more necessary that I should hunt some better place to get along; as I knowed I would have to move at some time, I thought it better to do it before my family got too large, that I might have less to carry."

He took his family, horses, cows, and all his worldly belongings and trekked across the mountains and settled at the head of Mulberry Creek, on the Elk River. Here he found the land rich and productive, the game plentiful, especially the deer and bear. In this new country he began to distinguish himself as a hunter. He rarely wasted a shot, supplying his family and many of his neighbors with their meat to be salted down and preserved for the winter months.

With his move to a new frontier, the fires of the dream had been rekindled. Something out there kept drawing him deeper into the wilderness, ever closer to hostile and warring Indians. However, David tried hard to become a faithful servant of the soil. He cleared the land, tilled the fields, hunted, and at night made ardent love with Polly. But rumors of better things and new experiences further west drifted to his ears. He again grew restless, uprooted his family once more, abandoned his land, and moved west into a more primitive frontier, this time to Franklin County, and took up land on Bean Creek.

Destiny had placed David Crockett in the wings of the stage that was to be his forte for the remainder of his life. His name will be henceforth on the tongues of everyone in the land, his powerful force felt in the halls of Congress, and eventually he will earn reknown in all the encyclopaedic columns of the world. He was now cheek-and-jowl with the northern tribes of the Creek nation; and the Indians having had their fill of the white man's encroachment upon their land and nation, were about to strike out in their defense.

The main body of the Creeks lived in northeast Alabama, at the junction of the Coosa and Tallaposa Rivers, where they unite with the Alabama River. Unlike the tribes of the far western plains, these Indians preferred not to roam. They were proud, of a high order of intelligence, accomplished in many arts, possessing rich credentials, and knew in full the history of their own race. They were well on their way to becoming "civilized" and finding a peaceful coexistence, and eventual assimilation with the whites. But, incited to war, they became savage enemies, haughty, ruthless, and very brave.

From their geographical and historical association with the white man the Creeks acquired a measure of his culture as well as his vices. Some of the tribes had

103

crudely modelled their governments on those of the white man's states. They built log houses and furnished them with chairs, tables, and bedsteads, and other conveniences of civilized society. They cultivated their lands, raised grain and vegetables, and products common to the latitude. They planted cotton, tobacco, grew rice and potatoes, especially the sweet variety. They kept poultry—chickens, turkeys, ducks; stocks of cattle, horses, sheep, hogs, goats.

The Creek territory was rich in timber and game. There was hickory, black walnut, ash, hackberry, locust, mulberry, pine, cedar, pecan, bois d'arc. For game there was elk, antelope, bear, and buffalo.

The buffalo was a most provident beast. For the frontier Indian the buffalo was all-important. Besides furnishing the staple food, it provided a variety of other important commodities. The brain and liver were used for softening leather, the horns and skull for ladles and vessels, the shoulder blades for hoes or pikes, the tendons for bow strings, the tail hair to make ropes and belts, the hide to provide bridles and saddles and to fashion shields and tents, traveling cases, shirts, moccasins, beds, and robes—a surprising array of gifts from one clumsy beast. In view of the buffalo's prodigal utility, it is little wonder it was the first animal to disappear from the wilderness and the western landscape.

The Creeks liked decoration and ornament and were fond of music and ball playing. The women were distinguished in character and intelligence, and were considered prizes whenever settlers could take them for their wives. They were taller, with lissome figures, high foreheads and, in general, lacking the Oriental cast of the eyes. They rode side saddle and dressed in the fashion of the whites.

In time of war, tall red poles were erected in the public squares of their villages. These poles were carried into battle by elders. Therefore the warring Indians were given the name of "Red Sticks." White villages—those with no red poles—were known as "peace towns." David Crocket will say years later in Congress that when he went to war with the Creeks, he was surprised to find so many white men pleasantly married to Creek women and living contentedly in the wilderness with their Indian brothers.

In proportion, as these Indians improved in intelligence and culture, wealth and enterprise, did the white man covet their country. Individually and in concert, by law and without law, the white man oppressed the owners of the soil and depredated their country. The formal resistance of the Creeks held off the white encroachment for a time, but in the end the sheer weight of numbers and advanced firearms, and the increasing ferocity and cruelty of the white man, overpowered the Indians and deprived them of their lands. The major problem of the settlers was not—much though historians would like to have it that way—their economic condition, their political rights, or the greed of land speculators. It was purely and simply what to do about the Creeks, upon whose land they were intruding and who resented the intrusion. Either the Indians must be bought off or they must be driven off. After the Fort Mims massacre there was but one way for the settlers. The Indians must be driven off, even killed off.

News traveled mysteriously in the wilderness. No tangible means of communications seemed to exist, yet among the few scattered cabins set deep in the forest events would be told that happened hundreds of miles away. Suddenly a name was on everyone's lips—Tecumseh. It went from fields to cabins to villages, echoing and spreading among the thickly wooded valleys. With the name came word that the Indians were gathering for resistance against the whites.

Tecumseh was a Shawnee, born at the ancient seat of the tribe in the Valley of the Miami. The power of the Shawnee had been broken before he was born, in earlier Indian wars, and he was determined to restore it. Magnificent in stature, far famed as a brave man and as a hunter, as a persuasive orator, Tecumseh had conceived an even greater plan. The many Indian tribes

105

had never been united; most often they had been at war with one another. Tecumseh proposed to unite them all, from the Great Lakes to Tennessee to Alabama to Georgia to Florida, in one warlike confederation. United they would exterminate the white settlers and hold the country for the Indians alone.

Until Tecumseh's visit the Creeks had come to be regarded as "good Indians." But gradually they had retreated as white settlers penetrated into the new country. Certainly no one could think they left willingly, though some had been paid as much as two cents an acre for their land. They had occupied this beautiful country for generations, and now they were obliged to leave behind their favorite hunting grounds, their splendid timber, their well-built towns and villages.

Tecumseh exhorted them to rise up and strike down the white invaders. Already, he assured them, the northern Indians had united and were pushing back the whites. A man, he told them, could not sell the land any more than he could sell the sea or the air he breathed. The Indians did not usually realize that when they accepted gifts for granting the right to use part of their tribal domain, they gave up their own right to use it.

Tecumseh's mind ranged far beyond the old argument about the ownership of land. He had a dream: the dream of his people adapting to white civilization. He foresaw that if the Indians could be united in their common interest they might establish a great state of their own, which would have the cohesive force to withstand the white man's advance. It was noble in conception. But it was foredoomed to failure—not only by the congenital inability of the Indians to submit themselves to the discipline that union demanded, but also by the irreversible force of American nationalism, which nothing could stay. Yet it was a lofty dream; for it represented the first attempt of the Indians to adapt to the new form of life that was overtaking the wilderness. If his plan could succeed only for a little while, Tecumseh believed, the Indians might save themselves from being debauched by the white man, and thus eventually escape being destroyed.

Tecumseh's oratory was lost on the older Indians. They could see little virtue in casting their lot with northern Indians who, after all, had never done anything for them. But the younger men, whose imagination had already been captured by the power of the Tecumseh legend, were enchanted by his majestic presence. The older men prevailed, however, for a time, and turned their backs upon the great Shawnee chief.

Tecumseh castigated them mightily. He called them cowardly names and, blazing in sudden anger, as he frequently did, shouted to them: "You have white blood!" Then he warned them with a prophecy. "I shall go," he said, "but soon I shall stamp the ground with my foot and shake every house in your domain."

Soon after his departure heavy tremors were felt throughout the Creek nation. They were caused by the mighty earthquake that sunk a vast forest in southern Tennessee and caused the Mississippi to flow upstream for twenty-four hours, flooding thousands of acres of land to form a lake that David Crockett was to name Reelfoot Lake. A good many doubters were ready to take up the hatchet at once. But there were not more than four thousand of them; and they were armed so poorly with such faulty firearms that they had to resort to bows and arrows and clubs after the first volley. They were hardly formidable, but they frightened the settlers on the frontier.

The great Shawnee chief who inspired the Creeks with his matchless eloquence was not destined to lead the warriors in their bid for survival. That destiny fell to one, like other foreigners before him who had risen to lead a nation to destruction, who was not a Creek. The mantle fell on the shoulders of William Weatherford, who was of Scotch, French, Spanish, and only one-eighth Indian blood. It is claimed by some scholars of geneology that a drop of blood compounded of greatness will often persevere and imbrue for many

107

generations. To comprehend the young chief-by-choice, Red Eagle, as William Weatherford chose to call himself, and who was stirred by Tecumseh's dream of an Indian confederacy stretching from the Great Lakes to the Gulf, one must look at his illustrious heredity.

Red Eagle boasted a romantic ancestry. His great-grandfather Captain Marchand came from the Gulf and established a French fort in Alabama territory. He married a Creek girl, and a beautiful daughter named Sehoy resulted from this union. Captain Marchand lost his life in battle and a young English Captain stole the fourteen-year-old Sehoy, whom he made his mistress. One day the Captain entertained a wandering and wealthy Scottish adventurer, Lachlan McGillivray. When the Scotchman departed he, in turn, stole Sehoy from the young Englishman. McGillivray fell in love with the lovely Sehoy and built for her on the Coosa River a great house and set her up in a life of luxury. From here he conducted a profitable fur trade.

The union was a happy one and Sehoy bore him a son and two daughters. Old McGillivray was very proud of his son, whom he named Alexander and sent to Charleston to be educated "so he can grow up to be a white man."

But Alexander, as his father regretfully said before he abruptly abandoned his home and family and went back to Scotland never to return, "fell back upon the culture of his grandmother and a career which French deceit, Scotch thrift and Creek savagery would see him far." The boy boasted that no Yankee blood polluted his veins. That drop of blood contaminated with greatness did see him far. His career was remarkable. He became a British colonel in the Revolution, a Spanish civil servant under Miro, and at last in the world of which David Crockett was born, he established himself as a Creek chief. But in the end he wound up as a "white man," and a brigadier general in the United States Army. When he died in 1793 he left a fortune in silver dollars and was given a Masonic funeral in Pensacola, where he was buried.

He left behind him a half sister who married a Scot trader. They had two sons, John and William. When the boys were old enough to understand their mixed blood ancestry, their father gave them a choice between two ways of life. William chose to be a Creek and rose in Indian councils as Red Eagle. Like Tecumseh himself, he was tall and dignified in bearing, a proud man and courageous warrior; he had light brown hair, black eyes, and was fair of skin. While he chose to call himself Red Eagle, the Indians gave him the tribal name of Hoponika Futsahia—Truth Maker. It was he who heard Tecumseh's passionate words and awakened to his vision.

The death blow to Tecumseh's dream would be delivered by another man in whose veins ran the blood of greatness, and to whom Red Eagle must finally bow. General Andrew Jackson was in bed at his home in Nashville, recovering from a wound in his left arm that he had suffered in a duel with his friend Colonel Thomas Hart Benton, when the news of the Fort Mims massacre reached him. The settlers demanded that Red Eagle and his Creeks be exterminated. Hardly strong enough to sit his horse, he answered the call.

Andrew Jackson was born ten years before David Crockett, at the Waxhaw settlement on the frontier of the Carolinas between North Carolina and South Carolina; and when he became famous both states claimed him, but as President he gave the nod to South Carolina. The Waxhaw territory offered little opportunity for formal education and such schooling as Jackson did have was interrupted by the British invasion of the western Carolinas in 1780-81. Jackson was captured by the British. Shortly after he was imprisoned he refused to polish the boots of a British officer and was slapped across the face with a sabre. That unsung officer's cruelty probably cost the British a victory in the War of 1812, thus preserving for the colonies the independence they had won in the Revolutionary War a little more than a quarter of a century earlier. Adding to this in-

109

sult, Jackson's mother and two brothers died as a result of the British invasion. These two occurrences fixed in Jackson's mind a life-long hostility to the British; and at the crucial Battle of New Orleans Jackson vowed he'd die in battle or defeat the despised Englishmen. His victory made him a national hero.

Jackson had fought the Indians in Florida and beaten them. Now that there was another uprising, he was called upon to exterminate the most civilized of all the southern Indians—the Creeks. And whom would he call upon to do the killing? Volunteers like David Crockett.

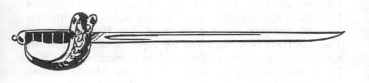

"Hey, I'll betcha I can swim to that log and back quicker'n you." Young Bonham pointed to a section of an old pine tree that had long ago fallen into the river.

"You're always trying to beat me at something. Like you wanted to race from my house to the river. I beat you, like always."

"Come on, when I say go."

"Naw, I told you I'll only beat you."

"I'll beat you this time. Come on! When I say go!"

"All right," the taller boy said, resignedly.

Young Bonham gave the signal, the two boys' naked bodies splashed into the water. They kicked, fought the water, propelled themselves in anything but the style of an expert swimmer, touched the log, turned and started back. Already Bill Travis was a head in front of Jim Bonham.

"I told you. But you're always so stubborn I have to convince you."

The two young friends lay half submerged in the red mud of the river bank, their legs extended into the water.

"Tell me, Bill, what you gonna be when you grow up?"

"I don't know, Jim. What you gonna be?"

"My pa says he wants me to go to West Point and become an officer in the United States Army. Says he's gonna ask your dad to speak to Mr. Calhoun about getting me in when I'm old enough."

"Lordy! That'll be a long time—six or seven years!"

"Pa says you have to start with politicians a long time in advance."

"Well, Mr. Calhoun stops at our house on his way to Charleston every time he goes to see his wife's relatives there. Last time he stayed over night. Him and my dad are old-time friends. My dad can fix anything with Mr. John Calhoun."

"What you gonna be, Bill?"

"I heard Dad and Mr. Calhoun talking about me. Dad wants me to be a planter like him. Mr. Calhoun said with the northerners fixing the tariff and everything in Washington, planting might not be so good a thing. He told my dad I ought to be a lawyer, like him. He said he could get me in Yale, where he went to study law. But shucks! I don't ever want to go away from here. Do you?"

"Yeah, Bill. I sure do. Tell you what. Let's run away. Just for a while. You want to see what it's like out yonder, don't you? Wouldn't it be fun to see what's down the Old Indian Trail? Just think, it goes all the way from Greenville to New Orleans. Gosh! New Orleans! Wouldn't you like to see New Orleans?"

"I don't know. I told you I like it here in Red Bank Church. Say, you coming home with me and spend the night?"

111

"Your ma got room? What about the new baby your pa found?"

Young Bill Travis' blue eyes momentarily clouded. "Something funny about that. Dad brought this baby—it's a boy, you know—in from the stables. Said he found him in a basket hung on the cowpen."

"Well, what's so funny about finding a baby?"

"I heard him and mom fussing about it."

"Fussing? Doesn't your ma want it?"

"She never minds kids. Lordy, look at my ten brothers and sisters. I heard her say, 'Mark, you know right well where that child came from. And if you say you don't, I'll ask your friend Colonel Harrell. Why, just look at its skin and eyes. Skin as fair as burnt ivory and the same bold, black eyes as that wench I made you send back to the colonel.'"

Jim was all ears, his eyes shining. "You don't reckon . . ."

Bill cut him off. "I don't reckon nothing! And you'd better not either, Jim Bonham!"

"Aw, Bill, I didn't mean anything. But go on—then what?"

"Then what what?"

"What did your pa say?"

"Not much. He just said, 'Jemima, you're always accusing the Negroes of things you don't know nothing about. Do you want to keep the baby or not?'"

"Are you gonna keep him?" Jim Bonham asked Travis.

"I reckon so. But mom sure put her foot down on one thing. She said he couldn't have a Travis name."

"What you gonna call him?"

"Dad gave him the name of William Barr."

Jim Bonham grinned. "Well, that name sure makes him sound like your half brother."

The two boys got up out of the muddy bank, plunged into the water to wash off. When they came out, Jim said, "Lookee here!" He pointed to his peter which had suddenly become erect and was pulsating up and down

112

impatiently. He cupped his fist around it. "Wonder what it's like to fuck a nigger? Have you ever, Bill?"

"Naw, and I ain't going to."

"Why not?"

"Mom says it ain't Christian."

"What's being Christian got to do with fucking a nigger?"

"I don't know. All I know is that mom sure is against it."

Jim was now giving his whang a gentle massaging. "Tell you what, Bill. Get yours up, and I'll bet you I can jack mine off quicker'n you can yours."

"You want to lose again?"

"I ain't gonna lose. I got a stiff up already."

"The last time we both got 'em up, you wanted to bet yours was longer than mine. You lost, remember? Now you wanna lose again!"

Jim Boham's gentle massaging had changed into a lively jack-stroking. His eyes were half closed, his face distorted. Suddenly his pelvis bowed out, his fist accelerated, and the thick, grey liquid came forth in quick spurts. "It's too late. You lose."

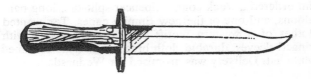

A week went by and Jim Bowie did not go to see Paula. He and Tex spent merry days enjoying New Orleans. Tex introduced Jim to a number of casinos where they had increased the two thousand dollars Jim received from the cargo of lumber to nearly five thousand, and to several elegant bordellos where they had reduced the sum considerably. New Orleans was a reawakening for Jim. He had remained in the Cajun woods too long. He began to realize that the importance of money was not merely in the possessing of it. He was, for the first time, experiencing what money could do for a man. Spending money was vastly different from fondly dreaming of money and getting money and hoarding money. He knew now that he would never allow himself to be without plenty of it; and he resolved to spend it as fast as he got it, otherwise life was a chase of pure futility which ended at the gate of the graveyard with nobody the winner.

"I've just realized," he said to Tex one morning, "how seedy we look, how far behind the mode we are in the bayou country. Do you know of a good modern tailor?"

Tex did, certainly. Within minutes they found themselves in the establishment of the much sought after tailor, Papillon. That thin, agile artist of the cloth considered Jim's shoulders and shook his head. He had some coats, to be sure, but they were designed for the ordinary figure, nothing for one as magnificent as this.

"Then cut me some to fit," Jim ordered.

For the next two hours, Papillon's assistants swarmed around Jim calling off measurements, which the master noted on paper with his little facile hands. Jim ordered a frock coat, a Spencer split-tail, long pantaloons, and one of the new Empire capes. Tex wanted clothes of a western motif: soft leather jackets with fringed sleeves, durable cloth breeches, a wide-brimmed white hat. Delivery was promised for Wednesday.

The two men from the Bayou country had discovered that it was not easy to strike up camaraderie with the natives of New Orleans. The Creoles regarded the Americans as barbarians, who lived, presumably, on a diet of gunpowder and whiskey, and had too much

114

natural violence to be permitted in polite company. Visitors in the city found it easier to fall in with one another. For several nights they had played *vingt-et-un*, which Jim knew as blackjack, with a group of Americans from Natchez, who were in the city on some banking business.

Papillon, indeed, had given Jim a new image and a rebirth of confidence. So on Wednesday evening when Jim pushed open the door to the *Casino L'Armoise*, Tex close behind him in his new western attire, he felt he was the gentleman that Papillon's clothes proclaimed him to be. The group from Natchez were awaiting him, hopeful of recouping their losses. Jim had assured them of a final opportunity before they had to return to Natchez.

A table was arranged and Jim found himself seated with Dr. Thomas H. Maddox, Major Norris Wright, and Reverend Robert Crain, all citizens of Natchez. Tonight there were two strangers in the party. Introduced, they were Henri and Alfred Fouchet, prominent New Orleans bankers. Jim noticed that Henri Fouchet wore a highly decorated dueling sword. Then he remembered. Henri Fouchet was talked about as one of the top ranked swordsmen of the city. Tex elected to remain out of the game and wandered off in the direction of the bar, leaving six players altogether.

"Gentlemen," Jim said, taking his place at the table, "Do you have an accounting of your losses?"

"Bowie, you're into me for one thousand, five hundred and forty dollars," Major Wright said gruffly. He was a burly man, with black hair brushed smoothly, and eyes equally dark that looked more piercing because of his florid face.

"I'm down five hundred and thirty-five dollars," put in Reverend Robert Crain, a hawk-faced old gentleman who wore his white hair to his shoulders.

Dr. Maddox, a stern-visaged man in his middle forties claimed losses of three hundred dollars.

The Fouchet brothers sat silent during this conversation, listening amusedly. Both were husky, athletic

115

types, with long muscular arms. By their small brown eyes and massive overhanging brows one would instantly take them for brothers, almost like twins.

Major Wright looked up into Jim's face, affecting an obsequious smile. "Comes to twenty-three hundred and seventy-five dollars, Bowie," he said putting his pencil and notebook away.

"Very well," Jim said, taking from his Spencer coat a handful of gold pieces. He counted out the exact amount. "You may make it a single hand. Or if you wish it simple and quick, one cut of the deck. High card."

A buzzing went around the table, a decision was reached, an equal amount of money was stacked alongside Jim's. "A single hand of *vingt-et-un*," Wright announced.

"Deal, Major Wright," Jim said. He was glad it would be a short session. He had no particular zest for these Natchez fellows. They impressed him as narrow and niggardly. He preferred the company of the chary Creoles, even if they did look upon *les Americains* with a condescending air. Such men as these visitors from Natchez, he reflected, had a lot to do with the Creoles' attitude toward Americans.

The cards were shuffled and cut and Major Wright slid a card towards Jim, face down, dealt himself the same; another to Jim, face up, another to himself. Jim's show card was a jack. Face down he had a five. Wright showed a king.

"A card, sir," Jim said.

Wright nodded, slipped a card across the table, face down. Jim glanced at it, motioned enough. It was a three, giving him eighteen.

Norris Wright studied his two cards, fumbled with the deck, beads of perspiration standing out on his brow. Slowly he took a card and more slowly looked at it. His face brightened. He turned over his down card: he showed a king, a two, and a five, a total of seventeen.

116

"Eighteen," Jim said. He gathered up the money and rose to go.

"Quitting us, eh?" Wright said sourly.

"It was so agreed."

"Just the same," Robert Crain said, "you won our money and you're cribbing out on us."

The muscles of Jim's face flicked with sudden anger. He looked fiercely across the table at the men, one by one. He sat down. "Name the stakes, gentlemen," he said, and emptied his pockets on the table.

"Count it," Wright said.

Jim quickly tallied and stacked all the gold pieces. "Five thousand, eight hundred and fifty-three dollars."

For the first time one of the Fouchet brothers spoke. Henri Fouchet said, "One hand against it all."

"In gold," Jim said. Already some of the players were opening their purses and fumbling with paper.

"It'll take a moment," Alfred Fouchet said, and left the table.

Tex returned and was tugging gently at Jim's arm. Jim lifted his face to him, Tex bent down and whispered, "Don't do it."

Jim shrugged him off.

Alfred Fouchet returned and began stacking gold pieces in the center of the table. Wright said, "Henri will deal."

Henri Fouchet produced a fresh deck of cards, shuffled them, slid the cards across the table to Jim, who cut them and pushed the deck back. Imperturbably, Fouchet dealt to Jim a deuce face down; for his next card Jim got a queen: twelve. A hard hand to hit. Impossible to stand on.

Fouchet glanced at his cards, seemed satisfied. "Another card, Monsieur?"

"Please."

The third card was a jack. Jim turned up his down card. He was broke.

"Hold it!" Tex said behind Jim. He snatched up the deck of cards from the table, began fingering them.

117

"Trimmed top and bottom for a sucker deal." He tossed the cards back on the table.

Greedy hands were gathering in the gold pieces and they quickly disappeared into pockets.

Henri Fouchet rose slowly, Jim with him. To Fouchet this was something very serious. Six men dead and four wounded; Fouchet had a reputation to maintain. His sword clanked in its decorated scabbard against the table as he swayed. The weapon which Fouchet always wore—mainly because of the rich gold and silver inlays in its hilt and font—had become a conversation piece among dueling circles, and Henri Fouchet had made it famous by his extraordinary skills; it was a seventeenth-century triangular rapier made in Naples by L. Palumbo. The contest would be without sport, Fouchet thought, and with little honor or exercise. But he felt he had to kill this outlandishly decked-out buffoon in order to maintain his status. Fouchet looked at Tex with an air of utter disdain. His lips curled. "Would you care to explain that?"

"No need," Jim said, easing Tex aside. He slid the cards through his fingers, tossing certain ones face down on the table. "Turn those cards," he said coldly. "They're the face cards, jacks, queens, and kings. Fouchet," he said, "your quarrel is with me, not with my friend."

It mattered not with the expert swordsman. Killing this backwoodsman would be as satisfying as killing the other. "Swords!"

Fouchet stepped back, unsheathed and lifted his blade, testing it.

"Your sword against my knife," Jim held out his hand and Tex laid his hunting knife in it.

Albert Fouchet stepped between the men. "But, Monsieurs, there are certain formalities."

"Forego the formalities," his brother said confidently. What chance did a backwoodsman with a twelve-inch blade have against a meter-long sword in the hands of an expert fencer?

"Pardon," Jim said, "I believe it is mine to lay down the terms."

Henri Fouchet shrugged. "It is Monsieur Bowie's privilege to choose the terms of his death."

Jim turned to Tex. "Find a room—empty and bare. It must be completely dark."

"What are you suggesting?" For the first time Fouchet's composure was penetrated.

"You and I will enter a dark room, barefooted, you with your sword, I with my knife. One of us will come out. The other will die."

Fouchet's nimble mind raced for an analysis, a reason behind such a ridiculous—insane—method of fighting. A barbarous backwoods custom? Such vulgarity! Certainly this frontiersman lacked all sensibilities of etiquette. No matter. He'd show his—the Fouchet—magnanimity. He'd kill this cockerel by his own terms. He gave a ribald laugh. "A duel in the dark! A novel idea!"

Tex was back. "I've found just the place. An empty store-room above. There's but a single window, a skylight and it's painted black. I've closed it. The room's dark as hades itself. Follow me."

In the dark, Fouchet's bravado began to fade. What had been a few moments ago an easy—too easy—kill was suddenly a strange and terrifying ordeal. It had seemed as child's play—something inwardly to be ashamed of or to roar with laughter about. But now he began to rationalize. The darkness. He had not considered the darkness. Never in all his life had he imagined himself without his eyes. They were his all! They told him everything: where to thrust, when to parry— how to survive! Above all they told him where the enemy was. Eyes!

The others had locked the door. Outside, in the light, they stood: Norris, Crain, Maddox, brother Albert, Tex, and a number of the morbidly curious who had left their gaming tables. One would die in that dark room. One would come out alive.

Fouchet sought to reassure himself. Was he not one

119

of the foremost swordsmen of New Orleans? A meter-long rapier in the hands of an expert against a back-woodsman with a butcher knife. . . did not the dullard value his life? He took a firmer grip on the hilt of his sword. One thrust and it would be over.

He felt the cold floor against his feet. He ventured a hand behind his back. He urgently wanted to feel the wall at his rear. A corner would be better, but surely his adversary had already found a corner for himself. That left him one chance out of three. No, he'd not gamble the odds. The wall. He had to gain the wall. With his rapier straight out, carefully he began to move backward. His silk-stockinged feet moving slowly and softly—not sliding but lifted and placed—touched barely on the floor at first and then gradually set down. It seemed an eternity but it was only a few steps and then he felt it, the cold cement of the wall against his shirt, damp with perspiration. Now he had an advantage. He need only keep absolutely still until the clod from the country made a noise—the tiniest sound—and then swish! He was prepared to make the quickest, most deadly thrust of his entire life.

He waited, the hilt of his sword at his thigh. His confidence began to mount. He—Fouchet—was still unharmed. He had the wall at his back. Bowie surely was frightened, cringing in his corner—it was just a matter of moments until his death. Thoughts flashed through Fouchet's mind of his reception in his club afterwards. He would be magnanimous; he would not bend to scorn the *Americain's* ridiculous code of fighting. And he began to believe, really, that he was a brave and noble fellow.

He waited. And nothing. If only the buffoon would give a sign—just one little sound of feet sliding over the floor, a faint click of his knife against the wall. He began to consider where he'd make the thrust. In the neck or the breast. It had to be a quick kill. He tried to think of something he had about him, a coin or perhaps a key in his pocket, that he might toss in another direction to make his enemy give himself away. A gold coin. Yes, there was one in his breeches pocket. But which pocket? Carefully, slowly, his free hand slipped into his left pocket. Empty. Did he dare change his sword from right to left hand long enough to get the coin from his other pocket? No.

Still no sound from the other. Waiting became painful. He began to perspire all over. Panic. It began in the guts—a burning, a nervousness; then a slight trembling of the limbs; finally a collapse of confidence. Sweat poured from his body. He began to imagine he could actually see his enemy in the darkness. Yes, there in *that* corner—crouching with fear, of course. Anxiety urged Fouchet to end the suspense, to get it over with quickly. Make the deadly thrust—now. Plunge the needle-sharp point of the rapier into Bowie's left breast, directly into the heart. He fixed his attention upon the corner where he was sure his enemy waited.

But Jim Bowie was not in that corner. He was not in any corner. When the door closed, clamping total darkness upon the room, Jim instantly planted his shoeless feet in the middle of the room. In a bent position, knife held at his waist, he moved only his head, slowly, from side to side. Otherwise he was as still as the darkness around him. Years spent in the loneliness of the woods had taught him certain traits of the animals. It was borne upon him that fear had an odor, and he had learned how to wait for its signal. He remembered, too, something his father, General Merriam's old swamp trooper, told him: if you want to know what a panther is going to do you have to think like a panther. He knew the panther would spring. He had only to wait.

Uncertainty and fear drained Fouchet of patience. He became even more tense, sweated more profusely. Was that a sound? Or was it a guess made into a sound? The guess grew and his mind *saw* . . . There! Frantically he stabbed. Only emptiness. But the action steadied him. He became bolder. He gripped his rapier firmly. He listened. Silence was absolute. Only the thumping of the pulse in his own ears seemed unnaturally loud. His confidence rose. Desperately he thrust in the dark, probing corners of the room. Nothing. He whipped the blade around.

There was a blow—a dreadful pain in his side. He felt the strength suddenly drain from his body. His sword clattered to the floor. It was the only sound that penetrated his ears in the blackness of the death chamber. And it was the last he ever heard.

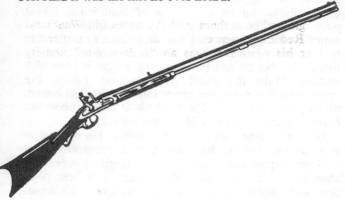

When the news of the Fort Mims massacre reached David Crockett, he was living about ten miles below Winchester, Tennessee. He had built a cabin which he called "Kentuck" on the banks of the tinkling waters of Bean Creek, where trout, crayfish, snapping turtles, and bullfrogs habitated. Deer, bear, and game were plentiful: this was virgin wilderness, the settlers had not been here long enough to kill off the game, and the Indians had never killed more than they needed for the day's sustenance. Roaming through the wood with his trusted rifle, he bountifully supplied his table as all settlers did in those days. Every first Saturday of the month a shooting match was held in Winchester with a beef or hog or sacks of flour as prizes. David won with such regularity that the fun for the other shooters went out of it all, and the matches were abandoned. But the settlers were not to suffer from boredom. A new excitement pervaded the town. General Jackson wanted volunteers to avenge the massacre at Fort Mims.

No one in David Crockett's country knew what set the Creeks on the warpath. But the names of Tecumseh and Red Eagle were sounds to inflame all backwoodsmen, although Tecumseh did not live to see the beginning of the war he so eloquently fomented. It was enough that white settlers had been killed by Indians. They blamed the war on the massacre at Fort Mims. Red Eagle had been there, and the name Bill Weatherford or Red Eagle was cause aplenty for any settler to shoulder his rifle. This was an "Indian War" and it caused inflammation everywhere; excitement ran like a prairie fire, from farm to farm, cabin to cabin, settlement to settlement. The tiger was loose. Nobody thought of anything but killing Indians. Fort Mims was the word—the catalyst. "Revenge Fort Mims!"

Fort Mims was not truly a fort. It was, in fact, no more than a stockade built around the fortified home of a planter by the name of Samuel Mims. Yet it was defensible and was garrisoned by eighty militiamen, commanded by Major Daniel Beasley. Rumors of an Indian revolt had packed the stronghold with five hundred and thirteen refugees from the surrounding countryside. These included rich planters, a body of white farmers, some half-breeds and Negro slaves. Among them were one-hundred-and-eighty women and children. It was the end of August 1813, one of the hottest summers in the memory of the settlers of southern Alabama. The fort was enjoying a quiet Sunday. Christian services had been held in the Mims house for a few of the devout. During the afternoon ennui some of the men had broken out bottles of whiskey and wine; others were engaging in a series of wrestling matches.

A Negro slave named Hosiah was outside the fort hunting through the watermelon patch for some small overlooked fruit. Suddenly his eyes caught a glimpse of a bright feather moving among the shrubbery. He dropped to his knees and listened, now and then raising his head to look. He made his way back to the fort and sought out his master, breathless.

"Massa! Massa! Dere's Indians outside!"

John Randon, Hosiah's owner, reported what he had heard to Major Beasley. The major had a whiskey bottle in one hand, was stripped to the waist, having been engaged in wrestling with a fellow officer, Captain Dixon Bailey. "Indians! Nonsense! My scouts have reported no Indians in this vicinity."

"But Massa Randon," Hosiah pleaded to his owner, "I done seen 'em! Dere all around de fort."

"I think, Major,' Mr. Randon said, "you ought to send out some scouts."

"Very well, if it'll make you rest any easier. But," he warned, shaking a finger at the trembling Hosiah, "if there are no Indians I'll have you lashed to the post and whipped!"

So threatening, he ordered a half-breed named Joe to select three men and scout the area. Joe chose three Negro companions and they went outside to look.

It being an excessively hot day Joe and two of his friends found comfort in the shade of a pine tree and sent the third Negro to "look around a little." Joe and his companions waited three quarters of an hour but their friend did not return; they decided he had run away, this being an excellent chance to make his bid for freedom, especially since they had heard Major Beasley's orders for such harsh punishment for reporting falsely. Whether the man had escaped or had been captured and killed by the Indians, Joe did not bother to speculate. He reported to Major Beasley that, indeed, the major was right, there were no Indians anywhere in sight. But when the two Negroes told their master that no scouting had really been done, and that they feared for their brother's fate, Major Beasley ordered these two, together with Hosiah, tied to the gate posts and severely lashed. There they would stay, he said, until Hosiah admitted he had lied about seeing Indians; if he had not done so by the morrow, another lashing

124

would be administered to all three of them. "The gate is wide open," he sneered, "If you see any Indians coming, just yell like the very devil!"

By the next morning Red Eagle had his braves in place, surrounding the fort. The whole establishment at Mims was lazy and unaware. As the noon hour was drawing near, Major Beasley with a party of his officers was engaged in a game of cards. The soldiers relaxed in whatever shade they found, the young girls and young men were engaged in the artful pasttime of entice and tease, while the thoughtless and happy children sported from door to door.

The hour of twelve arrived and the beat of the drum summoned the soldiers and officers to dinner. Red Eagle had waited for this signal, and now he gave the order to his one thousand painted warriors to storm the fort. Yelling ferociously, they charged from every side. Major Beasley and his officers rushed to close the gate, but the three Negroes tied to the gate posts prevented its closure. Half a hundred screaming Indians firing old muskets, bows and arrows, and wielding tomahawks and clubs raced through the opening.

The first to die was Hosiah and his brethren. They were clubbed to death still lashed to the posts and their scalps taken. The next to die was Major Beasley. As he raced for the safety of the blockhouse, he was overtaken and his skull laid open by a yelling Indian wielding a stone tomahawk. His legs carried him a few steps before he fell, his brains spilling from his cleaved head like cooked grits.

Captain Dixon Bailey took command and rallied the soldiers. Bravely as they tried, the red tirade flaming through the gateway into the fort could not be stemmed. On they came, screaming, shooting, clubbing—killing everyone in their path, soldiers, planters, farmers, children, women. They fell together in heaps of mangled bodies, the dying and the dead, scalped, mutilated, bloody.

At the first assault, the main body of women and

children and some settlers retreated to the blockhouse. Once inside they sent the children to the loft, while the men continued firing their muskets, rifles and pistols from the portholes. The women crouched behind the men and reloaded the guns, and did all that was possible to do in sustaining the courage of the men. They could hear the fearful shrieks of those outside, as they were put to death in ways as horrible as Indian barbarity could invent. The weak, wounded, and feeble were trodden to death as the Indians rushed the blockhouse. Hot volleys from the portholes turned them back, and they milled around, dancing and shouting, and clubbing the dead and dying.

The carnage completed, there came a lull in the fighting. Some of the Indians had broken into the officers quarters and found the store of whiskey. They ran shouting boisterously, swilling the fiery whiskey. They continued to club the dead with tomahawk in one hand and a bottle in the other. Some of the savages cut off the heads of Hosiah and the other two Negroes and had commenced a ball game with the gory heads.

As sunset approached, the Indians had not yet stormed the blockaded prisoners inside. Red Eagle had been summoned elsewhere, and they awaited his return. The victory was complete as far as Red Eagle was concerned, and he had left orders with his prophets to withdraw from the fort at nightfall and follow him toward Pensacola. But when darkness came the braves, emboldened by the whiskey and savaged by the scent of blood and death all round, were bent upon total carnage. They took their time. As long as no shots came from the portholes they were satisfied to continue their drinking, their butchery, and their games with the dead, fully aware that a houseful of fresh victims was at hand to add to their lustful pleasure.

Inside the blockhouse, the hapless prey waited and dreaded; there was nothing else they could do. The children in the loft cried for water, food, and their parents. The women did what they could to quiet and

126

comfort them. The men stood beside their portholes, knowing that doom awaited them all. The first alarm came from the children when the loft filled with smoke and drove them from their sanctuary.

There was no escape. Soon the flames swept over all, while the Indians danced around the burning building with savage delight. Those who charged out the doorway to escape the smoke and flames were shot down or clubbed to death like steers in the slaughter pen of the butcher.

While the men gathered in little groups in the fields and in the towns talking war, their womenfolk went quietly about their home duties of cooking, washing, weaving, sewing, milking and churning, gardening, bedding their husbands at night—always with leaden hearts, knowing that their men would in the end leave them for the excitement of war and the exhilaration of killing.

Polly Crockett, like the other women, knew and waited; but her time of waiting, as she had known from the beginning, was shorter than the others. She recognized the dreaded moment when she saw David coming out of the woods leading his horse Jeb, his rifle in the crook of his arm, and cross the field in long slow strides toward the house. Every step he took toward her sent her heart anew, each step foreboding a hundred leagues he would wander away from her. A feeling of absolute impotence possessed her, pressed her down. There was nothing in the world she could do about it. When his tall figure shadowed the doorway, she lifted her head and smiled, though her heart ached.

He stood there in the middle of the room, resting his rifle on the floor, looking at her. He remained still for a moment, searching for something deeply felt to say to Polly. A cloud reached the doorway, darkening his face. She spared him his words.

"Do you know when you'll be going, David?" She asked, turning away her face to blink back the tears.

"The men say there's a contingent leaving tonight.

127

I'll go into Winchester and volunteer. But I'll come back before I leave for good."

"I'll have your pack ready."

She watched him disappear. Then she retired into the darkness of the room and sank into the old worn chair beside the weaving loom. Long after he had gone the treadle could be heard whirring and clapping.

When the muster was called at Winchester, David Crockett was the first man who stepped out. A company of mounted riflemen was quickly formed. Most of the men had come prepared to move out immediately. They came riding their own horses, armed with their own rifles, in coonskin or foxskin caps, hunting shirts, deerskin leggins, the moccasins they wore for hunting, and their rolled-up packs of cooking utensils and blankets and extra powder and lead strapped behind their saddles. A rendezvous for the first night was named and the company moved out, while David went back to his cabin on Bean Creek, saying he would catch up with them.

Polly was not in the house. He saw that she had prepared his pack; it rested, neatly rolled up and tied, beside the door.

"Polly!" he called. "Where are you?"

"Here, David, down by the creek."

He went out the back door and a few steps carried him to as lovely and rewarding a sight as any man going off to war could wish for. Polly was standing ankle-deep and naked in the crystal spring, drops of water dripping from her, gleaming in the sunlight like jewels. She raised her head and her red hair, tumbling loosely about her shoulders, gathered in the afternoon light and threw it out again as golden sparks. He knew his Polly, knew she had planned it this way. He knew the depth of her passion, and seeing her before him naked in all her womanly glory, a heat like a small cannonball formed in his belly and caused his loins, his whole being, to ache for her. Images of a thousand nights of

128

making love with her seared across his mind. He went to her, tearing off his clothes, piece by piece.

He came into the water enfolding her in his arms. "Where are the children?" he asked.

"I sent them into the woods to hunt hickory nuts."

"You were waiting for me—like this?"

"Yes, David."

He drew her gently down in the shallow water on the sandy shore of the creek, and began kissing her lips, her neck, her sweet wet breasts. She lay there, a beautiful look on her face, half submerged, the water breaking over her body in sparkling bubbles in the fantastic light; in the water she was a silver siren, her hair streaming with pearls. "Take me, David. Take me good! I love you so much."

With a groan of mingled passion and despair he bent and kissed her wildly, feeling the throbbing in her thighs as she pressed against him. He remained there, feasting on her body, the very closeness of her. Her hands slipped down his back and felt the tensing and untensing of his hard muscles—up again to touch the long hair at the back of his neck that curled against her fingers. "Please, David, don't keep me waiting."

She opened her thighs and his knees went between them. She felt his body rest against hers for a moment before it was lifted, poised. Her hand found him and as she guided him inside a gentle moan escaped from deep within her. He stayed like that without moving, embedded in her, his body a part of hers, and then in a moment he began to move, inexorably and steadily.

She lay half-submerged in the water under him, her eyes closed, a look of heaven in her flushed face. Slowly she began to respond to his inthrust and outreach. She widened her legs, hoisted her thighs, struggled to engulf him deeper, fully, while keeping her movements perfectly to his rhythm. She became a wild, bold, sensual creature giving herself to him, demanding of him gluttonously. Never before when they had made love had she called out to him aloud, sobbing her love and her need as she did now.

129

Gradually she felt the cadence of his breathing and his thrusting into her increase; and by habit she matched her tempo to his. It came slowly at first—a warm, spreading exquisite sensation. Then it grew hot and with that warmth came the all-encompassing pain-pleasure. Beginning in her loins, it ascended up into her belly, down her quivering thighs—encompassing her entire body. There were long moments when she didn't know where she was, or cared; she was floating away into nowhere and nothingness. She heard his voice—from far away. He was saying, "I love you, Polly," and that was enough. Now she could send him away to his war and wait for his return in quiet pain and love.

"Polly, I'll be home in sixty days," were his last words to her as he left.

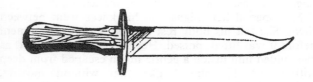

When Jim Bowie and Tex Delacey left the L'Armoise, the Natchez friends of Henri Fouchet were carrying his limp body down the stairs. No words passed between the two. Outside, Tex was the first to speak. "A bad lot," he said. "We haven't seen the last of that crowd." Then, after a pause, "We're dead busted, Jim. What do we do now?"

Jim did not answer, and they walked along in the darkness toward the Hotel de la Marine. The late moon, a pale pumpkin in the sky, bounced its yellow light off the cobblestones which glistened with the mist drifting in from the river. It was late and the streets were empty and lonely. There was only the sound of the men's feet on the ground. Suddenly from around a corner the form of a heavy-set man appeared. He thrust a cocked flintlock pistol into Jim's side and simultaneously delivered a powerful blow to Tex that sent him sprawling across the street, on the damp cobblestones.

"Goddamn you savage *American*," Albert Fouchet hissed in poor English. "You killed my brother. Now I'm going to kill you." He pulled the trigger.

There was a fizz and a little spurt of sparks but nothing else. The mist had fouled the powder in the flashpan.

Albert Fouchet swore and cocked his arm to strike Jim over the head with the heavy pistol. The blow never fell. Jim saw the point of Tex's Arkansas Toothpick suddenly emerge from Fouchet's neck. Tex had thrown it from twenty feet and it had penetrated clean through the man's neck from left to right. Fouchet's pistol slipped from his fingers. He coughed, swore once and crumpled to the street.

Jim bent down and drew the knife from the dead man's neck, wiped its blade and handed it to Tex. The two friends looked at the dead man, then at each other. There seemed nothing to say. An incident in the New Orleans night. They continued on their way to the hotel.

The next morning the city buzzed with the news of the duel and the death of the Fouchet brothers. The lobby of the hotel was filled with excited and curious people anxious to get a glimpse of the now famous knifeman from the bayou country. When Jim and Tex finally came down from their room they were hailed as heroes. Champagne bottles popped, cheers and words of approbation filled the lobby. Felicitations and drinks were offered. It was apparent that the celebrators were not devotees of the Fouchet brothers.

Jim had little to say, and tried to ignore the fawning

131

of the celebrants. He managed to have his breakfast in spite of the festive crowd and then slipped away and went up the stairs to his room. Pausing on the balcony, he gazed down upon the people below, still popping champagne and buzzing around as if celebrating a steamboat racing victory. What kind of people were these, who were anxious to see, hear, and touch someone who had only last night killed? Did these men represent the true character of the Creole? He remembered something his mother had once told him: isolated, a man may be a cultured individual, but in a crowd he is a barbarian.

That afternoon a clerk rapped on Jim's door. "There's a Negro downstairs, Mr. Bowie. Says he's got something for you."

The Negro was a strapping fellow, about Jim's own age, with a large, pleasant face and perfect white teeth. He was waiting in the street beside the hitching post with three fine horses provided with handsome saddles. The Negro handed Jim an envelope. Inside were two bills of sale and a note. One bill of sale was for the three horses and saddles, the other for "One Negro: name, Sam. Age, uncertain. Both instruments were marked "paid in full." The note was from Paula. Jim read it avidly.

Jim,

The news is all over town. It is also known that those people took all of your money. Maybe you don't want to see me. But I want to help—if you'll let me. Sam is a good domestic. Don't ever sell him. He will always remind you of me. The horses will get you back home safely.

Paula

Jim crumpled the note and pounded it with a fist. He looked at Sam. Instantly he liked the fellow. There was at once a depth and a gentleness about the Negro that greatly appealed to Jim. Here was a man with whom he could feel at perfect ease. "Take me to your mistress," he said.

132

Paula's house was plastered brick like its neighbors but larger, two-and-a-half stories tall, with a wrought-iron gallery on the second floor, overhanging the street. Sam pulled a rope at the gate. Somewhere inside a bell jangled and soon a slim young Negro girl hurried to admit them.

Paula had seen the two men from upstairs and was prepared to receive them in a reception room on the second floor.

It surprised Jim that she had changed so little. The same stubborn curls escaped the severity of her sleekly brushed hair. One of the dark whisps tumbled across her forehead just as he remembered it. The same level brow, the same dark eyes, lips as willful as ever. She wore a blue silken robe which clung to every curve of her body, a pale nimbus about her beautiful form. He always had thought of her as thin. That was no longer true. Still slender, perhaps, but maturity had rounded her. Her waist had remained small but her bosom had become fuller.

He found himself studying her, trying to read her with an almost cruel penetration. Time had added richness and poise but left her the luster of girlhood; opulence had given her assurance but had not taken away the awareness of poverty remembered. Her face seemed softer, her eyes brighter.

Her scrutiny was as penetrating as his. She took in the square set of his chin, the lines around his mouth, almost cruel now. "You've changed, Jim."

"Why not? It's been several years," he said amusingly.

She smiled. "I'm glad you're here, Jim."

He tossed the two bills of sale on the table in the center of the room. "I'm returning your property," he said gruffly.

For a moment she seemed hurt, then she said in a pleasant voice, "But Jim, you're my oldest friend. The only one I ever had, really. Friends prove their sincerity when one of them is in need."

133

"I'm not in need. I've done very well—since you ran away from me," he said, an edge in his voice.

He moved a little to keep his eyes in shadow. He didn't want her to read what was in them. She was talking about friendship, while memories were crowding back upon him: the smooth warmth of her skin, the clean fragrance of her hair, when he had held her close. Lost time. His eyes tried to search out the flaws time had wrought upon her. He couldn't find them. He could see the pulse beating under the soft surface of her throat. It angered him that she should stand there unchanged, bringing back with her the painful recollections of the past. It goaded him. He hated her in his thoughts; and yet it would be so easy to take her in his arms.

"You seem to mistake charity for friendship, Paula." He realized he was not making a lot of sense. He knew that she had not wanted to hurt, only help. But somehow he wanted to hurt her.

His words found their mark. The pain showed in her eyes. "I'm sorry, Jim. I really hadn't thought of it that way."

He looked around the room, took in the expensive decorations, the elegant appointments, glanced again at Paula's lovely gown. "So this is the pot of gold you always dreamed of?" There was no bitterness, it was said as a statement of expectations fulfilled. "A new life— that's what you wanted, Paula. You've certainly succeeded."

At that point a child came dashing into the room. "Mamma, mamma, Tilly won't let me play with my new doll. She says I've got to eat my dinner first."

The young Negro girl who had let Jim in at the gate came into the room. "Yessum, Miz Paula, she don't want to eat again. What I do now?"

"Nothing, Tilly. Go away. I'll send Pauline along in a moment."

Paula had long dreamed of telling Jim about his daughter. She had often thought of the pride she hoped to see in his face when he held her in his arms. Now it was impossible. She could not tell him.

"Jim, this is Pauline, my daughter," she said simply.

More surprises. It rasped Jim's nerves. A moment since he was prepared to either take Paula in his arms and tell her how much he had missed her during the intervening years, or to turn on his heels and walk out and hope never again to see her; he hadn't quite made up his mind which course to take. Now here was a mystery. "Pauline, this is your Uncle Jim," Paula was saying, almost cooing.

Jim stooped and the girl approached him. She had straight, dark hair that fell down her back, her eyes were brown but flecked with grey, her skin was of a high alesan color. "You're my uncle?" she asked. "Why haven't I ever seen you before?"

"Well, I—I've been away. I live in the upper country, on a bayou—in Bayou Boeuf."

"Do you have lots of oxen there? Is that why they call it that?"

"We have some oxen there—and lots of other animals, too."

Paula ended the conversation by taking Pauline by the hand and leading her to the door. "Go and find Tilly and eat your dinner. I'll come and see you when you're snug in bed."

She saw the question on Jim's face after her daughter was gone but ignored it. "Jim, you'll stay and dine with me . . . please."

"But—" he raised his arms, motioned around the place. "Isn't there someone—a man?"

"Nothing to worry you, Jim. I'll explain everything at dinner."

During the dinner and until late in the evening, Paula talked freely, telling Jim without shame or apology the events of her life since she left Bayou Boeuf. When she arrived on the wharf in New Orleans she met a seaman who took her in and kept her for a month, until he had to go to sea again. Before leaving he took her to

135

Madame Celestine's "Palace of Virtue," an elegant bordello frequented almost exclusively by the rich and prominent Creoles. Yes, Jim knew the place; he and Tex had visited it. They had met Madame Celestine, a plump, kindly Cajun who used to live in Alexandria. When the solicitous madame saw that Paula was getting big with child she took her into her own quarters to live away from the other girls until the baby came. Pierre Lafitte, a personal friend of the brothel's proprietor, met Paula there and by special arrangement with the madame, took her away and set her up in her own house on Rue Conti. While Pierre's brother Jean had a price on his head in New Orleans, Pierre was free to come and go as he pleased, serving as a valuable contact for the buccaneer's thriving enterprises in numerous commodities of contraband. At the moment Pierre was at Campeachy on Galvez Island. Paula expected his return by the end of the week.

Finally Jim asked the question that had plagued him all evening. "What about the child Pauline? Did Paula want to tell him about the girl's father?"

She remained silent for a time. Finally she smiled. "He was a man," she told Jim, looking into his intense grey eyes over the brim of her wine glass, "who in another world and in another time—if there be such—I will surely find."

Jim thought about this reply for long moments. He had to be satisfied with her answer, yet he ventured one more question, in the form of a statement "Paula, what you're saying is that the girl's father is dead?"

His question surprised her. It was a release and a relief "Yes . . ." she said thoughtfully, "that man is dead . . ."

Jim and Paula settled the matter of the horses and the slave Sam by Jim giving Paula his note in hand for payment at full value. It had become clear during the evening that Jim's interest in getting money was paramount in his thinking and accordingly Paula presented him with a bold idea.

When Jean Lafitte's stronghold on the Baratarian

coast had been reduced, he took his colony to a new location off the coast of the Mexican state of Texas, known as Galvez Island. He called his new stronghold Campeachy, after the large amount of logwood that drifted down the many streams which emptied into the gulf. It would one day become the city of Galveston. There, for the last time, the contemptible institutions of piracy and slavery met, the one living off the other. Jean Lafitte, as a young man had been captured with his child bride by Spaniards. As a result, his wife, whom he had loved more than most men love a woman, had died. It was then that Lafitte had sworn an oath that henceforth, until that time when he should be tucked under the good earth or slipped over the side on a weighted board, there should be nothing between him and the Spaniards but bitter and uncompromising war. The Spanish ships were his favorite prey, and he plundered them wherever he found them. Much of their cargoes was black ivory. Lafitte kept the pirated Negroes in slave pens on his island and sold them to whomever brought cash. In spite of the law forbidding importation of African Negroes, there were always men who, caring little for their good names or the dangers encountered, were willing to smuggle the slaves from the Mexican state of Texas into the United States, where the expansion of cotton and sugar lands created an insatiable demand for their labor.

Jim listened to Paula with interest and understanding. He had an instinct for central reasoning. "What you're getting around to, Paula, is proposing that I become a slave trader—to take the Negroes off Lafitte's hands. I do not wish to become a smuggler."

"There is a way—if you will hear me out," she pleaded, "to make yourself as rich as you desire without sullying your honor."

"Please go on."

"When President Jefferson signed the slave trade act—oh, a dozen years ago—prohibiting importation of Negroes, there was no provision covering the disposal of Africans apprehended by revenue agents. That mat-

137

ter was finally left to the individual states It followed, naturally, that Louisiana and most other southern states sell them on the auction block, just as demijohns of brandy and Jamaica rum and other merchandise confiscated as smuggled goods. Jim, I can arrange for you to buy the Negroes from Jean for a dollar a pound—average about one hundred and forty dollars a Negro—you bring them into Louisiana, turn them in as captured runaways. They are auctioned off and you get as bounty money half the price they bring on the block. The auction price runs from a thousand to about twelve hundred dollars per head. They cost you a hundred and forty dollars, you get six hundred; your profit is from four hundred and fifty dollars to six-fifty a Negro."

Jim thought for a long time, examining all possibilities. He asked many questions. Could Jean Lafitte be trusted? If Pierre sent him, yes. Was it safe to enter Campeachy with a large amount of cash on one's person? If one went there to do business, he could turn his gold over to Lafitte for safekeeping and it would be safer than in the Fouchet bank in New Orleans. This was an unusual statement but he did not doubt Paula's sincerity, although he knew the character of the men on Galvez Island: prison breakers, gallows birds, fugitives from justice, thieves, murderers, degenerates.

"I will arrange a meeting with you and Pierre," she offered. "I will tell him the price I quoted you, he will honor it. You can go with money for a hundred Negroes and no harm will come to you.

Jim was interested. He would remain in New Orleans until Paula's enamorato returned. They would talk.

Jim found nothing about Pierre Lafitte's appearance to indicate his calling. He was a tall, spare man, his complexion dark, his hair sleek, clothing rich in the latest fashion. He had warm sparkling eyes, and there was a gentlemanly courtliness about his manner that echoed his Creole background. Most of all Jim liked his deference and kindliness to Paula; this put the pirate warmly in Jim's favor.

Paula had refreshments awaiting but Jim was anxious to get down to business. They agreed on the price—one dollar per pound—and Jim would come with a party of four and bring the cash. There would be a short delay. Jim had to return to Bayou Boeuf and raise the cash necessary for the first transaction. Pierre promised the deal would stand "as long as the Spaniards have niggers aboard their ships for us to pirate." The two men shook hands, sealing the deal.

Paula saw Jim out. Before parting, the two stood facing each other inside the iron gate. Suddenly Paula flung her arms around his neck and kissed him passionately. It stirred Jim and, for one wild moment, carried him back to the bliss of their youthful romance. When she released him and drew away, he saw tears brimming in her eyes. She smiled them back, extended her hand. "Good luck, Jim, she said, and turned away into the shadows of the patio.

General Andrew Jackson was in command of the army: foot soldiers, horsemen, and militia. He had been hindered by official delays in moving south. The volunteers however, in advance, rode into Alabama, crossing the Tennessee River at Muscle Shoals where the water was shallow and camped on a high bluff overlooking the river, awaiting the arrival of the main body of the army.

Fully assembled the volunteers numbered well over two thousand, an imposing army of determined men.

Scouts were needed to venture into the Creek country and discover the movements of the enemy. The region swarmed with Indians, prepared for savage warfare. They were greatly and justly aroused. News had reached the Indian towns that a great army of whites had crossed the Tennessee, invading Creek territory with the purpose of destroying their nation. Any scout who was captured could expect nothing but certain death by the most dreadful torture.

David volunteered as a scout and was placed in command of twelve men for this difficult duty. The party made its way south through untrodden wilderness, and found itself among a settlement of Indians, which David was pleased to learn was a peace town. Here he found several families husbanded by white settlers. One of them, Jack Thompson, urged David to take his scouts, go away, and leave them alone. "This is a peace town, Jack Thompson pleaded. "But if the Red Sticks find out that we didn't kill you, they'll kill us."

Some of David's men insisted on retreating immediately.

"The first man who turns his head north," David said, "will get a rifle ball between his shoulders."

That ended any talk about giving up the scouting venture. David demanded to know the movements of any hostile Indians.

"Southwest," Thompson told him. "A band of painted warriors passed here and went that-a-way only this morning."

"How many?"

"About sixty."

"Well, that's just about right." David looked at his men. "Five for each of us."

He led his little band in the direction Thompson had pointed.

They rode quietly along for several hours, when after darkness fell they saw in the distance the gleam of campfires, and heard shouts of merriment and revelry.

140

David cautioned his men to remain under cover while he reconnoitered. He crept forward through the underbrush on hand and foot and reached the perimeter of the camp. He saw half a hundred Indians—men, women, and children—all in fringed, plumed, and brilliantly colored costumes engaged in various games and sports. Scanning the entire clearing, he saw no red pole.

The Indians, peaceful Cherokees, received David and his little band of men very cordially, took care of their horses and invited them to join in the festivities. Quite a number of them, with bows and arrows, were shooting at a mark, which was illuminated by the blaze of pitch-pine knots, a light which no flame or candle or gas could outshine. It was a scene of sublimity and beauty, of peace and loveliness, set deep in the green of the wilderness. David wondered how it could be that the brethren of these peaceful Cherokees could regress to a state of savagery such as at Mims. He would learn before this campaign was over that such retrogression is not exclusively the proclivity of the red man; he'd witness his white brothers degrade themselves just as shamelessly.

David and his men joined in the fun and sports, but some of the Indians began to feel anxious. The Cherokees tried to maintain a strict neutrality between the whites and the Creeks, lest they draw down upon themselves the vengeance of either side. One of the elders was delegated to ask David to terminate the fun and take his white scouts and leave. David's reply was: "Tell your brothers that I will keep a sharp lookout and if a single Creek comes near the camp, I will carry the skin of his head home and make me a moccasin."

When this answer was reported to the Indians they laughed in admiration of the jovial and brave white scout, and dispersed.

When David, wrapped in his blanket, was asleep, a Cherokee boy approached silently and whispered in his ear, "Red Sticks."

David was up instantly. There was no attack but he

141

learned what he wanted to know. A Creek runner had come into the camp and told the Cherokee elders that a war party of more than a thousand Creeks had crossed the Coos River at Ten Islands and were moving northeast. David gathered his men and left quickly, riding hard to cover the sixty miles back to the volunteer camp. When they rejoined the army, General Jackson had arrived.

David presented himself immediately to the commandant's headquarters. The General kept him cooling his heels outside for two hours before receiving him. His wounded arm still in a sling, the stern, long, yellow-faced master of the Hermitage and two hundred slaves, listened briefly to David's report, related in his customarily singular, and somewhat grotesque, language. The general scoffed.

"What's your rank, volunteer?"

"Why none, Mr. Jackson."

The general bristled. "Address me as Sir or General!"

"Well, all right with me, if that's the way you want it."

"That's the way it will be, volunteer!"

"Well, anyway, you know about them thousand Creeks and which way they're going, General."

"Go and prepare a written report for me."

David stood there, in his first encounter with General Andrew Jackson, sizing up the Tennessee politician-fighter. What he saw he didn't like, and, in later years in the halls of Congress, he would get his chance to stand up and oppose this iron-willed, acerbic fellow, Congressman-to-President.

"Sorry, General, I'm afraid I don't write that well. You'll just have to make do with what I told you."

The general turned on his heels, completely disaffected with this crude, cheeky backwoodsman, and left him to dismiss himself.

Jackson's army became paralyzed by a new enemy—hunger. An army of twenty-five hundred men re-

142

quired several hundred bushels of grain, tons of meat, gallons of whiskey, and many other stores each week. But provisions were arriving only in small quantities at irregular intervals. Food that was to come by river was halted because the waters were low in the autumn of that dry hot fall. Jackson watched the river like a hawk, hoping for arrival of supplies. His tall, inexorable, sparse figure could be seen striding up and down the great bluff as though he would wear the ground away by his impatience. His wounded arm pained him; he was sick with dysentary, short tempered, angered at the political incompetents who had failed him.

It was at this time that David Crocket became widely known among the volunteers. Beside the fires at night he would keep a whole company in high spirits by his tales and talk, poured from a memory which seemed absolutely never to have forgotten anything. In these days he was always merry. Bursts of laughter generally greeted his approach and followed his departure. His anecdotes were ever at hand. Though they were not always, indeed were seldom, of the most refined nature, they were nonetheless adapted to raise shouts of merriment in cabin or camp. If ever in want of an illustrative tale he found no difficulty in creating one. He talked of his adventures over the eastern mountains as a boy and pictured the odd people he had encountered in his travels. He told about Jacob Siler, who taught him the refinements of shooting, and mimicked the bizarre German of the Shenandoah Valley, and others of the waggoners he had known. He told of his adventures in hunting, and gave accounts of numerous shooting matches in which he had engaged. He had one story he continually told, and no matter how many times his listeners heard it they always laughed anew.

"It was in Cincinnati," he would begin. "Me and my buddy went into one of them fancy restaurants. The first thing that surprised us was that in this place they had girls waiting on the folks. Well, this real purty girl she comes a-slinking over to where me and my buddy was and slunk over our table. 'What'll you gents have?'

143

she says, and chawed away on her cud. 'I reckon I'll have me a glass of milk,' my buddy says. And you know what that purty thing did? She yanked out her tiddy and milked him a glass full right there and then. Then she says to me, 'Bo, what'll you have?' I says, 'Sister, when I come in here I knowed what I wanted. It was a glass of water. But I don't want nothing now!"

David Crockett's kindness of heart and good nature were inexhaustible. Those in want never appealed to him in vain. He would share his last pocketful of grain or piece of dried deer with a hungry comrade. He would without a moment's hesitation or consideration spend his last dollar to buy a blanket for a shivering soldier. He did it without reflection, same as he breathed.

Such was the David Crockett who, for the mere love of adventure, left his devoted and passionate wife and children in order to hunt and kill Indians in the wilderness.

Because the main army was stranded for lack of sufficient food, General Jackson decided to send out a contingent of riflemen to scour for warring Creeks under command of Colonel John Coffee. In addition to finding food, Jackson hoped they would discover and destroy some of the smaller Creek strongholds. The plan was for these men to make a wide circle and meet the main army farther to the south, on the Coosa River, where the general expected to move his army and establish a fort, when he received sufficient provisions. It was in this vicinity that the Creek war party was reported to be gathered. When David heard of Colonel Coffee's expedition, he volunteered as scout.

Colonel Coffee was a man who kept his own counsel. Neither David nor any of the other eight hundred men knew for sure the colonel's route or objectives, if indeed the colonel knew them himself. They were adrift in a strange and hostile country, forced to live off the land and by their rifles, seeking a subtle enemy whom they could not find, who might spring upon them in over-

144

whelming numbers from an uexpected quarter at any moment. These light troops, hardy men of iron nerves, knew only that they were ever riding southward, ever closer to the hostile Creeks. They passed through the heart of the Choctaw and Chickasaw nations unmolested. The men began to grow restless for some kind of action. Where were the hostile Creeks?

When the army reached the islands of the Coosa, where ten small green islands lay scattered in a wide river bed of shoals, David sensed what was in Colonel Coffee's mind. The little army would attack Pensacola, now within a day's march. This was a part of the plan for the revenge of the Mims massacre. It was the Spanish in Pensacola who were supplying Red Eagle with arms and supplies to carry on the war against the settlers. Pensacola would be a worthy prize to carry back to General Jackson, who, it was well known, nursed dreams of taking all the Southeast, including the Florida territory, for the Unites States.

David had divined Colonel Coffee's mind correctly. But when the army reached an imminence but a short distance out of Pensacola, it was learned that the city had already been taken by the British. The forts were strongly garrisoned, all the principal streets were barricaded, and the British fleet was anchored in the bay. David was sorely disappointed; thus he lost his chance of having "a small taste of British fighting," as he later wrote. He was not to be with General Jackson's army a few months later, when that lion-hearted soldier would march on Pensacola, compel the city to surrender its works and drive the British fleet out of the harbor.

But David Crockett was to have his gulletful of fighting—in its dreadful and most distasteful guise.

145

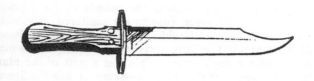

Jim Bowie, Tex Delacy and Sam, Jim's new slave, rode north along the road that had only recently been widened from an Indian path to accommodate the United States postal service now extending to a number of gulf towns. The sunlight, filtering through the moss-bearded branches of the trees, blinked across their faces as the horses trotted along.

"Tex," Jim said, "I've been thinking about those two knives of yours—"

"Wouldn't get dressed without them. Just like a part of my wardrobe."

"Both of your knives are so different. One for throwing, the other for gut cutting, in close. Why not have one knife combining the best features of both?"

"Hadn't thought of it that way. Where could a fellow get such a knife?"

"Might be something to consider."

That night after they had eaten, as Sam leaned over to pour coffee in Jim's cup, something extremely heavy in a leather pouch that was slung around Sam's neck struck against Jim's head. He caught hold of the pouch. "What's this, Sam?"

"Marse Jim, dat's my Zog piece."

"Zog piece? May I see it?"

Sam lifted the pouch from his neck, took from it a

dark and irregularly round object about three quarters the size of a man's fist. It was the heaviest thing for its size that Jim had ever handled. "What is it, Sam?"

"My Zog, he sent it to me, Marse Jim."

"Just who is this Mr. Zog?"

Sam was reluctant to say more. He seemed anxious to have his Zog piece back.

"Go on, Sam. Tell me about this lump. I've never seen anything like it."

Sam sat back on his haunches, looking into the fire, the flames casting their red flickering lights across his black face, and, caught now and then in the whites of his eyes, seemed to dance there like little red devils, mocking the world outside.

"About my Zog, Marse Jim. He fust come to me when I wuz a little boy in de Congo. He been comin' to me ever since. One night he come while I wuz sleepin' and he say, 'Boy, you goin' to travel a long piece, and you goin' to see many bad men befo' I comes to take you away wid me.'"

"Just a bad dream, Sam. We all have them."

Sam went quickly on the defensive. "Nosuh, Marse Jim! Twan't no dream. Zog he wuz dere. I seen him jus' as plain as I see you right now. He say, 'Boy, you keep watch in de sky. I'm gonna send you somethin' ain't no-body else got.' So I watches de sky, like Zog say. And I don't have to wait long. Three night later and dere comes a flamin' star—out ob de heavens, a-tailin' fire and sparks across all de world. I thought it wuz a-comin' to git me. But it went into de ground instead wid a powerful noise. De next day I went to see what wuz dere. All de trees wuz burned and turned to stone and dere wuz nothin' but a great big hole in de ground. I found dis lump and I knowed dat wuz de Zog piece. I kept it ever since."

"What did your Zog tell you to do with it?"

"When he know'd I wuz wearin' it round my neck, he say, 'Boy, dat's right. You jus' keep wearin' it around yo' neck until you finds a man dat thinks as

147

much of you as he does ob hisself.' Marse Jim, I ain't never found nobody like dat."

"I'm afraid you never will, Sam."

"But Marse Jim, Miz Paula, she tole me dat you wuz such a man."

Jim fell silent. Tex, who had been listening tolerantly, yawned. "Well, I'm going to turn in. Tell us more some other time, Sam," Tex said, and drew his blanket up around his eyes.

Jim held Sam's oblong lump to the fire and examined it. It seemed extremely hard and gave off a bluish hue in the firelight. Some kind of steel, Jim thought, but unlike anything he had ever seen. He handed it back to Sam, who replaced it in its pouch and reslung it about his neck.

Back home at Bayou Boeuf Jim laid out his proposition to Rezin. John was away in Arkansas. There was some trouble with the titles on some land grants they had acquired there some time ago. John had sold off some of the land, but the deals could not be finalized until the original titles were certified in the courts. Jim came to the point at once.

"I lost the money I got for the lumber gambling, and I killed a man, Rezin. But, hell, you know I'm bound to make a fortune, and I'm going to do it in a hurry. What I'm proposing requires bold action—but it means quick money for all of us. Lots of it. First we sell the sawmill and the land if necessary to raise the capital needed."

"What then?"

"We run slaves."

Rezin was stunned. Jim continued talking before his brother could raise objections. He explained in detail the scheme Paula had laid out to him. When he finished Rezin thought for a long while, then he said, "Smuggling slaves and then informing on yourself. It doesn't sound like the Bowies."

"It's simple arithmetic. A good nigger brings about twelve hundred dollars on the auction block. Our share is six hundred dollars and they cost us only one

148

hundred and forty. We'll buy them in lots of forty to sixty. I figure we can make a dozen gross lot deals a year. That's fast money—and big money, Rezin."

By the time John returned from Arkansas, Jim had convinced Rezin to go along with the slave enterprise. Rezin had talked with several potential buyers for the sawmill and offers were standing. John said if they needed quick cash someone ought to go to Little Rock and expedite the finalization of the land grant titles. You had to continually press the lawyers and notaries until the matter was settled, he said. There was ready cash in escrow when title to the sold lands were delivered. Jim decided that he and Tex would undertake this mission. The ready cash that John said was available decided him.

The day as Jim, Tex, and Sam were leaving for Arkansas, Sam came to Jim with a model knife he had whittled out of a pine board. "Marse Jim, I heard you and Mist' Delacey speaking about a new knife. Maybe one like dis model I done whittled out is what you want."

Jim examined Sam's creation. It was ingenious indeed. The blade was eleven inches long and an inch and a half wide. The heel at the back was exceptionally thick, about three-eighths of an inch there. But the innovation was in the point. It came to the exact center of the blade, and it curved to the point end convexly from the edge, and concavely from the back. Both curves were whittled to a sharpness equalling that of the blade itself, forming, in fact, a continuing part of the edge. Jim showed the model to Tex.

Tex turned Sam's pine knife over in his hands and marveled. "Never seen anything like it. With the right balance it ought to throw as well as kill out of hand."

"What we need," Jim said, "is a good blacksmith. Know of any?"

"Sure do. There's a good one who specializes in manufacturing knives in Washington—James Black. Ever been to Washington, Arkansas? It's a nice little town on our way to Little Rock."

149

Jim, Tex, and Sam drew their horses up to the building with the sign: JAMES BLACK FORGE.

It was a big shed of a building with double doors through which a wagon could run. James Black saw them sitting their horses and came out, wearing his black leather apron and wiping the sweat from his eyes with a forearm. He was a slender man, with a high slanting forehead, sharp features and jutting chin. His black hair was sleeked back, pompadour fashion.

"If you want your horses shod," he said, "this ain't the place. I do smithing only. Horse shoeing is out of my line."

"My name is James Bowie," Jim said, dismounting. "Tex here tells me you make a good cutting blade." Jim handed him the whittled model. James Black examined it as he led the group toward his office, which was in the rear of blacksmith shop.

"I'd like a knife made after that model that is springy, strong, and will take an edge like a razor," Jim continued. "And it must have balance—for throwing."

James Black was still considering Sam's model.

"You can vary that model, Mr. Black, if you need to."

"It won't need much varying," James Black said. "It's pretty perfect as it is. Steel is the thing. The worth of a knife is in the steel. Nobody since those fellows of Damascus has made a good blade steel. The secret seems to be in the refining. How to burn out all the impurities. Bar iron won't do. Wrought steel is better, but it still ain't good enough for the kind of knife I'd like to make."

James Black opened a drawer of his desk and took out a small oblong bar of iron and handed it to Jim. "That's the best steel I ever made. I refined it over a hundred times and it still ain't pure. But I keep trying. I'd say that piece comes as close to Damascus steel as any in the world today."

Jim hefted James Black's steel bar in his hand. It gave him an idea. "Just a moment. Sam, let Mr. Black see your Zog piece."

Sam took the object from its pouch and James Black examined it. He weighted it in his hand, he measured it, he filed it, he tasted it, he held it to his cheek. "A meteorite," he said. "A steel meteorite. Some are chiefly stone—balsic rock. Others are mainly rock and iron, full of impurities. But, by the heavens! this one is pure steel, smelted in the furnace of the heavens." His eyes drank in the meteorite. "Steel!" He sounded almost ecstatic. "Steel that's been purified by the oven heat of its passage through our air. Ah! If I could but use this in your blade, Bowie—"

"How about it, Sam?"

The slave stood behind his owner, his face solemn. After a moment, he said, "I reckon, Marse Jim, my Zog wanted you to have it. Yessuh. I'm done tired ob carryin' it round my neck so long anyhow."

James Black's eyes lit up. "I'll start to work right away. Come back in a few weeks and out of my own steel and this steel from heaven I'll make you a knife like none you ever saw before. Or will ever see again."

It had been four wearying weeks in Little Rock for Jim Bowie. But after numerous sessions with lawyers, notaries, and several court appearances, the claims to the grants were confirmed and the titles to the land John had sold duly transferred. The escrowed money was turned over to Jim: six thousand and eight hundred dollars.

Now he was eager to see what James Black in the little town of Washington had turned out of Sam's Zog lump.

The first thing Tex said was "Godalmighty!" He admired the ivory handle, the pommel with brass fittings, the hilt with balled ends. He ran his thumb along the hammered brass strip welded to the heel. "What's this for, Mr. Black?"

"Brass is softer than steel. It will catch a cutting edge. In parrying a thrust, the other blade won't slip away so easy. You did want a fighting knife?"

But Jim's attention was all for the blade. Its bluish

luster matched the blue of his blue-grey eyes. He took the knife and twanged it with his thumb. From it came a clear bell-like sound. He felt the edge. It was keen as any razor. He balanced the blade across his forefinger. At exactly two inches from the cross guard the balance was perfect.

"It is machined to turn once in the air of its own weight at thirty feet," James Black said.

"Let's test it," Jim said critically.

They took the knife outside, to the back of the shop.

"Try throwing it," James Black said. "That board yonder."

The knife sang through the air, struck, and gave a high vibrant note as it quivered in its target.

"It has character," its manufacturer said, withdrawing the knife and inspecting it. "The point did not blunt. The blade bent and did not break; it sprang back straight and true. It cut and did not chip."

"Mr. James Black," Jim said, holding the knife almost lovingly, "you have combined in this blade the right opposites. Stiffness and flexibility, hardness and softness. It is stiff enough to penetrate and yet flexible enough to bend. It is hard enough to take a razor-sharp cutting edge and yet malleable enough not to break or chip, and its point is sharpened at both edges." A cold look came into his eyes. "Sir, with this blade you can cut both ways. I never thought such a knife could be made."

"It won't ever again," James Black said. "There is no steel on earth like that of this blade. This knife came from heaven."

"Or from hell," said Bowie.

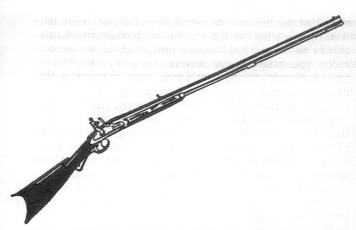

Approaching the Tallushatches settlement on his way
back toward the Ten Islands of the Coosa, where he expected to meet up with Jackson's main forces, Colonel
Coffee divided his detachment into two columns, for
scouts had reported that a large body of Red Sticks
were gathered there; the right column was stationed a
little way out of the village, with orders not to advance
unless given the signal to do so by the colonel; the left
column was to dismount and approach the village on
foot. The strategy, as Colonel Coffee saw it, would be
that the Indians, taken by surprise at the attack by the
foot soldiers, would retreat into the rifles and bayonets
of the horsemen, lying in wait for them. It would be a
total victory.

David was among the men of the left column, the at-
tackers. He dismounted and tied the reins of his horse
to a sapling in a little ravine, then began creeping
forward toward the village. In the distance a little way
ahead of him he saw the hamlet. In the clear, quiet
forest afternoon cool smoke hung over the huts like an
immense hazy umbrella. Only a few Indians were to be
seen out of the houses. It was a scene of complete re-
moteness; for encompassing the village in every direction, from the crest of the hillsides down to the banks of
the stream, over a vast area of valley and hills,

stretched the limitless forest. Except for the continually flowing creek at the foot of the little town, the settlement was a mere hole in an ocean of trees.

The scene before him was serene and calm. The inhabitants were completely unaware of any approaching danger. Several women were at the spring peacefully engaged in washing. Three other women had left their huts with buckets to fetch water. Having time to spare, they had seated themselves upon a log and were engaged in gossiping to pass the time of day. While these women carried on their idle conversation, David saw several men emerge from their houses, carrying rifles.

At the sight of the armed Indians a general whoop went up from the soldiers and the column rushed into the clearing shooting and yelling. The Indian men fell in the first volley. The women sitting on the log threw their buckets away and fled toward the huts. Two were overtaken and clubbed to death, screaming. The third, large with child, had fallen and rolled down a small incline. One of the soldiers leaped into the ravine and ran his knife into her, opening her belly. She lay moaning, her entrails covered with blood and cauliflowering from her. She moaned and screamed until her assailant clubbed her into stillness with the butt of his rifle.

The two women at the spring never had a chance to flee. They were shot instantly and fell into the stream, their blood staining the water red.

David's column crossed the clearing and gained the village. Warriors spilled from the houses firing arrows and muskets; their guns emptied, they threw them aside and charged the soldiers with tomahawks, hatches, and knives. Arrows whistled among the advancing soldiers, some finding a mark, many more spent needlessly. The soldiers, thoroughly inflamed by the fresh drawing of blood, shot, clubbed, knifed, and killed with the ferocity of madmen. As more blood flowed their violence rose. Many who were clubbing with their gun stocks and rifle barrels, finding this method of carnage unfulfilling for their bloodthirsty lust, threw their guns aside and began slashing and stabbing with their long knives.

154

The mounted men, hearing the whooping and yelling and the screams of the mutilated and dying, grew restless for a part in the carnage. Without waiting for an order from their commander, they burst forth, shooting and bayoneting runaways who sought any avenue of escape from the bloody scene.

An old Indian, a non-combatant, who sat on the ground at the edge of the clearing pounding corn in a mortar as though unaware of the tumult and danger around him, was an early victim. A farmer, a neighbor of David's, advanced upon the old man, placed the muzzle of his pistol to his temple and blew his head into a bloody mass. Too late David grabbed the man's weapon and struck him across the head with it. Lying on the ground, blinking his eyes to regain his senses, the farmer said, "Well, he wuz an Injun, wuzn't he? Besides, I want to tell the folks when I git home that I personally killed me an Injun."

A little Indian boy, five or six years of age, came running toward the soldiers with his arms outstretched. A volunteer struck him on the head with his rifle. The boy sank to the ground but quickly got up and tried to run away. The soldier knocked him down again, picked him up by his feet and, swinging him over his head, dashed his brains out against the edge of a large iron wash pot. Later when reported to an officer for barbarity, he replied, "Well, he would have growed up to be an Injun someday."

Barbarity now spread to the horse soldiers. They were all over the clearing and into the woods, shooting fleeing Indians, clubbing and knifing others who didn't have a chance of escape. From their saddles they terrified everything before them, clubbing the feeble, shooting the fleeing, trampling the wounded under the hooves of their horses.

As David watched, a young rifleman galloped his horse after a young girl, her long hair flowing behind her as she ran screaming for her life. Just as she gained the edge of the woods the rifleman impaled her on his bayonet. He then dismounted and, after cutting out her

155

scalp at the crown of her head, tied the bloody trophy to the bridle of his mount by its long glossy hair. Remounting his horse, with a victorious whoop he took out after another fleeing girl.

One of the elders, a prophet carrying the red pole, rallied his people as best he could—those who remained alive and able to flee—and herded them into a long storage house. The horse troops dismounted, joined the foot soldiers, and the entire command surrounded the house. Their thirst for butchery momentarily abated, they milled around, unsure what to do about the barricaded Indians.

While they waited, the door of the long house opened, and an old woman came out with a bow and arrow in her hands. She sat down on the porch, placed her feet against the bow, loaded the arrow on the string and, raising her feet, she drew with all her might and let fly the arrow. It struck with a sickening whoosh into the breast of Dick Moore, a volunteer standing beside David.

A yell went up from the soldiers and their lust for blood suddenly flamed anew. Someone produced a handful of pine knot flares and the house was quickly set afire from all corners.

As the flames encompassed the structure, not one warrior came out, preferring to die inside in the flames, women, children and all, rather than give the sanguinary soldiers the satisfaction of killing them as they emerged.

One Indian did get out, however. A small girl, her dress and half her body aflame, burst forth and ran toward the line of soldiers. She fell a little distance from the hot flames, grease issuing from her burning body. She looked up at the soldiers with large, brown, sad eyes, burning to death, yet not a tear flowed. No one made a motion to help her. David, with one instinctive reflex movement, swung his rifle to his shoulder and sent a ball directly behind her ear, ending the poor creature's suffering.

Surely it was not needful, in avenging the admittedly

156

savage, possibly drunken, massacre of Fort Mims, that the whites should imitate the crazed butchery of those warriors. It is claimed that the truly brave are humane, yet many war-ravaged regions can show that while soldiers will descend to the very depths of shameful degradation. Only the noble deeds are noted while the others are not recorded in the chronicles of action taken in war.

The slaughter was complete and terrible. Only five of the soldiers were killed and ten wounded. One hundred and eighty-six Indians were put to death in the battle of Tallushatches.

The army buried its dead, and Colonel Coffee gave the ten wounded men leave to return to their homes. The army had not moved more than sixty miles when the problem of rations was brought to the Colonel's attention. David had heard a rumor that in the cellar of the long house where the Indians had been burned to death was stored a cache of grain. He asked permission of Colonel Coffee to take a small detachment of men and pack horses and return and search for food.

They found a large store of corn underneath the ashes of the burned building. It was saturated with the drippings that had been fried out of the burned Indians. Notwithstanding, the detachment returned with a bountiful supply of corn, well-flavored with nourishing grease ...

While catching up with Colonel Coffee, David's marksmanship felled two large bears and half a dozen deer. The Colonel, much impressed with David's ability as a forager, detached him with twelve men to hunt and scour for more grain and meat.

On the afternoon of the third day, while David was inspecting some fresh trails, from a short distance in the woods came the call: "How do! How do!"

He listened, remaining still as a quail. Nothing. His horse was ten feet away, snorting softly; and his rifle was in its sheath, slung alongside the saddle. Silently he crouched. Then again, closer: "How do! How do!"

There was nothing to do but answer. The Indians knew exactly where he was. He stood up, in full view. "Howdy do! Howdy do!" he called.

Presently two Indians wearing breeches and hunting shirts and carrying rifles broke out of the tangle of trees and brush. They approached and took David's outstretched hand. They were, they said, out hunting for game.

David invited them to enjoy some smoked meat with him and his group.

While they sat around the fire after the meal, smoking in apparent perfect harmony, one of David's men whispered in his ear, "Them two's spies for the Creeks."

David assured his man that they were Choctaws, and certainly not spies.

The Indians indicated it was time to take their leave. David shared some deer meat with them, shook hands, and set about breaking the little camp. As he was engaged in this task, several blasts of rifle fire rent the woods. The two Indians lay dead not twenty yards distant.

"They wuz spies for the Creeks, like I said," announced the suspicious soldier, reloading his rifle.

The others who had joined in the execution agreed, saying, "Well, what'd we volunteer for? Wuzn't it to kill Indians?"

Two of the murderers drew their knives and took the scalps of the dead Indians.

The group was on a wide stream of water that separated them from an island on which several Indian huts stood. David, fearing that the inhabitants of those huts might indeed be Creeks and having heard the rifle blasts would trap them in an ambush, decided to lure them from their huts, and if they proved to be hostile, eliminate them. As the evening twilight was fading, he concealed his men in a dense canebrake, while he rode forward to the edge of the water, in full view of the

158

village. Nobody came forth. He called, and gave the sound of the screech-owl. A lone Indian woman came down to the bank on the opposite side and wanted to know, in signs and obscure language, what he wanted. He asked for the men. The old woman told him there were but two men in the village and they were out hunting. She was sure they'd be back soon for she had heard gunshots and assumed they had killed some game and were on their way home. He told the woman he had a dozen men and asked if they could come across and stay the night. She showed him where the canoe was, on his side of the stream; it was used that morning by the men who had not yet returned. With several crossings, all his men were in the village.

True to the woman's word, not a man was present. There were eight women, in all, in the little village. They gathered around in a group, some looking on silently and suspiciously. A few of the younger girls smiled and giggled, while the soldiers passed indecent remarks among themselves about the women.

About midnight David was awakened by a frightful piercing scream. He seized his rifle and rushed outside. There in the moonlight lay the naked form of an Indian girl, her life's blood draining from an ugly slash in her throat. Over her knelt her sobbing hysterical mother. As David took the girl in his arms, he felt her body go completely inert and leaden. He looked for some sign of life in her face but he saw only eyes that were half-closed, revealing slits of sickly white. He carried the dead girl into her mother's hut. The old woman, with signs, made David understand what had happened.

Earlier in the evening one of the soldiers had come to the hut with a bottle of firewater. The mother and daughter drank in a friendly manner with him, but when the soldier insisted on taking the girl to bed, the mother resisted and put him out of the hut. He returned with two companions and the three ruffians bound the woman, while all three of the men raped her daughter right before her eyes. As they left, the infuriated girl grabbed the old woman's bow and arrow and ran out of

159

the hut after them. She heard the girl scream but when she reached her side, it was too late. The girl's throat was cut. She saw two of the men running away. The third, she told David, was lying out there in the grass with an arrow in his back.

David routed the men from their hovels, tearing several away from the beds of squaws. He gathered them in the clearing, and demanded to know who killed the girl. Nobody admitted it. Try as he might, he could get no information from any one of them.

Finally he said, "The culprit will have to carry his guilt on his conscience for the rest of his life, and take his judgment before his Maker when he dies. If I knew who the guilty sonuvabitch is he would meet his maker tonight!"

If this was Indian war, David Crockett was rapidly getting his bellyfull of it. He had imagined going to war against the Indians as a stand-up fight to protect families and homes from such massacres as had happened at Fort Mims. But killing Indians for lust and sex and just plain meanness was something of which he did not wish to be a part.

He led his men in a circular route northeast, toward Colonel Coffee's army. As they traveled along the Chattachoochee River, he spotted in the distance across the river a large Indian village. Moving cautiously, he came close enough to see that it was a permanent town of some excellence. He observed a smooth green meadow on the western bank of the river, skirted by the boundless forest, wherein many fine Indian houses were erected. Luxurious corn fields stretched on either side of the town along the river. The Indian houses and lodges clustered on this emerald plain appeared to be unusually well constructed. He could determine that upon many of them much labor had been expended. Unquestionably Indians of an unusual culture inhabited this town. Surely there was a bountiful supply of grain and cured meat stored there. It was his duty to report such a find to Colonel Coffee.

When David rejoined Colonel Coffee's army of eight hundred men, he found that they had not moved for two weeks and had totally exhausted the fish and game in the vicinity and were again on low rations. Some, almost starving, began eating their beef hides. David's report about the prodigal Indian village on the banks of the Chattahoochee was cheerful news for the famished soldiers. The Colonel put the army in motion immediately. Their rifles were loaded and primed, and the flints carefully examined, that they might not fall into ambush unprepared before they reached the life-sustaining village.

The detachment approached the Indian town in Colonel Coffee's proven pattern—two columns encircling the area. This time it would be easy. The columns would advance upon the settlement from the woods. The Indians would have to stand and fight or be killed on the river bank. Among the soldiers there was not a single doubt about the outcome of the battle—after bloody Tallushatches.

The sun was just rising as the columns approached through the trees on either side of the village. Apparently at that early hour everyone in the village was sound asleep. Not a man, woman, or child was to be seen. Silently screened by the thick woods, the columns drew their battle lines. At a given signal, the attack yells burst from the lips of the riflemen, reverberating through the forest as both flanks rushed forward in the impetuous charge.

But to the intense mortification of the sanguine starving soldiers, not a single living being was to be found in the village. The huts were all deserted and devoid of food of any kind. There was not a grain of corn, a skin or an unpicked bone left behind. The Indians, the colonel told David, must have watched the movements of the foe and with their wives and little ones retired to regions where the famishing army could not follow them. The hungry men rushed into the cornfield only to find it stripped of every ear, every kernel. They had hoped to find stores of beans and grain, and quantities

161

of preserved game. In the impotence of their disappointment they applied the torch, and laid the town in ashes.

As he turned in his saddle, astride Jeb, and looked back at the burning beautiful village, David felt a sadness for the Indians who had spent so much care and patience in building their homes and erecting such a beautiful village and who would return to nothing save piles of ashes. A gratifying sense of relief came over him that there had been no one there to be butchered and burned. He had had enough of this type of war. He didn't think he could endure another Tallushatches.

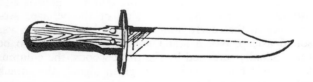

The four horsemen reined up side by side atop a small sandy hill overlooking the wide stretch of water separating Jean Lafitte's roost from the mainland of Texas. The four riders were Jim Bowie, Rezin Bowie, Tex Delacey, and Sam. Across the water they could see the low cluster of huts and hovels sprawled on the beach that housed the pirate's "Bloody one thousand." And behind them, upon a slight rise, stood a larger two-storied building painted a blazing red—the famous Maison Rouge, the lair of the buccaneer himself.

"Well, boys," Jim said, spurring his horse down the hill, "We'll soon know what kind of a welcome awaits us. That ferry yonder. That'll be Lafitte's men manning it."

Few questions were ever asked at the ferry. Anyone on foot or horseback who looked as if he might have on his person a few gold pieces could be taken across. Once in the power of Lafitte's murderers a man's life was worth no more than what he possessed.

Leading their horses from the ferry onto the sandy island the four men were immediately surrounded by ugly threatening faces—four aliens with four fine horses. And no telling what of value they might be carrying in their pockets. Jim led the way, pulling his horse after him in the general direction of the Maison Rouge. The motly crowd followed, hovering close, a little too close, Tex thought.

In an ever-growing circle the crowd followed, scoundrels of the scourings of the seven seas, attired in outlandish garbs—combinations of pilfered rich garments and filthy rags, silks and linsey, leather and velvet. Hand-fashioned shoes with silver buckles and bare feet were equally common. There were men in pantaloons of the latest cut and nothing else. One thing the surly crew wore in common was a sash into which a knife was thrust. They were men of all complexions, white, black, and all mixtures in between. Women, too, were among the mob—Negresses, Indians, Mexicans, Creoles, and a few who appeared to be of occidental blood. They were dressed in the same careless way, some half naked. Many were big with child. Dirty-faced brats of all crosses were in evidence.

Jim took note of an immense, barrel-chested fellow, bare to the waist and wearing red pantaloons, who carried a bull whip and wore a scimitar-like sword slung at his waist. The man's head was shaven clean, his face round and swarthy, and his bearing gave the impression of rank. Addressing the man, Jim said, "Lafitte is expecting us. Will you accompany us to the Maison Rouge?"

The man, as if expecting to be chosen, was at once at Jim's side, favoring him with a broken-tooth grin.

163

"Raoul, sir. Me name's Raoul Martin, overseer of the barracoon. Follow me."

The Maison Rouge was a huge square building, structured of heavy timbers, built on foundations of the old Maison Rouge that was levelled by a hurricane a few years since. A gallery shaded all four sides and above this were yawning ports through which muzzles of cannon glowered.

The buccaneer had seen his barracoon master approaching with the party and was standing by the door to receive them. Jim sought to measure Jean Lafitte by his brother Pierre, with whom he had dealt in New Orleans. Jean was shorter than his brother but not as sparse. His complexion was dark, his eyes black like his hair; his nose sharp and slightly aquiline. He wore a black mustache whose points sagged over a firm set mouth. His left eye, which had an habitual droop almost to the point of closing, seemed to flutter as he studied his visitors.

Ushered into the pirate's lair, Jim and his campainions were a little surprised at the luxurious appointments of the main salon. Tapestries and paintings, looted from many a gutted ship, adorned the walls; rich draperies, exquisite glass, and various objects of gold and silver met their eyes everywhere. The floor was thrown with exquisite colorful rugs from the Orient. Elegant furniture—too much of it, Jim thought—crowded the room. The man who had begun his career at a New Orleans anvil was living in what he thought was splendor.

Lafitte offered drinks and refreshments. But Jim was anxious to get down to business. Yes, Pierre had informed him of the arrangements. But would not the gentlemen remain for a few days as his guest?

"We'd like to select our merchandise and be on our way," Jim said.

"But you have traveled a long way, monsieurs. Surely one night as my guests—" His faulty eye opened and seemed to wink. "You have been without soft beds

164

and the touch of women for days. I can offer you both—and of the best quality."

"Thank you, sir. But we are pressed for time. May we see the Negroes?"

"You have the money?"

"In gold," Rezin put in, patting his waistline.

Lafitte and Raoul Martin accompanied them to the barracoon, a huge stockade of logs set upright in the sand. On each side of the gate were two ruffians holding shotguns in the crooks of their arms. Two more similar characters patrolled the perimeter of the stockade. Within the pen were several hundred Negroes.

"Most of these," Lafitte said, "are a fresh lot, arrived only yesterday. As you can see, they need a few days to get back their weight. And we have to cull out the sick and the malingerers." He glanced at Raoul. "How are you progressing with that matter?"

"The C pen still has a dozen or more. I had to lay the whip on good today. Several bad ones. I'll send maybe a dozen more to the C pen tonight."

Lafitte to Jim: "How many pounds, Bowie."

"I'll pick them by the man, if you don't mind."

Jim and Rezin spent the next two hours in the corral carefully selecting their Negroes, much as horse traders select the animals they are about to buy. They picked only strong, muscular fellows capable of heavy field work. Raoul, constantly at their side, now and then lashed out at a Negro with his long bull whip; needlessly, Jim thought. He appeared to derive a kind of depraved pleasure out of seeing the brawny men quail and flinch under his torment. Jim noticed that his face seemed to light up whenever his whip cracked across the naked bodies of the slaves.

The overseer spied a cadaverous Negro lying in the sand, propped up on his elbow. His body was thin, emaciated, his bones easily readable through his slack skin, his face emptied of expression. Striding over to the ailing man, Raoul proceeded to lay his whip on the man. The blows quickly raised long, lurid welts on his black skin; then, as Raoul continued the blows, blood began to cover his body. The unfortunate devil made no sound and hardly stirred, only to throw his head weakly back and forth. Jim had not seen this action at first, he and Rezin were inspecting some slaves in another part of the stockade. Raoul, unmindful of Jim's shout, continued his devilish work. As the whip snaked over the overseer's head, Jim caught hold of it, and yanking hard, sent its owner sprawling.

Jim strode out of the pen, seeking Lafitte, followed by the angry Raoul, who was cursing Jim under his breath.

"There is a man—yonder—in need of medical attention. Put him on my list," he said to Lafitte harshly. "Please see that his wounds are attended to."

Raoul drew close to his boss. "Captain Lafitte, am I not in charge of the barracoon?"

"As long as you please me, Raoul."

"Then, Captain, I suggest that the malingerer I just flogged be transferred to the C pen—at once. I've had to whip him twice already and he still fakes sickness."

"Just what is your C pen?" Jim asked, his curiosity aroused.

"Come with me."

Lafitte led the group to another pen, constructed the same as the first but much smaller, about sixteen feet square. Inside were a dozen Negroes, all lying on the ground; obviously they were either extremely ill or suffering from starvation and abuse. Some had horribly swollen joints, some had no belly, only a sunken hollow below their basket-like rib cages, the bellies of others were swollen and extended, resembling ripe pumpkins. Their faces were vacant of all manifestation.

"This is where we bring certain ones," Lafitte said, "for culminating."

"And what is that?" Jim demanded to know.

"We are merciful, monsieur," Lafitte said. "We give them three days to get on their feet—and then—" he lifted his shoulders expressively—"Raoul does what he has to do . . ."

166

"You mean he shoots them, like injured horses," Jim said accusingly.

"No, monsieur. Raoul puts the axe to their heads. It's quicker and it saves powder and lead, precious items here."

"Poor brutes," Rezin said. "It's enough to disgust a man with his fellow man. It turns my stomach."

Jim Bowie had never in all his life felt emptier, more completely drained of all power. He wanted to cry out in utter despair, for there was nothing else in the world he could do. He thought of his mother, sitting in her old leather chair reading her Bible to the children gathered round; and he saw in his mind the lonely figure of the man her words described, desperate and forlorn, standing on a mountainside, imploring, begging for someone—anyone—to hear him. . . . Jim turned away, trembling with rage at mankind's ignobility—and at his impotence to do anything about it.

Jim accepted Lafitte's invitation to stay the night. It would take the rest of the day to prepare the chains and shackles for the slaves. Lafitte's stewards prepared well for Jim and his party. Even Sam was allowed in the big house; but he kept his place, always hovering in the background or sitting on the floor beside Jim. It was quite obvious that Sam had come to worship his owner. Large silver trays were brought containing fish, roast pig, ham, fowl, and a wide variety of fruits, and bottles of vintage wines. The pirate enjoyed watching his guests partake heartily of his offerings. "I am always happy to have hungry guests," he said smilingly.

"We appreciate your hospitality," Rezin said.

"Nothing like it since we were in New Orleans, eh, Jim?" Tex said, pulling off the leg of a roasted chicken.

"Tell you what I'll do for you," Lafitte said, addressing himself to Jim, "since this is your first purchase. I'll boat you and the cargo as far as Calcasieu Lake. That'll put you on the Louisiana coast. Then you'll have only a couple of days overland to your destination."

167

Jim suspected some underlying motive for the pirate's sudden generosity. He wondered if a trap of some kind had been laid. "Surely, sir, you have a reason . . ."

Lafitte gave an odious smile. "The Kronks. I wouldn't want you to run afoul of the Kronks."

Tex suddenly became animated. "You mean the Karankawas? Them Indians that eat human flesh? I didn't know they ranged so far east anymore."

"They didn't until my men captured some of their women." His half-closed eye flicked open. "You know, some of those Kronk women are quite handsome specimens. The Kronks are vengeful savages. Only recently a raiding party of Karankawas took the men at the ferry. They staked and ate them almost in sight of the island. We found their carcasses the next day, picked clean."

Next morning the slaves were shackled and ready, eight groups of five each, waiting to be herded aboard Lafitte's schooner *Jupiter*. Jim and Rezin checked them, forty Negroes all told. Jim turned to Raoul. "Bring the sick man and put him aboard first."

Raoul's lip curled away from his broken teeth in a malicious grin. "Sorry, Mr. Bowie. That was a bad 'un. He died and we fed 'im to the sharks in the bay."

Jim felt the muscles in his neck tighten. "You killed him!" he growled savagely.

"Just a nigger—and a bad malingerer at that. In fact, I cleaned out the C pen completely last night."

Instinctively Jim's fist shot out and cracked against the man's jaw, sending him reeling against the log posts of the stockade. Two of his ruffian guards picked him up. Growling blasphemously, he drew his scimitar.

Wielding the deadly weapon over his head, he rushed upon Jim, but Jim ducked and the curved blade sliced the air scarcely an inch above his head. Raoul's momentum carried him a little way past Jim, but he quickly recovered and came on again. Jim caught the next blow with the brass spine of his knife, the metal that James Black had fashioned there for just such a

168

purpose. The scimitar clung in the soft metal, held for a moment, then slid down to the crossguard. Jim thrust both scimitar and swordsman away from himself in a mighty shove.

A crowd now had gathered and formed a circle around the fighters. Cheers and curses for both combatants were to be heard. It didn't matter to the villanous throng who won. Here was excitement vastly to the taste of connoisseurs in death, who were the onlookers. They, to the man, woman, and child, shouted for blood—either contestant's blood.

Lafitte, Rezin, and Tex stood at the back of the throng. Tex and Rezin were grim-faced and angry but dared not show the least intention of interceding on Jim's behalf. To do so would be fatal for all three. Lafitte seemed to be enjoying the combat with no less gusto for blood than his "children."

The two fighters circled each other. Raoul held his scimitar high, like a sugarcane cutter. Jim held his knife low, its pommel at his waistline. "Bowie, I'm going to kill you!" Raoul growled, and lashed out, aiming the curved blade at Jim's neck.

Again Jim ducked under the blow, but this time he was ready. As the blade passed over his head, he lunged forward. Raoul, surprisingly agile for his size and weight, avoided the full sweep of Jim's knife. Stepping back momentarily, Raoul rushed and swung again; Jim parried. Then, as Raoul raised his blade, Jim flicked his knife, slicing diagonally across the big man's chest. It was not a deep cut but it brought a wide flow of blood streaming down onto Raoul's belly.

Sight of the blood enraged the bull-chested man. A string of obscene oaths roared from his throat. Raging, he bent and scooped up a handful of sand and flung it into Jim's face. At the same moment, with a mighty bellow he lunged upon Jim, swinging his scimitar in a great arc. But the blow never landed. Jim's knife sliced clean through the arm that held the curved blade. The severed member still attached to the scimitar, carried by the vast momentum of the stroke, sailed through the air over the heads of the jeering crowd and fell to the ground far beyond.

Raoul stood looking stupidly at the neatly severed stub, blood pouring forth and staining the sand red around his feet.

"That'll put an end to that sonuvabitch's knocking niggers in the head," Tex muttered.

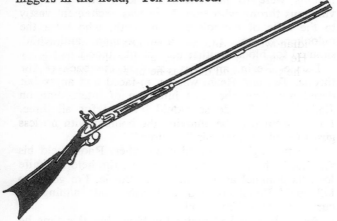

General Jackson finally received his long awaited supplies, along with six hundred regulars of the 39th United States Infantry, in which he took great pride. "With these soldiers I can end the war shortly," he proclaimed. He clearly lacked a zealous respect for the volunteers. He now moved his army into the interior of Alabama and established his headquarters on the Coosa River, and named it Fort Strother. Here Colonel Coffee and his eight hundred rejoined Jackson's main army.

David, sick at heart over Big Bloody, as the battle at Tallushatches was called by the exultant volunteers, had begun to think of Polly and the children—and his home on Bean Creek. He had told her he would be home in sixty days. His enlistment time was up. But, without consulting anyone, General Jackson had arbitrarily declared that all volunteers would serve a minimum of six months. David knew Polly; she would be watching for him to come riding across the field toward their cabin on old Jeb, any day now.

There were many of the soldiers in the same condition, whose terms of service had expired. They felt that they were free and enlightened Americans, and resented the idea of their being enslaved and driven, like cattle, at the will of a single man. Mutinous feelings were excited. The camp was filled with clamor. The zest of the volunteers' savagery had blighted David's enthusiasm for Indian warfare and had very considerably sobered him. He was over twenty-one, all his life he had gone where he pleased and done as he pleased. The next day an incident occured that decided the course he would take.

Paul Davidson was a seventeen-year-old recruit. He had volunteered in Alexander, Tennessee, a little port village on the Forked Deer River, a tributary of the Mississippi, about seventy miles northeast of Memphis. The little port will develop into the fourth largest town in Tennessee and change its name from Alexander to Jackson, in honor of the seventh president of the United States. Paul was engaged to his childhood sweetheart, Katherine Murray. The wedding was to take place at the end of his sixty day enlistment. Paul's time was up. In Alexander preparations were made for the wedding. He appealed to Colonel Coffee, who brought the matter to the attention of General Jackson; but Jackson stubbornly refused to hear of his leaving, not for any purpose, marriage least of all.

"You think that young scalawag would return?" Jackson scoffed. "Not by a damn sight would he leave a comfortable bed and a young pussy to go into the wilderness and fight Indians!"

When Colonel Coffee delivered the unfavorable news to Paul, the young soldier packed his roll and mounted his horse, determined to make it home for the wedding. Colonel Coffee grabbed the horse's reins to halt him and received a slash across the face by the hot-headed young man. When news of this incident reached Gen-

171

eral Jackson, that acerbic autocrat ordered the soldier's execution. Paul was shot the next morning.

Such harsh discipline may have been expected in order to exert a restraining force on the regulars, but not on the volunteers. Murmurs of dissent crescendoed and the volunteers whose enlistments were up looked to David Crockett for leadership.

David went to the general's headquarters, and after the customary wait, was received by Jackson. He stated the case formally for the men, then added his own opinion. "You ought to let them go, General. They will anyhow. If you let them go voluntarily most of them will return, after a visit with their families. They will need fresh horses and winter clothing so as to be better prepared for another campaign."

Jackson was quick with his refusal. "A man who deserts his ranks has no honor," he said with styptic shortness.

No use aruging with Andrew Jackson, David knew. Honor. It was just a word with Jackson. A high-sounding word, forced on those who accepted its sound as something sacred. An empty word used by generals and old men to cover weakness. A real man did what he had to do or wanted to do, as long as he was prepared to take the consequences for his actions. David turned on his heels and left Jackson's presence without waiting to be dismissed.

David Crockett, who had the uncanny instinct of knowing a man quickly, seemed to understand the character of Andrew Jackson, his merits and his defects. He placed himself at the head of the dissenting volunteers and prepared to challenge the general.

Jackson had every intention of keeping his word. He ordered a line of riflemen to be stationed on either side of a bridge that the volunteers had to cross, with orders to shoot the first man who reached the other side. That man would be David Crockett. "We had our flints picked and our guns primed," he wrote in his autobiography, "so that if fired on we might fight our way through."

172

When the column approached the bridge, they plainly heard the soldiers cocking their rifles. David held up his arm. "Hoo-oo!" he shouted, and signalled the volunteers forward.

Without looking to the right or left, with heads erect, fingers on the triggers of their guns, the column moved on across the bridge. Not a shot was fired. The soldiers were generally in sympathy with those who demanded their discharge, having faithfully served their term of enlistment. David Crockett had won this confrontation with Andrew Jackson. But there would be others, at other places, at other times. He would lose the fatal one.

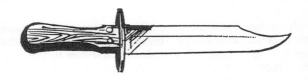

Tex didn't like it. All afternoon he'd felt they were being followed. It was the first day of the overland trek. The fading western light filtering through the moss-laden trees lent a cast of darkness to the timbers. He and Jim were at the tail end of the column, Rezin and Sam were at the fore, breaking trail. The slaves trudged along; the sound of the twigs and small branches breaking under their feet, mingled with the clanking of their chains, was the only noise that broke the stillness of the forest. Yet there was something. Tex had seen nobody and heard no strange voices. But there were signs: faint alien sounds that a man used to the wilderness can divine as not being native to the animals or nature. "Jim, we ought to call a halt," he said. "Pretty soon it'll be plumb dark."

"According to Lafitte, the campsite ought to be about here. Ride ahead and tell Rezin to call a halt. These poor devils must be tired and damn hungry."

Tex spurred his horse, and crashing alongside the laboring column of Negroes, trotted ahead. Jim reined his bay to a halt, waited and listened. Although he'd not allowed Tex to know that he shared his apprehension, he'd had his own suspicions. They were being followed, he thought, by two and maybe three horsemen. Indians? Not likely. Louisiana Indians were friendly and would have made themselves known to the party. Jim sat his horse and listened long after the sound of the column had disappeared up ahead. In the gathering darkness the stillness was absolute. The moss-draped limbs overhead lent an eeriness to the scene. Hearing nothing, he turned his horse forward. The bay walked gingerly, feeling her way and snorting now and then at the underfooting.

Shattering the stillness came the report of a pistol and a bullet whizzed by Jim's head. From out of the tangle of the woods crashed three horsemen in tandem. The front man Jim recognized as one of Raoul's shotgun men. His shot having missed, he spurred his horse, trying to get past Jim before his intended victim could retaliate. At the report of the pistol the bay reared high and whinnied but Jim held on and settled the animal. Now his knife was in his hand. As the horseman sped by, Jim leaned across the bay's neck and drove his knife into the man's chest. He tumbled from his horse, taking Jim with him.

Just as Jim retrieved his knife from the dead man's body, two more shots rang out. Both thudded into the ground near him. A second horseman came crashing down upon him. Throwing himself aside, Jim slashed out with his knife. He heard a harsh oath as the horse stumbled to the ground and its rider went sprawling into the underbrush. He dashed after him. The man,

174

seeing Jim's deadly knife covered with blood, opened his mouth to scream and tried to flee, but the tangle held him. It was too late. The blade, making a wide arc, cut off the man's voice as it sliced his head from his shoulders.

Jim turned his attention to the third assailant. But Tex, having heard the shots, was riding down upon the man. Seeing the bodies of his two comrades lying dead in the underbrush like a couple of huge rag dolls, he took his chances with the oncoming Tex. But Tex had already overrun him and as he tried to turn, Tex's long toothpick of a knife plunged into his skull from the base of his neck. The man loosed his hands on the bridle, slipped from his saddle, and lay on the ground slobbering and kicking. In a few moments he died with a whimper.

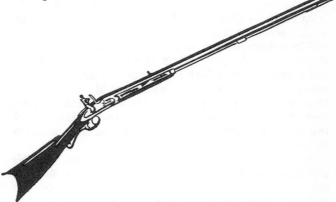

David was not to be with General Jackson's army when the general won his final victory over Red Eagle and broke the power of the Creek nation. In wars of civilization, a great general will always be willing to sacrifice the lives of ten thousand of his own troops if, by doing so, he could kill twenty thousand of the enemy. But it was never so with the Indian leaders. They prized the lives of their warriors too highly. They were always outnumbered both in men and in firepower. Indeed, the In-

175

dians were so careful of their ammunition that they rarely put more than half as much powder into a charge as a white man used. They endeavored to make up for their deficiency by creeping nearer to their prey. Red Eagle and General Jackson had clashed in several engagements before the final battle. There had been Talladego, where Red Eagle had lost two hundred and ninety warriors; and there was Emuckfaw and Entopachopco, which Jackson presented to the government as victories but which were really defeats for himself and victories for Red Eagle. Up to this point the United States had sent more than seven thousand troops into Indian territory, and in six months of activity had succeeded in killing eight hundred Creeks. Now events moved to a climax.

The day was March 14, 1814. Red Eagle had chosen to stake his fortune on a final stand at the Creek stronghold on the Tallapoosa River, with nine hundred warriors, accompanied by three hundred women and children. His position was protected on three sides by the bends of the river called Horseshoe Bend, and on the fourth side by a high log rampart. Jackson marched upon this wilderness fort with a field army of two thousand men. For all his considerable talents, derived from his Scotch, French, Spanish, and Indian blood, the wily and shrewd Indian leader was no match for Jackson.

It had always been Red Eagle's plan to save his warriors. He had provided himself with a fleet of canoes to carry his men away in case of trouble. But Jackson's first act, after he had surrounded the fort, was to send a detachment of scouts who swam the river and destroyed the craft. Then, using Colonel Coffee's proven stratagm, he lined up two columns of a thousand men each on the land side. He held the charge until the women and children were safely out of range. Then the drums burst out with the long roll signalling the charge.

In the gallant storming of the breastworks, Major

176

Sam Beasley was the first man to scale them. A bullet in the forehead toppled him backwards. Close behind him, a young soldier, sword drawn, pistol flashing, led the rush onward. Fifteen-year-old Sam Houston was displaying the fighting spirit that will win Texans their independence from Mexico at San Jacinto twenty-two years later. A barbed arrow drove deep into one thigh. When he was unable to tug free the jutting missile, he called on a brother Tennessean to help. Twice the volunteer tried, failed, and, sickened, gave up the attempt. Houston raised his sword.

"Goddamn you! Yank it out or I'll split your skull!"

The soldier wrenched the arrow out through torn flesh in a gush of blood. He then staunched the flow with a tourniquet. Houston leaped back into the thick of the fight.

The action now became general, and more than two thousand men struggled hand to hand. Arrows and spears and ball rent and filled the air; swords and tomahawks gleamed in the sun. The whole river rang with the yells of the Indians and the groans of the dying.

On through the afternoon the battle raged. The Creeks fought with valor. Jackson offered to spare the lives of any who would surrender, but the warriors, remembering Bloody Tallushatches, still fought on. Despite the valor shown clubs and tomahawks could scarcely prevail against bayonets at close quarters. Many took to the river but were picked off by sharpshooters. David Crockett might well be thankful that he was safely at home in his cabin with Polly and the children. What had begun as a battle turned into a merciless blood bath. Even the women and children were not spared in their place of sanctuary.

As darkness began to fall a remnant of Red Sticks manned a small covered fortress buried deep in a ravine. They beat off every attempt to dislodge them. It fell only when Jackson brought the war to full circle by ordering it burned with the defenders inside; thus

177

Fort Mims was twice avenged—at Tallushatches and here at Horseshoe Bend.

Of the nine hundred warriors who faced Jackson's army, five hundred and fifty-seven lay dead. On or about the river bank were one hundred and forty three wounded, while two hundred others were at the bottom of the river. Jackson lost forty-nine killed and one hundred and fifty-seven wounded.

But where was Red Eagle? Jackson did not find him among the dead or wounded. The general could hardly control his exasperation when he thought that the instigator of the Fort Mims massacre might have escaped to the safety of the Florida coast. He sent out searching parties to no avail.

A few days later Red Eagle presented himself at the general's headquarters, bereft of his Indian war paint and bright feathers. He wore the plain attire of a planter.

"General Jackson?" the figure inquired.

"Yes."

"I am William Weatherford."

"I am glad to see you, *Mr.* Weatherford," the general said. "You know you sealed your death when you came here."

"I am aware, General. I am in your power. Do with me as you please. I am a soldier. I have done your army all the harm I could. I have fought your men and fought them bravely. If I had more warriors I would yet fight. I have contended until the last. My warriors are all gone. I can only weep over the misfortune of their women and children. Dispose of me as you wish."

"I had ordered you brought to me in chains. But you came of your own accord."

It was said among the volunteers that General Jackson's magnanimity depended on the condition of his asshole. Red Eagle had surrendered when the General was at complete relief from his devastating dysentery. Jackson showed himself a generous victor, on this single occasion. He poured a cup of brandy for Weatherford and the two men exchanged promises.

Jackson said he would help the Creek women and children and would not punish non-combatants (a promise he never kept). Weatherford said he would preserve the peace. They shook hands and Red Eagle left the general's quarters, strode past the flabbergasted soldiers outside, and vanished into the wilderness.

Red Eagle kept his promise to preserve the peace. In later years, while Andrew Jackson was in the White House, William Weatherford was busily engaged in making a fortune as a planter with the labor of three hundred slaves.

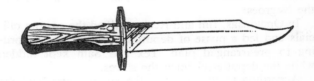

Jim Bowie's fight with Lafitte's barracoon boss, who was considered the "strong man" of the colony, had won for Jim the wholehearted esteem of the island's cut-throats. So whenever he appeared at Campeachy he was welcomed with warm admiration. Lafitte now had a new slave overseer, a man named Tom Jones, whom Jim considered to be regardful of the slaves and somewhat ruthless. Jones had done away with the infamous C pen. But Lafitte took all the credit for himself, proudly showing Jim the vacant space where the pen had been dismantled, and boasting, "After all, monsieur, I *am* a man with a heart."

Until the first trip had gone well (save for the perfidious attempt by Raoul to have Jim assassinated) Jim and Rezin had apprehensions and misgivings about the slave trade business. But now things were running smoothly and the money was rolling in.

Completion of the first transaction absolved all their doubts. When the slaves were landed from Lafitte's schooner *Jupiter* at the mouth of the Calcasieu River, they herded them overland on foot. Rezin and Sam rode at the head of the column, their rifles across their saddles, breaking trail through the wilderness. Jim and Tex trailed the column, their eyes on the trudging blacks. During the day they allowed the slaves to march free. Once in the woods, which were reminiscent of their native clime, they sang, happy to be out of the clutches of their former captors; they seemed to sense that some sort of better life lay ahead for them.

The final camp was about ten miles from Opelousas. Here they made sure the slaves were secure. Jim and Rezin went into town, leaving Tex and Sam to guard the Negroes.

In Opelousas, Jim and Rezin notified the custom officials and led a posse of deputies to the camp. According to prearranged plan, Tex and Sam kept hidden while the deputies claimed the slaves.

According to the statutes, the auction was held the next week. The average price was one thousand and fifty dollars, half of which went to Jim and Rezin. Their total reward amounted to twenty-one thousand dollars. They had paid five thousand and six hundred—a profit of fifteen thousand and four hundred dollars. They bought ten of the cheaper slaves from their bounty money and during the following days sold them one by one at a handsome profit.

Rezin wanted to visit Bayou Boeuf. He had been married only a short time and felt he ought to spend some time at home with his wife Meg. Jim, Tex, and Sam made four more trips to Campeachy. They were getting rich fast, just as Paula had told Jim they would.

On the next trip they took delivery of sixty slaves. After the first purchase they no longer had the courtesy of Lafitte's *Jupitor*, so they used the overland route for the entire trip: Galvez Island along the coast to Sabine, thence into Louisiana. This was a fine lot of Negroes, sturdy fellows whom Lafitte had captured from a slaver fresh from the African coast.

On the second morning, when they were still on the Texas coast, they awoke to find two braces of the Negroes missing. Somehow the ten slaves had managed to break their shackles and escape. Jim left Tex and Sam to guard the main body while he went after the runaways. There were tight lines about his mouth as he started in pursuit. The Negroes represented approximately five thousand dollars.

For two days he rode after them. They had left an obvious trail, easy to follow. On the evening of the second day he was closing in on the fugitives. In the distance he could see the lights of a campfire, and the noise of singing and chanting dimly came to his ears.

He approached what he assumed to be the slaves' campsite with caution, circled a little hill, and climbed to its crest on the far side. Creeping along on his hands and knees, he looked down upon a sight that chilled his blood.

The slaves had fallen victim of the Karankawas. Below him he saw the Negroes, all ten of them, hanging by their feet, side by side, on a common pole mounted on two tree trunks sunk upright in the ground. They were naked and nearly dead. Around them were about half a hundred Karankawas; the flames from the fire flickering on their painted and tattooed bodies made the scene all the more hideous. Leaping and dancing wildly about the fire, they could have been red devils out of hell's furnace itself. Others, in small groups sat apart, making weird music by means of blowing into long cane pipes, tapping with their fingers on small drums, and shaking gourd rattlers. The scalps of the Negroes had been taken and were fastened to poles painted in bright hues of blue and red, and these were paraded around by men who appeared to be priests or chief counselors.

Leaping and dancing, the Karankawas would approach the slaves strung upside down, cut off a piece of

181

flesh, take it to the fire, half-roast it, then eat it with great relish within sight of the poor victims. Chewing on the flesh as they danced lent a special satanic aspect to their grimacing faces. Swallowing the last mouthful of flesh, they would begin the process all over: another slice of flesh, more roasting, more eating, more dancing, and discordant cries. This would go on without cessation. Jim understood their ritual. Lafitte had explained the Karankawas that first night at Maison Rouge. The cutting and eating would go on until the victims died. In the end their bones would be distributed among the Indians to be sucked on for days afterwards.

He could not bear to see any more, and there was nothing he could do for the poor devils now. He left the scene, leaving the Karankawas to their fiendish feast at his expense—five thousand dollars worth.

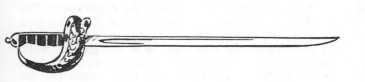

"I'm sorry, Jim," young Travis said. His voice was low, restrained. "I reckon we won't be seeing each other again."

Jim Bonham was stunned. The sudden announcement by his best friend that his family was removing to far away Alabama shocked him deeply.

"But I can come and visit with you," Jim insisted. "Or you can come and stay with me. My pa will arrange with your father. You always said you liked it here in

182

Red Bank Church. You don't want to go, do you, Bill?" Jim Bonham spoke with the desperate breathlessness of one drowning.

"I sure don't. But there ain't nothing I can do about it. My family is going and I have to go too."

"How come your pa wants to go way out there in the Indian wilderness anyhow?"

"It ain't like that, Jim. It ain't so wild. My dad says it's a real good move. He said when General Jackson whipped the Indians at Horseshoe Bend he made them give up their land. Dad says it's the best land in Alabama. And he bought the first land sold by the Sparta Federal Land Office. Mr. Calhoun told Dad that Alabama would be taken into the Union next year. It's in Conechuh County."

"Where's that?"

"Somewhere near Sparta, wherever that is. I heard Dad mention Claiborne."

"Bet it's not far to New Orleans or maybe Mobile!" Jim brightened.

"No, I suppose it ain't."

"Tell you what, Bill. When you get settled, we'll write each other. I'll run away and you run away and we'll meet in New Orleans, or Mobile, huh?"

"We'll see. What about your going to West Point?"

"Pa still talks about it. But I don't know. I don't want to be too far away. I'm gonna find you someplace, and we'll do something big and exciting together."

"Like what?"

"I don't know. Something real great. Maybe we'll become famous."

stood for long moments of time, his blue-grey eyes looking at something, someone, far away; his thumbs hooked in his waistband; his lips moving to words, or sounds. He felt the calm; it was over, and he picked up the knife, balanced the blade across his forefinger two inches from the cross-guard and . . . balance.

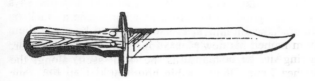

Precisely what ended James Bowie's slave running career was never determined. Some said it was because United States warships were closing in on Lafitte's stronghold at Campeachy. Others said that after witnessing ten of his slaves eaten alive by Karankawas he felt he was to blame for their horrible end and thereafter simply could not muster the stomach to carry on. Still others said that along about this time he had a change of heart and came to hate the entire practice of slavery. Whatever the reasons, abruptly end it he did.

But Jim Bowie did not give up the notion of making money. Having amassed a moderate fortune from their slave dealings, he and Rezin began investing their money in other projects, mainly land. The Arkansas land grants had turned out successfully, with John watching over the transactions. Jim, always of a certain prescience, espoused a theory to his brothers that people would grow sick and tired of the suffocating life they were forced to live in the crowded eastern cities and one day seek to break out. They've got to get out, Jim reasoned, and "out" was west, where there was still space and escape from too many laws and controls that eroded away man's last precious commodity—his personal freedom.

The brothers bought land wherever they could find

bargains. John acquired another land grant in Arkansas. Rezin picked up a tract below Thibodauxville on Bayou Lafoche. Jim purchased a plantation site in Rapides Parish, near Alexandria. As brothers they bought large shares in a new bank that was starting in Alexandria. They erected a sugar mill and Rezin began looking into the possibilities of operating it with steam power, something that had not been done before. If you can run a steamboat with a steam engine, Rezin expounded, why not a sugar mill?

Jim named his new plantation home Arcadia Manor, copying it after mansions he had seen along the Natchez Trace. It was a big house of two stories, four rooms above and six below, a wide center hall separating the rooms on the ground floor. The kitchen was a separate structure in the rear connected to the main house by a breezeway. Here Jim, Tex, and Sam lived contentedly for several years.

The various and expanding enterprises of the brothers constantly required new sources of credit. Natchez was the principal banking town, and so it was that Jim and Tex set out one spring morning for Natchez with a plan in mind of creating banking relations there. Arriving, they put up at Connelly's Tavern, sitting above the infamous community of Natchez-under-the-hill and overlooking the Mississippi River.

In Natchez, it didn't take long for Jim Bowie to discover that the entire banking business was in the hands of his enemies. As it was, Major Norris Wright, one of his old adversaries of the New Orleans duel, was the chief banker. Major Wright proved to be a man of lasting animosities. Upon learning that Bowie was in town seeking loans and credit, he called a meeting of his monied friends, including Dr. Thomas Maddox and Reverend Robert Crain, also instigators of the "dark room duel."

"That goddamn knife feller James Bowie!" Maddox said to his friends. "He's in town looking for credit. Don't even talk with him about money. I've already

185

shut him off in Alexandria by buying up the majority of the bank there. Let us stick tight here."

It was quickly agreed among Norris Wright's friends that all avenues of credit would be securely closed to the Bowies. Furthermore, Major Wright advised his friends that they should arm themselves while Jim Bowie was in town.

When news of this action reached Jim's ears, he went to call upon Banker Wright with the purest of thoughts: to see if some amicable way could be found to do business in Natchez. Through the window at the bank, Wright saw Jim coming and slipped out a side door, fearing violence. Jim saw the banker emerging onto the street and ran after him.

"Major Wright!" Jim called. "Major, wait!"

When Jim was within a few paces of him, Wright snatched from his pocket a pistol and fired point blank at Jim. Jim kept coming, grabbed Wright by the neck, lifted him off the ground by his neck and shook him like a rat. Friends of Wright came to his rescue, preventing Jim from killing the prominent banker.

"Why did you shoot me?" Jim asked, puzzled.

Wright gave no answer, hurrying back into the sanctuary of his bank. Wright's bullet had lodged in the pages of a book Jim had just bought to take to his mother, a copy of Wolfgang von Goethe's "Dr. Faustus."

Natchez-under-the-hill, that part of Natchez below the bluff, was the mecca of sin and profligacy, where crime was habitual, thieves, prostitution, and violence normal. It was the place where planters with money in their pockets went after dark to taste the evils of the universe and hoped to escape with their lives, some of their money, and their reputations untarnished. Here a man could indulge to the depth of his debauchery, for none was lacking in Natchez-under-the-hill. Here hired killers and notorious gun-slingers were available. For a very low fee one could purchase the demise of his enemy.

Stories drifted from bar to bar and brothel to brothel and dive to dive about the bad blood between Jim Bowie, the knife-fighter and Norris Wright, the uptown banker. And when Bloody Jack Sturdevant made a trip uptown and was seen coming out of Major Wright's bank, Colonel Samuel Wells, a prominent Rapides Parish planter and neighbor of Jim's, came at once to warn his friend that Wright had hired a pistolier to do him in.

"But you can't be sure," Jim objected. "Just because Sturdevant was seen in Wright's bank doesn't mean he's been hired to kill me."

"I'd call Wright out, if I were you, Jim. The man's a blackguard, I tell you."

"If it's Sturdevant who's going to kill me," Jim said judiciously, "then it's Sturdevant I ought to call upon."

John Sturdevant owned a small bar and casino called *Le Putois* where he sold rotten liquor and fleeced any misguided planter who might wander into his place.

The door of *Le Putois* swung open, admitting for a moment a breath of fresh night air and with it Jim Bowie, followed by Tex Delacey. Jim stood just inside the door for a few moments, giving his eyes time to adjust to the dimness of the place. Several men lounged at the bar and there were two tables of players, seven in all. Sturdevant was one of them. Jim went straight to the gambler. Sturdevant raised his eyes from the cards he held. "Hello, Bowie. Heard you were in town."

"Sturdevant, I'd like a word with you—private might be to your advantage."

"Whatever you have to say to me, Bowie, you can say here. These are my friends." He swung his arm around the room.

Jim came directly to the point. "The word is out that you've been hired to bushwack me. True or false?"

Sturdevant laid his cards down slowly, craned his neck all the way around and gave Jim a long malevolent look. Then he got up slowly, standing inches taller than Jim. He allowed himself time to reply, while he made a decision. The question: should he provoke Bowie and force a fight for all to witness. Or should he follow his original plan and ambush him. Bowie had practically called him out; there were witnesses. Sturdevant discounted Bowie's reputation with a knife. Luck, he reasoned. The man had had an inordinate amount of luck. Already he—Sturdevant—was better than anybody else in the territory with a pistol. To take Bowie in a knife duel would enhance his reputation on both sides of the Mississippi. Yes, let it be open, so everybody would know that it was Bloody Jack Sturdevant who killed James Bowie.

"Well, Bowie I ain't admitting anything. But it sounds mighty like you're calling me out."

"I haven't—yet. I'd like an answer to my question, Sturdevant. Has Norris Wright hired you to kill me?" Jim's voice was hard, demanding.

"Bowie, you've gone too far. I consider that a gross insult to my character. I'd like to teach you some manners. And a certain thing about a knife. Namely, that I can kill you with it."

"When, Sturdevant? Where?"

"Let's say tomorrow at two o'clock. Down at the riverfront. By then word'll be out and everybody can come to see me put an end to your reputation."

Sturdevant was right. A large crowd had gathered to see the fight. The handsomely dressed citizens from above the bluff had come down to stand in the daylight alongside the gamblers and thugs with whom they only rubbed shoulders after dark to watch the two men fight to the death. The gallery of Connelly's Tavern, which afforded an excellent view of the riverfront from its position on the bluff above Natchez-under-the-hill, was crowded with spectators. Most were the elite of Natchez; many were women for whom it was unthinkable to be seen within sight of the scum below the bluff.

The fame of Jim Bowie was wide. Men from far and wide rode to Washington, Arkansas, and begged James Black to duplicate the famous knife. Black could only

188

shrug and promise an inferior substitute. But Sturdevant had assured his friends that he would today put an end to this myth of invincibility. Both Bowie and his knife were vastly overrated, he smirked. The Arkansas Toothpick was the true killer. Sturdevant would prove it. He had a novel plan which he told nobody about and was saving for the last moment of the formalities. Bowie would not win this contest. Then Bloody Jack Sturdevant's fame would grow—as the killer of James Bowie and the despoiler of the legend of the Bowie knife.

The two combatants stood in the center of the space left by the crowd. Their coats were off and their sleeves rolled up.

Sturdevant flexed his powerful arms for the crowd. The oohs and aahs went up. Jim was quiet and seemed well composed. In the crowd he spotted Norris Wright, Dr. Thomas Maddox, and Reverend Crain. Also there were friends of his own present. He saw General Richard Cuny and John McWherter, and his neighbor Sam Wells.

"Somebody draw a circle, ten feet across," Sturdevant called.

Norris Wright came forward and with his cane drew a crude circle.

Now Sturdevant sprang his secret gambit. "Bowie, you challenged me. I name the terms." He tossed a leather thong to Wright. "Major, you'll kindly bind our left wrists together."

Jim made no sign of protest. Puffing, his face grimacing, Major Wright bound their wrists together with several turns of the strip of leather, and stepped out of the circle.

With his free hand Jim drew his knife, holding it with his thumb along the blade. Sturdevant's weapon was a hideous thing—a double-edged needle-sharp sliver of steel sixteen inches long. At the sight of it a murmur of awe went up from the crowd. It was a weapon to give a man confidence. It was a murder weapon, made for murder alone.

189

A signal was given. The two combatants came instantly alert, wary, facing each other at the full reach of their bound arms. Jim was well back, his body nearly erect, knife waist high. Sturdevant, showing no fear of the Bowie knife, was in a crouched position, his left foot forward, poised for a first, quick blow. The crowd saw his strategy and approved. Shouts of approbation gave him encouragement.

With a sudden bustle of activity, Sturdevant thrust his weapon—a savage plunge, aimed at Jim's belly. Sturdevant's action was as Jim expected and he was prepared for it. As the blade darted out, he twisted his body, yanking his middle clear of Sturdevant's thrust. A loud wail of disappointment went up from the crowd that expected to see Sturdevant's knife go home.

Instead they saw only the stances of the men change. Now it was Jim who was crouched, like a wrestler, well balanced on the balls of his feet. Sturdevant, suddenly realizing his momentary disadvantage, lashed out quickly at Jim's neck. His dagger clashed with the Bowie blade, clung for a moment then came free. Straining for all the distance he could command between him and the other, Sturdevant positioned his dagger for another and final desperate lunge. Useless in his position to try for the bowels. The neck. That would be quick and neat. This time his blow would not be parried. He steeled himself for the fatal lunge.

This was the moment Jim was waiting for. With a pantherlike quickness he shifted again to an upright position, jerking Sturdevant with all his might. Sturdevant's dagger slipped over Jim's shoulder. Simultaneously Jim's knife crashed into Sturdevant's ribs, through his heart, its point coming all the way out his back. The man collapsed instantly and lay like a sack of wheat at Jim's feet, only a glaze of white showing in his drawn eyes.

Sturdevant's deadly knife had slipped from his hand and lay on the clay soil beside his body. The sound from the crowd died away, and with that diminishing noise went the reputation of the Arkansas Toothpick.

From that day forward it was the Bowie knife that was copied the world over, and its creator praised internationally.

Jim yanked his knife out of the dead man's body, cut the thong that held their wrists together with the point of his knife. He wiped its blade on Sturdevant's silk shirt and returned it to its sheath.

With his friends Sam Wells, General Cuny, and John McWherter he left the scene.

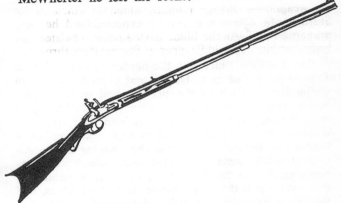

When the Creek war ended David Crockett felt a sense of relief. He had learned that killing Indians was no different than killing white men. One human being's life was just as precious as another's. He told Polly, "I'm glad I'm through with these war matters. I never liked this business of killing Indians. In fact, I don't believe I ever saw an Indian I couldn't like."

He spent the next years of his life in what was perhaps the most perfect state of happiness that he was ever to experience. He and Polly came to enjoy and love each other more each day. He told her, after they had made love one lazy Sunday afternoon, "You know, honey, I never felt right about that first night with you—in Pa's garret. Do you remember what I said then?"

"You said it would get better."

"Well, it has. Every time we make love, it's better than the last time. I've loved you more every day, Polly."

Came a day when David suffered a great blow. Polly fell ill, and after a short spell of hard chills and fever, she died on a warm afternoon while David fanned her face with a palmetto frond. In her youth she had contracted malaria from repeated infection of the *anopheles mosquitosa* which bred in the stagnant waters of the countryside. For many years that potential killer had lurked in her veins. Finally it killed her. His own account of this event does much honor to David's heart.

"At this time I met with the hardest trial which ever falls to the lot of man. Death, that cruel leveler of all distinctions, to whom the prayers and tears of husbands, and even the helpless infancy, are addressed in vain, entered my humble cottage and tore from my children an affectionate, good mother, and from me a tender and loving wife. It was the undoing of the Almighty, whose ways are always right, though we sometimes think they fall heavily on us. And as painful as ever even yet is the remembrance of her sufferings, and the loss sustained by my little children and myself, yet I have no wish to lift the voice of complaint. It appeared to me, at the moment of Polly's death, that my situation was the worst in the world."

For the rest of his life David carried a little pain in his heart, the stamp of Polly's overwhelming devotion and passion. Over her grave he erected a kind of cairn of limestone boulders.

The little cottage without her was too depressing. He found he could no longer remain in that domicile by the crystal creek, and he took his three children and moved again, still farther west, to new land on Shoal Creek. Here he met Elizabeth Patton, a very worthy woman who had lost her husband in the Creek War. David had known him, and fought alongside him at Tallushatches. Elizabeth had two children, a son and a daughter, both quite young. She owned a snug little farm, "much like Kate McCrory's," he thought. He wondered if she would make as good a bed partner as Kate had. But that did not seem to be of great import anymore. He felt sure that, after Polly, there would never be anyone with whom making love would mean a great deal to him. He dispassionately decided that he would make a good stepfather to her children, and she a good stepmother for his.

Sympathy is always an excellent opener. It is the oiled key that turns many a rusted lock. When David called upon Elizabeth Patton, her cup was filled and he was very thirsty. It proved to be a congenial marriage. The two families came very harmoniously together. Later, when he and Elizabeth had children of their own, and whenever all the children engaged in a brawl, as children are wont to do, David would humorously shout to his wife, "Come, Bess! Your children and my children are whipping hell out of our children!"

When the great earthquake of 1811 created the long, deep, winding lake in southwestern Tennessee, the country was wild and strange, with cypresses showing their black-green tops in lines above the water. The earthquake had shaken them many feet below the hillsides where they had grown, and when the Mississippi had reversed itself for two days and filled the abyss, a beautiful phenomenon was created. Soon the lake was covered by great yellow lilies, so that to come upon it suddenly was to find a yellow light glowing in the midst of the shadowed water. Mink, otter, beaver were to be found there. Wild geese habitated the shore. Here, too, were green snapping turtles with great heads and armored bodies that became Tennessee legend.

For a year and more, tremors continued to shake the country for hundreds of miles. At New Madrid, Missouri, a river town about twenty-five miles away, Robert Fulton's latest steamboat, the luxurious *New Orleans* was nearly destroyed by the violent reactions of the river to the tremors. The earth opened and the

193

banks began to crumble, but the *New Orleans* survived with Mr. Nicholas J. Roosevelt, Fulton's agent, and his wife aboard. Because of the strange disturbance of the land, the country where David had settled came to be called The Shakes.

In the spring of 1822 David Crockett set out with his family on foot for this wild country. There were now eight children, the two youngest so small that David carried them much of the way perched upon his shoulders or asleep in his arms, while the older boys led the horses. No one rode, not even Elizabeth. It was a journey of one hundred and fifty miles through almost a pathless forest.

He built a cabin on the Obion River, in the near vicinity of the great lake. It was a land David had dreamed about. Every stream that emptied into the lake was alive with beaver and fish. The brown bears battened on wild honey and chestnuts. Antelopes and deer drifted undisturbed through the secluded glades. Not a smoke showed above the forest. All was undisturbed silence, except for the growling of thunder in summer, the croaking of frogs, or the high hornlike honk of the wild geese in autumn, flying formation after formation ever southward. Here was a land, Elizabeth told him, that he could claim as his own—and here she hoped with all her might he would remain.

David, always good for a story, true or manufactured, soon began telling a tale in the lake country that changed its name from The Shakes to Reelfoot, According to David's legend, there had lived on the land before it was sunken a Chickasaw chief whose only son was born with a deformed foot that made him reel as he walked. The boy grew up unhappy because he was different from the other children. They jeered at him and called him Reelfoot. When he was older he ran away and lived with a tribe of friendly Choctaws. The Choctaw chief had a beautiful daughter, who saw no deformity in the boy to prevent her from falling in love with him. When the boy asked her father for her hand in marriage and was refused because he was a "cripple," he stole the princess and brought her back to his own tribe. The Chocktaw chief put a curse on him and all his tribe, declaring that the Great Spirit would destroy all his people. When the earthquake came this was taken to be the prophecy of the Chocktaw chief's curse. Adding credence to the story, from the very outset after his arrival in the Shakes country, David called the body of water Reelfoot Lake.

David Crockett was henceforth to maintain his home in the vicinity of Reelfoot Lake. His children were growing up and making their own friends. His wife Elizabeth liked the country and saw in it the kind of place she wanted her children to be a part of; and, in this new frontier, David was rapidly becoming a public figure and a political leader. He served as justice of the peace, state legislator, and now as a Congressman, representing a number of counties contiguous to the lake.

David's old adversary, Andrew Jackson, was in the White House. As President, Jackson exhibited that same vigor and determination in carrying out decisions that had characterized his conduct as commander of the army in the field. He made it clear from the outset of his administration that he was master. David knew what to expect of his old commander-in-chief, and he was right in his judgement of him. Jackson became so strong-willed and autocratic that David fastened on him the sobriquet of "King Andrew I," and caused his enemies in Congress to refer to his administration as the "reign" of Andrew Jackson.

At the time Jackson was elected president in 1828, the people had a firm faith in democracy and freedom. They were the product of a mixture of nationalities: English, Irish, Scottish, German, Dutch, French, and others as well. These folk were a self-reliant, versatile, ingenious people. Their main conviction was that young America was the pioneer in forging a new era for mankind. There were a number of experiments underway designed to broaden the area of freedom. They tested new religious faiths and philosophies from spiritualism to transcendentalism to Unitarianism to communionism. Secular education was widened, and its quality greatly improved, penal reforms were instituted, humanitarians ministered to the deaf, the blind, and the insane.

Jackson promised the country great things. He promised expansion in industry and culture. And he promised spiritual growth. New York City had a population of 123,000, Boston 42,000, Cincinnati 9,000, Pittsburgh 7,000, Knoxville 4,000. Jackson assured them that within twenty years these populations would quadruple. He said America would not remain a land of Jefferson's dream—merely a land of virtuous farmers. The growth of American cities, he said, meant the development of great centers of business and industrial power.

Although in Jackson's existence he had little time for the cultural side of life, he promised to provide the way for more aesthetic activities in the cities. It was the time of Washington Irving, Ralph Waldo Emerson, Henry Thoreau, Herman Melville, Nathaniel Hawthorne, Edgar Allen Poe, and Margaret Fuller.

Already, Jackson boasted, his own Nashville had a theater with a brick sidewalk in front. The town claimed a population of forty-eight hundred inhabitants, counting nine hundred slaves. Fifty municipally-owned Negroes kept the clay thoroughfares tidy in dry weather and passable in wet. The Nashville Inn, residence of judges and high political office holders, had adorned its front with a three-story gallery and its barroom with a billiard table. Davidson Academy had become Cumberland College, General Jackson contributing one thousand dollars toward the erection of new buildings.

Yet when Jackson became President the people felt oppressed; they sensed their liberties being eroded away and usurped by government. In their eyes the bureaucracy had been corrupted by its vested interest in its own power, and government became a means of promoting individual interests rather than an instrument

196

created solely for the service of the people. Big business had made a great discovery: the lobbyist. The people saw their mandate being bought up and taken away by the hirelings of powerful industries who resided in Washington and manipulated their representatives. Jackson, they believed, would rescue them from this dreadful danger. Old Hickory was a folk hero. The people called him and he came, like great folk heroes of other times, to lead them out of captivity and bondage.

Known to the nation as a military hero, Jackson came to the presidency with a clear and strong mandate. His immense popular vote arose from his military frame and from the widespread conviction of his integrity. Tall, thin, his white hair brushed straight back from his forehead, his face long and his eyes sharp and commanding, Jackson presented a noble figure. In his military campaigns he would consult his council of war, but never submit a question to vote. Similarly as President he would open up problems to full discussion, but in the end always made up his own mind. And once his mind was determined, no threats, no warnings of catastrophe, no persuasions could sway him. His strength derived not from books or academies but from his deep natural understanding of the people. "They were his blood relations," Vice President Martin Van Buren said, "the only blood relations he had." He believed that "to labor for the good of the masses was a special mission assigned to him by his Creator and no man was ever better disposed to work in his vocation in season and out of season."

Jackson bore the reputation of being intemperate, arbitrary, and ambitious for power. He did not crave power for power's sake, but for getting things done—cutting through procedure and red tape. As a general he had tended to do necessary things with great expedition and to inquire afterwards into the legality. Yet during his presence in Washington he proved to be a man of good service and of a particular distinction of manner.

When it came to a test of his nobility concerning the

Indians, however, Van Buren's assessment of Old Hickory lacked whole cloth substance. The folk hero, whose concern for the people's rights against the rich and powerful—and against a government that had become, in Jackson's words, "an engine for the support of the few at the expense of the many"—seemed to turn his evil side toward his red brothers. He confirmed in many people's minds what his enemies said of him: that he possessed a consuming hatred for Indians.

President Jackson was sponsoring a measure in Congress that would give him the power to dispossess five Indian tribes of the southeast of part of their territory, some nine million acres of rich fertile land; and by this action negate promises of security, ownership, and protection which he, as commander of the victorious Americans, had given Chief Red Eagle at the conclusion of the Creek War. David Crockett, the little slingshooter, again challenged the ramrod giant.

The American settlers had long coveted the Indians' rich cotton-producing soil. Suddenly gold was discovered in some sections of their lands. With the rapacious cry of "Gold!" the settlers, without law, without sanction, swarmed in to invade the Indian lands. These Indians were law-abiding citizens, many were prosperous. Moreover, the five tribes had shown themselves eager to adopt the ways of the white man. Yet David Crockett stood almost alone in opposing the removal of these tribes from their homeland. Being all his life a child of the wilderness, he felt a brotherhood with the Indians; he had spent most of his existence in the pursuit of an equal freedom for himself. He saw in the white man's invasion of the wilderness the end of the Indian world. As a Tennessee legislator, some years earlier, David had opposed the Jackson political machine on behalf of dispossessed settlers. Jackson, a land speculator himself. won that confrontation.

Again David stood up in opposition. He denounced Jackson's attitude as staining the national honor, and urged nationwide meetings of protest. Missionary-minded religious denominations, especially the Methodists and Quakers, belabored the treatment of the red brothers. In Congress David stated: "A treaty is the highest law of the land. But there are those who would not find it so. They want to juggle with the rights of the Indians and fritter them away. It is *wrong*! It is not justice. I would rather be an old coon dog belonging to a poor man in the forest than belong to any party that will not do justice to all."

The notice came to David through the speaker of the house: President Jackson requested the pleasure of Congressman Crockett at the Executive Office at ten o'clock on the morrow.

David appeared promptly, wearing his cutaway frock coat, frilled shirt, beige waistcoat, white stock, and pantaloons of grey twill. As had happened twenty-four years earlier at General Jackson's quarters during the Creek War, David cooled his heels long past his appointed time. Three-quarters of an hour went by before an usher appeared and motioned David to follow him.

President Jackson was pacing his office. His steps were firm, short, military. He stopped, gazed at his visitor with compressed lips and resolute expression. His lean face, David thought, had lined considerably since taking the office of presidency. Jackson waved David to a leather chair at the left of his desk. Pacing more slowly now, he began to speak.

"Crockett, I called you here to see if we can strike a kind of 'peace' between yourself and this office. I don't like your opposition to me in the house of Congress. I seek your understanding and cooperation in my handling of the Indian problem."

David opened his mouth to speak but Jackson cut him off. "I know all about you, Crockett. You're what one might call the 'delight of the naive.' You're a superficial thinker. In other words, a lightweight politician— a splendid representative for your constituents. You, like other congressmen, are elected and sent to the seat of government to represent the rights of your people. You are *de facto* the people's lobbyist." He paused to

199

look down upon David. "Fine. *Fine!*" Then almost to himself, "I wish to God it could remain so. But Crockett, do you believe that the people always know that they really want, what is best for them?"

"Mr. President—"

Again Jackson cut him short. "Take the Indian question in the southeast. What do your constituents in Madison and Obion and Gibson counties in west Tennessee care about the Indians in far-away Alabama and Georgia? There are certain things that are always best left to the judgement of the Executive. The southeast Indian problem is one such thing."

"But General . . ."

Jackson bored David with his powerful blue eyes. "Kindly address me as Mr. President, if you will."

David allowed a little smile. "You once ordered me to call you General or Sir."

"Things are different now, Crockett."

"Mr. President, I do not believe you understand the Indians. You are a man who frequently speaks of freedom for the 'people.' But does your freedom include your red brother? Let me tell you, Mr. President, that of all the virtues presumed by fancy or theory to be important to the human being, to the Indian his way of life is uppermost. He has always enjoyed the priceless boon for which all men of all times have yearned most profoundly—absolute freedom. Whatever his other circumstances, the Indian enjoys total freedom as an individual. His life is his surroundings—his land. He is peculiarly susceptible to every sensory attitude, to every natural feature of the wilderness—his home. He lives in the open, as responsive to the sun, wind, rain, snow, as any wild animal. He knows every glade, marsh, hillock, rock, spring, creek as only the hunter can know them. He does not consider one can deprive him of his surroundings anymore than he can take away his air or his sunshine. He has never grasped the principle that establishes private ownership of land. He feels himself as much a part of the land as the trees and streams. His homeland is holy ground, sanctified for him as the

200

resting place of the bones of his ancestors and the natural shrine of his religion. To take him away from his homeland is to destroy him."

"Let me explain my position to you, Crockett," replied Jackson. "What I seek is a maximum of individual freedom for *every* man. But none of us will long keep that freedom unless we are prepared to sacrifice *some* of our absolute freedom for a guarantee of the safeguards of our collective freedom. I visualize our constitution encompassing all the lands west to the Pacific and south to the Rio Grande. I see people—Americans by the millions—living out there, enjoying freedom under our way of life. I do not believe there are many Americans who realize the potential of our ever-expanding population. I want to see the people enjoy all the practical development of their sovereignty wherever they expand, to whatever limits they push their frontier. This will be possible only if we are united in defending our frontiers—as we expand. Whatever or whoever stands in the way of the ever-expanding population must of necessity give way. It is our destiny. Manifestly so!"

"Sir, the Indian is an American, too. The true American. One might say the *only* true American. He does not need to seek or fight for his freedom, or to develop his practical sovereignty. He already has it. His title to his homeland—and his freedom—is the most ancient, pure, and absolute known to man. Its date is beyond the reach of human record; its validity confirmed by possession and enjoyment antecedent to all pretense of claim by any portion of the human race."

"What the southeastern Indians have done with their title to land, Crockett, is repugnant to the tenants of the Constitution of the United States. They have set up a state within a state. The Indians thus situated can be regarded in no other light than as members of a foreign government. Therefore the ordinary legislation of the Congress in relation to them is not warranted by the Constitution, which was established for the benefit of our own, not of a foreign people. Subject to their own nation's control, they can by right make treaties and covenants with foreign powers. And in so doing would surely undermine the safety and freedom of our people."

"Sir, I can assure you the Indians have no such inclinations . . ."

Jackson raised an admonitory finger and a little vinegar smile crossed his thin lips. "I said you were naive, Crockett. Certainly they do have such inclinations. Every man has inclinations to get what he does not possess. Every man worth the few cents price of the elements of which he is composed covets what the other man's got. Call it the Devil's law—anti-Christian— what you will. But it remains a human fact. I concede the Indians have no *plans* at the moment of undermining the security and freedom of the whites. But once they align with powerful nations, you will see a different Indian. Power, Crockett. One must have power. And be prepared to use that power to protect one's freedom. Or to achieve the freedoms one longs for."

"You have the power to dispossess these people, therefore it is your right. Is that what you are telling me, Mr. President?"

"Toward these Indians I entertain the kindest feelings. I have repeatedly beseeched them in their own interest to allow us to extend the laws of the Federal government over them and their lands. This course promises them peace and happiness—and a continuance of their freedom."

David rose. "Sir, I appreciate your calling me here to give me your views. I respect them only as your views, not for their validity—or nobility. You have not changed my mind. I must warn you, I shall continue to stand up and fight you on this subject whenever and wherever I am able to do so."

"That, Crockett," the president said succinctly, "will not be in the halls of Congress. I shall put out the word in Tennessee that you are highly undesirable to me in Washington. You will not win in the upcoming election."

"So you're going to get me beat at the polls, are you?" smiled David. "Tell you what, Sir. You do that. And—as a wise old Dutchman called Jacob Siler would say—you can *leck mein Arsch* and go to hell. And, by God!—I'll go to Texas."

David Crockett turned on his heels, and as he had done over two decades ago with a truculent general suffering from dysentery in the wilderness of Alabama, walked out without waiting for a formal dismissal from the President of the United States.

John Calhoun had been right; almost immediately after statehood Alabama began to experience vast economic and cultural advancement. In half a dozen years within its borders six newspapers were published. Public and private schools were opened in the larger towns. Eight academies were chartered. Travis' own uncle, the Reverend Alexander Travis, founded the Baptist stronghold of Evergreen College at Sparta. Travis, however, did not attend his uncle's college. Instead, after sampling schools in the neighborhood, he enrolled in the academy of Professor Thomas McCurdy in Claiborne, which was now the principal town in the county. Situated at the head of schooner navigation on the Alabama River, it boasted a census of three thousand, six hundred and fifteen whites and one thousand, nine hundred and nineteen slaves.

Young Travis preferred Professor McCurdy's institution because it offered higher mathematics, Latin, and Greek, along with other curricula, and was not oriented mainly towards theology. Travis took great interest in the precise written word and the rhythm of oral expression. In later years his letters will ring with inspiring declarations of heroism—"freedom" and "liberty." It was here also at Professor McCurdy's that he acquired a taste for classical literature. He became a rapid reader. Professor McCurdy told his father that the boy could devour a five hundred page book in less than a single day; that he had read Homer, Milton, Shakespeare's *Hamlet* and *King Lear,* and sophisticated books such as *Rodenick Random.*

As a star pupil of Professor McCurdy's Academy he attracted the attention of Judge James Dellett, one of the ablest criminal lawyers of the state of Alabama. When he finished his studies at the academy, the judge offered to tutor Travis in the complexities of law. Judge Dellett became his substitute for Yale. In order that he might support himself while studying under the eminent judge, he took a job as school teacher in Claiborne.

Travis became recognized as the best groomed and most refined in personal taste of all the young men in the entire area. It was the time of fastidiousness in clothing for men, it was the day of Beau Brummel in England, and in his costuming Travis outdid them all. He continually kept the local tailors busy cutting and sewing. He had his own ideas as to cuts and designs of riding coats and cutaways and waistcoats and breeches and shirts. He was to be seen wearing a bright colored riding coat or a cutaway regardless of the time of day. He wore pantaloons custom made of green, blue, red, and tobacco brown, which was a popular color with the planters, over soft black boots. A favorite of Travis' costuming was the muffling cravat; often he wore two together, one of fine white muslin under another of black silk.

204

While others of his friends might wear shirts made at home by the good housewife or by slave girls under her supervision, Travis wore only shirts made by the "chemisier." He demanded that the sheer, linen cambric frills used on the bosom be rolled and stitched into the narrowest hems. He became intrigued by the "Garibaldi shirt," probably because of his admiration of the Italian liberator whose youthful exploits were being publicized in American newspapers and journals, and ordered three made for himself in the "Garibaldi red." That bright red color likely accounts for the "Italian red" or "fire-engine red" color still popular today.

William Barret Travis and Edgar Allan Poe both were born in the same year within a relatively short time of each other. In the span of their lives poetry was the elite literature. Everyone read and loved poetry. Those who thought they had a flair for the arts tried writing poetry. The Englishman George Gordon Noel, Lord Byron, was widely published in the United States and the young, stirred by the heroic beat of his rhythm, thought him to be a great poet. In his classes, Travis gave his pupils ample quantities of Byron, Shelly, Keats, and poetic works of the classics in which he was well versed and of which he was particularly fond. Had Poe been born and written his great works a few decades earlier, Travis would of a certainty have held him up to his classes as a great genius.

Rosana Cato was the daughter of a wealthy planter of the area and one of Travis' pupils. She was a quiet girl of fifteen and very impressionable. She never skipped Travis' classes and seldom took her eyes away from the always immaculately dressed, six-foot, handsome red-headed teacher, as he strode back and forth lecturing or reading for his students from a book. One day after he had dismissed Rosana's class, he noticed some papers that she had left on her desk. Gathering them up with the intention of putting them away for safekeeping, he saw, on the very top sheet, a poem quite neatly set down in her handwriting. He read it with interest, and it confirmed his suspicion that this young girl with the pretty legs and budding breasts had taken an interest in him beyond that in keeping with the decorum of pupil to teacher. He read the poem over several times.

MOON OF VENICE

When the moon is a golden gondola,
Afloat in the dull dark sky,
I sit at the stern and steer,
And like a singing gondolier,
Through the midnight waters ply.

I am lost in the midst of the heavens,
Where I ride till the dawn of the day,
At the tip of that gilded canoe,
On a broad pool of blue,
Till the blue has faded to grey.

And I am a poem of Venice,
Still sounding through the air,
So the centuries may hear,
Of the singing gondolier,
Who sings in the darkness there.

Had Rosana composed this poem herself? And had she left it to attract his attention? He'd been acutely aware of Rosana Cato because he suspected that she, as schoolgirls sometimes do, had fallen superficially in love with him. She seemed to be developed physically beyond her years and there were tantalizing curves of her body, as well as other assets, that stirred him deeply.

Travis was a healthy young man and no stranger to the luxuries which lay hidden underneath the young ladies petticoats of lawn, muslin, linsey, batiste, and mull. He had learned these secrets and much more long ago. First as a young boy in his early teens, when he and Jim Bonham used to tumble two pretty young slave wenches back in South Carolina. Often when one of his pupils caused him sexual excitement he'd close his eyes momentarily and allow visions of "Sugar Tit" and "Sweet Belly" to occupy his mind. In his fancies he'd fondle their firm, sleek bodies, caress their wonderfully smooth breasts; and he'd seen their little red tongues and thick lips as he bent to kiss them; always in his mind lingered their musical giggling laughter.

He frequently made trips to Mobile for Judge Dellett, and while there made a habit of visiting a tavern run by Joe Grady, a man of limited intelligence and still more limited scruples, and a paunch that could stomach anything. Above stairs, over the barroom, was advertised "Rooms to Let" but in truth was merely a blind for the four girls who were permanent residents to ply their trade. They were moderately youthful and immoderately brazen. One girl, however, named Margie, was less calloused than the others. Underneath her hard shell was a warm, softhearted, lonely person with a continual hurt look in her eyes, secretly reaching out for someone she could respond to. Travis was such a person for Margie. He, in turn, liked her and enjoyed sleeping with her; she offered a release for the pent-up passion that stirred and ebbed within him after days of standing before dozens of fetching and often sensuous young girls. Whenever he missed a trip to Mobile, he found himself growing restless, at times irritable, and unable to concentrate on his work. He would catch himself standing before his class, book in hand, saying nothing, while in his mind stripping Rosana Cato nude.

He read Rosana's poem again and again. Perhaps here was a girl with similar desires and feelings as his own. Could it be that she, too, saw him as a lover? Well, he'd talk to her about her poetry. The verses were not altogether badly written for a young girl.

He did not speak to her immediately. He wanted to observe her more closely for a time. During those days, whenever his eyes rested on her for too long, her eyelids fluttered and she lowered her head, appearing to busy herself with the books and papers about her desk.

207

He decided there were hidden pools of passion in the girl.

And at night he dreamed about her. She lay beside him in the moonlight. There was a faint, tender smile on her parted lips. Her eyes looked at him wide and solemnly, as they had sometimes done when she sat at her desk in school. She loved him! Why had he not known that before? For an instant her whole form glimmered into a bright, ivory light, glistening. He trembled toward her, the light, quick fire of his youth's desire flowing so that it possessed him. He half sat up and stretched out his hands to touch her. A mist began to curl about her ankles. It seemed to rush up her limbs and vanished with her like a smoke into the moonlight.

Sitting up in bed, awake, the realization of what Rosana meant to him came alive inside his pelvis. He longed for her intensely. He wanted to have her now, in his arms, to press her ripening little breasts against his chest, to fondle and comfort her, to be a boy and a girl together with her—to be a lover, a mentor, and a father to her.

The next day as the pupils filed out of class, he tapped Rosana on the shoulder. "I'd like you to stay for a moment."

After the others had gone, he sat down behind his desk. She stood a little way apart, her books under her arm, looking shyly at him then turning her eyes away, to the blackboard, to the windows, to the floor, back to him—the discomposure of the young. He pretended to busy himself with some paper work, a little nervous and slightly contrite, guilty because of his own deception.

It was Rosana who spoke first. "You wanted to see me, Mr. Travis?"

"Why, yes, Rosana. I believe I have something that belongs to you."

She came near his desk, took the proffered paper, made a little thank-you curtsy. "Where did you get it, Mr. Travis?" she asked with too obvious innocence.

"You did write that poem yourself?" he asked, ignoring her question.

208

"Yes, Mr. Travis."

"It's quite expressive, Rosana. Have you ever been to Venice?"

"No Sir. But I like to dream about far-away places."

"Have you others you have written?"

"Yes, Sir. I've a whole notebook of them. I love to write."

"Do you want to become a poet—someday?"

"If I am ever good enough."

"Very commendable, Rosana."

A silence fell between them. Neither seemed to find anything more to say. She stood there before his desk, growing restless, moving her weight from one foot to the other. Seeing that she was about to ask to be excused and leave him, he burst out, "Rosana, why haven't you asked me to help you with your poetry? What I've seen is quite good, you know."

Her elation almost gave her away, but she quickly took control of herself and became quite demure. "I really didn't think my poems were good enough to bother you with. But—if you would help me. . . . Oh, Mr. Travis—!"

"Of course I will, Rosana. Why don't you bring your poems tomorrow and after school we'll go over them together."

The next day Travis and Rosana remained at his desk in the schoolhouse discussing and revising her poetry until it began to grow dark. Both of them were so enraptured at being alone together that they had completely forgotten about the time. He walked her all the way home, to the lane leading up to her house. During the walk he told her that some of her poems had immense feeling. Some, he said, didn't quite come off. Just what he meant he failed to explain. But if she cared to work them over, he'd give her whatever time and assistance he could. She would be pleased. Her youthful little ploy was working!

One afternoon when Travis and Rosana had been together rather late, as they left the schoolhouse a thunderstorm suddenly broke loose. He grabbed her by the arm and they raced to his quarters, which were nearby, on Pace Street. Inside he insisted she take off her wet sandals, cape and jacket. He produced some cheese, bread, and canary wine, and while her clothes dried they ate, drank wine and let down the conventional barriers that still remained between them.

"Will your parents worry about you, Rosana?" Travis asked.

"No. I told them I'd be with you after school."

Outside the storm continued, it grew dark, he insisted on making her "comfortable" by taking her on the bed, his arm around her shoulder. All the diffidence of pupil-to-teacher disappeared; they were as boy and girl, he fondling her, flattering her, she trusting and coyly eager. Travis had known all along he would seduce her. He wondered if now was the time. Should he move in now, would he frighten her, alienate her and lose the advantage he had accrued? What he didn't know was that Rosana had already decided these things for him. She was here, in his room, on his bed, partially undressed. All that was lacking was initiative on his part. One little word, one little move and he'd see how willing she was. But Travis, the gallant, played it the gentleman's way: laughing, talking innocently, pretending to be completely casual but as each moment passed becoming more impatiently ardent for her.

"Bill," she said softly (it had been Bill for weeks now), "May I be perfectly frank with you?"

"Of course, Rosana."

"When you found my first poem that day . . . I—I really—I left it there hoping you'd read it. You know I wrote it for you, don't you?"

"I hoped you had, Rosana darling," he said and gathered her to him.

Before she could speak again his mouth came down over hers in a kiss that took her breath away. Her arms lifted, went around his neck and clung. His hand moved slowly and caressingly up her back, then began tugging at her clothes, loosening them and letting them fall from her.

"Rosana—Rosana." The words were half a groan. His hand found her breasts. If she might have protested, his lips covered her mouth, taking possession of it. But she did not want to protest. She craved him as passionately as he craved her.

"Bill," she whispered when he moved his mouth from her lips to her breasts, "are you sure? Sure about us? I've never done it, you know. Is this what you want—for us?"

"Yes!—Yes! Darling, I've wanted you—so desperately. All those torturous days, looking at you, craving you—"

"But . . . I mean—really want me?"

His hand had moved underneath her clothing. Now it found the soft fleece of her mons. "Yes! Yes, Rosana!"

"Very well, Bill. If you'll let me up for a minute, I'll take them off." He was struggling with the mysteries of early-nineteenth-century feminine underthings.

While she deftly and effortlessly solved the mysteries of buttons, laces, strings, straps, he was tearing off his clothes with the impatience of a drunkard rushing to a barrel of whiskey. No thirstier horse had ever been led to water, so avid was he for her body. Something like a hard knot grew in his groin and spread a burning flush over his entire body. The last of his clothes divested, he lay at full length on the bed, trying to calm himself. He felt her body, soft and warm, move next to his. Drawing her against himself, he began kissing her again, his hands wildly exploring her body, unable to decide which part of her was the loveliest to his touch.

Now Rosana arched up against him, half sobbing, not yet understanding the strange new emotion that he had awakened in her body. She was all too conscious of the pressure of his long, hard-muscled limbs against hers, of the feel of his bare chest against her tingling breasts, the crisp feel of his hair under her clutching fingers. Her head fell back and she began to whimper in her throat. Suddenly he let go of her, bent his head and

211

began kissing her neck, her breasts, his tongue tracing light, teasing patterns over their sensitive, firm peaks.

Impatiently but tenderly his hand moved between her thighs, stroking the smooth inner skin gently. She gave an instinctive, innocent cry as his fingers found her and he muffled it against his mouth.

"Be still, darling—"

She tried to relax, letting his fingers have their way, aching for something she couldn't yet understand or recognize until she found it. This is it, she kept telling herself. This is what I wanted. This is it—for now and forever! Her arms went around him to hold him closer, her body straining to open up and receive him. Then a killing, screaming pain and he was inside her. Now it's done, she told herself, it's over and he's mine. But it wasn't over, until she felt him grow tense and rigid, then fall limp, full length over her body.

The flood of desire drained away and the sobering realization came over Travis that it hadn't been everything he'd expected. He had tried to hold back, savor her for a prolonged time, but he had grown too tense, too excited. As he lay there allowing clarity and reason to chase away all passions, he began to worry about getting her home before her parents became alarmed about her absence.

But Rosana's feelings were far different. She was aware, without seeing them in the darkness, of the blueness of his eyes, of the redness of his hair, the shape and texture of his lips. He—all of him—would be hers for the rest of her life. He was hers now. She felt quite pleased with herself.

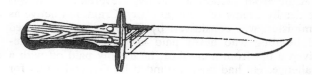

A horseman rode up to Arcadia Manor and without dismounting called, "Hallo! Hallo! Anybody home?"

A servant came out on the porch.

"Is your master home?" Sam Wells asked.

"Yessuh, Massa Wells. Lemme git 'im."

In a few moments Jim was on the porch inviting his friend into the house.

"I've no time, Jim. I want you to come into Natchez with me. I've called Tom Maddox out for a duel. I want you for my chief second."

In a quarter of an hour Jim and Sam Wells were riding toward Natchez.

For several years bad blood had been generating between the Norris Wright group and the Bowie group: Major Norris Wright, Dr. Thomas Maddox, and Reverend Robert Crain on one side; the Bowie's, Samuel Levi Wells, and General Samuel Cuny on the other side. The planters for many years had chaffed under the high interest rates exacted by the city bankers—the Wright-Maddox-Crain faction. On the other hand the bankers thought the planters proud and arrogant and feudalistic. And the factions were on different sides of the fence politically. The feud had begun some years earlier, over certain irregular election maneuvers. The Wright crowd supported John Quincy Adams and the

Bowie people were behind Henry Clay. Clay had carried Louisiana by popular vote; there remained only the formality of the state convention to name presidential electors. The Bowie people, assuming the issue settled at the polls, had not put anybody up as a candidate for the convention. But Norris Wright attended and switched the vote to Adams.

Aside from faction animosity, Reverend Crain was the deadly enemy of General Cuny. Crain, not active as a minister, was considered by Cuny as a white-haired old humbug who never paid his debts. When he received a bill from a creditor, he usually paid off with a challenge. He had been wounded by General Cuny for refusing to pay off a note held by the General.

Dr. Maddox and Reverend Crain were suspected of circulating some malicious gossip against the General. According to the stories, General Cuny was supposed to indulge in certain orgies said to take place regularly at Madame Celestine's Palace of Virtue in New Orleans.

When Jim had publicly shaken Norris Wright by the neck and subsequently killed the man suspected of being hired by Wright to assassinate him, the lid was off. During a meeting at the Planters Club, while drinking at the bar, Wells and Maddox had quarreled over whether Wright had really hired Sturdevant to kill Jim, resulting in the challenge.

Now Jim and Sam Wells were riding into Natchez to settle the matter between Wells and Maddox at gun point on the Vidalia Sand Bar.

"Jim," Wells said, "I wish this dual was between me and that blackguard Reverend Tom Crain. You know, he's not really a preacher at all."

"Come to think of it," Jim said, "I never heard of him holding a pastorate anywhere."

"He got a mail order diploma from some outfit in Nashville about twenty years ago, and he's been using the spurious title to get himself into the salons of busybody wives whose husbands neglect them for comely slave wenches or make frequent trips into Natchez and

New Orleans to get what they don't want at home in the fancy brothels there. From the stories I hear a lot of respected planters would shoot him on sight if they knew how often he'd bedded their lonely wives."

"And he borrows money from their unsuspecting husbands," Jim laughed.

"And the scoundrel never pays back a cent! Wish I'd killed him when we fought. But the bullet only lodged in his goddamn arm."

Vidalia was a long heavily wooded peninsula on the shore of the Mississippi, connected with the mainland by a narrow strip of brushy ground. Only the center was bare. It was here that men fought and were killed.

In the early part of the century, Joseph Vidal, a French settler and owner of the Concordia plantation, offered the peninsula as a place to settle disputes in duels. It was here that Governor George Poindexter of Mississippi killed Abijah Hunt. In this same clearing Major Ferdinand Claiborne had dueled with Captain Benjamin Farr. General Winfield Scott had here met Dr. Winthrop Upshaw, to answer for Scott's criticism of Captain James Wilkerson. These and others had fought and killed on the Vidalia sandbar. Now the hates of Wells and Maddox, Bowie and Wright, were to be tested on these sands.

James Bowie examined the pistols, after Norris Wright had inspected them. They were percussion pistols of the second generation of Josiah Shaw's models, the Philadelphia gunsmith who invented the percussion cap. Both weapons were oiled, properly primed and loaded with the same weight charge—beautiful pistols. "I'm satisfied, if you are," Jim said to Wright.

Maddox had chosen, besides Norris Wright as his chief second, Reverend Robert Crain, principal, and Dr. Paul Denny as his surgeon, and two political hacks who were in his employ, Harry Aimes and Cary Blanchard.

Wells' chief second, of course, was Jim Bowie, opposing Wright; others were General Cuny and George McWherter, principals, and Dr. John Cox as surgeon.

"Then let us proceed," Norris Wright said.

Whereupon Wells and Maddox stepped forward, each lifting a pistol from the case. The seconds and others formed two groups, one on either side of the line of fire.

"You have agreed upon the terms, gentlemen," Norris Wright said to Maddox and Wells. "I will repeat them so there will be no misunderstanding. You are to stand twelve paces apart, left side to left side. At the word 'Prepare!' you are to raise your pistols in opposite directions to each other. On the count of 'Three!' you are to face each other. On the command 'Fire!' you are free to fire at will. Will you take your places?"

Sam Wells stepped to the line assigned to him. As he stood, left side toward Maddox, he glanced at the heavy pistol in his hand. The copper percussion cap gleamed under the cocked hammer. The head, he thought. He would aim at Maddox's head. For a week he had practiced shooting, using a cabbage as target, and was able to send the ball to its mark three times out of five. Of the hated faction Maddox was the least offensive, but just the same he had to be killed, to seal his flannel-mouth.

Twelve paces away stood Maddox, wishing he had not got himself into this mess. He knew Wells was determined to kill him. Being a doctor, Maddox hoped that if he was the one to die the bullet would strike him in the heart. Head wounds could be messy and did not always kill; sometimes they left the victim in a stage of idiocy or blindness. It flashed through his mind that they both might die. But he found no cheer in this thought, either. Then a heartening possibility. Maybe a slight wound—only a little blood would be drawn. That should settle their differences. And he could go on living.

Through his mind passed the long list of grievances between the two factions. How trivial they seemed! Honor. Psha! He was supposed to be defending his

216

honor. Honor now seemed nothing but a hollow, dull word used by vain and pretentious men to assuage their transgressions. A man had to stand up and kill or be killed for honor. A senseless exercise. Norris Wright had the right idea. Kill your enemy secretly before he kills you. Like he tried to have Jim Bowie killed.

Wright's voice cut off Maddox's thoughts. "Prepare!" Maddox raised his pistol. He hadn't realized how heavy it was. Should he aim at Wells' head? Too risky. Better try for the body. "One!—Two!—Three!" He turned and faced his opponent. Wells' bitter features and grim mouth seemed inordinately close. "Fire!"

Maddox felt the jolt of his weapon. A puff of grey smoke obscured his enemy. The burnt powder drifted by. Wells was still standing. Surely his bullet had struck some part of the Well's body. He must collapse in another moment. No. The man was not hit. And for the first time, Maddox realized that Wells, too, had missed—Wells's bullet had grazed by his head.

The seconds were in a huddle. "Sam Wells, are you satisfied?"

Wells shook his head. The pistols were reloaded and the formalities repeated, this time Jim Bowie giving the words.

Once more Maddox took his place, once more he contemplated death, once more he saw the grim visage of Sam Wells facing him, once more he saw the huge black bore of Wells' pistol. And once more both men's shots went wide.

Maddox left his position. "Wells, I think we both have proved our courage. I'm satisfied if you are. Will you shake hands?"

"He's a right to continue if he wants too," Jim called.

"Then Maddox will stay here all day if your man is not satisfied," Wright shouted testily.

Wells glanced from Jim to Wright, saw the bad blood beginning to boil. He stepped forward and took Maddox's hand.

"I had hoped it would end this way," Maddox said,

relieved. "Excuse me for one moment, gentlemen, please."

Maddox stepped to the edge of the woods and returned with a large wicker basket. Lifting the lid, he said, "I think everybody will find some wine to suit his taste, and a few delicacies for your palates. Let us make this an occasion to end our quarrels.'

"I'm agreeable to that," Jim said. He was still holding the discharged pistol Wells had handed him. He placed it in the case. But Wright was busy reloading the one he had taken from Maddox. "Why are you reloading, Wright? It's all over," Jim said.

"I told him to reload the pistol," Reverend Crain said. "I don't think it's over. I have no love for your friend, Sam Cuny. I'm still carrying his bullet in my arm. Now's a good time to even that score."

Crain snatched the pistol from the case and began hastily to reload it.

General Cuny, holding a glass of wine in his hand, became aware of the dispute and started toward the three—Jim, Crain, and Wright. "Stay away, Cuny!" Reverend Crain called, leveling his pistol.

Jim stepped between Crain and Cuny. At that moment a pistol shot rang out. Jim felt it jolt his hip. His leg seemed suddenly to lose its strength, and he began to sink to the ground.

Lying on the sand Jim saw the smoking pistol in Norris Wright's hand, saw General Cuny throw aside his wine and draw forth from his pocket his own pistol. He heard the *click-cluck* as Cuny cocked it. Wright saw what Jim saw and quickly hid behind Reverend Crain, still holding the empty pistol with which he had shot Jim. Crain aimed the now loaded pistol and fired at General Cuny. Cuny fell beside Jim, his hands clutching at his breast, the look of a stricken animal on his face.

Jim picked up the dying man's pistol and fired it point blank at Reverend Crain's head. He saw the left side of Crain's skull explode, spewing bloody gray matter.

Jim shook his head to clear it, and began levering

himself up, pushing with his hands on the ground and dragging his wounded leg. Miraculously, his leg supported him. He unsheathed his knife and started for Wright. Two shots rang out about him. He hardly knew who fired them but he felt the quick impact in his left shoulder. It did not stop him. He kept going for Wright.

Norris Wright, with nobody between him and Jim, saw the wild man with the murderous knife coming closer and closer. In one last desperate act to save himself, he hurled the empty pistol at Jim. The butt of the heavy weapon struck Jim in the temple and he again fell to the ground.

"Harry! Harry!" Wright called.

Harry Aimes came between Wright and Jim, jerking at his pistol, which was caught in his coat pocket. Once more Jim shook his head and rose painfully. Wright's henchman, Harry Aimes, tugged and tugged. In his excitement he cocked the pistol while it was still caught in his coat. Jim was close. The pistol came out. Aimes thrust it against Jim's breast and pulled the trigger. The hammer fell on the bare nipple. The copper firing cap had come off in Aimes' pocket.

Jim's knife plunged into Aimes' soft belly, slicing upward. Aimes staggered backward, trying to hold his cauliflowering entrails in with his hands. He looked wretchedly at Wright and sank to the ground.

Another shot rang out and Jim fell to his side. Vaguely he heard someone cry, "Jim, watch out!"

Jim turned on his side and with clear vision he saw it. Wright had snatched from Dr. Denny his goldheaded cane, and was drawing from it the long sharp sword it concealed. Throwing the case aside, his murderous face grimacing, Norris Wright rushed upon Jim with the blade.

Jim, prostrate, saw the gleaming needle point as Wright swore and delivered the villainous thrust. Jim felt the sharp pain and heard Wright's rasping voice: "Die, you son-of-a-bitch! Why don't you die?"

The blade was deep in Jim's body. Wright stood over him trying to pull it out. One more thrust and he'd

219

close those fierce eyes for good. Wright pulled and pulled. Each effort sent excruciating pain through Jim's body. Furious, Wright put a brutal foot on the wounded man's chest and with an oath dragged once more. The handle came off in his hand.

Wright stood frozen for a moment, looking abjectly at the gold-headed object in his hand. Then his eyes fell on the steel rod sticking up out of that great heaving chest. A cry that was both a curse and a prayer escaped from his lips as he felt Jim's powerful grip on his wrist.

Wright pulled backward, tried desperately to free himself. He felt the mighty jerk, felt himself falling, felt the blunt end of the sword crash into his own chest, felt it tear into his heart. A final cry came from him. "Goddamn you, Bowie! You've killed me!"

Dr. John Cox and McWherter approached the two forms.

"Both dead?" asked McWherter, as Dr. Cox pulled the corpse from Jim's body.

"Jim's alive. Help me with him."

But Jim Bowie, snatching strength from hell itself, staggered to his feet, covered with blood and driven with fury. He began tugging at the steel blade still protruding from his body, gigantic, fearful, reeling savagely in the clearing where four men lay dead. Gary Blanchard and Dr. Paul Denny, the last of Wright's crowd, were sure Jim, too, had mortal wounds. Yet they knew he was deadly dangerous until he died, and so they slipped away into the woods.

Lying on the sand under the trees where McWherter and Dr. Cox had brought him, dimly Jim heard the professional pronouncement: "The blade deflected and missed the heart . . . passed through the lung before protruding out the dorsal side of the body . . . hmmm . . . I'll have to saw it off and pull it through the body from the back . . . pneumonia will set in for sure . . . he can't possibly live."

It seemed indeed as if Fate were withdrawing her last skein of lucky thread from the eye of the broken needle. But Mephisto, sitting brazenly on the wall of the Alamo in faraway Texas, laughed hilariously, took up the slack, and drew the red cord all the more taunt . . .

Elve Bowie came to Arcadia Manor and nursed her son through the critical days of his convalescence. Jim Bowie was alive only because his body insisted upon survival. It was as simple as that. The wounds he received in the Vidalia Sand Bar fight were slow in healing, and Elve stayed on. She lived in the room adjoining his on the second floor. At night when he suddenly cried out in pain, she was instantly at his bedside. She prepared his meals, changed his dressings, and read to him.

But Elve was worried about his drinking. Since they brought him home to Arcadia more dead than alive, he had continually demanded whiskey be kept on the table beside his bed. The bottle had to be replaced every day, sometimes oftener. This was unlike the son she had always known who, as Rezin liked to say, "only took a glass in a merry mood to chase dull care away." Now he drank almost continually; never, however, to the stage of drunkeness, just nipped all day and into the night, until he fell asleep.

When Elve spoke of her concern, he smiled. "Don't you worry about me and old John Barleycorn, Ma. I can lick him anytime."

Elve searched him for long moments. "Son, there are lots of things in life a man can fight and win out against—enemies, disease, poverty, reverses of all sorts," she said gravely. "But once a man takes his first drink, he can never win a victory over John Barleycorn. The very best he can hope for is a draw."

That was the last word Elve ever had to say about the matter.

One afternoon, when Jim was well on the road to recovery, Elve closed her "Dr. Faustus" from which she had been reading aloud to him and suddenly said, "Son,

221

I believe I know the answer to all your troubles—your fighting."

He looked at her, almost pleadingly. "Ma, you're blaming me. I never started a fight in my entire life. You don't want me to tuck tail and run, do you?"

"Tain't that, Jim, I'm talking about. It's the cause—the *why*. It's because you haven't got a woman. Look at Rezin and John. Both married and raising families. Neither one of them has ever killed a man. What you need, Jim, is a good woman." She nodded at the bottle beside the bed. "And that ain't no substitute for a woman."

He smiled a little rakishly. "Well, Ma, I certainly have nothing against women. In fact I like them a lot."

"That ain't what I mean, either," Elve snapped. "Tell you what, Jim. I know a woman—just the kind of woman for you. Her name's Mary Forbes, a neighbor of mine. Her husband died of snake bites. I'm going to send her over to look after you. I've got to get back home anyhow."

"Sure, Ma. Why not? I'm feeling really strong now. Is she pretty?"

"She's a real fine looking woman, young enough, the kind to make you a good wife and a fine mother of your children. If you're up to it and she'll let you, you ought to take her to bed. Maybe you'll both find you're suited for each other."

Jim laughed. "Ma, you're a devil in linsey-woolsey. I love you!"

A few days later, while Jim, Tex, and Sam were sitting on the front veranda, a buggy turned into the lane and proceeded up to the house. Sam said, "Lawdy, Marse Jim, look at the purty lady a-comin'."

Mary Forbes was not really pretty, in any classical sense; but she was, as Elve said, "just the kind of woman." In that good woman's interpretation, meaning: young widow; childless; attractive with good figure; excellent health; needing sex; forebearing sex; good wife possibility.

Mary Forbes made herself at home forthwith, occupying the room next to Jim's that Elve had vacated. She was always pleasant, congenial, and seemed to find much satisfaction in ministering to Jim's needs. Often to his annoyance. Careful not to scold him for his imbibing, she sometimes joined him in a drink or two in the evening. She never let the bottle run empty, always notifying Tex of this danger in plenty of time for him to forestall the disaster.

One night when she and Jim were sitting in his room having their evening drinks, Jim said, "Mary, you tend me, you minister to me, you mother me, you never deny me. You're too goddamn perfect. A man likes to be denied by a woman once in a while."

"I only want to please you, Jim Bowie."

He gazed at her wonderingly, his eyes swimming a little. "Why?"

"I—I—I really don't know."

"Well, I do," he said recklessly.

"You do—?"

"You want to get married. You want a man." He peered at her through foggy eyes. "Don't you, Mary?"

"A husband—yes."

"I said a man," he repeated gruffly.

She remained silent, not choosing to make a distinction.

Jim took her glass, set it aside and drew her onto the bed and began to take off her clothes.

"Jim—oh, Jim . . . do you think you are well enough?"

The next morning he awoke early and lay in bed thinking about Mary Forbes, asleep in the next room with the door ajar between them. She was a good woman and would make some man a dutiful wife. She would always be there when her man needed her. She would succor him, feed him, care for him in sickness, bear his children. And, like his mother had said, she needed a man. Last night, he reflected, she had gotten deep satisfaction in making love with him. In the best and worst sense she would worship her husband. All she wanted was to be accepted casually, trusted, and be allowed like a friendly and slightly foolish dog to come to him and receive a pat on the belly or be stroked on the head. But she could never satisfy a man like himself, Jim thought. Her lovemaking had been dutiful, clinical, casual. Goddammit! He had to have a woman of ingenuity—of fire! A woman like his lost Paula!

He poured himself a large drink. Another. Euphoria. Sensuous thoughts of Paula. He went to the desk and wrote a note.

Paula,

I'm sending this to you by Tex in the hope that you'll let him bring you here. If you can possibly do so, please come to Arcadia. If I thought words would bring you I'd say I need you. Tex will tell you that isn't true. But I do want very much to see you.

Jim

Then he went looking for Tex.

Telling Mary Forbes the truth was an embarrassing but not a painful task. If nothing else Jim Bowie was forthright. Mary packed and left the same day, maintaining her pleasant and cheerful attitude. If he ever needed or wanted her for anything, she assured him, all he had to do was just let her know.

Tex had been gone nearly two weeks and Jim began to give up hope that Paula would come. After all, it had been a long time; and there was her child Pauline to think about. Women just don't pick up and run to a man because of a few scribbled words on a piece of paper. It was a rash, foolish act, sending Tex all the way to New Orleans to make such a request of a woman he hadn't seen in so many years. He began to feel contrite about it. But where was Tex? If she wasn't coming Tex would have been back by now.

The next afternoon when he saw a carriage approaching in the distance, he knew it was bringing

Paula, and his heart lifted. He was waiting with Sam in the yard when she stepped down from the cabriolet.

She hadn't changed really, still slender, with just the right contour of hips, still small of waist, and her bosom—promise enough. Looking at her the intervening years seemed to fall away. His heart sang again, as it had long ago when, on Sundays, he'd find her waiting for him in the glen. His joy at seeing her here on his plantation, in his own manor, his woman, completely his, even if only for a little while, made her seem more beautiful than ever.

Paula smiled her happiness at seeing him, then she greeted Sam, whose white teeth gleamed behind his broad smile.

As they went into the house she clung to Jim's arm, asking questions about his wounds, his health. He assured her that he was perfectly sound once again. She stopped at the head of the staircase to admire the great salon below them. "It's lovely, Jim. The decor is yours, I'm sure. It's so—so virile, so manly. So indestructible. It's you."

While Paula unpacked Jim looked her over once again and thought it somehow unfair that she wasn't marked. He felt old and she looked as young as ever. Now that she was here he wondered anew what he really wanted to do about her. During the days he waited for her, afraid she'd not come, he had convinced himself that he ought to make her his mistress, if there was still no way he could marry her. He was now in a position to own—and keep—a quadroon woman. Most men he knew who commanded his wealth kept a mistress, and most of them were married men. But he hated himself for the thought of owning Paula. Somehow, in spite of her frequent reminders, he had never been able to think of her as a black woman, a Negress.

That night Sam and Tex had seen to it that the servants prepared a wonderful meal. It consisted of turtle soup, saddle of venison, broiled wild duck, and hickory-smoked ham, with jellies, hot bread, yams, sauces, and wines, the dessert followed by nuts of many deli-

cious varieties. But Jim hardly knew what he was
eating. His eyes were all for Paula and the longer he
looked at her the more muddled his thoughts became.
He was trying to arrange in his mind a train of action
for his future. He had been thinking a lot about Texas,
and he and Tex had just about decided on going out
there, at least to look around a bit. According to Tex it
was the country of the future, a land of vast opportunity. Could he persuade Paula to uproot herself
from New Orleans and go with him? What about her
daughter Pauline? And how attached was she to Pierre
Lafitte? His mind boggled.

After dinner Jim, Paula, and Tex sat on the veranda
and talked. Jim had little to say, listening for a clue as
to Paula's interest in what Tex was saying about Texas.
He learned little. His drinking was light. He wanted his
head to be clear while Paula was with him; he wanted
to enjoy her with all his senses.

In his room Jim, undressed, waited for Paula to
come to him. At last the door adjoining their rooms
opened and she appeared, wearing some sort of chiffon
peignoir, very sheer and soft, light red in color. Her
face was flushed and her eyes shone even in the
dimness of the room. He stood up, faced her, feeling his
pulse beat in the veins of his neck, her soft savage
beauty almost taking his breath away. She came to him
and he held her.

"You're trembling, Paula."

"It's been a long time, Jim."

He kissed her, at first tenderly and lightly, savoring
the sweetness of her mouth. Then the tumultuous desire
raging inside him caused him to enfold her intensely.
He noticed a little startled catch in her breath as he
drew her hard against him and his hand ran down her
arched back with a sleeking motion, encountering the
stunning soft abundance of her hips.

Crushed mouth to mouth, perfumed, hot as fire, her
lips trembled under his. Always in his embrace she had
become inflamed with a strange barbaric passion. Again

226

the same primitive force was at work. But had the years in between robbed her of its naturalness, its innocence? As if reading what had flashed through his mind, she released herself from his embrace. "Jim," she said, "I want you as passionately as you want me. But I must know something first."

"Anything, Paula."

"In a few moments we will be lying there on your bed, very close in each others arms. But, Jim, will we be close—really?"

"What are you trying to tell me, Paula?"

"Will there be between us—in your mind—half a hundred other men?"

He sat heavily down on the bed; a low groan escaped from him. "Paula . . . my dear Paula, you have an exquisite capacity for torturing me."

In the dimness of the room she could see the steel in the grey of his eyes. "Jim," she said softly, "if you can feel about me—even a little bit—as I do about myself, it won't matter. I've done what I had to do with my life. And I have no regrets."

"Paula, you should have listened to me—years ago. Before it was too late."

She came and placed her arms around him. "Jim . . . dear Jim . . . don't you realize it was too late the day I was born."

She lifted his chin and kissed him. "Let's don't talk about it anymore. Just say that you love me—still."

The nightgown fell from her body and she eased him back on the bed. "Jim, a woman never forgets her first love, or the first man who made her a woman. I will show you the depth of my love, my darling."

He glanced down. Paula was bending toward him, her dangling breasts descending between his knees, blazing passion lighting her eyes, her face beautifully colored with excitement.

He felt her mouth on him, her lips and tongue teasing—ardently, titillatively, until he groaned. She raised her head, and began moving her breasts over his body, their tips brushing lightly his skin. In a moment her

227

mouth was back where it was before but now engorging him savagely—deep in her throat.

He was amazed at her skill. What a sensation! It was an intoxicating experience, filled with ecstasy—poignant, exciting, excruciating. It was easy to let physical sensation take over, closing his mind to all else. Such prowess! Such finesse! Such expertise!

Over and over again she brought him tumultuously to the brink of consumation only to hold him quivering at the edge of the world yet not allowing him to go over. Deftly she gave him all the sensation of fulfillment while maintaining him on the brink of eternity. She would let up momentarily, when it seemed he could stand no more, then in a few moments she would begin all over again.

In this manner she kept him teetering between heaven and hell for a long period of exaltation. Only when she sensed that he was becoming completely exhausted did she lift her head and lay alongside him.

"Why didn't you finish the job?"

"Darling, there's more to come. You shall have everything you desire. Look at me, Jim . . ."

In the gloom he drank in her exquisiteness. Pulsating throat. Rising breasts. Swelling thighs. Up-cast mons, embroidered with dark curly fleece which half-revealed the delicious lips of her sex.

"You're so lovely," he said with the adulation of a connoisseur viewing rare and precious objects of art. He bent and kissed some of these objects. Then he reclined his head on the pillow beside hers.

"Jim, you kissed my throat and my breasts. Am I not beautiful down there, too?"

"You are lovely all over, Paula."

"Then why do you not kiss me there?"

He did not answer. But he needn't. She knew that there would always remain between them the spector of a gallery of men to separate them forever.

While Paula packed for the trip back to New Orleans, Jim fretted. She had stayed a week, a little

228

longer than she planned. During that time he had been unable to speak of what plagued him most. Suddenly he snatched the dresses from her arms and flung them aside.

"Paula," he said impatiently. "I know you have to go back to your home and daughter. But hear what's on my mind. Tex and I are going to Texas. I want to take you with me. I'll come to New Orleans and get you. There'll be a new beginning for us out there . . ."

She put her hand to his lips. "We've been through that, Jim. My blood would be just as black in Texas as it is in Louisiana. But in New Orleans people care less. No, Jim, it cannot be."

He took her by the shoulders and had trouble restraining himself from shaking her. He made her look into his eyes. "Listen to me, Paula. It's no fault of your own that somewhere in the past a white man amused himself with a slave woman. And each succeeding line submitted to the same degradation by a white man bearing daughters nearer and nearer to the pure white strain, but never becoming absolutely white. Try to look upon it as your good fortune. For me, you are as white as I am. We'll have children and they'll be white."

She drew away from him. Oh God! how he was wrenching her heart! Now was the finest—and last—opportunity to tell him that Pauline was his child. For one wild moment she saw herself rushing into his arms and breathlessly babbling all about their daughter—how lovely she had become, already in her teens. But she shrank from telling him.

Striving to calm her heart, she said, "I have my life, Jim. And my daughter. Neither can possibly fit into your plans."

She began packing her clothes into her portmanteau.

He poured himself a drink. Gazing at her with mixed fury and frustration, he gulped it down. Poured another. His eyes followed her as she moved from the closet to the bed with armfuls of clothes, bending, packing her cases. And all the while his dream of cutting

229

out—casting his lot with a new set of people in a vast new country—was becoming more and more of a resolution to be undertaken at once.

Wherever James Bowie went, his reputation was sure to have gotten there first. And so it was in Texas. Wherever there were people he was received with much enthusiasm.

"James Bowie? Is that Jim Bowie?" Texans stared open-mouthed, treated him everywhere with profound respect, approached and addressed him with ceremony. His exploits had been told and retold. Now that he appeared among them in the flesh, they found nothing to disappoint them. His size, great shoulders, powerful arms, and steel grey eyes fulfilled the legends concerning him.

Tex chose the route that took them through Nacogdoches, just across the Louisiana frontier. Here was the landlocked part for the newly arrived settlers from the United States. Many stayed and put down their roots, without venturing further into the vastness of Texas. This was an odd town, half old, half new. The many recent buildings of new lumber seemed curiously out of place among the old adobe houses. Many Mexicans were here, but it had lost its character as a Spanish town. There remained a few gentry clinging to the elegant pretensions of the past, but this was only a thin top crust; below, the new town seethed—bawdy, vigorous, pollyglot.

Tex would tarry, looking up old friends and acquaintances; but Jim was impatient to push on. Tex's stories of San Antonio de Bexar had captured his fancy.

On the way to San Antonio they stopped at San Felipe de Susting, and put up at Peyton's Tavern. Jim liked the independent aggressive American colonists and their easy-going hospitable manner. Their way of life and dress appealed to him. Before leaving San Felipe he purchased at Dinsmore's buckskin breeches, western boots and hat, and several hunting shirts.

During the stay at Peyton's they met some of the

frontier's most distinguished citizens: Three-Legged Willie Williamson, the Jack lawyers, Noah Smithwick, Ben Milam, Father Michael Muldoon, G. D. Williams, and Gail Borden, Jr., William Barret Travis and David Crockett had not yet come on the Texas scene.

Jim called upon Stephen F. Austin at his home on Palmetto Creek. Austin wanted to talk about Jim's duels with the famous knife, which he examined with great interest while they talked. Jim wanted to discuss politics and the risks of purchasing land in Texas. Austin said he was prepared to take the case of any disputed claim to the government in Coahuila, and direct to Mexico City if need be. Jim left Austin with an agreement to take a headright of approximately a million acres, and a letter of introduction to the Vice Governor Juan Martin de Veramendi, in San Antonio.

Jim found San Antonio de Bexar, the capitol of the province, everything that Tex had promised—and much more. Tex had called it the queen city of Texas, and seeing it for the first time, Jim thought the compliment well deserved. Mexican leisure, Mexican laughter, Mexican happiness characterized the city. It was the largest town in Texas, four thousand men, women, and children, nearly all Mexicans. It was a sleepy town, a place of leisure. Everyone was leisurely. Men idled in the streets or *cantinas*, the soldiers from the barracks swaggered aimlessly through the markets and lounged in the plazas. Women languidly washed clothes in the clear, sparkling water of the tree-lined San Antonio River, which meandered through the heart of the city. Jim liked the white limestone buildings often stuccoed over with a plaster of pale pink, the quaint old bridges spanning the river, the gardens and orchards, the carved front doors and the barred windows of the houses where the affluent lived.

Jim and Tex took up lodging in Soledad Street, near the L-shaped two-story stone palace of the vice governor. The elegant building with its great cedar doors was only a few steps away.

231

Vice Governor Juan Martin de Veramendi's family was of Spanish nobility, and they lived in regal style. Veramendi was a rich man, owning vast estates in both Texas and Coahuila, but his principal seat was in San Antonio. He maintained a summer villa on a mountainside in Monclova, where the Veramendis retreated during the hot months. In Monclova the air was clear and cool and was believed to be very healthful.

Jim spent the first few days wandering about the town, acquainting himself with its charming narrow streets, quaint shops, markets, taverns, and *cantinas*; he saddled his horse and rode out to the abandoned old missions on the town's outskirts: San Jose, Espada, Conception, Capistrano, and the Alamo.

Though he made no special effort, he found friends among the Mexicans. Faces broke into smiles when he entered a *cantina*. With them he drank aqurdiente and tequila, and he always displayed plenty of silver. Any man present was his companion and became his guest. His Spanish improved rapidly and he strove continually to refine it.

One day he doffed his buckskins for the more elegant attire of his grey broadcloth suit, linen shirt, brocaded waistcoat, and fine beaver hat, and presented himself at the palace of the vice governor, Austin's letter in hand. He was ushered into a large room with massive dark furniture and great oak beams across the ceiling. Behind an ornate desk sat the vice governor, a man with a lean, intelligent face, black hair, handsome features, and piercing dark eyes.

Don Juan Martin de Veramendi read Austin's letter, looked directly at Jim. "What are your intentions in Texas, Señor Bowie?"

Such directness. Such curtness. But Jim did not resent the vice governor's instant probing. Just as directly, he replied, "Land, Your Excellency. You have plenty of it, it is available, it is cheap, and I believe one day it will be of great value."

The ghost of a smile appeared on the vice governor's lips. "Only land, Señor?"

232

"I am not interested in nor am I involved with any schemes or plots against your government, if that will relieve your mind."

"You know, don't you, that in order to own land in Texas you must swear to protect the Mexican government and enter the Catholic church?"

"Mr. Austin so informed me. I am willing."

Veramendi smiled. He liked this American's unadulterated and direct dialogue. He rose and Jim did also, believing that the interview was over. However, the vice governor motioned him to remain seated. He pulled a bell rope and a servant appeared. "Señor Bowie will do us the honor of lunching with us. Please inform Señora Veramendi."

It was at lunch that Jim first laid eyes on Ursula Veramendi, an event that changed the course of his life. An invisible shutter clicked in his mind and he was looking upon a ghost from out of his past. Deep brown eyes. Acorn-ivory skin. Short upper lip, full mouth. Soft black hair. Tall, slim-waisted but well-formed. Paula! Paula of long ago, Paula of Bayou Boeuf.

The girl's neck and shoulders were bare, half revealing ripening firm breasts, like succulent pomegranates. She wore the costume of the country, the pretty *china probino*—a very full skirt of bright crimson trimmed in white a, sheer white waist wrought with red embroidery, and pink satin slippers. As he gazed at Ursula Veramendi the tinkling of a tiny bell began in the cathedral of his heart, that of the little bell he carried there just for Paula.

It was only natural that Jim should form a speedy friendship with Juan Veramendi, who, like himself, was interested in land investments. Through his friendship with the Veramendi family he met the elite of San Antonio. The vice governor's was a proud circle. Jim attended a procession of dinners and balls where the silk and satins recalled those he had seen in New Orleans and Natchez and in the great plantation manors of the south. Along with the news of local and regional poli-

233

tics, talk of Continental affairs had its place in the conversations.

Jim found Ursula to be a charming young lady of impeccable manners. But she was also lively and versatile. He saw her pensive and quiet, laughing impudently, discussing serious matters with intelligence and spirit, gleaming barbarically, pure, audacious, daring. Through the social whirl he everlastingly monopolized her time. They were endlessly in each other's company, and were always expected to show up at the same places. Friends of the vice governor's family waited discretely for a formal announcement of their bethrothal.

Jim took the first step. The records of the Church of San Fernando show that on June 26, 1828, James Bowie, a citizen of the United States, was baptized by Padre Refugio de la Garza in the Roman Catholic faith. His sponsors were Don Juan Martin de Veramendi and his wife the Señora Maria Josefa Navarro de Veramendi.

Though Jim Bowie had been brought up and schooled by his mother Elve as a Presbyterian, in order to get the two things he wanted most in the world—Ursula de Veramendi and leagues of land—he had to embrace Catholicism and declare allegience to the Mexican government. The second step he would take later; that would be harder for a man of his patriotic background.

As the days went on, the weeks, the months, Jim continued his quest for land. He acquired eight hundred and eighty-five acres near the old mission of San Jose, where he commenced building a large home, and another tract of eight thousand, eight hundred and fifty-seven acres about thirty miles down the San Antonio River. He purchased a tract here and a tract there, seeing nothing of any of it but the titles. He lived the life of a respected man about town, toasted in the salons of the noble families, frequenting the public gathering places, taverns, *cantinas,* talking politics.

When a state of courtship between Jim Bowie and

Ursula de Veramendi became recognized, the aristocratic Veramendi family, aside from requirements of certain formalities, demanded a long waiting period. The nuptials were not to be celebrated for nearly two years.

There were tales of lost treasure—silver mines discovered and developed by the early Spaniards, then abandoned and lost to record because of Indian peril. Stories of rich lodes and smeltered bars, hidden away in caves of shafts that the Spaniards had filled in before being routed or massacred by savages. The story which most interested Jim Bowie, because it obviously was based most firmly on fact, was the one of the lost San Saba mine. Tex, too, had heard credible tales about this mine and had always dreamed of finding it. He suggested that Jim have a look at the Miranda report in the vice governor's office, which dealt with the San Saba silver.

Juan Veramendi was not enthusiastic about his prospective son-in-law "chasing wild tales about lost silver mines." But he nevertheless produced the Miranda records. The report, prepared eighty years earlier by General Jose de Miranda, stated that a little way north of the old Spanish presidio San Saba, at a place called Red Hill there was a cave, which he named Cave of Saint Joseph of Alcasar, that led to a fabulous vein of pure silver, and that here mining and smelting operations were carried on before the Indians drove the Spaniards from the diggings.

Jim reported to Tex what he had read of the Miranda report. "So," he announced, "we'll go and find this Red Hill."

"The Lipans," Tex said. "No man goes that deep into Lipan country who values his life."

"There must be some way . . ."

"I know a Lipan chief—Zolic. He brings his people into San Antonio every summer to trade. And they always come loaded with lumps and bars of silver. Can you lay hands on a fancy rifle? I owe the old fellow one.

He once lent me the use of one of his wives for a week, while he was in town. An Indian never forgets a promise. With such a rifle we just might get safe conduct."

"And I know of such a rifle," said Jim. "It hangs on the wall in the study of the Veramendi palace. It is ornamented and engraved beautifully. It would delight the eyes of any Indian. I'll have no problem convincing Juan Veramendi to let me take it."

When the Lipans came to San Antonio, Jim and Tex went to the edge of town where the Indians had spread their wares. The beautiful rifle was in the crook of Tex's arms. They found old Zolic dozing in the shade of a cottonwood tree, his four wives attending to the business of trading. Tex sat down beside Zolic and nudged him awake. Zolic blinked his eyes at the rifle, reached for it. Tex withdrew the prize.

"My gun," the old chief said. "You promised and you remembered."

"Yes, Zolic, my old friend. But there is something I want of you."

Zolic looked in the direction of his wives. "Take Papikita. She's the youngest. Large bottom, two large tops. Plenty woman for any man." Zolic reached once more for the gun. Again his hands were denied the delight of that shiny weapon. "Take two wives. Keep both for six days."

"No woman this time, Zolic."

"Skins? Furs? I have plenty."

"No skins, no furs. This is my friend, Jim Bowie. He comes from far away. He would like to hunt in your country."

Zolic's eyes searched the two men. "What will you hunt?"

"Deer. Buffalo. Wild game."

"How long?"

"One week—two weeks."

"How much deer and buffalo you take?"

"Only what we can carry on one pack mule."

"*Bueno.*" Zolic reached again for the rifle, from

236

which his eyes had not strayed. Still Tex held it from his grasp.

"Safe conduct for us, my old friend. Give us a word, a token, that will satisfy your braves."

Zolic reached inside his shirt, fumbled there for a few moments. When his hand emerged it held an odd-shaped medal of three points with interlocking Z's graven on one side and interlocking S's on the other. "All Lipans and friends of Lipans honor Zolic's talisman."

Tex took the medal and let go of the rifle.

The two men rose to leave. Zolic halted them.

"But you must watch out for *El Tres Varges*. That one does not honor Zolic's talisman. *El Tres Varges* is bad Indian. I cannot promise safeguard against *El Tres Varges*."

On the way back to their quarters, Tex explained *El Tres Varges*. He was a Lipan chief, about Jim's age, with a sworn hatred for all white men. As a young man he had been bethrothed to a beautiful Indian maiden named Kopana. One day when Kopana was bathing in the stream a little distance from her village, two settlers captured and raped her, and in her shame and anguish she hanged herself from the limb of a tree beside the creek. Her bethrothed found her still alive and cut her down, but it was too late. She gasped out her tragic story and died in his arms. The young chief tracked down the villains, tied them end to end to a fallen tree log, cut out their testicles and ate them before their eyes. He then scalped them and cut off their penes and left them to die horrible deaths. He smoked and dried the two penes, which he ever since wore around his neck as a constant reminder to hate and kill whites. Therefore his name: Three penes—*El Tres Varges*.

Two days later Jim and Tex rode side by side north-east from San Antonio into Lipan country, toward the location of the old San Saba presidio. On the evening of the third day they were surrounded by a party of twelve Lipans. Tex approached their counselor and displayed

237

the talisman Zolic had given him. The counselor held a brief parley with the braves, they raised their weapons in salute and rode away. Twice more they were intercepted by hostiles, Zolic's medal sparing them. Meanwhile they killed and bled an elk and several deer. Their pack mule soon became loaded. But they had at last reached the ruins of the San Saba presidio: heaps of broken stones and part of an old wall, blackened and overgrown, final testament to a savage massacre.

All the hills around were red.

"No wonder nobody ever found the mine," Tex said. "*Which* red hill? There are dozens."

"We must look for a cave at the base of a hill north of the presidio," Jim said. "Miranda called it the Cave of Saint Joseph of Alcasar."

They spent futile hours circling the hills, searching, digging, and scratching with the spade and shovel they had brought along. Nothing.

On the verge of giving up, Jim spotted a small rectangular space in which shrubbery grew only stubbornly. Digging into the top soil he turned up several darkened stones.

"Fired," he said, showing then to Tex. "These stones must be part of the Spaniards' smelter."

"Then we must be close," Tex said, excited.

"The cave has to be nearby."

With spade and shovel they probed, dug, hastily thrusting aside shrubbery and undergrowth. Tex did not see the opening in the side of the hill until his spade slipped completely inside, disappearing from his hand. They cut an opening in the thick growth and, stooping, entered what appeared to be a natural grotto. Lighting a cedar torch, they followed the winding passageway, which twisted and turned, always leading toward the center of the hill. At last it widened into a chamber about forty feet by forty feet.

On the floor was broken pottery, rotted bows and arrows, rusted pieces of iron; and among the ruins were the littered skeletons of humans. Stacked against two walls were innumerable blackened bars of some metal.

Jim scraped away the dark tarnish of several.

"Silver!"

Tex began to scratch. "Solid silver. Every bar! What do you suppose it's all worth?"

Jim make a quick estimation. "Enough to load seventy-five, maybe a hundred pack mules. Tex, this silver—if we can ever get it out—would make us the richest men in America!"

"Goddamn!"

Jim sat down on a stack of silver bars. "Yeah, that's the hitch. Getting it out."

"The Lipans will never let it be taken away," Tex said dejectedly.

"They never took any more at one time," Jim said, "than they could carry in their hands. They could have been very wealthy Indians indeed. Murderous, yes; rapacious—no."

Jim decided they should follow the example set by the non-rapacious Indians. He and Tex took only two bars each, one in each hand. Later, of course, a way would be found of removing all of the treasure.

They hastened back towards San Antonio, and on their last night out made camp on a hummock between two live oaks, about a quarter of a mile from a clear creek of tinkling water.

Next morning Tex awakened to find that he had made his bed over an ant hill and his clothes were infested with the pesky insects. While Jim broke camp, he went down to the creek to shake out his clothes and divest himself of the ants.

When a long time passed and Tex did not return, Jim went to see what was delaying him. As he approached the creek, the gentle snorting of a pony sent him to his knees. He crept stealthily forward until he could get a view of the creek.

Before him he saw a chilling scene. Tex, naked, lay dead beside the stream. Two Indians were working over his body, one taking his scalp and the other cutting away at the lower part of his body. Jim had come away without his rifle but he had his knife.

Drawing it, he rushed toward the savages. He plunged the knife into the breast of the scalp-taker. Dangling at the other's chest Jim saw the hideous token of *El Tres Varges'* hatred: two dried and shriveled penes stuck together—probably so melded in the curing process—and strung on a slither of rawhide around the savage's neck.

Quailing at the sight of Jim's deadly knife, *El Tres Varges* fled. Running with the swiftness of a deer, he leaped astride his pony and sped away.

Although only a day's ride from San Antonio, Jim buried Tex there beside the creek. He knew that Tex would not want anyone to view his body in its mutilated condition. Afterward it seemed to Jim that a ribbon between him and a way of life was cut. There was reflection and bitterness as he rode back toward San Antonio. The knife. It had taken possession of him. It had been Tex who first schooled him in the use of a knife as a means of survival. It had become his murder weapon, and a symbol of blood for the young men of the nation. Schools of knife fighting had been opened all over the southwest in his name. The knife had become bound up in him and would not let go. He tried to think of the future and all of his thoughts were centered around Ursula. She was the bright aura of all that was left for him. He decided there would be no place for the knife and its attendant blood after his marriage to her. A cleansing thought, fraught with nobility. But futile. He was never to separate James Bowie from the spellcraft of the knife.

The discovery of the San Saba silver and the long delay of his wedding to Ursula decided Jim on a trip back to Louisiana. He told nobody, not even Juan Veramendi, about the discovery of the mine. With Tex gone he would need somebody he could rely absolutely upon to help him bring the treasure out of Lipan country. He would convince Rezin—and perhaps even John—to return with him. Together they would remove the silver. It would make them rich—very rich. One thing was clear in his mind. He'd sell his holdings in Louisiana and Arkansas. All that wealth meant nothing compared to the vast riches that lay hidden in the cave of Saint Joseph of Alcasar.

When Jim told Ursula of his impending trip, she cried, "Oh, Jamie—you're always going away."

"But only for a little while. Then—never again, *mi rosa de San Antonio*."

Jim reached Arcadia in time to help his family celebrate the Christmas holidays.

His father had died in his absence. "So the old Revolutionary warrior finally made it to the happy fighting swamp he always talked about," Jim said to his mother. "I'm truly sorry, Ma, that I was not here."

"Son, your pa understood many things far better than you ever realized. He would not hold it against you for not being present at his funeral."

Although Elve's hair was streaked with grey and she seemed to have shrunk in size, she was still vigorous and spirited. When Jim told her about Ursula Veramendi her eyes shone with pleasure. "Jim, without seeing her I just know she's the right girl for you. I hope you start a family right away."

"But Ma, I thought you'd object to my marrying a Mexican girl."

Elve pulled him down to her height and kissed him. "Son, when you and your brothers lay me beside your pa, you can write on my tombstone: Here lies Elve Bowie: She Loved Her Fellowman. And, son, that don't mean only them that's got white skin."

Rezin was intensely interested in the San Saba silver. Certainly he would come to Texas!

Jim remained at Arcadia for several months making arrangements for the sale of his holdings. In the spring he took Sam and set out for Helena, Arkansas, to visit John and his family and to dispose of his property there.

John had put on considerable weight and was growing balder. He looked like the prosperous man he was. He was nearing his fortieth year and had no inclinations to pull up stakes and go to Texas, silver or no silver.

On a May day, while watching the loading of barges at the Helena river landing, Jim noticed a bearded man leaning against the cabin of a flatboat talking with two other men. Jim's eyes remained on the fellow because of his magnificent head and powerful body. As the boat bumped against the wharf, the man straightened up, and Jim drew in his breath. The man was a giant. Great massive arms and legs; broad powerful shoulders. He wore a stained leather shirt with fringes on the sleeves, and a wide-brimmed wool hat with a feather in the band. His expression told Jim Bowie this man was of no ordinary mold.

The big man threw a rope at Jim. "You there! Lend a hand!" It was an order. From a man used to giving orders.

The big fellow came ashore and Jim got a closer look at him. Large square mouth, large nose to match his prominent features. Underneath heavy bristling brows were a pair of unforgettable eyes. They were opalescent, light blue—or were they grey? Jim couldn't tell, so bloodshot were they.

"Can you direct me to the nearest saloon?" the giant said gruffly.

"Certainly," Jim smiled, glad for the opportunity of getting to know this man. "It's only a few steps. This way."

"Goddamn! You're a gentleman. Let us hasten. Please to be my guest. My name is Sam Houston." He poked out a ham of a hand.

"Mine's Jim Bowie."

"Now I will be goddamned!" The man rumbled. "What in the name of the devil is a man like you doing in an asshole of a place like this?"

"I might ask the same of you, Sir. Me? I'm on my way back to Texas."

They had reached the tavern, a ramshackle of a place with a crude bar where a fat bartender with a greasy apron poured forty-rod whiskey. Houston ordered a bottle, and ignoring the glass the bartender set before him, stuck the neck of the bottle down his throat and gulped several long draughts. He belched, spat some of the vile liquid out, swore, sucked at the bottle again. Then he passed it to Jim.

"Bowie," he said, wiping his bearded mouth with his sleeve. "So you've been to Texas. Want to tell me about that country? Andy Jackson has been writing me about it. Maybe I'll go out there myself."

The two men drank and talked away the afternoon. Jim liked this huge, rough man. They undeniably had a lot in common. Both were strong-willed, independent-minded, bold men. And there was another analogous link in their lives. They both loved beautiful girls half their ages.

Houston, a fighter in his own right, at the age of thirty-three had been a major general, member of Congress, and governor of Tennessee. He had married blonde, beautiful Eliza Allen, daughter of Colonel John Allen of Gallatin, Tennessee, in her teens. A few weeks later, upon the eve of his second election as governor, they quarreled and he walked out, saddled his horse, and in a blinding rain rode off to live with his Indian friends in the wilderness of Arkansas. Why? It was a mystery. Neither Houston nor his bride would reveal the secret.

Jim explained the political posture of Texas; he described the character of the Peace Party and that of the War Party. He delineated the political positions of many of the members of both parties.

"And where do you stand, Bowie?" Houston wanted to know.

"Right now, on middle ground. Under the Constitution of 1824 the colonists can enjoy most of the freedoms they were accustomed to in the United States. But Santa Anna, once he consolidates his power in Mexico City, might change all that."

Houston took another swig from the bottle, gazed at a knot in the crude bar for a long time. At last he said,

"That's the danger. Put a swashbuckling sonuvabitch like him on a horse and give him a few thousand armed men and you have a dictator."

"Or worse—a tyrant."

When Houston spoke again it was from deep in his memories and experiences. "The only way to deal with a man like Santa Anna is from a position of greater strength."

"General," Jim said, "I must leave you now. But I'd be honored if you'd join me for dinner in the tavern tonight."

"Come to my boat—about eight—and we'll see."

That evening the two men dined and drank whiskey. During the course of the meal Jim got around to telling Houston about his forthcoming marriage to Ursula Veramendi.

"She's about half your age, you say?" Houston mused reflectively.

"She's eighteen—about."

"I've been through it, you know," Houston said.

"Yes. I've heard several accounts of your marriage."

Houston snorted. "None of them correct."

"Want to talk about it, General?"

"No. I shall never speak of it to any man." A longing came into his face. "She *was* lovely. Blue eyes—dark blue—some called them violet. Blonde hair that flowed down her back. Sometimes she braided it. A fine horse-woman. How that girl could ride!"

"My Ursula is a great one on a horse, too."

The conversation seemed to end there. The two men sat looking into their drinks.

It was Houston who next spoke. He said he ought to be getting back to his flatboat.

Jim walked to the wharf with him, and they shook hands. "I hope the next time we meet, General," Jim said, "that it will be in Texas."

"Never can tell, Bowie." Houston went up the gang-plank. He stopped, a new train of thought entering his mind. "How old did you say she was?"

"My Ursula? Nearly eighteen."

"Umm . . . about half your age," he repeated. Come aboard with me. Lets have a nightcap together."

Inside the cabin, Houston knocked the cork out of a bottle of Monongahelia, and the two men settled down to drinking and talking. But Houston did most of the talking. Looking thoughtfully at the rough planks in the cabin floor between his legs, he began slowly.

"She was the freshest and prettiest school kid I ever laid my eyes upon," he began, remembering Eliza when she was a student of literature and languages at Gallatin Academy. "That was when she wore her blonde hair in braids. And how she'd gallop her black and white pony about the Allen place, across the big lawn of bluegrass and around the bend of the Cumberland River."

"I know. You ought to see my Ursula . . ."

Houston cut him off, not hearing his words, transported by visions of his lost Eliza. "Right after the wedding we left Gallatin for Nashville on our horses, a distance of about forty miles. We hadn't gone far before it began to snow real hard. It was January twenty-second. We stopped at the home of Mrs. Robert Martin, a friend of the Allens. Heavy snow fell during the night, but in the morning we continued on our way. We paused next at the home of Robert McEwen, a cousin of mine. We stayed there for two days. Three nights passed and I hadn't slept in the same bed with my bride. The first night, at Mrs. Martin's, Eliza complained embarrassment because Mrs. Martin and her husband were sleeping in the next room, so I slept on the couch. At my cousin's, she protested on the dubious ground that she felt like a stranger in the house of my relatives. So I slept in my cousin's study.

"But the fourth night we were alone in my quarters at the Nashville Inn. We had a fine dinner with good wine and retired early. I was sure Eliza was virtuous and naturally was not surprised to encounter the usual inconveniences accompanying first nights of love."

Houston paused to pull at the Monongahelia. Look-

245

ing Jim in the eyes as if seeking understanding, he continued, "Jim, without shame or boastfulness I can tell you that I'm built more to the scale of a horse than a man. The size of my joint has always been a source of embarrassment to me. Ever since a boy swimming in the river with the other lads, I've been both derided and admired for the great size of my dong. They used to call me 'fire-hose Sam.'

"Well, the goddamn thing was so big and Eliza so small, there was just no way to consumate the union. We tried everything and every device——oil, soap, force. Eliza cried, claiming I hurt her. But let me tell you, it couldn't have been any more painful to her than it was for me. But try as I did——mightily, I can assure you——I couldn't make even the slightest entry. So finally I gave up and went to sleep. In the morning I tried again, thinking maybe she'd loosened up during the night. My efforts were absolutely useless. By now we were both pretty sore. And that goddamn joint of mine, if it wasn't already embarrassingly oversized, began to swell even bigger from the abuse I had put to it, trying to get it into Eliza.

"That night I slept on the couch. Eliza begged for a little time to let the soreness of her jigger abate. The next day I made several determined attempts but still it wouldn't go in. For a week we hardly left the inn. But nothing happened to relieve the situation. Eliza just cried more and more and my peter got sorer and sorer.

"Well, as you can imagine, I was half out of my mind. Every glance at my lovely young bride sent me into a fit of frustration and despair. But since I was on the tail end of a gubernatorial campaign for my second term as governor, I left Eliza alone and went on a three week electioneering trip."

"General," Bowie ventured, "you've spoken at length about your urgency to consumate union with your young wife. But what about love? Did you love her, really? And are you sure she loved you, or did she marry you because her family pushed her into marriage with you?"

Houston dropped his head limply in a rueful grin. "Love? I can only speak for myself. Certainly I loved Eliza. Always will." He lifted his head suddenly. "Jim Bowie, let's face it. When men reach our age and station in life all eighteen-year-old girls are loveable. Men like us are capable of loving any of them—and carrying that love to the grave with us." Without giving Jim opportunity to respond to this statement, he continued, "When I returned to Nashville, I had renewed hope that I would be able to consumate my marriage. But no.

"By this time I had begun to wonder if the fault was entirely the size of my joint. After all, I had had lots of women in my time. To be sure, there were sometimes complaints but never a complete failure, such as this one with my young bride. So I talked Eliza into letting me take her to Dr. John Shelby, who was a friend of mine as well as the Allen family physician. After examining Eliza, Dr. Shelby reported that she was born with an abnormally small opening.

"So there we were. Gargantum and Lilliput. Me with the biggest dong in Tennessee and Eliza with a pipkin no larger than a whiskey jigger. Dr. Shelby said our effort was as useless as trying to force a plow handle into a peg hole."

"So . . ." Bowie said, taking another drink of Monongahelia and passing the bottle to Houston, "where did that leave you?"

"There seemed to be absolutely no need of trying anymore, and for the sake of both our well-being we agreed to sleep apart, and after the election we'd separate. But until then we'd keep up appearances.

"Jim Bowie, you can't imagine the torture I went through—living in the same quarters with Eliza, viewing her beautiful body as she dressed and undressed. Pretty young breasts. Slim waist. Perfectly formed legs and thighs. And God Almighty!—that stubborn demitasse that wouldn't give a goddamn millimeter winking saucily at me from the lovely dark blonde triangle in which it lay half-hidden, challenging me, tempting me.

"At last it reached the point where I simply couldn't bear it anymore. So one evening when we returned from an election rally and dinner, while she was undressing I threw her across the bed, dragged her legs apart and buried my head between her thighs."

Houston halted the story while he lifted the bottle to his lips, took a long pull.

"Well, Bowie, I just about scared poor Eliza out of her dignity. There she was, a girl in her teens, spreadeagled on the gubernatorial bed with his honor himself feasting at her little honey pipkin."

Both men took time out to chuckle.

"So, how did your young bride take it—your feast, I mean?"

"She was fit to be tied, angered beyond words. She didn't know whether to scream, pray, or curse me. So naturally she cursed me. 'No! No, don't,' she cried, pushing at my head and crossing her legs.

"But now that I'd tasted the honey in the pot I wasn't to be denied the glutton's full indulgence. I tore open her legs again. 'You brute—you wild animal!' she wailed. I held her still with my hands on her breasts, my fingers playing with her virgin little nipples, and went about the job as I had learned it from my Cherokee wife Tiana, back when I lived with the Indians in Hiwassie country."

"Did your bride relax," asked Jim.

"She began shaking all over, completely helpless. Her body writhed, her head rolled from side to side. Unthinkingly her fingers caught my head, held me, pulling me closer to her. 'Ohoo—' she moaned, her middle gyrating wildly. 'Oh—damn you, damn you!' Then she drew me up over her and begged me to try again to get it in."

"And did you succeed?"

"No, goddamnit. Even now with Eliza's enthusiasm we couldn't get it in. I then placed my hand on her head and gently nudged her down toward my upreared joint and suggested that she do for me what I had done for her." The big man looked at Jim with a hurt look. "And you know what that high-born haughty bitch did? She lept out of bed, highly insulted, and began berating me with all the scorn of a short-changed whore in a Natchez whorehouse.

"The next morning my mind was made up. Election or no election—I'd had enough. To hell with everything! So I packed my saddlebags, mounted my faithful mare and set out for the Hiwassie country in Arkansas to find my wife Tiana, whom I hadn't seen for eleven years."

"Did you find her?"

"She was waiting. Said she knew I'd come back some day. We're now living together in Chief Jolly's wigwam."

Jim Bowie had one final question. "Tell me, General, do you have trouble fitting there?"

"Hell no. Tiana's big as a washtub."

For fifty years, from about 1820 to 1870, the river steamboat dominated the economy, agriculture, commerce, and social customs of the middle areas of the United States. Few phases of 19th century North American life had so wide and vivid an influence on the region and people around it as the "palace on paddle-wheels."

New Orleans, the queen city of the Mississippi, owed its greatest opulence and growth to the steamboats. They determined the direction and development of the Mississippi valley; they made fortunes for their owners and the plantation masters; they brought the old south in touch with the world and aided in the expansion of slavery and the cotton economy.

After Henry Miller Shreve of Shreveport, Louisiana realized a completely new concept for the riverboat by drawing up the engine and mounting it on a hull as shallow as that of a barge, adding a tall second deck and placing paddle wheels at the sides, river traffic boomed. The trip from New Orleans to Natchez, for instance, was cut from five and one-half days to one day and seventeen hours. The number of steamboats arriving in New Orleans increased from less than twenty a year to over twelve hundred. The New Orleans waterfront was called "the master street of the world." Nowhere else could be found such concentration of steamboats; they stretched for four or five miles, curving with the river itself, two and three deep. At the height of this commerce the banking capital of New Orleans exceeded that of New York, and its port ran ahead of its eastern rival in tonnage.

Never had the title Captain represented so much authority. The steamboat captain was an omnipotent person, a man with vast authority over the conduct and affairs—even the lives—of his passengers. He encompassed the power of sheriff, mayor, judge, and pastor. He could remove a passenger at a word, and tales were told about luckless ones being dropped at marsh edges. He lived in splendor on land and water, receiving one of the highest salaries of the day. A man of many anecdotes and of prodigal hospitality when in a good mood, but of sulphurious rages and thundering orders when others crossed him.

When Jim Bowie left Helena, Arkansas, he took passage on the *Natchez*, a stately third generation steamboat of the same name—truly a floating palace of the Mississippi. With bells clanging, the majestic white craft floated out into the main current. Jim stood on the deck waving good-bye to John and his family, his wallet stuffed with nearly thirty thousand dollars in bank notes from the sale of his Arkansas property.

After dinner Jim went to the men's cabin. It was brilliantly lighted, for darkness had fallen on the river. At several tables men played cards, some for the fun of the game, others wagering heavy stakes. At one end of the room was the polished mahogany bar, attended by two Negroes in white jackets. Numerous people were here ordering drinks. Jim stood at the bar, apart from the others, drinking alone and slowly, listening vaguely to the ceaseless thrumming of the engines below.

His thoughts were of Ursula, the Veramendi family and other friends he had made in Texas. After seeing the flat wet country of Arkansas and experiencing again the whimsical climate of Louisiana he would be glad to lay eyes again on the sunny plains of Texas. Visions of Ursula increased his anxiety to get back to San Antonio. She was very young. She was pretty. And she was much sought after, being the vice governor's daughter and of one of the noblest families. Would she await his return? He was plagued by a mounting eagerness to see her.

The hands of the clock behind the bar reached one o'clock and Jim paid his bill and left to go to his stateroom. He paused on the deck to gaze at the distant shore, dimly seen through the gloom. It was then he saw the girl. A figure in night clothes. She rushed from a cabin and was trying to climb the rail, apparently with the intent of throwing herself into the channel. Just in time Jim snatched her back. She clung to him sobbing.

"I'll take you back to your stateroom," he said, when she had become somewhat quieter.

"No! I won't go back there," she cried. The girl turned distressed eyes upon Jim.

He gently guided her into his own stateroom. She was very young but fully matured for her age, which he judged to be about sixteen. Her hair was dark and flowing, mouth rich, lips full. Her large dark eyes were filled with distress and brimming with tears. "Perhaps you care to tell me who you are and why you cannot go to your stateroom," Jim said.

"I can't stand it any more," she said and began sobbing anew.

Jim waited for the storm to abate. "Now tell me, Miss . . ."

"Pauline."

"All right, Pauline. What can't you stand anymore?"

The girl gazed into his eyes, hesitated, making up her mind whether to trust him or keep silent. His grey eyes reassured her and she slipped the straps of her negligee from her shoulders and let the garment fall. Jim's breath drew in angrily. Across her back were rows of long ugly welts.

"I didn't know he was like that," she said, readjusting her nightgown. "And I'm sure if Madame Celestine had known she wouldn't have let me go away with him."

Jim rose—angered, confused. He took the girl by the shoulders, looked her firmly in the eyes. "Your name is Pauline. Pauline who? Where did you come from? What are you doing here? Please begin at the beginning and tell me everything. My name is James Bowie, and I'm on my way to Natchez."

The girl lifted her head. "James Bowie? *The* James Bowie?"

"That's right, Pauline. Now begin by telling me who you are."

"Just Pauline . . ."

"Don't you have a last name?"

Hesitatingly, she said, "Well, one might call me Pauline . . . Lafitte."

Realization slowly dawned in Jim's mind. His jaw fell momentarily slack. "Your mother's name is Paula? You live in Rue Conti in New Orleans?"

"My mother's name was Paula, and I used to live in Rue Conti."

"You said your mother's name *was* Paula . . ."

"My mother died two years ago—the fever. Afterwards, Pierre sold the house and I went to live with Aunt Celestine."

Jim allowed time to collect himself. So Paula was dead. Gone. Her lovely body placed in the ground to become one with mute, unloving earth. At last he asked, "Did your mother ever speak of me? Do you remember me? I was in your home, when you were very small."

"I know who you are, Mr. Bowie. I know that my mother knew you well."

"Is that all? . . ."

252

She often spoke of you. But I don't remember anything in particular . . ."

"You're not afraid to talk to me?"

Pauline looked up at Jim. "No, not at all."

"Now, Pauline—about those welts?"

Pauline had gotten control of herself. She seemed quite calm and relaxed. "This man—he's the son of a very rich importer. His name is Angus Mann, Jr. He came to Madame Celestine's in the company of several other young men. He saw me and made arrangements with Madame for me to accompany him on a trip to Louisville. He doesn't really mean to hurt me, Mr. Bowie. Whipping girls is just his way."

Jim's jaw clenched, his temples flamed. "Come, Pauline. We'll go to your stateroom."

When they entered, Angus Mann, Jr. was reclining on his berth smoking a cigar, his coat and waistcoat off. He sat up, put his cigar in a tray and poured himself a drink from a cut glass carafe. Jim's eyes took in the flagellum consisting of three long cowhide thongs that lay on the floor of the stateroom. Mann glanced at Jim. To Pauline he sneered, "Just who is this customer you've picked up? And how dare you bring him to our stateroom!"

Jim seized the flagellum from the floor. "Get up, Mann!"

Pauline stepped between the two men. "No, Mr. Bowie! You'll only please him."

Jim threw the whip aside and jerked the young man to his feet and slapped him viciously across the face time and time again. The blood came in a trickle at first but soon covered his face. Finally Jim let him sink to the floor barely conscious.

"Pack your things, girl!" Jim commanded.

When Pauline had packed her cases, Angus Mann had recovered and was sitting on the side of his berth, spitting blood into a silk handkerchief.

"Will you give me your card, sir?" Mann said to Jim.

"I have no card. Name's Bowie. Jim Bowie."

"You realize, Bowie, for the sake of my honor I must

demand satisfaction. With your reputation a knife combat would not exactly be fair . . ."

"I concede to you the choice of weapons, Mann."

"Pistols. And I reserve the right to set the formalities."

"Agreed. Provided it is now. Do you have pistols?"

Mann went to his traveling trunk and produced a case containing a set of polished Allen's patent, ivory-handled pistols, the very latest thing in hand guns for dueling purposes.

"On the deck. In twenty minutes," Jim said.

Jim took Pauline to his stateroom, awoke Sam and sent him to fetch the captain.

Captain Jonathan Jones appeared almost immediately. Jim explained the situation briefly to him. The captain agreed to officiate the duel. "Whatever happens, Captain Jones," Jim said, "I want you to see that this young lady gets safely back to New Orleans."

"I name the formalities," Angus Mann said to Captain Jones, loading his pistol.

"I so agreed," Jim acceded.

"Twelve paces," Mann said. "At the command 'Prepare' we stand right shoulder to right shoulder. At the count we turn left shoulder to left shoulder. At the command 'Fire' we shoot at will."

One glance at young Mann and Jim saw the diabolical design in this unorthodox formality. Mann's pistol was in his left hand. The man was left-handed. The formalities as laid down meant that Jim had to fire from an awkward, unnatural posture across his left shoulder—an impossible shot. Mann would be firing a straight, direct shot from a position quite normal for him.

"You mustn't go through with it, Mr. Bowie," Pauline begged. "He's sure to kill you."

"Many times, Pauline," he told her, "I have contemplated my death and always found it unimportant. So it is now. Death can be accepted easily—if there is some way to make other matters sure."

254

They stood twelve paces apart, the duelists, in the gloom of the deck, facing each other, pistols at their sides. The distant shores were almost indistinguishable in the darkness, but the bright sparkle of the navigation lights showed that the *Natchez* was booming along at full speed down the center of the channel. The only witnesses: Pauline, Sam, and Captain Jonathan Jones, who was officiating.

"Prepare!"

Both men moved their bodies half a turn to the left; now they stood right shoulder to right shoulder, pistols at their sides.

"One— Two—"

The men turned, left shoulder to left shoulder.

"Three—"

Mann's pistol came up. At arm's length it was aimed at Jim's head. Jim's pistol remained at his side.

From Angus Mann's pistol came an orange tongue of flame and a sharp report. Pauline and Sam watched in disbelief as Jim made no effort to fire. They saw him still standing when the blue smoke drifted away, leaving a clear outline of the two men in the dimness. Captain Jones looked from Jim to Mann's smoking pistol. "Mann, you missed. You know that now Bowie is entitled to a free shot."

Mann was heard muttering.

"Are you counselling God?" Captain Jones asked.

"By Christ, no! I was cursing myself for aiming at the head."

He needn't have. Never again would he miss. Jim turned, took deliberate aim and sent his bullet into Mann's heart.

The *Natchez* had docked at Natchez. Jim and Pauline stood on the upper deck by the rail. Sam was below getting the horses ashore.

"What will you do, Pauline," Jim asked, "when you get back to New Orleans?"

"I'll leave," she said. "I want to go east someplace.

255

Madame Celestine has lots of connections. I'd like to go to Mobile or Montgomery."

Jim took out his wallet and counted out five thousand dollars. "Pauline, your mother once came to my rescue when I needed a hand. When she died she still held my note to the amount of thirty-one hundred dollars. I reckon by now, interest and all, this ought to cover it." He pressed the money in the girl's hand.

They stood silent for a moment, looking down upon the passengers leaving the boat and being greeted by those awaiting them, the Negroes loading and unloading cargo. While they watched, attendants carried the covered body of Angus Mann, Jr. from the boat. Pauline turned her face up to Jim, a soft, lovely face. As her eyes encompassed his countenance, they filled with tears. He cupped her chin in his powerful hand.

"Could it be, Pauline," he said, "that you have tears for that dead scoundrel?"

"No! No—never! I—I was thinking how narrowly he missed you. Oh, Mr. Bowie . . . what if he had killed you? . . ."

Jim held her close. After a moment he spoke, a man talking to himself. "Had his bullet found its mark and entered my temple and passed through my brain and out the other temple, I still would have found the strength to fell that young blackguard. That was my firm determination."

Pauline stood on her toes, placed her arms around Jim's neck, pulled herself up and kissed him. "Jim Bowie," she said, smiling, "I shall always be happy to have known you. In my memory you will always be a great shining hero—and the kindest gentleman in all the world."

"Good luck, Pauline," he said huskily.

And they kissed again, tenderly. Neither knew or ever would know that it was the most treasured kiss of all—the kiss of a father and a daughter.

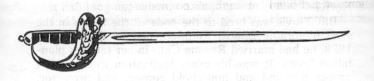

In the early eighteen hundreds there appeared a cult of young men born of the best blood of the eighteenth century and bred to be gentlemen of the nineteenth century. But as often happens in the breeding of a dog for show and prize-winning purposes, when too much attention is given to the begetting of beauty, swagger, and flaunter and far too little to behavior, the well-bred dog will sometimes defile the most precious carpet and might think nothing of putting his teeth into a friend of the family. So it was with certain carefully bred young gallants at the turn of the nineteenth century. These young coxcombs took it as their privilege to perpetrate transgressions and expect no voice from heaven nor the lightning to fall. To them the legend of divine justice, immediate and fell, was like old wives' tales—to be lightly discarded. They did wrong, and nothing happened. They still seemed one with the innocent. Relieved at their supposed immunity, they rejoiced. Finally they became elated and boastful, dangerous even to themselves.

Such a young blade was Andrew Norris. Generations of good Spanish and Hugeunot blood had been immaculately selected and blended to flow into his veins. Carefully groomed and schooled, he was put out to collect admiration and applause in the salons of Southern fedual mansions. The prizes he picked up himself, in the form of favors of young—and often not so young—ladies. It mattered not to Andrew Norris if the trophy belonged to another. Rosana Travis, it was whispered behind French silk and Japanese lacquered fans, was a recent prize who had fallen to Andrew Norris.

Bill Travis was bred to the code of the South in the most honorable Baptist tradition, and on October 28, 1828, he had married Rosana Cato in her father's plantation home. It was his every inclination to become a proper husband and household consort and protector, and at the same time apply himself all the more diligently to Judge Dellett's law library. Within the shortest period of time the judge saw to it that he was admitted to the bar and licensed to practice in the state of Alabama. He became a credible lawyer, winning many cases. Within a year after his marriage a son was born to Rosana, whom he named Charles Edward. The couple was accepted by the town's elite and always received engraved invitations to the plantation balls and house gatherings. It seemed that the future held bright promise for this handsome young couple.

Yet Travis found no personal happiness in this union. Something had gone wrong and it puzzled him greatly. He was a young man in his early twenties, and thoroughly virile. He sensed that Rosana loved him, perhaps only perfunctorily, but it was without passion. And of women he demanded all. He respected the slight nervous shadow that crossed her face when he came too near her. But there arose out of this denial the pangs of doubt, that ghost of suspicion which, in the most compatible relationships can make even a whole lifetime devoid of the contentment and satisfaction that a wholesome response to passion can bring. He wrote in one of his letters to his friend, Jim Bonham, who was practicing law in Montgomery:

Jim, my oldest and dearest friend—my "brother" of childhood. Can I tell you how I feel? I must.

258

I am perfectly wretched! It's Rosana my (cherished?) wife. Remember how we were in our youths? How *manly* we thought we were, how we tried to prove it to each other. Well, as it turned out I *am*. You know exactly what I mean. Maybe you don't really. So without boasting I'll tell you. During the first year of our marriage Rosana and I made love every night—sometimes *twice* a day. At night and when I awoke in the morning with the bright hope of the day manifest in the hardness of my manhood, Rosana was always understanding, at least cooperative—at best enthusiastic. That was *then*, in the first bloom of our marriage. Now, on her part there is no enthusiasm at all. I am forced by the urgency of my own patent nature to seek the surreptitious beds of others—unhappy wives and comely wenches of which there never seems to be a scarcity in these parts. I feel like a lonely, deserted, crippled Lord Byron. Oh, Jim! Dear Jim, how I wish we weren't so far apart. How wonderful it would be just to talk to you, old friend and chum. I feel—like—

> One who treads alone
> Some banquet halls deserted.

Yrs. in brotherhood.
Bill

To this letter Travis, three months later, received the following enthusiastic reply:

Bill! My old, old, dear, dear "brother!" News! Good news! Wonderful news! We can be together again, for a few days. Can you come to Mobile? I am leaving Montgomery on the 19th inst. and expect to be in Mobile on approximately the 22nd. I have some legal transactions to handle there that will take me several days. I understand the distance from Claiborne to Mobile is approximately 75 miles. Meet me if you can. I will be staying at the Clark House.

Hopefully,
Ys. in brotherhood.
Jim Bonham

Would he meet Jim Bonham? The Devil himself couldn't keep him from going to Mobile. How long had it been? Too long—and too many years! Bonham, too, had become a lawyer. It would be a happy reunion indeed!

When Travis reached at the Clark House there was a note from Bonham saying he would arrive on the twenty-third, which was the morrow. There was nothing to do but wait. Travis took a room at the hotel and went down to the waterfront.

When the door of Grady's winked open and closed, letting in Travis' six-foot frame along with a whiff of fresh air that hardly diminished the smell of stale beer, Grady arose from his cane chair and came forward to greet the long-absent visitor. He took Travis to the polished wooden bar and ordered the bartender to open a bottle of the best Madeira. The grey-aproned bartender popped the cork out and poured for both his boss and the newcomer. Travis sipped, set the glass down on the bar and stared down into the rich body of the wine.

Grady, having waited for his elegant customer to elect the topic of conversation, finally burst out, "Margie! You want Margie. But, my friend—" he kissed the tips of his fingers in mock ecstasy— "I've a new one—a beauty fresh from New Orleans. I can tell you, she's something special. An octoroon of elegance, my friend!"

Travis was interested. He turned sideways towards Grady, leaned on the bar, "And how do you happen to come by such a wench, Grady?"

The tavern proprietor continued, anxious to impress his immaculately attired friend. "She was one of Madame Celestine's select girls. Surely, my friend, you've heard of the famous Palace of Virtue in New

Orleans—a *bagnio* for the select only. Well, this delicious morsel—name's Pauline—was on a steamboat trip with a rich young blade, scion of an influential Creole family, and on the journey—Ah!"—Grady feigned sadness—"the poor fellow got himself killed in a duel—shot straight through the heart."

Travis laid a commending hand on the proprietor's shoulder. "Grady, I certainly am interested—for a friend. Now you place that little beauty in iron-clad reserve for tomorrow night. My friend will be here, and he's always hungry for just such a feast as you describe."

"Done, my friend! She's yours," Grady said with pride and enthusiasm.

"Is Margie still here?" Travis asked, turning his gaze back into his wine.

"I'll go fetch her," Grady said, anxious to accommodate Travis in every way. "You wait right here." Grady finished off his wine and hastily climbed the staircase.

In a few minutes Grady reappeared. "Give her a few minutes. She's putting on her prettiest dress for you." He hastened behind the bar, took a damp cloth, went to the back of the room and wiped off the top of a table, rushed back to the bar, grabbed the bottle of Madeira, got two clean glasses, and ushered Travis over to the new place. "Do you want me to bring you some food? Some fresh gulf flounder maybe?"

"Whatever Margie wants, Grady."

"I'll fix the flounder. She loves it."

During the meal Travis noticed a new awakening, a brightness, in Margie. The curtain behind her eyes had been lifted. Afterward he spoke about it. She responded brightly.

"Oh, you see it, Billy—does it show so much?" She smiled at him and he thought the faint freckles on her nose and about her cheeks made her more attractive; they gave her broad face an earthy, friendly look.

"I've met a man, Billy. A good man. He's a seaman, and he's quitting the sea and taking a section of land

261

about five miles east of Mobile. And he wants to marry me."

"That's wonderful, Margie. You can be happy on a farm if you try."

The curtain in her eyes lowered a little. "There is something . . ." she sought his eyes beseechingly. "Billy, why have you never asked me about my life? Who I am, where I came from, what I'm doing here? Most men do. They ask a lot of questions."

"Do you tell them?"

She traced an aimless pattern on the table with the wet bottom of her glass. After a moment she began, speaking slowly, painfully. "I came from a farm. And when I left I never wanted to see the dirt of any farm again. I was the only girl. There were three brothers, all older than me. We were poor sharecroppers, not much better off than the landowner's slaves. Poor white trash. That's what we were. I had to work just as hard as the boys, hoeing the cotton and corn, clearing the land of trees and stumps." She paused, traced some more patterns.

"And you don't want to work hard like that again?" Travis said.

"It's not the work. I think I could be content with Silas anywhere, doing anything. He's a good man, like I told you. But something else happened on the farm. My brothers used to force me to make love with them. Two of them would hold me down while the other one did it to me. Then, when I got older I got pregnant."

"What about your father? Didn't he do anything about it?"

"I never told him what my brothers were doing to me. They would have hurt me. When my old man found out I was going to have a baby, he beat me good. He beat me with a stick of stove wood, and I lost the baby—thank God! Then I ran away. I never wanted to see another farm as long as I lived."

Her head was bent down. Travis took her hands in his. She lifted her head and he saw that the curtain had fallen behind her eyes. "I'm sorry, Margie."

She wiped a tear from her cheek, forced a bright smile. "Don't be, Billy. I'll be all right." She lifted her wine glass. "Here's to us, Billy. Welcome back!"

He raised his glass. "Happiness, Margie."

She placed her hand on his, squeezed it. "Come, Billy. You want to take me upstairs, don't you?"

"But I thought——"

"Silas won't be back for another month. Besides, I like you, Billy, very much. Nothing has changed between us."

She arose and led the way to her room.

Later, in the early hours of morning, with the perfume of jasmine and magnolia blossoms drifting in through the open window, Margie turned on her back, her arm thrown across Travis' chest. She seemed quieter now than hours before, when she and Travis had come up to her room. Her eyelids were heavy and a warm glow underlined her face underneath the freckles.

"Billy," she said, a question in her voice, "am I not desirable anymore? Are you displeased that I told you about Silas?"

"Margie, please! You're wonderful. The fault is not yours."

"Then something is troubling you. I wish you'd speak about it."

Travis turned on his back, placed his hands behind his head on the pillow. He heard the girl beside him sigh.

"I was thinking, Margie——"

When he didn't continue, she asked, "What were you thinking?"

"Why does a man's wife lose enthusiasm for her husband?"

"In what way, Billy?"

"In making love. Why can't my wife give me the satisfaction you do? It's always wonderful with you, Margie." He kissed her lips lightly.

"What is the difference?"

263

"Well—you're always *with* me. You come when I come, you come over and over again."

"She does not?"

"She just lays there. I might just as well be sticking it in a mudhole, like I used to do on the river bank in South Carolina, with my friend Jim Bonham."

"Do you still come with your wife?"

"Well—yes. But I have to imagine I'm with somebody else. I often think of you when I'm doing it with her. It helps me get it off."

"You don't come too quickly with her? Are you sure you're doing it good enough with her?"

"Margie! You know very well how I fuck."

"Then the fault is not yours, my Billy."

"Well . . ."

"Another man, maybe."

Travis fell into an angry silence. Margie let him revel in the rage in his mind. Then she moved against him, began doing the things she knew he liked so well. Soon he was over her, making violent, angry love with her.

Jim Bonham arrived in Mobile shortly after Travis had had his noonday meal and was reclining on the veranda of the Clark House, his long legs stretched out, his feet resting on the railing. Travis watched his childhood chum riding slowly up the dusty street, looking for the hotel. Such an attractive head. He was tall, as tall as Travis himself, with wide, powerful shoulders. How handsomely he sits his horse, Travis thought. His heart burned with love and admiration for his childhood friend, now become a beautiful man!

The two old friends fell into each others arms. Travis could not resist kissing his old pal on the cheek. Both men blinked back tears of joy at the reunion. After Bonham had checked into the hotel, had a tub bath and changed his clothes, they went into the Clark House bar, and with a carafe of red wine on the table between them, began bringing each other up on the important events of their lives since the old South Carolina days. A stranger coming into the bar would have taken the

264

two men for brothers. Both were strikingly handsome and it was obvious that they were well aware of their natural gifts. Both were over six feet tall, both commanding in presence. They both had curly hair, Travis' now turning from red to auburn, Bonham's black. Bonham's eyes matched his hair; Travis' a blue, the same kind of blue as the slate at the bottom of the creeks in his native South Carolina.

"Tell me, Jim," Travis said, "whatever happened to your dreams of going to West Point?"

"Pa stopped talking about it rather suddenly. Maybe it was because he changed his mind about some of John Calhoun's political doings. Anyway, as you know, I went to South Carolina College." He allowed a rueful grin to creep across his broad face. "But, Bill, I never told you—I was booted out."

Travis smiled.

"I see you're not surprised," Bonham said.

"Not at all."

"Well, the students—we felt we ought to have more choice in the curriculum, more say-so as to what studies we chose. Too goddamn much arithmetic, theology—a lot of useless junk. The students grumbled among themselves but nobody did anything about it. So—"

Travis' grin widened. "You led them."

"Well, yes, something like that—and I got booted. But I went on studying law and was approved for practice by the board in Sparta. I then got in trouble with a woman and had to leave."

"So you left the state?"

"The whole affair sort of ruined my practice. So I went to Montgomery and opened a law office."

"How is it there, in Montgomery?"

"Dull, and I don't like the town or the climate."

Travis sat silent for a while, then he began to chuckle. "Jim, you haven't changed one goddamn bit. You're still a rebel. And I love you!"

After having dinner, Travis and Bonham climbed on

their horses and rode the half mile from the hotel to Grady's tavern on the waterfront. They tied their horses to the hitching rail and went inside.

In the tavern this March night there were four youthful men, all having the appearance of culture and genteelness. Their dress and bearing was in harsh contrast to their present surroundings. Their clothes, including hats and boots—and even the polish to which they owed their gloss—simply had to be of English manufacture. They each wore a clawhammer tail coat with black velvet collar, but each of a different color, a bottle green, a black, a red, and a tobacco. Their waistcoats were uniformly white, however, and their trousers fawn, their high top hats black. Their dress might assert that they had just left their ornate box at the opera, but there was not an opera house in Mobile. In truth they were dressed for a wedding reception at a plantation manor which lay between Claiborne and Mobile. At the moment they were engaged in a game of sledge, while two of Grady's girls attended them, one sitting on the chair arm of one of the men and the other leaning against the shoulder of another. Travis recognized one of the young men as Andrew Norris of Claiborne. He had never particularly liked nor disliked Norris. He considered him a contumelious young wastrel.

Upon seeing Travis enter, Andrew Norris raised his head. Recognizing Travis, he gave an ingratiating smile. Travis touched his hat in a small salute of recognition and led Bonham past the men to the bar. Grady appeared and set before the two Travis' favorite wine. Bonham ordered brandy. Travis introduced Bonham and invited the tavern keeper to join them in a drink. Grady was delighted.

"How long they been here?" Travis asked, tossing his head in the direction of the table where Norris and his companions sat.

"Half an hour, or so," Grady said, careful to keep his eyes averted from the men's table, for Andrew Norris was craning his neck in the direction of Travis. "Mr.

Norris comes here frequently. They're waiting for Margie and Pauline."

"Did you tell them they can't have Margie and Pauline?" Travis' voice was sharp.

"I told them they'd have to make it short with the girls. I didn't expect you gentlemen until much later."

"Tell them, Grady, they can't have Margie and Pauline."

"But sir, they won't be long, just half an hour upstairs with the girls and they'll be gone."

"No!" Travis' voice cracked like a pistol. "Tell them to go away, Grady. My friend and I will have none of their leavings."

Grady demurred. Travis gave him the glint of his eyes, and strode over to the gentlemen's table.

Touching his hat to them, he said, "Gentlemen, I haven't had the honor. My name is William Barret Travis." Then to Norris, "I understand you are awaiting the girls Margie and Pauline. For your information, and so that you may not waste any more time, they won't be joining you tonight."

Andrew Norris pushed his chair back slowly, stood up and faced Travis. "It would appear to be a free market, Travis," he said petulantly. "First come, first served, wouldn't you say?" A superfluous smile covered his face.

"Not this night, Norris!"

Andrew Norris' smile remained but rearranged to insolence. "You can't abide seconds, Travis?" Then the smile disappeared, and he chuckled in his throat. "Thought you'd be used to them by now."

The base of Travis' brain became suddenly hot. A red screen flashed before his eyes. He raised his hand and brought it sharply across Norris' face. Blood gathered in the corners of the smitten man's mouth and trickled down his chin and dripped onto his white waistcoat. Norris' friends stood up, appeared as if they would enter the quarrel. Bonham stepped between Travis and Norris. He moved Travis aside and flung his card on the table among the men. "My name's James Butler Bonham. I'm at the Clark House—at your pleasure." Nobody picked up Bonham's card.

Norris had taken a handkerchief from his pocket and was wiping his mouth. He looked at the bloody linen. "Travis, goddamn you, you've hurt me!" He raised his arm.

Before he could deliver the blow, Bonham's fist struck him in the face with the speed and force of a trip-hammer. Norris' top hat flew in one direction while its owner, driven by the force of the blow, sailed into the corner of the room and landed on the floor. Instantly the other three were in the melee. Travis caught one of them in the middle with a quick swift blow and he doubled up groaning. Bonham struck the other two in their faces, and before they could collect their heads their skulls were being cracked together between the powerful hands of Jim Bonham.

The three companions of Andrew Norris, completely subdued now, lifted their friend from the floor and slapped his face to revive him.

"I'm at the Clark House," Bonham repeated. "Anybody want to pick up my card?"

Nobody did.

"Come on, Andy," one of his friends said. "Let's get on out to the wedding reception."

As they left, Norris turned to Travis. "I'll not let this go by unnoticed, Travis. I have ways . . . I'll catch you in the dark of the moon." He slipped out the door quickly.

After the four gentlemen had left, Margie and Pauline appeared. Pauline was all that Grady had promised, and much more. Travis was greatly pleased. He watched his friend as his eyes swept over Pauline. She was young, about seventeen, he guessed. That she was octoroon was evidenced by the tint of her skin and the liquid hue of her eyes. She had large dark eyes filled with brilliant highlights and her skin was the exact color of polished old ivory, and just as smooth. She was a tall gleaming girl, slim-waisted and well formed. Her black hair fell streaming down her back, caught away from her face by a blazing rhinestone fillet, rendering the color and curve of her cheek more perfect. Her light blue gown, cut low in front and back, revealed soft smooth shoulders and high, round, swelling breasts. The effect was vivid, almost barbarically beautiful. Bonham's eyes came to rest on Pauline's mouth, the perfect mouth, the mouth of a Messalina or a Paphain or an errant Jezebel, with a short upper lip and full sensuous lower lip. It was a woman's mouth, promising untold delight for the man who kissed it. Poor Grady; he had vastly underpublicized this girl.

Travis led the party to a table in the rear of the room. Grady brought drinks. He asked if the ladies would dine. Bonham insisted. In the course of the evening, delicacies such as mutton, fish, fowl, salads, and a variety of vegetables, pies and sweets were served. Grady was surpassing himself.

When Travis spoke to Margie about Andrew Norris and his friends she told him, "You needn't have worried. We had no intention of joining them."

"Does Norris come here often?" Suddenly there was a lot Travis wanted to know about Andrew Norris.

"Often enough. He never comes alone, always brings his friends. They're all like him."

Travis wanted to ask Margie if Norris had slept with her; he wanted to know for a purpose. But he didn't want to know just now. He'd learn more later—in bed with Margie. There was a great deal he wanted to know—would know—about Andrew Norris. And if Margie had slept with him, surely the young braggart had babbled—about the many women he had seduced. There was little doubt left in Travis' mind about what lay behind Rosana's sexual indifference toward him.

In the early hours of the morning, when Travis and Bonham left the respective beds of their ladies and came downstairs, Travis had the answer to his connubial troubles. To further inflame him, he discovered that somebody had sliced off the tail of his horse. As

269

for the name of the villain who had done this cruel and knavish deed, he need not guess.

Travis remained in Mobile until Bonham had concluded his legal business and was ready to return to Montgomery. Every night they drank, revelled, made love with Margie and Pauline. It was a warm and happy reunion. The old friends promised to meet again soon, and reaffirmed the life-long bonds between them.

When Bonham left Mobile he purchased a fine gelding and saddle for Pauline and took her with him. In Montgomery he set her up in a fashionable women's wear shop. She called it Maison de Pauline and in time it turned her a tidy fortune. She will, in later times and long after Travis and Bonham have died in the Alamo, become the mistress of one of Jefferson Davis' cabinet members and render valuable service to the South as a spy, planted in Washington during the Civil War.

The faintest streak of sapphire was appearing behind the hills beyond the Norris mansion. A profound silence wrapped all the buildings; only a faint breeze set the magnolias sighing. The opalescent pre-dawn mist still lingered about the whitewashed slave quarters behind the high, sprawling mansion. Reuben was the first servant up and about on this morning. He had been awakened by the whinnying of a horse down by the hitching rack at the lane gate. This was unusual. Reuben was proud to be a Norris Negro and he liked all things at all times run orderly. Somebody had failed to stable one of the horses.

"Why, dat's Mist' Andrew's horse Victor," Reuben said aloud, as he caught the loose reins of the animal, which was straying aimlessly about by the gate. He led the horse to the barn, unsaddled him, rubbed him down and fed him. Then he started across the lawn to the kitchen; he sure was hungry.

He hadn't gone far when he noticed a form lying under a big magnolia tree. Approaching gingerly, he saw that it was the body of Master Andrew Norris. There was a bullet hole in his head.

Reuben ran the rest of the way to the mansion, scrambled around to the back, banged on the kitchen door. "Massa! Massa!" he cried.

Julie swung open the door, busily setting her five-pointed madras in place in the mass of black hair piled atop her head. "Reuben, you old fool!" she admonished. "What for you makin' so much racket befo' de folks is up? You know de Norris folk likes to sleep in de mornin'."

"Git de massa! Git de massa! I done seen de young Mist' Andrew layin' out dere—daid!"

"Reuben, you been sniffin' or are you jus' plain lyin'?" Julie peered at Reuben with suspicious eyes. "What you been up to, Reuben?"

Reuben was trembling with fright, quite beside himself. "Julie, I ain't done nothin'. Especially kill Mist' Andrew. I found him daid."

Reuben's words uttered in confusion and consternation became his condemnation. The household was alerted, the body brought into the house, and a slave dispatched into Claiborne to fetch the sheriff and a doctor. The sheriff came quickly, but it was later in the morning before the doctor arrived. It was determined that at the time Reuben reported finding the body, Andrew Norris had been dead for approximately four hours by a ball from the young man's own pistol, which was found about twenty feet from the body.

In questioning the servants, the sheriff elicited from Julie and several other slaves that they had seen young Norris, on several occasions, horsewhip Reuben, and not infrequently strike him across the face with his riding crop. When the sheriff asked Reuben if he hated Mr. Andrew, Reuben replied in simple innocence, "I shore didn't like him. He wuz an evil young gentl'man. A bad man—he whipped me for nothin'. But, nosuh! I ain't killed him."

The sheriff concluded that since Reuben found the body, he must have murdered him. And besides, the Negro hated Andrew. Hadn't he said as much? Reuben

271

was taken to the jail in Claiborne and charged with first degree murder. Whipping a slave certainly was no excuse for the delinquent to take reprisal against his owner! These blacks had to be taught a lesson.

Reuben's trial was set in Judge Dellett's court, and the judge appointed his star protege, William Barret Travis, to defend the hapless Negro. It mattered little, now, that young Andrew Norris had not been a demi-god of virtue, and that many respectable citizens of Claiborne and planters from Monroe County to the Gulf secretly felt that the purity of their young females was considerably more likely to remain undisturbed so long as the young man remained safely in his grave; after all, Andrew Norris was a "gentlemen," a *galant-nomo*, an aristocrat, and therefore someone had to answer for his murder. Reuben would do quite nicely; the public conscience would be mollified, and neither mankind nor society would be noticeably diminished by the demise of the Negro; viz: Reuben (Norris); age 48?; African; Owner, Hon. Benjamin J. Norris; Value, $875.

Travis tried valiantly to save Reuben. He was well aware that the Negro's fate rested with the consciences of the jurors and their concern of how the citizenry in general would accept their final judgment. He saw his problem clearly: he had to set their consciences to working against their own circumspection. Rightly or wrongly the concensus of opinion was already set against his client: a citizen (white) had been murdered, a suspect (black) had been arrested and a motive established—jury do your duty. It was a simple case, neat, pat; and the public didn't expect or want any complications. Nobody had ever won a case of this nature in Monroe county, and nobody expected Travis to win this one. He had no witnesses but the case against Reuben was purely circumstantial.

Travis argued passionately. His address to the jury was brilliant, but to no avail.

Afterwards, Judge Dellett told Travis that he had made an eloquent speech—an inspired, moving appeal.

"In any other trial and before any other jury," the judge told him, "you would have won a brilliant victory. I'm setting the hanging for the tenth."

The night of the ninth Travis went to Judge Dellett's house.

"Come on in, son. I was kind of expecting you." The judge led him to his study. "I wondered why you waited so long. Tomorrow's the hanging, you know."

"Yes, I know."

"Well, what's on your mind, Bill, my boy?"

"I want you to give Reuben a stay of execution."

"A reasonable request. Provided you've got grounds. Have you prepared a brief?"

"No, sir. I come with no brief. I need some time. I'm asking that you give Reuben a stay."

"You've got to give me some grounds, son."

Travis clenched a fist and pressed it hard onto the judge's desk. "Give me some time, Judge! I'll find a way to clear Reuben. We just can't let him die. You've got to stop the hanging!"

The judge was calm; he spoke quietly and authoritatively, looking Travis levelly in the eyes. "Son, I don't have to do anything. The man was arrested, charged, tried by law, found guilty by a jury, and sentenced to be hanged by the neck until dead—by me. Now, unless *you* can show good reason for the contrary, the mandate of the law will be carried out in the morning."

The two men looked at each other in silence. "What can I do, Judge?" Travis said hollowly, more to himself than to the judge.

"Unless you can come up with some new evidence—" The judge looked directly into Travis' eyes— "or a new suspect, Reuben will hang."

Travis rose to his feet. He pounded a fist. "Judge—!" He placed his hands on the desk, leaned toward the judge. "I know Reuben is innocent!"

"Sit down, son." The judge's voice was gentle, consoling. Travis slid into the leather chair and looked across the cluttered desk at the judge. "You say

273

Reuben did not shoot Andrew Norris," the judge continued. "Yet you bring me no evidence of his innocence." He peered into the younger man's eyes. "How do you know Reuben did not kill young Norris?"

An overwhelming impotence crept up inside Travis' chest; he felt a diminution of himself, a complete frustration; he felt like a man fleeing from a host of enemies who suddenly finds himself trapped in a blind alley. He raised his eyes helplessly to his friend and mentor.

"Judge Dellett, you can't let Reuben die. It was I who shot Andrew Norris."

A profound silence fell between the two men. It lasted a long time. Travis sat with his legs apart, his hands clasped between his knees, his head reclined. Finally Judge Dellett spoke. "I know, son."

Travis lifted his face. "You knew!"

"Yes. I knew you killed Norris."

"And you let the trial go on, let the jury convict poor Reuben?"

"I had no evidence—until now—to do otherwise."

"But you knew."

"Like everybody else in the county, I was quite convinced you killed Norris. But until you admitted it, I had no evidence."

There was another silence in which Travis, now that he had got it off his chest, began to regain his spirits. He asked, "Sir, what do we do now?"

The judge arose, went to a sideboard, poured two brandies, handed one to Travis.

"Drink that, son, and then I'll make a little speech."

Travis tossed off the brandy and Dellett refilled his glass. The two men sat down.

"Now, son, as I see it, you have three options. One, you can keep your mouth shut, as other Southern gentlemen have done in similar cases. Two, you can let your confession stand and go on trial for the murder. Three, you can leave Alabama for good." Taking a fatherly attitude, the judge added, "If you want my advice, I'd say take the first choice. Your confession will

274

never go beyond these walls. After all, the black man has no soul and so it is of little consequence."

"And if I take the last choice—leave Alabama. What happens to Reuben?"

"I'll see that he is cleared and promise you his freedom."

Before dawn of the following day, Travis, under cover of darkness, swam his horse across the Alabama River bound for the Mexican province of Texas.

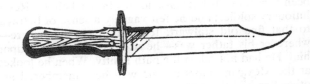

The morning James Bowie left Arcadia, beginning his return trip to Texas, a clear wet air washed the hoary outreaching arms of the trees streaming with gray moss. A dew lay like jewels on the bushes. Painted faintly by the early sun, a beautiful procession of clouds strayed up from behind the hills like a wandering flock of sheep. A lovely new day.

Rezin had agreed to come to San Antonio as soon as he finalized certain business transactions now pending. Elve had extracted a promise from Jim to bring his San Antonio rose to Arcadia on their honeymoon.

They, Jim and Sam, had new horses, new saddles and new equipment, and new garments on the pack horse Sam led. A new life. Texas. San Antonio. And Ursula.

As the two men rode west with the sun pleasantly on their backs, Sam burst into song:

"If you ever monkey with my Lulu gal,
I'll tell you what I'll do;
I'll carve you wid my Bowie knife,
And shoot you wid my pistol too."

"Where did you hear that song, Sam?"

"Why, Marse Jim, ev'body dey sings dat song—and lots more about de knife."

"Go ahead, Sam!" Jim shouted happily. "Sing it loud and clear. And say goodbye to the old life. We're on our way to Texas—the land of the beginning again!"

As they rode, Jim thought of the day he swore Mexican allegiance. He had taken it soberly, hesitating over this crucial step. He had always carried a deep loyalty to the United States. An intense patriotism had been a part of his background, his father being a Revolutionary soldier; and he felt vaguely a sense of betrayal to that fine old stalwart, felt that from somewhere—wherever his father was—he was frowning down upon him. He had not taken the oath lightly. When he looked at the Mexican colors on the wall he remembered another flag and the words came hard. But he wanted Ursula more. She represented a new angle on the future. "A man owes his loyalty to his family and the place he lives," he told Juan Veramendi. "Now I am a Mexican. I will be a good one."

Back in San Antonio Jim went at once to the Veramendi house. He found the family in excellent health and spirits. When Ursula came down the stairs his eyes embraced her warmly. There was little change in her: the same curving line of cheek, the same youthful contour of bosom, the same softness of her neck at the back where a few dark tendrils defied the brush. Her bright smile came instantly. "You're back, Jamie!" she cried and rushed into his arms.

She led him through a door out onto the patio, clinging to his arm. They walked to a remote part of the garden, her wide skirt brushing his ankles. Like a web, he thought, enmeshing him. She was just about the age

276

Paula was when, after making love, they had walked along the bayou with her clinging to his arm, loving him—feeling both possessed and possessive. Ursula's voice, the shades in her dark eyes, the intimacy of her manner—materializations from another time, another girl. Ursula was in his blood, his bones—like a hunger.

Could he by merely reaching out his arms once and for all possess her? He craved reassurance. "Ursula," he said and choked on further words.

She let go of his arm. "Yes? . . ."

"I have been away . . . some time. Before I left, you promised to become my wife. I am a great deal older than you are. . . . There are many beautiful young men who seek your hand—"

She cut him off and looked up into his eyes. "What are you trying to say, Jamie?"

"Only that I want you more than ever. I only want to be sure that I haven't lost you in my absence."

A smile of relief came to her lips. "I have waited for your return, Jamie. Do you wish to make me completely happy that I did so?"

"With all my heart."

"Then tell me the one thing that all women of all times want only to hear from the lips of the man they adore."

As he gathered her in his arms and pressed his mouth over hers, he said the words. "I love you, *mi Urseltia*."

Jim found that nothing could be rushed in San Antonio, not even the wedding of a daughter of a highborn family. Custom decreed that such arrangements should be very elaborate. Linens and many variety of cloths must be embroidered; it would take months to assemble a fitting trousseau for such a young lady.

In the meantime, Jim finished building and furnishing the handsome house on the outskirts of town, near the old San Jose mission.

On April 22, 1831, Jim Bowie appeared before the *Alcalde* of San Antonio, and drew up a contract

277

concerning the marriage dowry. In part the contract read:

James Bowie, being about to undertake marriage with Ursula de Veramendi; and with due consideration for the virtue and other praiseworthy qualities of said wife, he offers her in addition to her dowry by way of marriage, to make whatever use she may of it, and in case the marriage shall be consummated, the sum of 15,000 pesos, which may be selected from his possessions which he lists as following:

—In the territory of Arkansas, in the United States, 70,000 arpents of land at four reales each at lowest price.

—In legal obligations and sufficient notes made by C. C. Walker and Wilkins Bros., residents of Neches and of the United States.

—Certain individual notes in judgment or suit.

—Certain cotton and wool machinery in possession of C. Angus McNeil in the state of Boston.

—Besides certain furniture and articles in use in his house.

—Land under contract and to be acquired in this country ... good title to 15,000 arpents of land on the banks of the Colorado River, and in the Teche in Louisiana, valued at 75,000 pesos.

So he binds himself to pay in money to his future wife or her representative in case the marriage be terminated for any legal cause.

The dowry contract having been witnessed by Jose Manuel de la Garza, Jose Cardenas, Juan Maria Flores, and Ignacio Frechey, preparations for the nuptials went forward at the vice governor's palace.

Three days later Ursula Veramendi and James Bowie were united in marriage at the Church of San Fernando by the padre Refugio de la Garza. Ursula wore a lace gown of white, with a lovely white mantila covering her head. Jim wore an elegant suit of dark blue broadcloth, a blue silk waistcoat, and a white stock. All the notables of San Antonio were present.

The bride and groom retired to the Veramendi palace, where a huge formal dinner was prepared. For three days feasting and dancing continued in the palace; most of the elite of San Antonio passed through the great cedar doors on Soledad Street.

The festivities at an end, Jim took his bride on an extended honeymoon. They traveled by carriage to Copano, and took passage on a schooner for New Orleans, where they stayed at the Hotel de la Marine.

For a week Jim showed his bride the wonders of the city—the clubs, the casinos, the markets, the famous sights; they dined in the finest restaurants and bistros.

During their gaiety Ursula's laughter often brought memories of the past. At night when they made love, her brown shoulders and soft body caused ugly twitchings in his mind. But in these moments of intimacy the brilliant luster in her eyes, the wonderful ripeness of her breasts and thighs—they were more than his memory had bargained for. In her response, in her profound love for him, he found Ursula: he came to recognize the woman herself in her full majestic power.

Before returning to Texas, Jim kept his promise to his mother Elve and brought Ursula to Arcadia. Rezin said, "Jim, Texas has done something for you. You're sure of yourself. I see in you the fulfillment of a promise. In a few weeks I'll be joining you in San Antonio."

When Jim and Ursula said their goodbyes, Elve stood on the veranda, Ursula's warm hand in her own. She adored this lovely girl, and was sad at her departure.

Elve looked up into Jim's grey eyes. "Son," she said with solemnity, "in olden times there were angels who came and led men away from the city of destruction. Today we see no white-winged angels. Yet men are led away from threatening desolation. A hand is put into theirs and they are led gently forward to a calm and happy land."

She placed Ursula's hand into her son's.

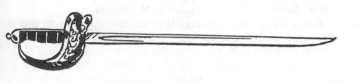

It was early in the year of 1831 that William Barret Travis arrived in Anahuac, Texas, a gulf port in the Galveston Bay. The territory of Texas was at that time a province of Mexico. He was admitted as a settler, and bought land from Stephen F. Austin, the man appointed by the Mexicans to administer the area. For fifty dollars he received eleven hundred acres in the Buffalo Bayou area. He was only required to pay ten dollars in cash. He gave a note for the balance. *"Having been admitted by S. A. Austin as one of the settlers under his contract with government, I agree to pay said Austin on order ten dollars on receipt of my title for land as a settler under said contract and forty dollars for one year thereafter."*

So the tall auburn-haired Travis who had been born with a forthright sense of justice and who thrived on challenges, chose to settle in Texas where the action was. If nothing else, the surroundings would serve as an antidote to remembrances. Whatever the vast Mexican province held in store for him, Travis intended to make the most of it. There would be no turning back.

When Travis arrived in Anahuac what greeted his

eyes was far different from the comfortable, well-built houses and mansions and edifices of the old established towns of Alabama. What he saw were forty log cabins, a few shops, and the shacks erected to house the garrison, which numbered about three hundred men. Stretching beyond the town he saw no rolling, green fields and lush forests, but an almost level plain of brown scrub and buffalo grass, live oak, mesquite, and scattered cottonwood and pine trees. The town itself had only about one hundred Americans in it, and the garrison was made up of outlaws and hunted men. A Mexican law read: "Vagabonds and disorderly persons shall be taken in preference for military service." With this type of men in the garrison any newcomer to the settlement could quickly see that they were insolent and overbearing, and that conflict with settlers, who were independent and hotheaded, was inevitable.

Within a short time he got himself established. He adapted quickly to Texan ways and from the outset threw in his lot with the colonists. Together with another young lawyer from Alabama, Patrick C. Jack, as partner, he opened a law office. Jack had practiced in Jefferson County, Alabama, three years before coming to Texas with his brother William, who had settled farther west, in Stephen F. Austin's capitol town of San Felipe. Both the Jack brothers were capable civil leaders with a patriotic tradition in their family background. Their father had commanded a Georgia regiment in the War of 1812.

Travis was quick to attract the brilliant, the romantic, and the rebellious. William Williamson was one of those young men who thought Lord Byron was a great poet, and he, like the Englishman he so admired, was a cripple. An illness at fifteen that kept him confined for two years had drawn his right leg back at the knee so that he was obliged to use a wooden appendage and carry a cane. A fastidious dresser, he had his trousers tailored to accommodate the three legs and wore a shoe on the appendage as well. It was inevitable that he would acquire the appellation of "Three-Legged-Willie." But neither the name nor the disability affected Williamson's fun-loving and gregarious temperament. He was a gifted storyteller, an excellent singer, banjo player, and could "hold his liquor," which quality among his friends Travis greatly admired. He was also literary. Since arriving in Austin's colony he had published the *Texas Gazette*. He was fond of printing Byron's, Shelly's, and Thomas Moore's poems. Travis once said of him, "Three-Legged-Willie may be halt in his leg, but he's bright as a whip." But most important to Travis, Willie was, like himself, a rebel.

The American colonists had been left to themselves, to rule themselves. Before the rise of Santa Anna, they had been granted a seven year tax exemption. Now Santa Anna concerned himself with ways and means to raise revenues out of the state of *Tejas*. But most of all, the Mexicans had become alarmed at the influx of Anglo-Americans. At first, as is always the case with benevolent oppression, the measures were designed to appear mild and inoffensive, even noble.

From Mexico came a proclamation freeing the slaves (later rescinded). This was not motivated by humanitarian scruples but rather because it was thought it would tend to stop the entry of colonists. But the real concern in Mexico Ciy was caused by the fear that the United States was determined to get possession of Texas.

Laws were enacted to bring the Texans under control. One article authorized military occupation of the province; for this task convict soldiers were used. Another prohibited further immigration of Anglo-Americans to Texas.

Money would be needed to defray the expense of enforcing these measures. The stage had been set for the next act—the collection of taxes. The colonists would pay for their own subjugation. To do this posts had to be established. Four such posts were created. The most important one was the garrison at Anahuac.

The others were placed at Valasco, San Antonio, and Goliad. The garrisons at these posts were immediately reinforced. Now the work of collecting revenue began.

John Davis Bradburn, a stocky man of gaunt and vulpine visage, was a renegade from Kentucky. He was by nature a rascal, without honor or respect for the law or the rights of others. Run out of the United States for stealing slaves and reselling them, he escaped to Mexico and was recruited as a convict soldier. In a short time he rose to become a colonel in the Mexican army. Because of his knowledge of the English language and through his ability at chicanery, he secured the post of commander at Anahuac. Once established, he resorted to all sort of repressive and tyrannical measures. It followed as the night the day that John David Bradburn and William Barret Travis would clash.

The list of Bradburn's audacious acts included illegal arrests, seizure of supplies from citizens without paying for them, and forced labor of citizens. To add to the problem was what to do about certain squatters who had crossed the frontier and settled vacant lands near the coast. The Mexican government had promised them title to the lands they had cleared and improved, but failed to keep the promise. Travis and Jack, as lawyers, represented many of these people, and finally, they succeeded in getting the government to send a commissioner to survey and give the settlers title to their lands. Bradburn took it upon himself to stop the operation. When Travis protested and threatened to go to Mexico City with the settlers' grievances, Bradburn had him arrested and thrown in jail. Jack, Travis' law partner, enlisted the air of Three-Legged-Willie Williamson, who took the matter to Stephen F. Austin, and Travis was released.

The gauntlet was thrown. Travis decided that Bradburn had to go. He and his partner set in motion a series of ploys and gambits designed to ridicule and discredit the tyrant. They spread tales that bodies of men were marching toward Anahuac for the purpose of hanging Bradburn; that gun-slingers had been hired to assassinate him; that his ex-convict soldiers were about to murder him. These false stories and rumors exposed Bradburn for the poltroon he was and caused him to set up absurd and embarrassing safeguards for himself.

Finally Bradburn's nerves caved in and, suspecting Travis and Jack as being behind all his troubles, called out his soldiers, marched them to the office of the two lawyers and ordered their seizure. In full view of the citizens of Anahuac, the soldiers beat them and then dragged them off to prison. When threats of storming the prison to free the prisoners reached Bradburn's ears, he had the most rebellious of the pair, Travis, shackled hand and foot to the stone floor of the prison cell.

Travis' voice roared defiance. "Go ahead, men! Break it down!"

The mob stormed the door, pounding, beating, shouting, cursing, some emptied their guns into it.

Over the tumult, Bradburn's voice was heard. Williamson! Williamson!"

Willie quieted the men down somewhat. "What do you want, Bradburn?" he called.

"Tell you what. Git your men away from that door. Send 'em home, and you and me, we'll see about these traitors, eh? What do you say?"

"You'll release them?"

"I said we'd talk about it. Good enough?"

"Not good enough, Bradburn. We're coming in."

"Hold it, Williamson! Just git that mob away from here and I'll do what you say."

Willie dispersed the crowd, believing he had won. But he was disappointed. During the following days Williamson and Bradburn talked. Bradburn stalled for time, and all the while had his soldiers completing the transformation of an old kiln into a prison-fortress that no mob could possibly break down. This done he transferred Travis and Jack to the fort and had them manacled to the walls by chains. In the next days he arrested and imprisoned half a dozen prominent citizens who had taken part in the assault on the jail.

The episode was related in a letter written by Travis to his friend James Bonham, after Travis and Jack were finally freed.

August 20, 1832
Anahuac – Province
of Texas

Dear Jim:

If ever I really needed a friend like you—a fighting friend—I needed him lately. But as it turned out, I have many friends here—and they are ready to fight. For fifty days I have languished in jail—in the most horrible of prisons—the captive of a fiendish despot named Bradburn, an American in the services of the Mexican army. I was arrested and held on a trumped-up treason charge, me and my law partner, Patrick Jack. You want to know if I was guilty? In my heart I certainly was—and am! Jim, I'll be eternally guilty of opposing tyranny in any form. Do I need tell *you* that? The government in Mexico seems to have adopted a tyrannical oppressive policy in dealing with the colonists. Somebody has to rise up and fight. And many Texans seem ready and willing, as was evidenced in my own and Jack's case.

Appeals to Bradburn's decency and humanity failed (he had none), then a mob of citizens moved on the jail with no success, only inciting Bradburn to further mischief. Three-Legged-Willie Williamson—oh, yes, he's a compatriot, a marvelous fellow—escaped the knavery of our jailor and went to San Felipe to enlist aid in saving us. He sent Pat Jack's brother, Bill Jack, who also is a lawyer with an office in San Felipe, to try and obtain our release. Bradburn ordered him out of

285

town in fifteen minutes on pain of being arrested and jailed.

Pat's brother Bill had little choice except to obey the tyrant, but as he left Anahuac he spread the alarm all up and down the coast and let people know the danger they faced. As a result an "army" of about 120 men assembled at Lynch's Ferry, on the San Jacinto River, with their rifles, pistols, knives, and swords, determined to march on the garrison and free Jack and me. Three-Legged-Willie took command of the men.

As the men marched on the town Bradburn took refuge in a special redout where he had mounted several cannon, and requested a conference. A committee from the army went to interview him. His position and the cannon—the army of 120 had no cannon—made him obdurate. But the committee was just as stubborn. They warned Bradburn there would be an attack unless he relented. Bradburn the poltroon turned to clever tactics. He persuaded the committee to move their men to a camp eight miles away, up to Turtle Bayou, on a promise that he would then release Pat and me as well as the other prisoners.

The committee did not realize the full treachery of Bradburn, for the army of 120 had no more than got clear of the town when he came out with two 18-pounders and opened fire on them.

The colonists began to realize that the situation meant war—and they were quite determined to see it through. Then Three-Legged-Willie (a head that one's got on his shoulders) made a speech to the men. He pointed out that they were entirely without legal support, that they stood in open defiance of he Mexican government, that if they continued on such a course they would be guilty of the same crimes they were fighting to prevent, and that they would surely bring down upon themselves hostile acts from Santa Anna.

Then Willie proposed that the army adopt what he called the Turtle Bayou Resolutions—a clever bit of strategy. He already had the Resolutions written out, and then and there drew the paper from his pocket and read it.

The Resolutions proclaimed to the world that Texans would fight against all forms of tyranny and tyrannical officials that Mexico sent into the province. But it declared they would only fight on the side of Santa Anna and for the Mexican Constitution of 1824. After a short discussion The Turtle Bayou Resolutions were unanimously adopted—and given wide circulation. When Santa Anna heard about them, he was pleased, and granted a two year extension of tax exemption. (I'm enclosing a copy of the Resolutions.)

Soon the army of 120 grew to an army of 300; and, emboldened by the favorable reaction of the settlers to the Resolutions, it attacked and defeated the forces at Valasco and subdued the post at Nacogdoches. As it approached Anahuac the coward Bradburn fled; a new commandant, Colonel Predrars, was named, and he immediately freed Pat and me as well as all other colonists jailed by Bradburn.

What all this means, Jim, is that Texas has got to get its freedom from Mexico. At the moment the people are divided into the Peace Party and the War Party. The Peace Party is headed by Mr. Austin, in San Felipe, who still has a lot of land to sell. He does not seem to realize that war with Mexico is inevitable. He refuses to see that the colonists, with their backgrounds, their love of justice, their ideas of how an orderly society should be conducted, cannot get on with the uncertainties and the tyrannies of the Mexican government.

Jim, I wish you were here. This is where it all is—in Texas. I'm moving my law office to San

287

Felipe. That's where it really is, at the moment.

Ys. in brotherhood
Bill
(Rubric)

Encl.

THE TURTLE BAYOU RESOLUTIONS

RESOLVED That we view with feelings of the deepest regret, the manner in which the Govern't of Mexico is administered by the present dynasty —The repeated violations of the constitution—the total disregard of law—the entire prostration of the civil authority; and the substitution in the stead of a military despotism, are grievances of such character, as to arouse the feelings of every freeman, and impel him to resistance—

RESOLVED That we view with feelings of the deepest interest and solicitude, the firm and manly resistance, which is made by the highly talented and distinguished Chieftain—General Santa Anna, to the numberless incroachments and infractions, which have been made by the present administration, upon the constitution and law of our adopted and beloved country.

RESOLVED That as freemen devoted to a correct interpretation, and enforcement of the Constitution, and laws, according to their true Spirit— We pledge our lives and fortunes in support of the same, and of the distinguished leader, who is now so gallantly fighting in defense of Civil liberty.

RESOLVED That the people of Texas be invited to cooperate with us, in support of the principles incorporated in the foregoing resolutions.

Rising in a salt region in the Texas panhandle near the New Mexico border and flowing in a southeasterly direction, the Brazos River extends approximately nine hundred miles to the gulf. Navigable for more than two hundred and fifty miles above its mouth, the river provided an excellent location for the site of Stephen F. Austin's proud centerpiece, San Felipe de Austin, a name honoring both its patron saint and founder.

Built along half a mile of the west bank of the winding Brazos amid moss-draped trees and surrounded by lush green meadows, and eighty miles from the gulf by land and one hundred and seventy by the course of the river, it held promise of becoming a splendid capitol for the state of Texas. It never had the opportunity to achieve such glory. After the massacre at the Alamo General Sam Houston will burn the town on his retreat toward the Louisiana frontier, hotly chased by Santa Anna's army.

When William Barret Travis packed his saddlebags and headed toward San Felipe he had been in Texas a little more than a year. During that time he developed a consuming animosity and a keen wariness of Mexicans in general. Approaching San Felipe by way of the Atasconsito Road Crossing, he spurred his horse to the crown of a hill, halted, and looked down upon the little town, which was laid out in Mexican style by the surveyor Seth Ingram. He saw across the river below him a village built around four plazas and two water wells. He counted approximately forty houses and more than a dozen business structures. The residences all seemed to be constructed of unhewn logs with clapboard roofs. Most were double-winged with an open passage through the center, called dogtrot, separating the two.

Both the town and the landscape wore a different aspect from anything he had ever seen. Nothing he observed before him seemed permanent. It was all a beginning, a natural condition subject to immediate change. The present town, rude as it was, was a triumph over what had not been there only a few years before, and he could see gardens and grain where there had been nothing but prairie. His angle of sight was cast in the future. For a brief moment his mind held a glorious and majestic vision. He saw stately cities of magnificent buildings rising tall and shining in the pristine Texas air under the brilliant and ever-shining sun.

As Travis sat his horse contemplating his new home, he unaccountably thought of his wife Rosana and his son Charles Edward. (Word had reached him that since his leaving Alabama his wife had given birth to a daughter, Susana Isabella.) For an instant his heart panged for Rosana—and his son. The little town seemed to invite families. What a lovely place to bring up children. As quickly as the ache had come it was gone. He had put all that behind him—Rosana and Alabama—and for William Barret Travis there was no turning back—ever.

That night when he made his summary decision in Judge Dellett's study, he went home and wrote out statements assigning all his "real and other goods" to Rosana and his son, packed his personal belongings in saddle bags, told his wife simply that he was leaving her on the terms that he had married her "for better or for worse." There had been no accusations, no recriminations, no confessions. And there were no pleas for him to remain. And he was gone. He had sacrificed all, he thought. But now, at twenty-two he was struck with the exhilarating realization that he had a hell of a lot of living to do. Do we ever sacrifice anything, he asked himself, save what we know we can never attain or what some secret wisdom tells us would be uncomfortable or saddling to possess?

Travis urged his horse down onto the road and crossed the river on the ferry run by Hugh McFarland. He noted the several small craft unloading and taking on cargo at the wharf. The boats were all moored by means of long ropes fastened to a large tree on the bank; he was to learn that the tree was named "Steamboat Tree."

He rode past Smithwick's blacksmith shop on his left and entered Constitution Plaza: crossing this, he came to Peyton's Tavern and hotel; then, just beyond, Coopers and Cheevers Saloon and billiard hall. He was surprised to note that the saloon was the only frame building in the town. On his right were two stores, Dinsmore's and White's. The two stores offered for sale just about everything one would need to set up a life of relative comfort on the frontier. As he rode by Travis glimpsed cutlery, plows, hardware of many descriptions, axes, groceries, guns and powder, wines and liquors, bolts of cloth—all manner of commodities. He will discover that Dinsmore's specialized in luxurious materials from the eastern markets, and be pleased to learn that women rode fifty miles to a ball carrying in their saddlebags dresses made in Boston, New York, and New Orleans and sold at Dinsmore's. With his preoccupation for dress and his fondness for gift giving, Travis will become a regular customer of both Dinsmore's and White's. In his diary six months hence, he will write. "Purchased at White's six yards of domestic at thirty-one and one-fourth cents, a yard of linen at $1.75 and thread for shirts, one pair of suspenders at thirty-seven and one half cents, one pair of stockings at $1.00, and one vest, with the total bill amounting to $10.00."

Between Dinsmore's store and the Whiteside Hotel was a fine house, which he took to be the residence of Stephen F. Austin. But he learned it belonged to Gordon B. Cotton, and that Austin had built his home, a spacious double log cabin with a chimney gracing each end, half a mile out of town on the west bank of Palmetto Creek; there he would insure himself of privacy and be less accessible to colonists with grievances.

Travis rode back to Coopers and Cheevers saloon, tethered his horse to the hitching rack, and went in. Cooper was behind the bar, a portly man with a melon stomach. Travis had a brandy, handed over a silver dollar and Cooper laid down ninety-five cents change on the bar. Travis introduced himself.

"Heard a lot about you, Travis," Cooper said. "You sure gave a lot of people a good scare. Everybody, you know, don't like what you done at Anahuac. Most folk here in San Felipe don't favor your war policy."

"I'm not sure, Mr. Cooper, I have a war policy," Travis countered.

"We're Mexican citizens. Travis. All colonists are.

291

We had to take the oath of allegiance to get title to the land, and we had to declare to the Catholic faith, too. But people don't pay much attention to that, except nobody can get married unless Father Muldoon performs the ceremony. If we get into a war with Mexico, we just might lose everything. Me, I like it here. And I'm with Mr. Austin. He's for peace under the constitution."

"I'm for peace, too, Mr. Cooper. But not for peace without liberty. I cherish my personal liberties."

"What's your business in San Felipe, Travis?"

"I plan on opening a law office here."

"Oh, you're settling here?" Travis thought he saw a little frown on Cooper's forehead.

"Yes. Any recommendations as to which hotel I should favor?"

Cooper rubbed the bar with a rag while he thought a moment. "I suppose Peyton's would be the right place for you, Travis. Your kind of crowd stays there. One of your friends lives there, Three-Legged-Willie—and a lot of his hot-headed friends, too."

"If Willie stays there, it's the place for me. Thanks, Mr. Cooper. Be seeing you."

There could have been no other than Peyton's Hotel for Travis to take up lodging. In addition to Three-Legged-Willie Williamson, Patrick Jack, Travis' fellow sufferer in the Anahuac prison, had joined his brother in San Felipe and the two lived at the hotel. Peyton's was the rendezvous of the leaders of the colony. Sometime later, in one of his letters to Jim Bonham, Travis would write: "It is the headquarters of the most distinctive men in Texas. What it lacks in size it makes up for in comfort and prestige. Its register has carried the names of Jim Bowie, the Warton Brothers, James Fannin. I'm afraid all of us have spoiled Meg, the little Peyton daughter, who is always a pet of the guests."

Here was everything Travis sought. First there was the excitement of the people—diverse people from diverse places, with a multitude of dreams and fears and passions running through them. All the many cross-currents of emotions and thoughts which ran through

292

them, now ran through Travis. Regardless of the reasons—and there were all kinds that brought the colonists to Texas—it was Austin's ardent wish to "receive none but persons of good respect." For the most part Austin's colonists were a respectable lot. Yet there occurred cutting scrapes, duels, shootings, and varied acts of violence. Here in San Felipe, William Barret Travis was prepared to move in a stimulating atmosphere and daily rub shoulders with bold and interesting men, not unlike himself.

There were memorable and notable men among those who stopped at Peyton's. Prominent was Henry Smith, the redhot War Party member who was destined to become Texas' first executive and the first one to be impeached. There was Father Michael Muldoon, the hard-drinking parish priest and the sole cleric in San Felipe who could perform marriages. Because the territory he served was extensive, he was often absent from the country when a couple decided to marry. In his absence they signed a bond with the *alcalde*, whose office was that of a combination mayor and judge; then they set up housekeeping and awaited the priest's return to make their marriage legal. In the meantime if the two decided they were incompatible, they destroyed the bond and each went his own way. Sometimes the couple would have a family started by the time Father Muldoon returned. Muldoon was a man who knew the price of legalized love. Twenty-five silver dollars was his standard fee. Gordon B. Cotton, the newspaperman, was Father Muldoon's drinking partner. A bachelor at fifty, Cotton was a huge man. Editorials appeared in his newspaper, *The Cotton Patch*, signed "G. B." Once when a curious reader asked what the letters stood for, Cotton replied, "Why, goddammit, man, can't you see? Great Big Cotton."

One of the most picturesque and eccentric characters was Captain James "Brit" Bailey. He died a year after Travis arrived in San Felipe. In his final instructions to his wife he demanded to be buried standing up. He told her he had never stooped to any man. He didn't want

293

anyone to look upon his grave and say, "There lies old Brit Bailey." His widow had a ten foot hole dug for his casket and slipped him in feet first.

Benjamin Franklin Milam was one of the first citizens of the United States to come to Texas. He arrived in 1818. Aside from being a rebel, he was a colonizer like Austin. Shortly after arriving in San Felipe, Travis will obtain from him a grant for a league of land, some 11,428.4 acres. Milam, a barrel-chested man with blond hair and a broad ruddy face, was the "friend and protector" of Jane Long, who ran a tavern and boarding house in San Felipe. Jane Long was the widow of Dr. James Long, the dreamer-adventurer who attempted to found a republic of his own in Texas territory. With a company of sixty men he entered Texas by way of the mouth of the San Antonio River and built a fort at Point Bolivar across the channel from Galveston Island. He left his wife Jane, her small daughter Ann, and a young Negro slave girl named Ruda alone at the fort while he and his army attacked the bastion of La Bahia at Goliad. The fort was captured, but after a few days Dr. Long was forced to surrender and taken to prison in Mexico City. He was released, and then shot down by a Mexican soldier. His widow Jane bravely held out in the fort at Point Bolivar during the winter, and was careful to keep a flag—her red flannel petticoat—flying, and each morning fired a small cannon that had been left behind by her husband. She was finally rescued by settlers on their way to San Felipe. Respected for her courage, she was often called "The Mother of Texas," and many claimed her red petticoat as the first Texas flag of independence. Jane Long was one of those beautiful women who grow more beautiful with maturity. She had many admirers, and Ben Milam, not without justification, frequently became violently jealous of her.

Gail Borden, Jr. who operated a blacksmith shop next to Noah Smithwick's, was a young man with ideas of better things. He came to Galveston Island in 1829 from Norwich, New York, and was surveyor for Austin, preparing the first topographical map of Texas. He founded the *Telegraph and Texas Register,* the major propaganda vehicle for the revolution. Gail Borden Jr. will become the first collector of the port of Galveston under the Republic of Texas. And he will perfect the milk formula that will make his name a household word. In his honor will be a county formed in Texas—Borden, with its city seat named Gail.

These were but a few of the men Travis will become associated with in San Felipe. They were men of ideas, adventure, and action. They were men who dreamed of empire and planned rebellion, and this alone gave Travis a common denominator with them. He had been of one passion with them only a year and already, in his heart, he was the best Texan of them all.

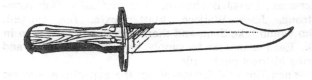

When Josefa Veramendi, Ursula's mother, laid eyes upon her daughter after her return to San Antonio from the honeymoon, the image of the inelegant clumsy child she had carried in her mind was swept away forever. The long legs and awkward knees were homogenized into a woman of perfect grace. The almost grotesque and hungry face of the child had become sublimely beautiful. Her whole nature appeared gentle and mysterious and oddly wise. Josefa knew, then, that her daughter was pregnant. She gathered Ursula into her arms and wept silently; and for the first time in her life

Ursula felt compassion and humility for her mother. The two women clung together without words, transported and exalted in a new kind of love and respect for each other.

Jim's house was ready for occupancy and Josefa and the Veramendi servants together with Sam's smiling assistance quickly got the couple settled in their new home.

While Jim impatiently awaited the arrival of Rezin, he went over and over a long list of friends, evaluating, appraising, deciding on who and how many to include in the expedition to the San Saba treasure. By the time Rezin arrived he had his selection narrowed to seven men.

Rezin reached San Antonio in October and by the last of the month preparations were completed. At first Rezin was in favor of a strong force, but Jim convinced him that a smaller group was much wiser both from the standpoint of travel and maneuverability, and discretion. The compact was well chosen, worthy brave men Jim trusted and who could fight, if called upon to do so. They were Cephas Ham, a stalwart, raw-boned frontiersman, David Buchanan, Tom McCaslin, Bob Armstrong, Jesse Wallace, Matt Doyle, Jim Coryell. Jim would take Sam, and there was Rezin—ten men in all. Each man was to supply his own equipment and bring his own pack mule.

When Jim told Ursula about the expedition, she sat beside him for a long time, a lonely look upon her face. "It will be dangerous and I will worry about you. But I understand. You love danger—and you must go. Each day you are away I shall go to San Fernando and say a prayer for you." She touched her cheek against his shoulder. "Oh, Jamie, I've had you with me such a little time . . ."

Jim led his small force out of San Antonio with no great apprehension concerning the mission. He took them over much the same route he and Tex had taken. It was early November and the last heat of summer was fading from the plains. The days were pleasant, the nights cool enough for the comforts of their blankets and buffalo sleeping robes. They shot an occasional deer or wild turkey for their fresh meat. Traveling at a leisurely pace, by the night of the nineteenth they were about thirty miles from the ruins of the old San Saba presidio. Jim estimated that they were about seven miles north of the Llamo River, well towards its source. The broken country, covered with live-oak and scrub cedar, was cut across by a shallow valley at the bottom of which a stream of clear water twisted through groves of taller trees. Jim decided to make camp there.

As the party was having breakfast, galloping out of the early risen sun was a lone horseman. Everybody stood in the circle of the fire waiting for the rider to approach.

"A Mex," Cephas Ham said, as the man rode into the camp, dust-covered, eyes bloodshot and weary to the bone. He was in breechcloth and moccasins, but otherwise naked.

"Have you come alone?" Jim asked.

"No, Señor. Ten men are with me—there." He pointed in the direction from whence he had ridden.

"What do they want?"

"They are friends of Zolic. They want to see you, Señor."

"Lipans?" Cephas Ham asked.

"Twakoni," the Mexican rider said.

"Bring them in," Jim told the boy.

"Slave," Cephas Ham said, when the boy rode off.

"Slave?" Rezin said. "Why doesn't he escape?"

"Probably all he knows. Strange power of the wilderness. I've known of white women captured by the Indians and taken as squaws, who refused to return to civilization when they had a chance."

The Mexican came riding at the head of a group of Twakoni. Immediately behind him was the prophet. Jim hailed them into camp, offered food. While they gorged, Jim talked with the prophet. He showed Jim a

297

medal, a duplicate of the one Zolic had given Tex a year ago.

"Zolic dead," the chief said. "You not safe here. *El Tres Varges* now chief of Lipans. Go. Leave Lipan country. Many warriors trail you."

"How many?"

"Hundred—two hundred."

The prophet hailed his men and they rode off at a rapid pace, trailing a cloud of dust.

"What do you think, Cephas?" Jim asked.

"How far to that old presidio?"

"About thirty or forty miles—up this valley."

"If we could reach it, we can give the Lipans a goddamn good fight there."

"We'd better get going."

They broke camp quickly and soon were headed for San Saba, driving the pack mules before them at a sharp trot.

The floor of the valley was covered with broken rocks and the horses and mules soon began to limp because of the sharp flints underfoot. By nightfall they were still miles away from the ruins of San Saba presidio. Jim reluctantly gave orders to halt. He scouted the area for a defensible campsite, settled on a small hummock, at the foot of which a little stream, tributary to the San Saba River, ran. The valley here widened into a broad almost barren level. Up ahead the steep canyon and the stream curved around a dense oak thicket about forty yards in depth. Just south of this was the place Jim had chosen for the campsite, which was covered with thirty or forty live-oak trees, some with a trunk about the size of a man's body. Good protection, with one danger: across the narrow stream was another small hill with a growth of timber. If they had to fight here it might shelter hostile sharpshooters.

Under Jim's direction the men prepared the place for defense. Rezin and five of the men cut a trail through the thicket about ten feet from the creek and cleared a space in the center large enough to accommodate all the men and their equipment. The horses and mules were hobbled in the grove. Every available bucket was filled with water and pickets were established before they settled down.

When night passed uneventfully Rezin, rolling up his blanket, said, "Looks like a false alarm. We might make that old presidio after all."

The horses were saddled and they were about ready to move out when Cephas Ham gave a yell. "Indians! Goddammit, Indians!"

With the sun at their backs, over a rise about eight hundred yards distant, came a long line of mounted braves. In the fore of the line was the tracker bent low, his nose to the ground, a human track dog leading the warriors straight to the camp.

Quickly the men dismounted, led the animals into the thicket, tethered them. They took up their rifles behind Jim.

The line of savages came on, their paint and fluttery feathers bright in the early sun, a cloud of dust rising behind them.

"How many do you figure?" Jim asked Cephas Ham, who was at his side.

"I count a hundred and sixty—so far."

"About sixteen to one, eh?"

The Indians had halted their slow march, and accompanied by yelps and war whoops, dismounted and began stripping off their surplus clothing, preparatory for battle. A dozen still mounted rode forward to reconnoiter, circling close enough so that Cephas Ham could make out their markings.

"There's some Caddos among them," he said. "I can tell by the cut of their scalplocks. They've always been friendly. Maybe they'll parley. If we use the right talk they might go on and leave us alone."

"I've still got Zolic's talisman." Jim held the quaint medallion in his hand.

David Buchanan pressed forward. "I know some Caddo. I'll go out with Jim."

299

"Give me that double barrel shotgun of yours, Rezin. And—all of you men—keep us covered."

Together Jim and David Buchanan, their right hands uplifted, walked toward the twelve mounted warriors. They ventured about two hundred yards, close enough to carry on a shouting conversation.

From their protected positions among the oaks the men heard David Buchanan call out in the Caddo tongue.

There was a brief silence. Then a horseman, brandishing aloft a handful of bloody scalps, shouted: "How-do! How-do!"

A friendly sign. The men in the grove relaxed. It was false hope. A musket blazed away. David Buchanan jackknifed. "The sonuvabitch shot me, Jim."

Jim pulled the hobbling man backward, keeping face to the Indians. David Buchanan slumped to the ground. The Indian who had fired the shot rode toward Jim yelping and aiming a lance. Jim raised the shotgun and fired both barrels at close range. The horseman's head exploded in a small cloud of brains and skull and blood.

Jim stopped, knifed his wounded companion across his shoulder and started running back to the grove, with volleys of shots spattering around them. He felt one tug at his hunting jacket, felt two more thud into David Buchanan's body. Rezin, Cephas Ham, Tom McCaslin, and Jim Coryell came running to Jim's assistance, the eleven remaining warriors bearing down upon them. On they came. Fifty yards. Twenty yards, lances gleaming. "Fire boys!" Rezin said, raising his gun on the run. Four rifles cracked. Two Indians toppled from their saddles. Two horses stumbled, whinnying fearfully, their mounts kicking in the bushes. More bullets thudded among the men.

A volley of shots went out from the trees. The Indians jerked their mounts around and veered off, bending low over the animals' necks.

David Buchanan had been shot in the body and both legs. Jim was missed narrowly. Blood was oozing from

300

a deep crease above Rezin's eyes. In the excitement he had felt nothing. Everybody gave his attention to the seriously wounded David Buchanan, who was bleeding badly but conscious and angry.

It was the wounded David Buchanan who saw the Indians prelude to the next assault. They had gathered in a group just out of rifle range whooping war cries, a swirling mass of bright plumes, war paint, gleaming weapons. "They're coming, boys! Leave me be and load up your guns!"

The Indians began to advance in a closed line, led by an exceptionally painted and feathered warrior who rode back and forth before the rank exhorting, shouting. Led by the inspiring prophet, the Indians spurred their horses and dashed forward at full speed.

"Who's loaded?" Jim asked.

"I am," Cephas Ham said.

"Think you can kill the prophet?"

The frontiersman's rifle came to his shoulder, he sighted down the long barrel. A flat report. Indian and horse went down. The prophet freed himself from his fallen horse, hooped around on one good leg, brandishing his shield and yelping at the other warriors.

"Give me a loaded rifle," Jim said.

A gun was pressed into his hand. He aimed, the rifle spurted fire and lead. The prophet went down, kicked twice, and lay still.

The line of horsemen, carried by its momentum, overran the fallen leader and came within fifty yards of the grove. From behind tree trunks the men fired. Every shot toppled a warrior, emptied a saddle. Seeing their leader dead and the riderless horses among them, the Indians drew up and welled around uncertainly. Jim's men, their ramrods clicking in the barrels of their guns, were quickly ready. Another volley. More riderless horses. The line of braves rode back to a hillock, out of range.

The Indians milled around the hill, then a group rode forward. "Get ready!" Rezin shouted. "Here they come again!"

"Hold your fire," Cephas Ham said calmly. "They only want their dead."

A volley of rifle shots suddenly rang out from the clump of trees across the stream that Jim had earlier spotted as a good place for sharpshooters.

"Tom! Tom! By God! I'm hit!" Matt Doyle's gun slipped from his hands, his face fell in the dirt.

"Matt—Goddamn!" Tom McCaslin lifted the wounded man's head. The pupils of his eyes were sinking away like two cornflowers in milk. The bullet had entered his right breast and passed out his back.

Tom McCaslin and Matt Doyle had come to Texas together. Between them, both Irish, there was a warm friendship.

"Matt, I'm gonna get that bastard redskin that shot you!" Tom McCaslin cried with rage. He spat, looked around wildly, picked up his rifle and ran toward the creek.

"Come back!" Jim shouted. But Tom McCaslin had crossed the stream and was coming out on the opposite side, muddy and wet, his rifle swinging.

An Indian crept out of the timbers, and from a kneeling position drew back the string of his bow, loaded it, and sent the arrow through Tom McCaslin's neck, dropping him to the muddy creek bank with blood spilling from his mouth.

Robert Armstrong, who had started after Tom McCaslin, raised his gun but a ball from the timbers splintered his gun stock, almost driving it out of his hands. But he raised it again and fired. His bullet splattered the skull of the Indian who had killed Tom McCaslin. "Die, you bastard! Die!" he screamed.

The warriors on the hill in the fore of the men, having picked up their dead and wounded, were being assembled for another assault by a new leader. They swarmed around this highly painted and plumed leader with renewed vigor, yelping louder and more fiercely.

Jim strained his eyes against the direct sunlight. Could that be *him?* He called for Sam.

"Sam, you've got uncommon eyes. See that brightly painted chief on the white horse?"

"Yassuh, Marse Jim. I sees him."

"Can you see what that is around his neck?"

Sam shaded his eyes, gazed a long time. "Marse Jim, he's got somethin' hanging from his neck about the size of my old Zog piece."

"That's no Zog piece, Sam. That's two human penes. That's *El Tres Varges.*"

Jim sized up the situation quickly. "They're going to charge in full force this time, boys," he said. "We've got to get to the clearing Rezin made in the thicket. First we'll have to clear those Indians from the trees across the creek. Men, draw back and concentrate your fire over there."

The men crept back from the protection of their tree trunks, moved along the edge of their wooded concealment and, as they went, shot the Indians in the head as they raised themselves to pick a target. Very shortly the braves abandoned the wooded position and tried to flee out of rifle range. As they strove to scramble up the canyon wall they were neatly picked off to the last man.

Carrying the wounded David Buchanan and Matt Doyle, the men made their way into the prickly mass of chaparral and undergrowth.

"Rezin, you're a damn fine engineer," Jim said with a grimace. "Your work here last night just might save all our lives."

Improvised bandages staunched Matt Doyle's bleeding and he seemed to rally. One of the balls had broken David Buchanan's leg. Rezin with some help from Jim Coryell lined up the bone and bound the leg in an improvised splint. Painful but endurable.

His snipers having been killed off, *El Tres Varges* saw too late his mistake at not charging the men when his braves had them flanked. Now in order to get at them he had to attack from the open plain.

He launched fifty men in a thunderous, yelping run at the thicket. Jim's men were ready. A volley toppled six from their saddles, brought down two horses. Before the Indians could pull up and retreat nine more were dropped. In the thicket only the noise of ramrods against steel, the cracking of guns, the exuberant oaths of the shooters, plus the cutting whine of enemy balls whizzing into the brush, could be heard.

El Tres Varges immediately launched a second attack of thirty men, fifteen came back.

The resolute chief was not through. He initiated a new strategy. No more attacks by mounted warriors. He began sending them out on foot, taking advantage of every gully, every little hillock, every scrub tree, always creeping closer to the thicket. After a time *El Tres Varges'* gunners had the thicket completely surrounded. They waited for the men to fire, then shot back at the point where rifle smoke rose. Jim Coryell took a bullet through the arm.

Jim Bowie realized that he had to counter this latest tactic, and quickly, or the little force would be wiped out. It was just a matter of how long it would take *El Tres Varges'* braves to pick them off one at a time.

Jim crawled to the center of the men. "The instant you fire," he told them, "move five or six feet before attempting to reload."

This counter tactic undoubtedly saved the expedition.

The day wore on. Bullets continued to thud in the thicket. But they were blind shots. Several of the mules and two horses were killed. The marksmanship of the Americans was deadly. All morning and into the afternoon they fired, moved, reloaded, swore, and killed Indians.

Nature and the weather gave *El Tres Varges* an assist for his next move. The wind changed and began blowing from behind his warriors. Between his gunners and the men in the thornbushes was tall, dry grass. He set fire to it. The wind carried blinding, choking clouds of smoke into the thicket. Jim's men lay on their faces, coughing, almost blinded. *El Tres Varges* launched an attack behind the fire and smoke screen. His victory, total to be savored, was practically in his hands.

But *El Tres Varges* was no meteorologist. As the wind rushed into the canyon, the horseshoe bend of the walls caused it to veer, carrying the fire away from the thicket toward the creek. There it swept along the bank of the stream and died out where the brush became greener.

Seeing the failure of his strategy, *El Tres Varges* now sent the full force of his warriors across the blackened and still smoking plain. Bullets lashed through the thicket, clipping branches, ricocheting and zinging away.

As Jim watched, he saw that this was to be *El Tres Varges'* decisive assault. Violent determination was displayed in his gestures, his every motion; it was in every yell of his braves, who saw the madness in their chief and lent their own ferocity to the all-out attack. Carry this charge into the thicket and it was all over. On they came, rakishly, howling, shooting, taking to bows and arrows after discharging their muskets. Emboldened by their invincible chief, they still charged when their weapons were impotent.

Jim and his men lay in the bushes firing and reloading. No time now to shift positions. Jim fired, began reloading. God! What a time to be with an empty weapon! Through the branches he saw the murderous face of *El Tres Varges* nearing. Of all the Indians who rode on that thunderous charge, *El Tres Varges'* was the only face his eyes encompassed. Frantically Jim worked at the recharge, all the while that vicious face looming closer and closer. No time to finish the load.

Jim leapt to his feet, rushed out of the thicket, plunging toward *El Tres Varges* with his rifle held by its barrel. The Indian fired. The ball thudded into the ground at Jim's feet. There he was, the chief, almost eyeball to eyeball with Jim. On the run Jim leapt in the air and simultaneously swung with his rifle. The stock of the weapon struck the chief in the center of his breast. No longer would the mummied amulet incite to the killing

305

of white men. The rifle butt shattered the dried and flinty trophy like Dresden china. *El Tres Varges* had barely fallen to the ground when the Bowie blade plunged through his chest.

The eyes of all the braves had been on their chief as he led the charge toward the thicket. They saw him felled from his horse by a lone man on foot with an empty rifle. They saw him ignominiously murdered before their very eyes. The warriors reined up their horses in jolting jumps, milled around silently, making no effort to harm Jim Bowie, who stood over their slain chief, his dreadful knife in hand.

The Indians withdrew but remained visible on the hill in the distance. The two forces had been engaged for fourteen hours. The men were tired and hungry, but Jim insisted on building an earthwork around the clearing. By ten o'clock the fortification was breast high.

They buried Tom McCaslin by the creek, while in the distance the Indians carried on their death chant, their quavering yells continuing throughout the night.

Jim and Rezin did all they could to ease David Buchanan's pain. The jagged wound in his leg was throbbing and he was feverish, but he still clung to consciousness. Matt Doyle, shot through the chest, seemed to be in fair condition despite the seriousness of his injury. Jim Coryell, who had managed to staunch the flow of blood from the hole in his arm, assured Jim he was perfectly able to fire his rifle, when the battle resumed. Rezin had developed a severe headache from the wound over his eyes, otherwise he felt quite fit.

The next day the little group stood ready to take up their defense once again. But no attack came. Shortly before noon a scouting party of fifteen mounted warriors appeared on the border of the burnt plain, reined up briefly, turned and rode away.

During the night David Buchanan's leg had taken a turn for the worse and Matt Doyle's fever would not subside. There seemed nothing for the party to do but remain in camp and attempt to nurse the wounded to a condition which would enable them to travel.

Later Rezin Bowie wrote a report concerning David Buchanan's wound and his recovery.

Having no surgical instruments or medicine of any kind, not even a dose of salts, we baked some live-oak bark very strong and thickened it with pounded charcoal and Indian meal. We made a poltice of it and tied it around his leg, over which we sewed a buffalo skin, then traveled along five days without looking at it. When it was opened, the wound was in a fair way for healing, which it finally did, and the mortified parts all dropped off. His leg is now well as it ever was.

On the sixth of December, Jim Bowie and his little band of silver hunters straggled into San Antonio. They had not reached the Cave of Saint Joseph of Alcasar, because their horses and mules were nearly all destroyed and their wounded needed care.

With Ursula's first child on the way and the harrowing experience he had just survived, Jim pushed back in his mind any further plans to rescue the San Saba silver. But by no consideration was he abandoning the notion of recovering, at his leisure, the vast riches. Meanwhile, the treasure, he felt, was perfectly safe. If he, Jim Bowie, could not get it, certainly nobody else could.

Indians coming into San Antonio to trade reported that the western country buzzed with stories of the San Saba battle. No less than eighty-two Indians, killed and wounded, had gone down before the little band of ten Americans.

In San Antonio the San Saba battle became the topic of the day. Jim Bowie was the most discussed, most gazed-upon man in the town. The Bowie knife became a must for all frontiersmen. Many of these knives were manufactured in England, inferior copies of the James

307

Black original, and sold all over America. Ursula did not chide Jim about his latest adventure. Perhaps more than all others she understood his need for adventure, the taking of risks. But she was happy to have him safely home. The baby was due in the spring and she wanted to have her husband at her side for this crucial event. She caused candles to be burned in San Fernando church for poor Señor McCaslin, as she had done earlier for Señor Tex Delacey.

Jim and Rezin decided it would be folly to venture into Lipan country while memories of the recent fight still rankled, so Rezin returned to Louisiana to await a more propitious time for the raising of a second expedition. Jim resumed trafficking in land and became more seriously involved in the political activities of the colonists. He made trips to San Felipe, Washington-on-the-Brazos, Nacogdoches, and other settlements, where he attended meetings and talked with important members of both the War Party and the Peace Party.

Came a day in April when the big white house was filled with women and activities which reduced Jim to maddening uselessness. Dona Josefa took affairs in her own capable hands, and shooed him from Ursula's bedside.

At last he heard a stir from within, female voices expressing joy, and a tiny cry—the protest perhaps of a new born soul born into a troubled world. When finally he was admitted into Ursula's chamber his concern was not for the small bundle pillowed at her breast—a tiny head covered with straggling black hair, a wrinkled grimacing face with tight-shut eyes—but for the girl to whom he had become husband, father, brother. She smiled at him with happiness flowing from her drained face, and only then did fatherhood begin to take possession of him.

Ursula gave their daughter the name of Jaima Juanita, honoring the two finest men she knew: James Bowie and Juan Veramendi.

When Jim Bowie strode into Peyton's Hotel the big

man standing at the mantlepiece beside the fireplace called, "James Bowie!"

With his beard shaved away Jim did not at once recognize Sam Houston. He seemed younger and somehow more powerful. His opalescent eyes clear, he seemed the man in command, as his military bearing suggested. The two men greeted each other as long lost brothers.

That evening while they ate dinner together in the Peyton dining room, Houston asked many questions. Was it true that Santa Anna had revealed himself as an oppressive dictator? What was the attitude of the colonists? How did the Texans feel about the United States? When Jim told Houston that the colonists would welcome assistance from the people in the States, Houston's cat eyes lighted.

"Andrew Jackson is profoundly interested in the welfare of the Americans in Texas," Houston said.

Jim looked sharply into the general's eyes. "Did he tell you that?"

"He did."

"This might cause my Mexican friends some alarm," Jim said.

"It shouldn't—not yet. The president will probably make a purchasing offer for Texas. The United States is a creditor nation with no national debt. The money is no real problem. But Jackson has a unique idea. He has a notion of forcing the bankers to come up with the wherewithal to buy the Texas territory. He has no love for the big money people."

Jim sank into thought. Houston, a most perceptive man, wanted to know what was on his mind.

"My father-in-law, Juan Martin Veramendi, the vice governor. I'm wondering how he will take the news."

"What I've told you, Jim Bowie, must go no further—for now. There's one thing we must wait on."

"And that?"

"Jackson's got a small political problem. Congressman David Crockett. Those two, it seems, were born to

309

be adversaries. In opposing Jackson on the Indian land question, Crockett took the popular stand, and Jackson's political enemies would like to set the illiterate backwoodsman up as presidential candidate in opposition to the Jackson party. Andy feels that Crockett is woefully unqualified. He's put out the word he wants him defeated in the next election. After that he will act on the Texas problem."

While they talked Houston noticed three men who had entered the dining room and were approaching the communal dining table, at which Jim and Houston were the only guests so far. Houston knew one of the men well. He was James Walker Fannin, a young man from Georgia looking around with a view to settling in Texas. Before taking their places at the table, Fannin introduced his companions. They were William Barret Travis and Dr. Amos Pollard. Fannin, in his late twenties, had a long, serious face, black hair, and black eyes that shifted from side to side whenever he spoke. Dr. Pollard, Massachusetts born and New York trained, was a man Jim judged to be in his mid-thirties; his hair was brown and wiry, and he parted it low on one side and combed it straight back over his head. His large eyes matched the color of his hair, though lighter. Jim instantly resented Travis' garish attire: red pantaloons, green frock coat, beige waistcoat, bright red shirt, and double stock, a white-over-black.

The men seated themselves and Fannin said to Houston, "Well, General, I've made up my mind. Texas is the place for me. I'll go at once back to Georgia and fetch my wife Minerva and the two girls. This is a good place to raise a family."

The talk quickly got around to politics. Travis and Fannin were the most vocal. The two men, youngest at the table, were in militant agreement that the Texans would have to form an army and fight. They bitterly denounced Santa Anna as a despot with whom it was impossible to come to any satisfactory terms. Travis savagely proclaimed that the Mexican president-general had thrown aside his mask and revealed himself for what he was—a tyrant of the worst order. Fannin heartily agreed. Dr. Pollard had little to say; Jim listened with a silent dudgeon resentment of Travis the firebrand; Houston seemed somewhat amused.

Finally Jim said, "Travis, I do not agree with you. You are voicing only the opinion of a very few of the War Party, the hottest hotheads. For the moment the Peace Party holds the majority opinion, and Austin is acting as its representative of the laws of Mexico, which all of us have sworn to uphold. We should wait until his return from Mexico City and hear his first hand impression and counsel."

"Classical literature is filled with stories of war parties and peace parties," Travis countered. "History shows us that all the peace parties ever did was barter away man's individual liberties. I tell you we'll have to fight." He tapped the table with his forefinger. "Hear me good, right this moment we ought to be busy organizing a Texas army."

"The time may come when all you have proclaimed is right," Jim said tolerantly. "But for now I don't see it."

"Nor do any of the other big landholders," Travis said succinctly.

Jim gazed coldly into Travis' eyes. "Understand one thing, Travis. Should the time come when we Texans must take up arms to defend our liberties, you will find Jim Bowie will fight just as diligently as any of you young firebrands."

Travis addressed Houston. "And you, General, will you remain in Texas and join the struggle for independence?"

"I must return to the States for a time. But I will come back."

For the first time, Dr. Pollard spoke. "I hope you don't get struck by the pestilence, General."

"What pestilence?" Houston asked.

"The Asiatic cholera. It's been ravaging parts of the States since last summer."

"What parts?"

311

"Mostly the Mississippi Valley area—Saint Louis, Memphis, Vicksburg, Natchez, New Orleans. It hit New Orleans real bad. The doctors were helpless. In ten days six thousand died. The dead were stacked in the streets like cordwood. They buried them in great trenches and burned many of them."

"Good God!" Houston exclaimed, a sudden dread crossing his mind. "If it hits the Indian settlements it'll wipe them out."

"It's already got to some Indian areas. Killed them by the hundreds."

"Where did it start?" Jim asked.

"It came from Asia, reached Russia by way of China, Manchuria, and Mongolia. From Moscow it spread into Germany and across the North Sea to Great Britain last year. Then it was carried to Canada, and from there it came into the Mississippi Valley. Some say a sailor was brought ashore from a ship at Fort Dearborn stricken by violent vomiting and diarrhea, agonizing cramps in his legs and arms, abdomen, and back. From there it spread down the river."

"Has it reached Texas yet?" Travis asked.

"A couple of cases in Nacogdoches."

"What are the symptoms?" Jim wanted to know.

"Voice husky, clammy skin, horribly sunken eyes, imperceptible pulse, anxious and pathetic look on the face. A peculiarity of the disease is that the body of the victim stays warm for a time after death. Its temperature may even rise. Sometimes, too, after life is gone the legs and arms keep moving, as if even in death the body is still tormented. It's a most horrible disease."

"How can one best escape it?" Jim asked.

"Avoid contact. Stay clear of the area where the victims are—even the dead."

When Jim left San Felipe for home, Houston went with him. He wanted to meet with some of the Indian chiefs who came into San Antonio. As they rode along Houston told Jim about James Walker Fannin.

"The fellow's hankering for military recognition. He

had some training at West Point, was admitted to the academy under the names of James W. Walker. As a small boy, because of some question as to his legitimacy, he was adopted by his maternal grandfather, James W. Walker, and brought up on a plantation near Marion, Georgia. He wasn't too bright a student and quarreled constantly with the other cadets. One day he and another boy had a fight on the banks of the Hudson. It seems that Fannin got the worst of it—in truth, the other lad beat hell out of him. Rather than face the derision he feared would come from his fellow cadets, he ran away. So they booted him out of the Academy. I understand he went to Cuba and made a lot of money dealing in slaves. Now, he's here, in Texas, seeking a military career."

In that ambition James Walker Fannin will succeed beyond his fondest hopes. He will be commissioned full colonel by Stephen F. Austin and given command of Texas' largest army in the field. But he will learn that he lacks ability to command large bodies of troops. He will become disillusioned with both his command and the Texans. He will write to a friend:

I have not so much confidence in the people of Texas as I once had. They have been called on and entreated to fly to arms and to prevent what has now been done. I have but three citizens in the ranks and tho' I have called on them for six weeks, not one arrived, and no assistance in bringing me provisions. Even Texas (the government) refused me. I feel too indignant to say more about them. If I was honorably out of their service, I would never re-enter it. But I must now play a bold game. I will go the whole hog. If I am lost be the censure on the right head, and my wife and children and children's children curse the sluggards forever.

Fannin will be defeated by Santa Anna's troops, and surrender on ignoble terms. On Palm Sunday, March

27, 1836, he will see his army slaughtered like chickens on market day. His final request before his own execution will be that he be shot in the breast, that his body be given a decent burial, and that his watch should be sent to his family. Instead, the watch will be kept by the Mexican to whom it is handed; he will be shot in the back of the head like a criminal; and his body will be placed with the others and burned.

In San Antonio Jim put Houston up at his home. Ursula was delighted with the general, both as a gentleman and as a guest. Houston fell in love with little Jaima Juanita, whom he called J.J. The entire household, servants and everybody, became quite fond of the big man.

When Jim took Houston to the palace to see Juan Martin Vermendi, the vice governor asked Houston the same question he had asked Jim when they first met. "What do you want in Texas?"

Houston explained that he was in Texas to hold parleys with the Comanche Indian tribes and confer upon certain chiefs medals of friendship on behalf of the President of the United States.

Vermendi, speaking with his usual candor, remarked, "If the Comanches are wise they will turn their backs upon any Andrew Jackson medal. Jackson is an imperialist. He robbed the Florida and Alabama Indians of their lands without mercy. Jackson is a man who speaks of the 'manifest destiny' of America."

"Would you explain that, please?" Houston demanded just as directly. "You know, Sir, that I served in the Indian wars under General Jackson."

"Certainly," said the vice governor. "Jackson apparently believes it is America's manifest destiny to overspread the continent allotted by providence for the free development of America's yearly multiplying millions. Manifest destiny!" Veramendi scoffed. "It's just a pontifical expression—words—designed to disguise a theft. A hypocritical way of proclaiming the right to deprive the Indians, and anybody else who

314

might stand in the way, of lands that Washington covets."

One evening Houston asked Jim for paper and pen. The letter he wrote was addressed to Andrew Jackson, President of the United States. In part the letter read:

Dear Sir:
Having been as far as Bexar (San Antonio), in the province of Texas, where I had an interview with Comanche Indians, I am in possession of some information that will doubtless be interesting to you, and may be calculated to forward your views, if you should entertain any, touching the acquisition of Texas by the United States. That such a measure is desirable by nineteen-twentieths of the population, I cannot doubt. Mexico is involved in civil war, the government is despotic, the rulers have not honesty, and the people have not intelligence.

Texas has already beaten and expelled troops of Mexico from her soil, nor will she permit them to return. She can defend herself against the whole power of Mexico. Her want of money, taken in connection with the course which Texas must and will adopt, will render a transfer inevitable to some power; and if the United States does not press for it, England most assuredly will obtain it by some means.

If Texas is desirable to the United States, it is now in the most favorable attitude to obtain on fair terms.

Yrs. obiediently
Sam Houston

Jim received a letter from Meg, Rezin's wife, urging him to come at once to Arcadia. Rezin was going blind, she wrote, as a result of the wound he received in the San Saba fight, and the only doctor who could help him was in Baltimore. Jim was needed to take his brother there.

Jim was reluctant to leave his family at this time. Ursula's second child was due in July and he wanted to be with her when the baby was born. However, Ursula insisted that he go to his brother's assistance. She would be just fine, she assured him. "And when you return," she said, "I'll place in your arms a son. I've already decided on his name. We shall call him Juan Rezin Bowie."

Jim did not want to alarm Ursula about the cholera plague. Already it had creeped near. Several had died of it in Victoria, including the important land holder, Don Martin de Leon. And at San Felipe it had taken John Austin. Eighty were reported dead in Brazoria. Jim extracted a promise from Juan Veramendi that he would take the entire family at once to the villa on the mountainside at Monclova, where the air was always fresh and healthful.

A few days later, the entire Vermendi family, together with Ursula and Jaima Juanita, left by coach for the south, while Jim took the horseback trail for the east. As the long trip began already he was looking forward to Monclova in the fall. Ursula's last words to her husband was the beautiful Mexican farewell, which is also a prayer, *"Vaya con dios—go with God."*

To Jim the long journey up the Mississippi and Ohio Rivers by steamboat seemed endless; the churning paddle wheels carried him always further from Ursula. In Baltimore Dr. Valentine Mott helped Rezin. They were there for two months. Jim chaffed at the delay. He wrote Ursula a long letter every week, telling her all the little incidents that happened and describing the scenes and people he encountered. He could not be sure she'd ever receive any of the letters. But it relieved him to write them. He addressed them to Meg with a note: "Maybe you can find someone going to Texas. If you do send these along. If they ever get to San Antonio, I have friends who will forward them."

When he and Rezin left Baltimore, Rezin had recovered partial vision and Dr. Mott promised further improvement, provided his treatment was continued.

Ursula died in September. It was January before Jim knew. The dreaded plague reached into Coahuila, into Monclova. The Veramendi household had been stricken in the first week of September. Juan Veramendi and Josefa had died the same day. A week later Ursula and the two children had all died. Jim received the news when he rode into San Felipe. The *alcalde* had received a letter from San Antonio with the news. Jim refused to believe the terrible truth. That night he set out for San Antonio. Two and a half days later he stumbled into his house haggard and unkempt. He shook Sam for the truth.

"Marse Jim, I's shore sorry, but I knows dey's all daid."

Jim broke the neck off a bottle of brandy and poured himself a powerful drink.

James Bowie became a roughed-up loser, traveling through the dark lit only by the beacon of the most futile dream of all—the desperate illusion that one can escape from himself. He drank. He drifted. He dropped out of human relations. He wandered from place to place—the hunter, seeking that which he knew he could not find. He drifted to Nacogdoches, to Natchez, to New Orleans, to Arcadia, and back to San Antonio. There the weeks passed, the months, two years . . . yet he found nothing but the bottom of the jug.

He was seen with eyes like coals, fierce with drink, as he strayed along the dry banks of the river or through the ruins of the old missions. Sam had found him upon the river bank asleep or dazed with liquor, wet with dew under the stars. He was seen swimming midstream in the craggy, twisting San Antonio River. He was picked up from alleys outside *cantinas* and mercifully carried home by friends. A loser with nothing to lose.

Late one night when Sam found his master wandering aimlessly about the old Alamo, he took him gently by the arm and led him towards home. Passing by a familiar street that in Jim's mind dimly reminded him of drink and conviviality, he pulled away from Sam. After a little way he stopped and stared down the street toward the *cantina,* like a dog that wants to go away, but is reluctant to offend his master. Sam took him by the arm and gently led him home.

Next morning Sam saw that Jim bathed and ate some solid food. Afterwards Sam said, "Marse Jim, I want to tell you somethin'."

"First I'll tell you something, Sam."

"Yes, Marse Jim?"

"Get me a drink!"

"Marse Jim, can I talk to you first?"

"I want it now!"

Sam went into another room and brought back a bottle of brandy. Jim snatched it from the servant's hands, ignored the glass Sam had brought, lifted the bottle to his lips, and gulped throatily. He put the bottle down, gripped the edge of the table; revulsion shook him. Then he poured a moderate amount in the glass and sipped it slowly.

"Marse Jim," Sam said, "things ain't so bad. Dey ain't so bad as all dat." He nodded at the bottle.

"Sam, I killed Ursula, the children—the others. It was I who sent them to their deaths."

"Marse Jim, de vomito wuz here, too. Just de same as it wuz dere."

"Everything is bad, Sam. I can see only bad things —everywhere."

Sam remained silent for a time. At length he said, "All things are good, Marse Jim. Things ain't always what they seem."

Jim lifted his head. "What about Ursula? Was there good in her being taken away?"

Jim Bowie had always thought of Jim Bowie as a pragmatist. Wherever he appeared things happened, things began. He made his own fortunes, caused his own defeats in life. He was a judicious arbiter of his own behavior. He felt responsible only to his own will and might. But now in his loneliness, looking back in desperate longing for his lost Ursula that faith in himself was badly shaken. Two women, infinite treasures of his life, had been taken from him by a power beyond his might and will: Paula by the prejudice and ignorance and hypocrisy of society; Ursula by the Almighty. Suddenly he felt completely helpless, a tiny being with no headland. Fleetingly he saw himself as a small child kneeling at his mother's lap, his eyes overflowing with tears, begging her supplication. He lifted his head to his servant. "Sam, for God's sake, help me!"

Sam silently reached for the cork, drove it into the bottle, and took away the liquor. "Marse Jim," he said, "let's see if we can do without this for a while."

Antonio Lopez de Santa Anna Perez de Labron was an opportunist excelled by none. All his life had been spent in perfecting the art of taking the option best suited to furthering himself up the ladder of power. At the age of twenty-two he had achieved a record of better than six years of military service in some of the most brutal and bloody conflicts on record, always surviving and coming out a step ahead, a rank higher. Along the

319

way he learned two things vital to survival and gaining power: A man must have absolutely no scruples about making a promise he had no intention of keeping, and he must have the loyalty of the army behind him. Always uppermost in his mind was the glorification of Santa Anna.

He will write in his autobiography: "In the hearts of most men there lurks a sentiment which they carefully try to conceal from their fellow man. This foolish sentiment is that which causes men to aspire constantly to immortality. Not all men, however, succeed in inscribing their names on the walls of the temple of glory."

His hero, Napoleon, had succeeded admirably in inscribing his name on that wall. In spite of Santa Anna's many rides toward fame, holding the golden sword of immortality aloft over his head, he never in all of his eighty-two years gave up the struggle for a lasting place in the temple of glory. He was nonetheless an excellent example of the nineteeth-century *caudillo,* the great political-military boss, the *personalisimo* leader in the Mexican frontier period. He was a product of his era— one which included Napoleon Bonaparte, Simon Bolivar, Andrew Jackson, Augustin de Iturbide, Louis Napoleon, Prince von Metternich, and Otto von Bismarck.

Santa Anna was a *criolo*—a Creole—in the sense that he was of Spanish parentage but tainted by the fact that his birthplace was geographically in New Spain, a colony of the New World, and erroneously regarded by Spaniards to be subject to the degenerating influence of the tropics.

When Santa Anna was born on February 21, 1794, Mexico was firmly a colony of Spain. It remained a part of Spain until 1821. Santa Anna came on stage at just the right time to play an important role in the political changes that brought on Mexico's independence from the mother country. His birthplace was Jalapa—"water on the sands." Capital of Vera Cruz, the town was named for the Jalapa plant, a most energetic purgative and an important ingredient of castor oil. As for Jalapa, it has been called an "Eden in the sky." And well it might be. Set in a perfect garden country, it is tucked in the folds of the mountains five thousand feet above the pestilential inferno of Vera Cruz. Towering majestically over it is Mt. Orizaba, dazzling in its snow-capped brilliance at eighteen-thousand feet. Santa Anna remembered Jalapa as being lush and convolvulus and brilliant everywhere. Acacia trees, roses in negligent profusion, red and purple bougainvillea, brilliant azalea, carnation, begonia, zinnia, and exotic orchid gorged the senses with a riot of grandeur. There were mango trees, banana plants with their green semaphores, and from the public square one could see orange and lemon groves, apple and peach and pear orchards, and higher up even fields of wheat. It was a spa for the health-seeking rich, and a lovely place of refuge to maintain a second wife or to hide away a mistress.

It was in the sylvan tropical clime of Jalapa that Joel Poinsett of South Carolina, the first minister from the Washington government, discovered the beautiful brilliant plant which bears his name, and which flourishes in southern wintergardens, the Poinsetta Pulcheriman.

And it was in Jalapa that the hushed word "independence" first gained respectable utterance.

The Mexican revolution really owed its beginning to Napoleon Bonaparte. In 1808 Napoleon put out the Bourbon king of Spain and installed his brother Joseph on the Spanish throne. The people, who had long bowed under the iron rule of their tyrant kings, had nothing to lose in the change. But it was the ruling class who aroused the nation against the foreign French usurper and drove Bonaparte out of Spain. These political upheavals in the native homeland had their almost seismic disturbances in Mexico, especially in the towns and regions where the rich, the educated, the autocratic dwelt.

The Catholic Church began to stir like a huge leviathan. The church in Mexico was fabulously wealthy.

321

It held in lands and property and gold almost one-third of all the riches of the country. Spain was impoverished after the wars of Napoleon, and had lost many of its South American colonies; and the leaders in Mexico feared that the wants of the mother country might lead to a levy on the Mexican church's wealth.

There were more than six million native Indians in Mexico, and only a few hundred thousand Spaniards and persons of Spanish blood. These millions of uneducated peons were the slaves of an aristocracy which flourished under Spanish rule. The wealthy autocrats and the autocratic church party conceived the idea that they could best care for themselves by overthrowing Spanish sovereignty. So they planned an independent despotism where a coterie of Spanish families and powerful clergy would rule over the millions of Indian vassals. Their ambition was to make Mexico safe for autocracy.

Santa Anna grew up in the province of Vera Cruz, at the family residence in the port city of the same name. His father was an official of the port. During his early schooling Santa Anna got a smattering of Voltaire, Montesquieu, Diderot, Raynal, and some of the classics. His father wanted him to pursue a commercial career in the city of Vera Cruz, and farmed him out as an apprentice to a merchant named Jose Vaca, but the boy did not last long in this position. Jose Vaca had a pretty twelve-year-old-daughter, and young Santa Anna, failing in his attempt to seduce her, forcibly raped her. He escaped punishment by joining the Spanish army as a cadet in 1810.

The young cadet saw his first action under the command of Joaquin de Arredondo, when his unit fought and captured a band of insurgents, which Arredondo summarily ordered tortured and put to death. In a later expedition against marauding Indians, Santa Anna suffered an arrow wound in his left arm, for which the Spanish king recognized his loyal service, and the young cadet was promoted to second lieutenant. When Arredondo began his Texas invasion in 1813, Santa Anna was advanced to first lieutenant.

The trouble in Texas had started with the Louisiana Purchase. After the deal was made the United States and Spain got into a controversy over the southwest boundary and compromised by creating the Neutral Ground—a strip of territory between the Aroyo Hondo and Sabine Rivers which neither nation occupied. It had no legal authority, no police system, and a population consisting mainly of Mexicans, Indians, and American adventurers, free-booters, and riff-raff. Yet this motly populace sought to overthrow the power of Spain in the New World. Arredondo led a Spanish army into the province of *Tejas* to suppress the riff-raff.

It was undeniably hot that cruel August when young Lieutenant Santa Anna rode his mount over the desolate and sun-afflicted plain north of Laredo with Arredondo's two thousand-man army—about seven hundred and fifty troops, the rest mounted. There were no villages to give them rest, not even a ranch. As Lieutenant Santa Anna plodded through barren valleys and over rocky hillocks in the blinding glare of the sun and choked on the dust from the advancing army, far away in a totally different world were his real and deadly adversaries—Travis, Bowie, and Crockett. And little did he dream that twenty-three years later he would put them to the sword, and by his act of extreme barbarity inscribe their names on the walls of the temple of glory which he so ardently coveted.

At that time David Crockett was serving with Andrew Jackson's forces in the Alabama wilderness against the warring Creek Indians and dreaming of going home to his wife Polly and their children. Jim Bowie was riding alligators in the bayous of Louisiana and making love in the glade with a beautiful quadroon girl, with whom he had fallen in love. William Barret Travis, barely weaned from his mother Jemima's huge teates, was getting his runny nose and smelly behind wiped by the young black house girl, whose firm round buttocks and sleek legs kept his father, Mark, in a state of constant amorousness.

It was on that bloody expedition that Santa Anna received, first hand, his initiation in the barbarity of dealing with insurgents.

Approaching the Medina River, near San Antonio de Bexar, General Arredondo concealed the main body of his army in a V-shaped ambush in a chapparal which was filled with many oak trees. An advance guard of several hundred men was sent ahead with strict orders to avoid battle, to skirmish, to retreat slowly and draw the enemy back with them.

Seeing the Spanish soldiers falling back, the rebel force swept forward, rushing blindly into the cul-de-sac. Caught in a withering cross-fire, the Americans, whose slogan was "we never retreat," provided the backbone of the resistance. But they fought with hopeless ferocity. Arredondo's troops closed the vice and butchered the eight hundred resisters so efficiently that only ninety-three escaped to bring the story back to Neutral Ground.

During the fighting Santa Anna elected to remain continuously aloof on a hillside at a safe distance from the firing. When he saw that the rebels were thoroughly routed, he gave the bugler the order to blow the *deguello*—a motif that was to be the theme song of his life.

When the young lieutenant entered San Antonio with Arredondo's victorious troops, he witnessed more brutality. Three hundred citizens were rounded up and stuffed into a small inadequate jail. The next morning he watched the troops drag out those still alive. He saw them perched on timbers thrown across a long ditch that had been dug by the soldiers. He calmly stood by as they were unmercifully shot and tumbled into the mass grave. Troops under his command filled in the ditch.

Afterwards the merchandise, wealth, and women of the town became the prize of the victors. It was the old tradition of Spanish cruelty, a tradition from ancient Spanish warfare—the essay of the *deguello*.

The whole campaign built up in the mind of Santa Anna two illusions that were to cost him dearly at a later date. One of these was that the way to handle rebels was by terrorization, and the other was that the Texans were inefficient fighters and could easily be defeated by Mexican troops.

During the years that followed the Texas campaign, Santa Anna was in continuous service. Sometimes he participated in long marches against scattered bands of insurgents, to which he showed the same degree of mercilessness he had learned under General Arrendondo in Texas. But his ambition was not entirely concerned with the military. His mind remained occupied mainly with politics. He became one of the most successful chameleons of Mexican political history—posing successfully as a royalist, a republican, a centralist, a federalist. His adroit changing of colors—at the right time—brought him to the rulership of Mexico on eleven different occasions during his lifetime.

As an officer in the colonial army of the King of Spain, he was sent to deal with the mobilizing patriots supporting Augustin de Iturbide. The rebels invited him to join them. His answer was wholesale slaughter. At two o'clock of the day of the victory he joined the rebellion. His terms for joining included promotion of a full rank. Prior to this *volte-face,* however, he reported his victory—for what it was worth—to his superiors. Word came back that his reward was a colonelcy. Accordingly, he made the revolutionists bid higher for his services.

And there was the Gothicism at Zacatecas. When the Zacatecans rose in revolt, Santa Anna conducted the kind of campaign for which his training had fitted him in the earlier Texas invasion. Here were the same great distances, the same climate, and somewhat the same sections of the country. So he employed the same tactics that Arrendondo had been famed for. After delivering a crushing defeat upon the local troops, he allowed his soldiers to plunder the city, rape the women, murder the civilians wholesale.

The aristocracy and the church found in Augustin de Iturbide a suitable patriot to act as leader. He had been a successful commander of the Royalist forces, and had been called the Prince Rupert of the Spanish Army in Mexico. Iturbide had the sympathy of the clergy, the secret well wishes of the aristocracy, and the noisy enthusiastic support of the proletariat. He became the first emperor of Mexico.

At the time of Iturbide's ascendency, Santa Anna was a power in his own milieu of Santa Cruz. Sitting on the fence waiting to see which way to jump, he was invited to the capitol by Iturbide. There at a reception he met the emperor's sixty-year-old sister, in whom he saw an excellent opportunity for advancement. He proposed marriage to her, and took her to bed. "She looked lovely," he later told his brother-in-law, General Martin Cos, "with her waist held in with corsets, her bosom scaffolded by whalebone, and the crowsfeet around her eyes concealed by layers of paint. But in the bedroom, stripped of her accoutrements, she was a flabby breasted, dried-titted old tub of lard with rotted breath over which I labored with considerable disgust. Afterwards I made two vows: I would henceforth gain my stars on the battlefield, and never as long as I live make love with a female beyond the age of twenty."

His first wife, Inez Garciea was fifteen at the time of their marriage, his second, when he was a middle-aged man, thirteen; and like his hero Napoleon, wherever his campaigns carried him, he always found a teen-age *amante*.

Santa Anna had come a long way since the Texas campaign of 1813, making the necessary sudden hairpin turns in his politics and loyalties to push himself up the ladder to glory and power. He had stood by while rivals were exiled and watched with apathy when old friends were shot. But he had survived. Through a series of revolutions and betrayals he emerged as a full general and a five-alarm national hero.

In 1833, at the age of thirty-nine, he assumed office as President-General of Mexico. His aim was absolute dictatorship. In the process of this achievement he dissolved the Mexican congress and appointed stooges of his own to rule over various states and important towns. In a word, he abolished the United States of Mexico, deprived the states of all autonomy, and substituted for the old constitution one authorizing absolute control.

Three years after his ascendency to the dictatorship of Mexico he will again march into Texas, at the head of his most powerful army. No one will ever know the magnitude of his ambitions when he begins the invasion. He will suggest to one of his aides that he intends to "plant the Mexican flag in Washington." But just forty-six days after his triumph over the Alamo defenders, his army will be ignominiously defeated at San Jacinto. In later times he will read an account of the battle written by one of General Houston's soldiers and become enraged at the "inaccuracies" chronicled by that amateur historian. Especially will he become incensed at the vignette of himself being forced to stand before Houston, stripped of all rank and finery, and Houston, wounded and lying propped against the trunk of a cottonwood tree with a jug of whiskey by his side, levelling at the defeated Mexican dictator a bitter and scathing but pontifical tirade because of the massacre of the Alamo. Santa Anna will declaim that Houston did no such thing; that the painracked general raised his bleary eyes, looked him up and down with abject disgust and uttered a single objurgatory word: "Shit!"

Santa Anna will remain in American captivity more than a year but will eventually be returned to Mexico through Washington. Later he will emerge to fight the French occupation forces at Vera Cruz. Wounded, he will lose a leg to incompetent battlefield surgeons; a hero, he will again become president only to be exiled to Cuba for incompetence and extravagance.

In the Mexico-United States war, after a secret agreement with President James K. Polk, Santa Anna will again assume the presidency. But as commander of the Mexican forces he will prematurely rush his troops to the north, where desert campaigning, complicated by a drawn battle with General Zachary Taylor, will cost him his army. He will be returned to exile in Jamaica and New Granada. In 1853 governmental chaos will once more recall him to become president, but age will have exaggerated his shortcomings and he will be banished in 1855.

Ten years later Santa Anna will seek United States support in ousting Austrian Prince Maximillian; at the same time he will offer his services to Maximillian. But by now he will have prostituted himself too often; both proposals will be refused.

As an old man, nearly blind, he will live in penury on Staten Island, New York, awaiting permission to return to his native Mexico, where he will die in poverty June 21, 1876, at the age of eighty-two.

While residing on Staten Island he will eke out a livelihood by importing chicle into the United States from Central America. Ingenious Americans will introduce to the world a new, senseless produce made of this substance; therefore, Santa Anna might seriously be called the "father of chewing gum." Nearly a century later, a crusty Texas governor, irate and profane because of sticky wads of the pesky gum continually fouling the soles of his shoes, will declare: "The most heinous thing old Santa Anna ever did was to import into the United States that goddamn stuff Mr. Wrigley makes chewing gum out of."

As General of the Army, on his way to absolute power, Santa Anna lent a sympathetic ear to Texans' grievances and made them many promises to protect their rights and liberty. But now, as President-General, he was watching them with an eagle eye and taking advantage of every opportunity to exercise his power. He sent Colonel Juan N. Almonte, one of his loyal stooges, to tour Texas presumably to reassure the colonists of his continued sympathy and to determine their needs but secretly to estimate their strength, vulnerability to attack, their various assets, and to gauge their loyalty.

Santa Anna had an uncommon perceptive sense. He saw as clearly as William Barret Travis that war was inevitable. But he needed time to recruit a powerful force and supply it with the extraordinary equipment necessary for the invasion of Texas. In furtherance of this scheme he appointed his brother-in-law, Martin Perfecto de Cos, as commander of the Eastern Provinces.

When the two-year tariff exemption ended, Santa Anna reopened the custom houses. Captain Antonio Tenario was sent with a detachment of soldiers to occupy the post.

Although Captain Tenario was not a real knave, he was having his problems with the settlers at Anahuac.

329

The Americans simply rejected repression of any degree. Tenario sent a request to General Cos for reinforcements. In reply General Cos sent word to Tenario that troops would depart immediately for the Texas coast; the dispatch also stated that "the revolutionists will be ground down . . ."

Spies of the War Party intercepted the dispatch and turned it over to Travis and his friends. Santa Anna was opening the way for war. Travis was elated and he took immediate action. He called for volunteers to march to the relief of Anahuac. Travis' excitement became infectious. Meetings were held. Leaders of the Peace Party talked. Hot heads of the War Party talked. Travis proposed to raise three hundred men, march to the coast and reduce the garrison at Anahuac and seize the arms and ammunition for the cause of the colonists. He was shouted down by voice of the Peace Party. He called them fools and stalked out. Completely convinced that now was the time for action, he began to recruit secretly. He felt his friends in Anahuac were being persecuted.

Thirty stalwarts agreed to follow Travis. They quickly pooled money and supplies and formed an army, such as it was. They elected Travis captain, chartered a forty-five ton sloop and two yawls, loaded a six-pound cannon mounted on a pair of sawmill truck wheels on board the sloop and set out for the bay.

Travis had the good fortune to discover a fine Prussian sword that some German settler had traded to Mr. Dinsmore for more needful commodities. It was an unusual and handsome sword. The scabbard was of black leather inlaid with gold trimming and hung with a twisted red cord. The sword was a *Kavallerie* saber made in Solingen, Germany. It had a wrapped leather grip and a pommel fastened by a silver capstan rivet, and a gold guilloche and knuckle bow. The blade itself was made of carbon steel and was shallow-hollowed down the center to give it lightness. Near the hilt on the blade, graven into the steel, was the symbol of a running wolf and the letters *Inglred,* denoting its origin.

This sword was a source of great pride for Travis. He considered finding such a beautiful and rare weapon as a good omen. He now donned it as a symbol of his command.

In the chill that presaged the coming of dawn, the little sloop *Ohio* heeled over slightly. Travis pulled up his collar. The damp fog, light and opaque, drifted in from the gulf. A full moon sailed rakishly through a sea of small blue clouds, touching the brown water of the estuary with highlights. It was still night. Travis listened to the creaking of the cordage and timbers, and dull wash of the waves, and thought solemn thoughts. The six-pounder, lashed securely to prevent it from rolling and slipping, cast an incongruous shadow on the deck in the white moonlight. The presence of the cannon lent a certain bravado to Travis' thoughts. The inert bulks of the men sleeping here and there warmed his breast. Some Texans were ready to fight. Bedamned! he thought, why couldn't the farmers and the ranchers see that they *had* to come forward and support the War Party. But they, the bone and the sinew of the country, were against it.

Stephen F. Austin, it was rumored, had at long last been set free in Mexico City and was on his way home to Texas. Travis wondered what Austin would have to tell his followers when he arrived in San Felipe. It had been a year and longer since Austin made the journey to Mexico to present a list of reforms to the government. Among them was the important proposal that Texas be separated from the state of Coahuila, to which it was attached. Texans didn't like this connection because it was Coahuila and not Texas that made the laws. Other reforms Austin hoped to accomplish were the repeal of the law prohibiting further immigration from the United States, and certain improvements in the judicial system. But for his concern he was called a traitor, arrested, and confined to solitary imprisonment, a sick man suffering from amoebic dysentary.

It was the farmers and ranchers who were most anx-

331

ious that Austin go to Mexico to seek a compromise with the government. They were the strength of the Peace Party. But they were all doing well and Travis knew that as long as people are prosperous they stand opposed to any change that might disrupt their state of affluence. He reflected sadly on how public opinion was so much against his own. He had to find a way to convince the people that independence, their very lives, hung on Santa Anna's sword. Austin's return might open up such a way—if he was now convinced that only by fighting could Texans gain their liberties.

Travis thought back on his years in San Felipe. Since his arrival there he had become a name among the *norteamericanos,* and for that matter to Mexican officialdom. He had established himself as an attorney of incisive ability and quite a social blade. Success and popularity came naturally to him; he was bidding fair to fame and fortune. Underneath, though, he burned with his belief that Texas—and William Barret Travis—would only achieve true stature under the Anglo-American government. He had written to Jim Bonham: "I think that Texas is forever ruined unless the citizens make a manly, energetic effort to save themselves from anarchy and confusion, which are the worst of evils . . ."

But there were brighter things. He remembered the day he got lost on horseback and came upon a saw-and-grist mill on the bank of a creek he had been following. Logs were racked everywhere and a few slaves busied themselves, but not too energetically, with the chores of the mill.

"Where is your master?" Travis called to them.

An old darky pointed to a doorway that apparently led to an office. Travis dismounted and went into the building, calling "Hallo! Hallo! Anybody here?"

"In here!" a ringing voice called back.

He entered the office and found, standing before a high counter and bent over a set of books, an auburn-haired woman whom he judged to be in her mid-twenties, wearing a hunting shirt and leather breeches. She turned around, gave him a perfunctory glance.

"What can I do for you?"

Travis said nothing at the instant. He was somewhat surprised to find a woman in a saw-and-grist mill, dressed in men's clothing doing a man's job— bookkeeping. And such an attractive woman. At least, the parts of her that were not concealed by her clumsy attire. He saw wide brown eyes, unblemished skin, a firm chin, and full soft lips. Austin's colony was pre-dominantly masculine; women were supposed to be confined to the kitchen, bed chamber, spinning wheel, and garden. Their prime function on the frontier was to provide men with man-children to help men tame the wilderness, not to don men's clothing and man men's businesses. The woman smiled slightly, the smile re-maining on her lips as she gazed at him with that singu-lar expressive look which women often give a new man, the look that mirrors neither curiosity nor expectation, but a judgement secret and withheld.

She extended her hand. "I'm Rebecca Cummings. My brother John and I run this mill."

Travis took her hand, made a little gentlemanly bow. "I'm William Travis. I'm a lawyer and I've been with a client a little distance east of here. I seem to have lost my way. I live in San Felipe."

"You're only seven miles from home, Mr. Travis."

The man who walked through the door, Travis knew, was John Cummings, but he had none of his sister's openness of face. His eyes, in contrast to hers, were small and did not look into Travis' as he talked but constantly changed focus, shifting from Travis to his sister. A most circumspect fellow.

"Oh, yes," John Cummings said, having entered the room on the latter part of the conversation. "Travis. I've heard things about you."

Travis smiled. "Nothing greatly edifying, I'm sure. Only perhaps that I'm an overdressed dandy or that I'm an undeclared enemy of Santa Anna's."

This brought forth from Rebecca Cummings an

333

amused smile and caused her brother a little rueful grin. It disarmed them both.

"Now that you're here, Mr. Travis," the brother said, "and it's getting nigh onto dark, pray stay and snack with us."

In addition to the saw-and-grist mill, the Cummings owned and operated the Mill Creek Inn, which constituted the main portion of the large building, of which the mill was a lesser part; the inn also served as home for the Cummings. A Negro slave took Travis' horse and led him to the stable, which was located on one side of the slave huts behind the inn. John Cummings led the way to the main part of the building.

While the evening meal was being prepared, Travis and John Cummings sat in the parlor talking. Rebecca had gone abovestairs. Their conversation quite naturally centered on politics. John Cummings was a confirmed Peace Party man. He wanted nothing to occur that would change the status quo of the settlers. In addition to the mill and tavern, which he said were quite profitable, he had taken a headright on a large section of land. War must be avoided, he said. The settlers had to "get along with those fellows in Mexico City." Travis, since he was a guest, kept his violent feelings mostly to himself.

When Rebecca came down the stairs Travis was completely overwhelmed. A transformation divine. Her hair had been combed out and set in a neat bun at the nape of her neck, which gave more expression to her great, soft eyes. She had changed her mill attire for a New York manufactured gown of soft blue that was high-waisted, low-cut Empire fashion, and the loveliness of all the world was in the cleft of that bosom, half concealed, half revealed.

Modesty was not a bedfellow of Travis'. He was quite aware that he was practically irresistible to women, and he took a personal pride in keeping a record of the number he had slept with. Only two days ago he had recorded in his diary: " . . Made love with Luise S———, which is number fifty-seven." As he

334

feasted his eyes upon that magnificent bosom he wondered what number Rebecca Cummings would occupy in his diary.

"May I say, Miss Cummings, not since I left Alabama have I beheld such loveliness!"

"Pooh! Mr. Travis, I'm just a farm woman." Her throw-away remark was without conviction: the flush under her skin gave her away. "Come, I think dinner is waiting." She led the way into the dining hall.

After the meal, John Cummings excused himself, saying that some chores awaited him at the mill. Travis and Rebecca retired to the parlor.

"You've never married, Miss Cummings, I believe you said?"

Travis worked at being charming, giving his best smiles at the right time and holding his best pose. In her eyes was an equivocal little light: he knew she was debating what treatment she should accord him, and wondered if she was finding amusement or admiration in his extravagant tailoring: red pantaloons and flamboyant waistcoat.

"I didn't say, Mr. Travis. You are putting words in my mouth. No, I've never married. If you were asking why I never married, the answer is, I suppose, I've never taken the time. My father died some years ago, then my two younger brothers, William and James, after them, then my mother. There's only John and myself left to manage the mill and tavern. I really haven't had time to think about marrying. And, please, Mr. Travis, I'd feel more at ease if you'd call me Rebecca or Becky, whichever you prefer. How do your friends call you? William, Willie, Will?"

"They call me Bill. I think I like Rebecca for you. You, with your gentility . . . why, Becky is just not right for you. Too earthy, too farm-girlish. Rebecca, yes! That's right for you. Rebecca it shall be!"

"Pooh! Mr. Travis, you're a flatterer. I'm sorry . . . Bill. But suit yourself." She looked at him with a level gaze. "Are you a bachelor?"

Taken aback, he didn't answer right away. That

question was impertinent, he thought. But, on reflection, he didn't mind, really. Men either had families or were single. She was single; therefore, his marital status was important to her. He answered her in a tone that was both judicious and kindly. "Let's say, Rebecca, that my wife is married."

She gave a bright little laugh, quite inoffensively. "Now, that *is* clever, really! If you're something of a rake, Bill, and living with your wife I'd take that as a rather ribald answer. But quite obviously you're not a rake, and just as obviously you are a gentleman, and so I take it that you are a 'single man'."

Travis reddened, then put his embarrassment aside with a smile. "Thanks, Rebecca. For putting me in my place. The facts are simple. I left my wife and son in Claiborne, Alabama, three years ago. I understand that shortly afterward a daughter was born to her. I do not love my wife. It was an unpleasant relationship. I expect to be divorced."

His reply was so frank and bold that Rebecca felt a quiet embarrassment. "I'm sorry," she said softly. "I didn't mean to pry."

Rebecca lifted a small bell from the table between them, tinkled it; after a few moments a Negro girl entered.

"Mehetibel, go to the barroom and bring a bottle of that red wine from under the counter, one that has a dark brown label on it. You understand which one, Mehetibel?" Quickly to Travis, "Oh, pardon me. It's a very good port. But perhaps you prefer whiskey?"

"Port will be just fine, Rebecca."

After a few glasses of the rich red wine, Travis lapsed into a conversation about his own interests: his law practice and life in San Felipe. He spoke of drawing up wills, collecting bad debts, and handling probate matters. He told Rebecca about how he prevented the sale of a blind horse to a widowed farm woman: how he recovered a stolen chamber pot; how he cleared the title of some slaves for a planter and received a young

336

Negro boy as fee. He owned four Negroes now, he told her—Jack, Simon, Peter, and Jared, the small boy. The problem was what to do with them. He had a small problem with Simon. The Negro liked to drink, when he could lay hands on liquor. He had had to whip him three times.

John Cummings returned, scoffed at the wine, ordered Mehetibel to bring him a bottle of whiskey, and the conversation quickly got around to politics. Travis was in his element. He talked about his friends and their revolutionist views: Three-Legged-Willie, the Jack brothers, Noah Smithwich, Henry Smith, James Robinson, Ben Milam and others. John Cummings expressed the view that "those hotheads will have to come to their senses before they cause a war or we will lose everything we've worked like the devil for."

Travis thought, for the sake of being invited again, he'd best turn the conversation to the social side. He got on the subject of gambling, explaining to Rebecca some of the points of poker, euchre, faro, monte, and brag. He told of winnings and losses, taking both lightly. He spoke of Mrs. James Long. She was, he thought, a woman of great beauty, charm, and intelligence. He said he had left his young Negro boy Jared in her keeping. He talked about some books he had read recently: four volumes of "Febrero," "Westward Ho!". One of his favorite authors was Sir Walter Scott. He was, he said, now reading "Ivanhoe." Would she like to borrow some of these books?

John Cummings was not interested in Travis' gambling friends or his reading habits. He seemed concerned only with keeping the War Party in check. He was interested in Travis' adult slaves, though. He offered to take them off his hands and pay a nominal fee and their keep if Travis wished to farm them out for work at the mill. Travis agreed almost too quickly. This would give him good reason for visiting Mill Creek Inn often.

"I allow," John Cummings said, bringing the conver-

337

sation back to his favorite topic, "we had better let Mr. Austin set our sails for us. He'll get what's right for us. He'll work something out with Santa Anna. You'll see, Travis. Just stick tight with Mr. Austin."

Travis could not let his host's remarks go without at least a mild rebuttal. "When I arrived in Texas," Travis said, "I wanted separate statehood for Texas under the Mexican Constitution of 1824. When Santa Anna first came to power it seemed we'd get it. But now we see our independence being constantly eroded away. Every day we delay in taking up the fight for our rights is a day taken away from us and given to Santa Anna in his scheme to suppress us."

"I'm a man of peace, Travis." There was impatient hostility in John Cummings' voice. "We—our whole family—came to Texas back in '24. We hoped to make our fortune here—and be happy in this land. We took an extensive head-right with Mr. Austin, and all that's left of us is Becky and me. But we'll do all right. The land will be worth a fortune someday—unless your hotheaded friends get us into a war. No, Travis, I'm for peace."

"John, I'm afraid you're nursing an old fallacy, and a dangerous one—peace at any price. You're only beguiling yourself. When you start paying for peace piecemeal with your personal liberties, you begin selling off your manhood."

John Cummings bristled. "Manhood!" He gave Travis' dandified clothes a disdainful look. "I've got plenty of manhood. And I don't have to prove it by going to war."

"Nobody said otherwise, John. But we're talking about our liberty. That is something we have to fight for every day of our lives or it is eroded away."

John Cummings took a drink of his whiskey, gave Travis a little benign smile. "I ain't lost no liberty yet, as I can see. We Texans have to be quiet and peaceful. And when Santa Anna sees that we are men of peace

338

he'll be a right sort of fellow himself and let us have our due."

Travis' face flushed. This was the kind of suicidal talk he heard every day from Austin's people. It wasn't easy for him to restrain himself. But he was enamored of John's sister, who had politely remained silent while the two men engaged in their political encounter. Perhaps she, too, he thought, was playing the same game: leaving the way open for him to come back. Travis rose, smiling at Rebecca.

"I trust our 'man talk' has not bored you, Rebecca."

To his astonishment, she said, giving him a supporting smile, "Not at all. I thoroughly agree with you. I've never been able to make John see it, though. Maybe with you on my side we can change him."

Travis' heart warmed. He suddenly had a different feeling for Rebecca, and he rebuked himself for his initial thoughts about her. "It's late," he said. "I'd better start for San Felipe."

"Not a t'all!" John Cummings said. "You're staying the night—as our honored guest."

Travis thought back on all this, standing on the slanting deck of the yawl in the misty pre-dawn. He glanced around at the sleeping men, bundled in their blankets and jackets. The *Ohio* was sailing smoothly into wider waters, and the sky was growing lighter. Ahead in the bow of the ship he saw two figures, up and about.

He was pleased that others were up and astir. He made his way forward over the coils of rope and other obstructions on the dim deck. The two men were his first lieutenant, Ritson Morris, and John W. Moore, orderly sergeant.

"I thought I saw a sail out in the bay," Riston Morris said. "Out there—"

Travis squinted his eyes, looking in the direction Morris was pointing. The mist was lifting.

"There she is!" Morris exclaimed. "She's closing in."

"Lieutenant, take four men and one of the yawls and

intercept her," Travis ordered. "If she's Mexican, delay her as long as you can."

They were now in sight of the shore. Everybody was on his feet and the little sloop was astir with excitement. The men were wolfing down bread and salted meat. Some ingenious persons had heated coffee in an old iron wash pot and the men were scalding their throats with the steaming brew. All the while they were anxiously watching Lieutenant Morris and his little crew of four as the yawl reached out toward the oncoming sail.

Travis ordered the six-pounder readied for action. Sergeant Moore was in charge of the cannon. He quickly saw to its charging and had it aimed toward the Mexican barracks, which were now discernable in the first light.

"You may fire when ready, Sergeant Moore," Travis commanded, his hand resting gallantly on the hilt of his Prussian sword. He felt the role of an officer and, in red pantaloons, green waistcoat over his Garibaldi shirt, and in a high beaver hat, he looked impressive, if not authentic.

Moore lowered the burning fuse to the vent. The cannon roared, lurched backward, blazing forth its charge in a long column of fire and smoke. A cheer went up from all on board. Moore was already busy recharging the cannon. Travis ordered it fired again, and again. Every man aboard strained his eyes toward Anahuac. There was no sign of a reply.

A little way to the south of the *Ohio,* Lieutenant Morris was approaching in the yawl and directly behind him was the sailing boat. Attention of the men now turned to this development. The yawl and the sailing boat came alongside. Travis stood at the rail of the *Ohio,* his sword drawn.

"They're friends," Lieutenant Morris called. "They want to come aboard."

The men of the sailing boat were a crew of fishermen, and Travis received them cordially. They were as anxious to rid the coast of Mexican troops as were Tra-

340

vis and his men. The *Ohio* and its satellites now moved in closer to the shore.

The cannon shots, at least, had brought an audience, whether friendly or unfriendly. The shore was now lined with people. And in the background the first rays of sunlight glinted on the guns and trappings of Mexican soldiers marching before their barracks.

Travis ordered the cannon and its makeshift wheels loaded on the two yawls. During the procedure he and a contingent of sixteen men, armed with their rifles, shotguns, and pistols, pushed ashore in the fishing vessel. They expected to be met by fire from the Mexican troops. Strangely, and to Travis' confusion, the soldiers were not rushing toward the landing. The Mexicans could have put up a fierce fight among the driftwood and debris while Travis was getting his men and the cannon ashore. But Captain Tenario's soldiers fired not a shot.

In the fewest minutes the landing was completed. With the cannon hastily assembled and remounted on the truck wheels, the little American force, with their brilliantly attired captain, sword drawn, advanced upon the Mexican barracks.

There was caution, there was mumbling, there was the sound of the cocking of rifles and pistols—and there was courage aplenty. Any moment withering blasts of gunfire were expected from the walls of the Mexican fort.

Suddenly a lone civilian was seen running toward Travis, waving a piece of white paper. Travis raised his arm, halting his men. The runner approached and Travis took the paper from his trembling fingers. It was a note from Captain Tenario but was signed by Judge William Duncan, the highest civilian official of the colony. The note demanded reasons for the action and directed the Texans "not to disturb the tranquility of this municipality."

Travis dispatched a verbal reply: he would answer in thirty minutes. He asked for a pen and paper. Lieutenant Morris quickly produced them. Travis penned a

341

curt order, demanding the surrender of the garrison, together with arms and supplies, and a written statement that the officers and soldiers would never again serve against Texas.

All day Travis waited for a reply, his men within rifle shot of the garrison, his six-pounder loaded and aimed at the garrison gate. Sergeant Moore was ordered to keep his lighting taper burning at all times. No shots came from the fort, no messenger emerged.

When darkness descended Travis decided that no reply was forthcoming. He formed his troops in battle lines, with a six-man advance guard, followed by a man bearing a torch, next riflemen, and lastly the cannon crew. Travis shouted the order and, leading the force with sword in one hand and a pistol in the other, he advanced against the fort at a gallop.

Not a shot halted the brave little army. They reached the gate and broke it down to find the garrison deserted. Tenario with his men had retreated into a woods behind the garrison. Travis took possession of the fort, and ordered Sergeant Moore to turn the cannon on the woods where he suspected Tenario and his soldiers were hiding. Half a dozen shots blasted into the woods and an officer from Tenario's forces came out waving a white flag on the barrel of his rifle, accompanied by a sergeant bearing a torch. Travis received the pair into the fort. Tenario, said the captain, requested that Travis meet with him on the river bank for a conference.

Travis agreed; a place was named and a time set for the meeting. Having no faith in the honor of the Mexican, Travis had three sharpshooters accompany him unseen at a distance. He halted his men in a clump of shrubbery about thirty yards from the river with the instructions to pick off Tenario at the first indication of treachery. Then, alone, Travis advanced to the bank. In the moonlight his silhouette was distinctly visible. But the moonlight did not reveal the outlines of Tenario or his men.

Travis called in his best Spanish: "I'm here, Captain

Tenario. You can see me clearly. If you are the knave I think you are, you can shoot me down. If you have any honor you'll come out and talk."

There was silence, only the river returned a reply, a faint echo of Travis' voice.

"I'll wait sixty seconds, Tenario."

In a few moments the Mexican answered, the voice in English coming from a place of concealment. "You want to keel me, *Americano?*"

"I said we'd talk."

"No . . . I no come out. You want to keel me, no?"

"Where are you, Tenario? I'll come to you."

"You come here—where I am, *Americano?*"

"Just keep talking. I'll find you."

It could have been a trap, but Travis seemed not to know the name of fear. He found Tenario crouched in a declivity, covered with buffalo grass. When Travis convinced the Mexican he was alone, Tenario came out. The two men talked face to face. Tenario asked what Travis wanted, what terms.

"Captain Tenario," Travis said ostentatiously, "I have fired the first shot of liberation. No longer will Texans be ground under the heel of the tyrants of Coahuila. Texas will be a state of its own. We demand a return to the decency of the reform laws of the Mexican Constitution of 1824. Short of this, all Texans are prepared to join in the fight for complete separation and independence from Mexico. Immediately I demand your surrender at my pleasure. You will deliver up your arms and all supplies, and I will guarantee your safe departure for Mexico."

There were indeed powerful words, particularly from a young man not yet twenty-six years old, standing alone against a disciplined company of Mexican soldiers, with only thirty unruly civilians playing soldier to back up those high-sounding words. No Napoleon, no Caesar, or Frederick the Great would have risked a similar situation without powerful legions flanking him.

Tenario asked to be permitted until morning to con-

343

sider Travis' demands. This would be fatal and Travis was soldier enough to know it. He sumarily refused.

"Captain Tenario, you have fifteen minutes." Travis made the pronouncement levely, authoritatively.

"And if I do not?"

Travis played his last card. The entire gamble depended on his final word. "Then, Sir, I regret to inform you that you and every one of your men will be put to the sword."

Even in the pale moonlight Travis saw his words go home. Tenario's face became sickly, he coughed, his eyes shifted.

"Agreed," he said hoarsely.

The next morning the two men signed papers of capitulation. Tenario surrendered "sixty-four stands of arms (muskets and bayonets) and twenty-one cartridge boxes," which Travis distributed among his men. Tenario begged to be allowed to retain twelve muskets for his men to protect themselves from Indians while on the long march to Mexico.

Upon his return to San Felipe, Travis found, to his dismay, that he was by no means welcomed as a conquering hero. The news of his action had spread rapidly. The colonists were shocked and frightened at his audacity. Austin was expected any day now, and a great many of the colonists, despite the many ominous indications to the contrary, still believed that Santa Anna would deal justly with them. Austin, they felt, would bring with him an acceptable peace plan. The immediate result of Travis' action was to draw the members of the Peace Party closer together, while raising doubts in the minds of the less dedicated of the War Party.

And, it being the nature of organized man to ever seek a villain as the cause of mankind's ills, Travis was their self-made culprit. While others had grumbled and protested and threatened among themselves. Travis had taken the bull by the horns and thrown out the garrison command: practically open rebellion. Few were ready

344

to go that far. Travis was leading them much too fast. They pinned the entire blame on him and condemned him for his precipitate behavior. The dissent would not die away, the grumblers would not be quiet, so finally Travis, against his better judgment, and swallowing bitter gall, published an open letter to General Martin Cos, Santa Anna's occupation commander in San Antonio. He wrote:

" ... If you will condescend to open a correspondence with me on this subject. I think that a good understanding may be brought about. I assure you the inhabitants are in the best disposition for it. The reason I ask this favor of you is because I think it will produce the most beneficial results, both for the government and for the people of Texas."

This cooled many tempers temporarily, but everyone awaited General Cos' response.

Travis told himself he had been too busy meeting with groups and organizations and friends explaining his position to go to Mill Creek, although Rebecca was constantly on his mind. But in reality he felt too embarrassed to face her just yet. During the two years intervening since he had met her, he had been almost a steady weekend guest at the Mill Creek Tavern. The course of his romance with Rebecca had not at all times run smoothly. It had never been Travis' nature to deny any woman the pleasure of company. And women came to bed easily with him. He took them as if they were gold pieces to be gathered up from the pavements of heaven. In dress he was fastidious, in appearance impressive, in grooming meticulous. He wore pumps and stockings to balls instead of the usual boots worn on the frontier and used ointment on his hair and such perfumes and toilet waters as bergamot and lavender. And, of course, in manner he was always charming. In his diary there were listed names of women, some prominent

345

names of the colony, some nobodys, some Negro slaves, with whom he had shared his six-foot, handsome body, and there were many he had not listed for reasons known only to himself. Among those of prominence that he did list were: Juanita Gonzales, Louise Sixts, Senorita Herta, Millie Wolf, Helen Stokes, Carolyn Moore, J. Long.

Stories of Travis' amours were tittered in corners of drawing rooms, at "quiltings," at the bars in taverns and inns, and in the fields by farmers and planters. And they had reached the sensitive ears of Rebecca Cummings. She was especially incensed over his reputed affair with Jane Long. Try as he might Travis found it difficult to explain away the deleterious rumors by claiming that Jane was merely a good friend who sometimes made him shirts from materials he bought at Dinsmore's and kept his slave boy Jared. It was surreptuously said in taverns when the bottle got on the empty side "Old Ben Milam's gonna shoot the nuts off'n that dandy Bill Travis one of these nights, when he comes to Jane's and catches him friggin her."

Travis became engaged to Rebecca after a six weeks complete abstinance of her—and all others. Jane Long's Negro girl, Ruda, had grown into a pretty sixteen-year-old, well-matured, with firm, round chocolate-colored breasts, and brilliantly white teeth, which were ever in evidence because of the wide smile she wore for the male guests at Jane's inn. This girl Ruda was undoubtedly the magnet that brought so many transients to the inn. Her name was passed along from lip to lip with a sensuous grin by male travelers far and wide. Jane had few women guests.

Ruda was part-time servant to Travis, and so was daily in and out of his rooms, picking up his clothes, taking them away for cleaning or bringing them back and straightening up his quarters.

One late afternoon Ruda was in Travis' rooms while he was getting dressed for a ball at the Warton brothers' farm. She had brought his freshly laundered Garibaldi shirts. Lounging on his bed and watching him

346

as he primped and perfumed himself, she said, "Marse Travis, how cum you don't never want no hoochipat from me?"

Travis turned toward the girl, amused. "Ruda, when did you have a bath?"

"What's a bath got to do with it, Marse Travis? I washes myself down dere all the time, ever time I frigs somebody."

Travis burst out laughing, but he sat on the bed beside Ruda, unbuttoned her waist. "You're quite attractive, Ruda," he said, passing his hand over her shoulders, her breasts, and abdomen. "I had no idea what you really had underneath those ugly clothes." He was amazed at the smoothness of her body; never had his hands felt such fine texture of skin.

While his hands were busy. Ruda was looking up into his face with her sparkling black eyes, a wide innocent-looking smile on her face. Suddenly, without expecting or inviting it, there it was again—that old devil, itching away at his crotch.

"All right, Ruda. Get your skirt off. But if you ever tell Miss Jane, so help me, I'll bullwhip you to within an inch of your black little life! You understand?"

"Yessa, Marse Travis. I ain't gonna tell Miss Jane. I ain't gonna tell nobody."

That's how it began with Ruda. Travis found this young Negress completely responsive, uninhibited, and ravishing. She was always there, it seemed, when he felt the need of sex. There never was the necessity of nonsensical preliminaries, she was always ready, she was always willing, always smiling—and always delicious. And, as it turned out, Travis noticed that his clothes were getting laundered a lot more frequently. They were cleaner, always done promptly. It seemed that everytime he returned to his rooms, Ruda's smiling face greeted him.

But, as Travis' uncle, the Reverend Alexander Travis, in his best Baptist tradition would have exhorted: "The Wages of Sin Are Death." So it was that Bill Travis took his sins to Dr. Amos Pollard. The good doctor

347

bade Travis take down his breeches and lay on the examining table, while he pressed his fingers in the patient's groin, gently squeezed his testicles, and, finally, milked a light yellow substance from his urethral channel. He straightened up with a look of a professor who had just discovered a fatal error in an examination paper. "My boy, you've got a fine case of gonorrhea!" he announced almost gleefully, it seemed to Travis.

"Goddamn!" Travis sat up. He put his elbows on his knees, pressed his hands to the side of his head. "Goddamn that wench! And she told me she washed after every fuck."

"What wench?" Dr. Pollard was intense, all ears.

"Why? Want me to kiss and tell?"

"Not at all. Yours is the third case this week. One man had already let his advance to a stage of epididymis. Awful mess. If I can treat the carrier we might prevent an epidemic."

"What's epididymis, Doc?"

"That's when your testicles get about as big as falconet cannon balls."

"Any danger of it getting to mine?"

"You came to me in time. Now, when did you have your last exposure?"

Travis inclined his head, trying to remember the sequences. He was at Mill Creek two weeks ago, slept with the Gonzales girl after that on Tuesday night, then the next day there was Susana. That would be twelve days ago. But in the meantime, there had been Ruda, who was always underfoot.

"How long ago, Doc?"

"Normally it takes from two to ten days for the disease to show up, after exposure."

"I'll send the carrier in to you this afternoon. No! I'll bring her in myself, to be sure you stop it where it is. Now, how about me?"

"I'll put you on an elixir of my own. It's a compound of several drugs and chemicals, with a base of potassium. It'll make you piss a beautiful blue, otherwise you won't notice a thing. But——" Dr. Pollard held up

348

a finger of caution. "No sex! You'll only spread the disease and prolong your recovery."

"How long will I be out of action, Doc?"

"With luck—and your complete cooperation—six weeks."

So Travis stayed away from Mill Creek religiously. During that period he went through the three stages of gonorrhea hangover: first, shame and mortification; then remorse and regret; finally reform. Why did he always have to possess so many women? he asked himself, with sincere contrition. Never had he drawn the line as to age or comeliness. If she was a woman and available, he always tried to take her to bed; all women were his target. Why could he not be content with one woman? Rebecca certainly gave him wholesome and complete satisfaction and love. Her body was luxurious—soft round hips, great warm breasts, tender, sweet mouth. A fine wholesome woman. He resolved firmly that, once he was rid of the disease, he would eschew all others. Yes, he'd marry Rebecca and put an end to his profligate life. It would be different this time. There'd be no repetition of the unhappiness he'd experienced with Rosana.

When Dr. Pollard pronounced him well and fit, he immediately put in an appearance at Mill Creek, making what he thought to be a logical explanation for his absence. And he swore to Rebecca—and he could do so with a clear conscience—that he had not been with Jane Long or any other woman during his neglect of her.

"I love you Rebecca. These weeks away from you have opened my eyes, made me see things about you I didn't know."

"What things, Bill?"

"That I want you for my wife. I want you desperately. Only you, Rebecca. I do love you. Yes, I love you, Rebecca!"

Of a certainty he did love Rebecca, he told himself, and he really did want to marry her. (He even told this to himself the next morning, after having slept with her.) But her brother John was reticent and sullen toward Travis. How could he, John Cummings wanted to know, still married, propose marriage to a fine, virtuous woman like Rebecca?

"But my wife has made application with the Alabama legislature for a divorce," Travis protested. "I should get notice of its finalization any day now."

That night, when her brother was sound asleep, Rebecca—as she always had done whenever Travis was their guest—came softly to his room in her bare feet. Never before had she been so passionately in love with him and never had she shown so much ardor in her lovemaking. When she had to leave his bed at daybreak to be safely back in her room before her brother awakened, he was positive in his resolutions to forsake all others—a noble resolution but one that it was not in his nature to keep.

A week went by after Travis' open letter to General Cos appeared in the *Texas Gazette* and no reply came from San Antonio. Rumors of Austin's imminent return to San Felipe were everywhere. Would the leader of the colony upon his return alleviate or exacerbate Travis' situation? He had hoped to have a meeting with the Mexican commandant before Austin's arrival, an assuagement of things. So, Travis waited, his status shaky at best.

As Travis was leaving his office Simon approached him with a note. It read:

The news is all over that you're back. Looked for you every day. Please come—today if you can. Will expect you at four.

Rebecca.

Travis hadn't gone to see Rebecca, he told himself, because he had been too busy. But that was only a good excuse for the real reason. He was afraid to face Rebecca and her brother since his Anahuac expedition. He knew what John Cummings' attitude would be. But what about Rebecca? Would she too condemn him?

Here was a mystery. A request to come, at a stated time. Today. The entire tone of the note was formal. Was his disgrace so complete that she wanted to break off the engagement?

If Rebecca's note was a mystery, it was a small one compared to the surprising letter he received the day before. Rosana's brother had written him that his wife was preparing a trip to Texas and was bringing their children with her. It was true that he had requested custody of his son, Charles Edward, in the divorce proceedings. But the boy could have been sent to him alone. Why was Rosana coming at all?

It would take an hour to ride up to Mill Creek. That meant he could not start until shortly before four, and it was only twelve-thirty. An eternity, the intervening hours.

He ate lunch with Pat Jack, a fast friend in whom he had solid support. He said nothing to him of Rosana's coming, although it was prominently on his mind throughout the meal. When Jack left him to go back to his office, Travis went to his room, not knowing exactly how he would fill the time until four o'clock. Ruda was there, cleaning up. That was fine.

"Ruda, I want you to go out in the back and bring that big oaken wash tub. Then go into the kitchen and heat lots of water. I'm going to take a good, long soaking."

Travis sat in the tub, his legs drawn up so as to get both his feet and bottomside in. Ruda stood behind him pouring hot water over his head while he soaped and scrubbed. The girl took the wash cloth and scrubbed his back.

"Marse Travis," she said, "mind if I ask you somethin'?"

"Go ahead, Ruda."

"How cum you don' ever want no more hoochipat from me?"

Travis laughed. "I'm going to marry Miss Cummings, Ruda. I decided if I loved Miss Cummings and plan to

351

marry her I shouldn't have any relations with other girls."

"Dat's funny."

"What's funny, Ruda?"

"De married men. Dem's de ones dat's always after me."

Ruda didn't see the grimace on Travis' face. "Besides, Ruda, we had a bad experience. Remember? You caught a disease from that drummer that comes to San Felipe to call on Mr. White and Mr. Dinsmore— the one you told Dr. Pollard about—and you gave me that disease. I ought to have whipped you good for that but I didn't. It was my fault as much as yours. I hope you've learned your lesson, girl. You just can't lay down for every man who asks you."

"Marse Travis, I don't hoochipat wid all of 'em. Just dem I likes and dem dat gives me a quarter."

"You took the medicine Dr. Pollard fixed for you, didn't you? You got well, all right?"

"Yessuh. Dr. Pollard, he makes me come back to see him every now and den, to see if I done caught it again."

When Travis emerged from his room, he wore a white ruffled shirt, burgundy cravat, and cinnamon coat. Once out of town, leaving behind the critical words and recriminating glances, he began to feel confident once again. He was an excellent horseman and it felt good to be astride his favorite mare once again. It had been some days since he had ridden her and she seemed full of energy and was quick to respond to his every motion and reflex. He had started early; there was plenty of time. The tubbing had envigorated him and the bergamot toilet water was still faintly in his nostrils. He felt great, a healthy animal running to his mate. He was hungry for Rebecca, ready for her. If only she still was on his side. Well, he'd soon know the answer to that question, so vital to him. As for her brother, the best he could hope was that he would still be received cordially as a guest at the inn. But as long as Rebecca gave him sympathy and support he felt he could survive anything, even the appearance of Rosana in San Felipe. But his immediate concern was the time of month. He was afraid he was coming during Rebecca's "bad days." That's what she called them. The last time he had slept with her she told him that he "just made it. Another day would have been too late," she taunted him. He struggled in his mind to tally up the days. Be damned! Could it be that he was coming right in the middle of her "bad days?"

He allowed the mare to jog along easily, at loose rein. As he listened to her hoofs trodding softly on the dry path, he thought of Rebecca. It was no secret that she had had a lover or lovers before him. That much she had not denied, but she gave no names, made no explanations. "Take me as you found me, Bill," she told him. "I can offer no more."

"And if I don't?" he asked.

"Then stop coming to see me."

Well, who was he to demand—or even expect—chastity? Nonsense! Did it really matter? Rosana was immaculate when he took her. It did not presage compatability or happiness, nor did it ensure a satisfactory sex life. But Rebecca—oh, God! What a passion! He rested his hands on the pommel of his saddle and half-closed his eyes, remembering their first night together.

It happened at the mill. He had ridden out in the early afternoon and found her alone in the office. John, she told him, had taken the Negroes down the creek. They were to load some cut logs aboard the barge and pole them back to the mill. They would not possibly return before dark, at least.

Rebecca made some tea and they sat on a narrow wooden bench, close together, their thighs touching, each feeling a strong desire for the other. On other occasions he had kissed and fondled her and was aware of the deep wells of passion within her. There were times when he sensed they were roiling and trying to overflow. But she had managed to keep them tightly

353

capped. He knew this was his day but somehow he couldn't seem to get around to making just the right move. He strove to keep a rather innane conversation alive that neither of them cared about. He felt that she perceived as well as he did what was about to happen. Should he speak of it? Come right out and say, Rebecca, I know how you feel and you know how I feel, and go on from there? Or should he say nothing and simply proceed to take her as if he were completely sure of her?

Without further debate with himself, he set his cup aside and let his arm fall over her shoulder, then around her waist. He waited a moment before doing anything else. She put her cup away and turned her face to his. As his mouth fell hard on hers his hand clasped her breast. She took away her lips and gave him a perplexing look. Was this a disapproval, a signal to stop? Never mind. He would not, could not, stop now.

His hand ripped open her waist and found her naked bosom. In an instant her arm came from around his shoulder and he felt her hand sharp across his face. A coldness passed up his spine and he would have released her, but in the next moment her hands were clinging to him. The chill passed and he became hot all over, his mouth pressing hard over hers. Her mouth opened and began grinding against his, her tongue darting in, exploring, searching. He heard the silk of his shirt tear under her clutching fingers, and he felt the muscles of her back tense; and then her head fell helplessly back under the assault of his mouth on hers. She clung to him and he bent her body backward; he could feel her large, firm breasts against his chest as her lush body, all its pulsating parts, strained against his. She let his knee slip between her legs, and then somehow they had almost fallen on the pinewood floor, still kissing.

Another knee went between her legs and her thighs opened, and he was over her, penetrating her tenderly and deeply. She made no cry of pain, only a great sigh of ecstasy escaped from deep within her. She shifted her

354

body, making some slight adjustment in their position, and began to respond to his every thrust and act.

It was only afterwards, when they lay panting and exhausted together, that he heard an almost inaudible sob. This gave him a cutting sense of humility. He turned his eyes away from her and closed his own while realization came fully to him that here, after all the others, he had at last found the complete woman. He had to make her his own, and his alone. He felt a deep humbleness in his intimate presence of this woman, and when he noticed that they had not even taken the time to undress completely this made his humility cut deeper.

"Rebecca," he said softly, "I love you."

"Oh, Bill! But now you know. How can you say you love me?"

"It's true, Rebecca. I love you."

She sat up, wiping away the tears with her hands. Her eyes sought his. "Doesn't it matter?"

"What, Rebecca?"

"That there was somebody before . . .?"

He brushed away a tear from her cheek with his finger, kissed her. Then he looked her tenderly in the eyes. "Let that be the last word that is ever spoken about it."

She clung to him. "Oh, Bill! Bill! You do love me. I'm happy, completely happy."

Travis took his watch from the pocket of his waistcoat. It was time he was getting on to Mill Creek. He put his mare into a trot. For the hundreth time since Simon had handed him her note, he hoped that Rebecca would not rebuke him for Anahuac. He let himself imagine for a moment that she would even be proud of him. To be sure, he'd have a lot of explaining to do, and he took consolation in the hope that she would give him the comfort that he so sorely needed now. He would have to tell her, too, of Rosana's coming to San Felipe. This would be difficult, since he himself could not fathom his wife's purpose in coming all the way to

355

Texas to see him. But, in the face of all his troubles, he was resolved to remain steadfast in his devotion to Rebecca and firm in his resolution to marry her.

Travis arrived at the Mill Creek Inn at exactly four o'clock. Rebecca was expecting him, dressed in a form-fitting skirt of a light red material that drew her waist in sharply, and a loose blouse with bloomer sleeves drawn in and caught her the wrist.

"I wanted you to come at four so we can talk while John's away," she said, greeting him on the porch.

"I appreciate your consideration, Rebecca. I'm most concerned about how you feel on account of the Anahuac expedition."

"Bill, whatever you do I approve. I cannot do otherwise. I love you."

Travis' heart lifted. This was what he hoped to hear from Rebecca. It cheered him, put iron in his back. Not just anyone to stand up and cheer him, pat him on the back, but Rebecca.

"That deserves a drink!" he said with a very pleased smile.

Rebecca led him into the parlor, excused herself and went to the barroom and returned with a bottle of canary and glasses. Travis took them from her, placed his arm around his fiance's waist. "Let's drink it in your room."

Travis, sitting at the head of her bed, and she, reclining at the footboard, drank the wine and talked. He told her every detail of the Anahuac episode; she delighted in his heroism, which he was careful not to exaggerate.

It grew dark and he put the decanter and glasses aside, moved down near her, and took her in his arms and began kissing her. When he laid her across the bed, she slipped out of his arms. Thinking she did so in order to take off her clothes, he began stripping off his own. When he glanced at her she had not loosened a single button; instead she had taken a more distant position on the bed and was quietly watching him, with an

356

amused smile, as he meticulously, piece by piece, placed his clothing on a chair beside the bed.

"Come, darling, undress. Its' been a long time and I'm hungry for you."

"Bill . . ." Her voice was apologetic.

"Yes?"

"It's my . . . 'bad days'.'"

"Bedamned! Bedamned!' he swore, sitting back on the bed. "I was afraid so."

He lay back, his long body supine across the bed.

"Are you so terribly disappointed, darling?"

"Bedamned!" he repeated, staring glumly into the ceiling.

She got up and sat beside him. Taking his hand, she kissed it and placed it inside her blouse on her breast. He turned on his side, took off the blouse, pulled her to him and began kissing her breast, one of them, then the other, until both points slowly extended, creeping timidly at first from their declivities, then standing rigidly out like miniature pink cannon vents. Her hand found his throbbing sentinel, which stood fully at command.

"Poor Bill," she murmured. "You're really suffering. Let me try something."

He was reclining half on the bed, his feet resting on the floor. She dropped to her knees between his legs. Leaning over him, she placed his upreared phallus between her breasts and, squeezing them together around it, simulated lovemaking. After a time relief came to him—only a tiny emission at the beginning. But as she worked, moving her breasts rapidly up and down, it came thick and white, the warm fluid of manhood, in several separate hot ejections, spurting over her breasts, reaching her neck and chin. As she raised her body, she felt the warm and sticky fluid coursing down the valley of her bosom. She placed her head on his abdomen, holding his phallus against her cheek. It diminished and softened as the deep contentment she felt within his belly spread throughout his body, soothing him like a vial of cocaine in his veins.

"Oh, Lord!" he murmured. "How I do love you, Rebecca."

Suddenly they heard heavy footsteps outside, then a loud banging on the door.

"Rebecca? Rebecca! You in there?"

"Oh, God help us! It's John!" Rebecca whispered, snatching her blouse from the floor. "Yes, John," she called. "One moment . . . please!"

But it was too late. The door flung open. John Cummings stood in the doorway; an instantly angry black look encompassed his face. Rebecca had barely covered her breasts with her garment. Travis lay half naked across her bed.

"Oh, John! How could you!" Rebecca cried.

Travis pulled himself up, sat on the side of the bed. He made no effort to reach for his clothes. "I suppose you are considering getting your gun and shooting me," he said. "I wouldn't blame you but I beg you to consider just two things. I love Rebecca and she loves me. We would be married but for the delay in the arrival of my divorce papers."

"Travis, you're a scoundrel—a blackguard!"

"Do you want to call me out?"

"I just want you to get out!"

Rebecca placed herself in front of her brother. "For heaven's sake, John! Bill and I love each other. He's to be my husband. You can't order him out—just like that."

Travis was now pulling on his clothes. "He can, Rebecca, if he wishes. But I'd be gratified—and mighty humbled—if he'd accept my apologies."

"John . . .?" She looked hopefully at her brother.

"Your apologies are accepted in the spirit you offer them. But it does not make right your conduct toward my sister—"

"John, it was all my doing," Rebecca said. "Not Bill's."

John Cummings continued, addressing himself to his sister. "I think it best he stay away until such time as he can come to us prepared to marry you."

358

Rebecca walked with Travis to his horse. "I'm sorry about John," Rebecca told Travis. "I don't know why he came back."

"Simon undoubtedly told him I was coming. Somebody in town must have given Simon whiskey. He talks when he's drunk. I'm going to whip him again. I bought me a bullwhip just to use on those slaves. Sometimes they need it, to keep them in line."

"I'm sorry he told John."

"Rebecca," Travis said, "I received word that my wife Rosana is on her way to San Felipe. I don't know what she wants. She's bringing my son Charles Edward, whom she has agreed to turn over to me, as you know. I'm hopeful that she will also bring the finalized divorce papers. The Alabama legislature should have acted on them by this time. As soon as I know I'm free, we'll be married."

She turned her face, damp with tears, up to him. "Bill, don't let John keep you away from me. Come back. I'll talk with him. I'm sure I can bring him around."

Travis climbed on his horse.

"Wait, Bill!"

She began tugging at a ring on her finger. It would not come off and she thrust her finger in her mouth, thoroughly wet it and tugged again; the ring slipped off into her hand. She reached up and took Travis' hand from the pommel of his saddle, tried to slip the ring on a middle finger; it wouldn't go. Finally she forced it on his little finger.

"It's a cat's eye, Bill. Some people say it's ill luck. But for us it won't be. It will always tell you that I love you."

She kissed the ring on his finger. He turned his mare, spurred her, waved back at Rebecca as he rode away. She stood there, watching the outlines of the man and the horse until they became one with the darkness. It was the last time she would ever lay eyes on William Barret Travis.

Now Travis got an answer to his open letter to General Martin Cos. Santa Anna ordered Cos to arrest Travis and bring him into San Antonio for trial. Also to be arrested were the officers of his little assault group and some outspoken members of the War Party. In all, eight prominent Texans were to be tried for treason.

Santa Anna, although a brilliant manipulator and clever politician, had failed completely to understand the character of the colonists. He thought that by executing a handful of hot-heads he would frighten the Americans into submission. He had had considerable success with such a policy in certain holdout areas in Mexico, yet Mexicans still rankled over "Bloody Zacatecas." Santa Anna was to learn that Mexicans and Americans were a strikingly different breed.

The most important and historical human event in the minds of all Americans in 1835 was the American Revolution. The parents of many of the colonists had fought in the Revolutionary War. The Declaration of Independence and the United States Constitution were new documents but already the whole world had begun to recognize them as the most powerful and important expressions of man's desire for individual liberty and collective freedom ever penned. The colonists simply refused to turn Travis or anyone else over to General Cos.

A reissue of orders for these men's arrest came from San Antonio, and a group of prominent citizens asked the general to negotiate with them. General Cos replied he would negotiate with no man of Texas until the offenders had been surrendered. Now members of the Peace Party began to see the fire on the horizon. Although they had rebuked Travis because he seemed to them to be provoking a fight, now they began to see the situation through his eyes. They feared an infinitely greater threat—martial law, military occupation, the arrest of good friends. Who would be next? Almost overnight the pendulum swung the other way, and the people turned violently against Santa Anna.

Stephen F. Austin returned from Mexico in July.

Since arriving at his home in San Felipe he had remained closely indoors, recovering from his long illness of amoebic dysentary. All eyes were turned on the leader's cottage on Palmetto Creek and all ears were awaiting word from the man they were anxious to mount on the horse to lead them in their quest for independence.

The first sign from the colony's leader came in the form of an invitation from Austin to Travis for the young rebel to call upon him. Wearing his most conservative clothes, Travis went to pay his respects to Stephen F. Austin.

A kindly old Negro took Travis' black top hat and led him into the north wing of the cottage. Austin, a slender man of five feet, nine inches, with a long, lean face, high forehead, and keen penetrating eyes, slipped the Indian blanket from his shoulders and extended a bony hand. The grip was hard and positive. Travis observed the man closely, seeking clues as to which way he would go. He had always clung firmly to the doctrine of the Mexican Constitution of 1824. The fate of Texas was here—now. Travis was looking at a man in whom time and experience had stored up and kept for him the rarest of all commodities, wisdom and tolerance. Somehow in himself he did personify the achievements of what these people had come to Texas to get—freedom, ease, vastness, and abundance.

"Wine or whiskey, Travis?" he asked his guest.

"Neither, Sir."

"Then we'll get to the proposition."

"Thank you," Travis said. "Sir, I would like to explain to you my actions at Anahuac and what lay behind them—"

Austin cut him off. "You needn't. I understand quite well enough."

"I am at your pleasure, Sir."

Austin began, talking slowly, looking sometimes at Travis and sometimes through the window, as if trying to see out there somewhere what he was seeing in his mind. "I left Texas in April 1833 . . . I rigidly adhered

361

to the instructions and wishes of my people ... I was arrested and have suffered a long persecution and imprisonment. ... Upon my return I fully hoped to find Texas at peace, but regret to find it all disorganized, and threatened with immediate hostilities. The people here are not to blame. They have endeavored to sustain the constitution and the public peace. The object of Santa Anna is to destroy the Federal Constitution of 1824 and establish a dictatorship. In order to accomplish this he must foremost subdue and control absolutely the Texans. If not stopped he will annihilate all the rights of the people. Something must be done, and without delay."

Austin rose. He caught his hands behind his back and paced slowly back and forth, his head bowed; he stopped, looked down upon Travis.

"My decision has not come lightly," he said, his gaze penetrating Travis' anxious blue eyes. "Indeed, it has been a painful one. I am convinced that Texans must fight if they are to be free men. I shall announce my decision to them, and, if asked by them, shall lead them in their fight."

Travis' heart beat fast. Barely could he control his elation. At last! Everything he had come to Texas for was suddenly within his grasp: glory, fame—immortality! Austin's somber voice brought him back to earth. "But all these things must be done orderly, properly, legally. I shall ask the people to elect delegates from every settlement and call a convention. I will ask them to draw up a declaration of independence."

Travis spread the good news. It went like floodwater, sweeping before it the debris of dissension. Texans could now unite. Three-Legged-Willie front-paged Austin's declaration in bold type. Gail Borden gave it even greater prominence in his *Telegraph and Texas Register*.

Austin's decision swung the power to the War Party. The *Texas Gazette* told the people they had three courses to consider: to leave the country, to remain passive and accept whatever government Santa Anna imposed upon them, or to load guns while asserting their rights. The almost unanimous decision was to resist at all costs the measures which were stiffling the freedom and prosperity of the colonists. A committee of delegates was formed, and on October 5th a formal declaration of war was published in the committee's name. By that time hostilities had already broken out, and Stephen F. Austin was on his way to take control of the fighting.

The first shot of the war was fired at Gonzales. Back in 1831, that community had been given a cannon by the Mexican government. Its purpose was defense against Indian attack. The old six-pounder had been neglected and sat rusting in a peach orchard. The citizens now brought it into the town square and set about refurbishing it and putting it into firing condition. General Cos sent Lieutenant Antonio Castaneda with a detachment of one hundred and twenty men to take the field piece away.

When Lieutenant Castaneda and a group of officers appeared formally requesting return of the gift, Almeron Dickinson, a young colonist who was celebrating the second birthday of his daughter Angelina, told the Mexican officer that the cannon was a gift of the Mexicans to the citizens of Gonzales and that they had no intention of giving it up. Dickinson then invited the officers to join the birthday party. Castaneda refused the invitation and insolently demanded the six-pounder. Dickinson's reply was historical:

"Come and take it!"

Castaneda remained with his army of one hundred and twenty a little distance from Gonzales, undecided what to do. Meanwhile, Dickinson sent out messengers to tell the settlers that the town was besieged by a force of Mexican soldiers. The colonists, guns loaded, began pouring into the town. Castaneda closed the roads, but that night many more slipped across the Guadalupe River, and in the fog-shrouded dawn the determined colonists grouped toward the Mexican camp.

Castaneda, Dickinson learned, had planned to attack that day.

The fog lifted and the Americans and Mexicans faced each other only three hundred yards apart. A shot went off. No one knew who fired first. But it precipitated a rattle of musketry. There were shouts of alarm in the Mexican camp. The Texans halted uncertainly. Castaneda sent a messenger asking to talk about the cannon. The reply Dickinson sent back: no more parleys. Both sides waited. Suddenly a few shots from the Mexican side. A howl went up from the Americans accompanied by a hail of musket fire. Next the cannon roared, spouting a shower of nails and bits of old horseshoes at the Mexicans.

The unanimous roar: "Come and take it!" The Americans charged.

The Mexicans broke for the road back toward San Antonio.

Ironically, William Barret Travis was not on hand for this historic moment. The flu virus, respecting neither the great nor the lowly, had laid him low. He was in San Felipe, in bed with fever, severe headache pains, and an inflamed and sore throat, being attended by Jane Long and the faithful Ruda. Nevertheless, the "Lexington Shot" of Texas revolution had been fired.

The colonizers responded generously to Stephen F. Austin's call to WAR. The clarion call was heard afar, as well.

A frenzy of "Texas meetings" swept the land everywhere. Baltimore mobs burned Santa Anna in effigy. Bostonians jammed the Concert Hall to hear Major General John S. Tyler denounce the Mexican tyrant. At Tammany Hall in New York over two thousand people roared their "loyalty" to Texans. In New Orleans excited groups swirled about the decorous lobby of Richardson's Hotel, planning great things for Texas, raising money, recruiting volunteers. On the waterfront gangs of slaves labored and sweated in the mid-winter sun loading cannon and kegs of powder on the schooner *Columbus,* bound for the port of Galveston. At the Arcadia Coffee House a group of planters pledged $10,000. At Mobile's Shakespeare Theater a rally, called by Jim Bonham who, in answer to his friend Travis' summons, was enroute to Texas to fight in the revolution, quickly produced $1,500 and forty volunteers.

And at about this same time Rosana Travis arrived in San Felipe with her two children, and put up at Jane Long's inn.

The first inkling of the news that his wife and children were in San Felipe came to Travis through a medium known, in that time, as "dark laughter." During the slave days "dark laughter" was an expression used by the owners of Negroes to describe that mysterious, silent look of malevolent satisfaction that lurked behind the eyes of their slaves when there was scandal, trouble, or disaster brewing for the slaveholders. The darkies seemed to know of or sense this kind of calamity long before it surfaced among the whites. Travis saw the dark laughter in Ruda's large, black eyes—the secret mockery, the silent gratification of impending trouble for him. All the while she bathed him, changed his bed linens, brought his food and medicine, there was that smug air about her, a secret not shared, that disturbed him. Yet he knew better than to probe her; it would be absolutely useless.

It was Jane Long who broke the news to him.

"I've some lovely new guests, Bill," she told him with the air of a woman who is trapped into speaking of a wife whom she is certain cannot or does not give her husband the kind of satisfaction she thinks she is capable of giving him. "Your wife, Rosana, and your children are here. They're at my place. Your daughter, Susana Isabella is simply a *darling* little girl!"

Travis groaned. "Oh, God!"

"That bad for you, Bill?" Jane asked too sweetly.

"Promise me one thing, Jane. Keep them away from

365

here until I'm on my feet." He grabbed Jane's arm, squeezed it as if trying to wring a promise from her.

"Certainly, Bill. If that's how you want it. I'll try to keep her away. But she's come a long way. Maybe she'll insist."

"What has she said? Do you know what she wants?" Travis was half out of bed, resting on his elbow.

"I'd say, Bill—you."

Travis groaned again.

"Why, Bill—shame! She's a lovely woman, and the children are adorable."

"Please, Jane," he begged. "Tell her I'll see her as soon as I can. Maybe tomorrow."

"Dr. Pollard says it will be longer before you can get up. Maybe two or three days more."

Travis got out of bed the next day. He felt a little wobbly at first, but after tossing off a brandy felt steadier. He dressed somewhat conservatively: dark frock coat, brown breeches, white shirt, beige waistcoat, and white stock. It was but a short distance from his quarters to Jane's inn, about a quarter mile, but it seemed a long way. The closer he came the greater his consternation at Rosana's presence in San Felipe. In the short time she had been there she must have picked up all the gossip about him; surely she knew of his engagement to Rebecca Cummings. She would be expecting him, he'd sent word by Jane he'd arrive at three o'clock. He was exactly on time.

When he entered the room Rosana looked at him a long while, her eyes very still, taking him in fully. He too was very much interested in how she looked, how she had developed. It had been a long time. She had matured, for one thing; her features had ripened. Her face had lost its oval childlike look; and in it there was a quiet beauty that he had not been aware of. She was in a dress of old gold and blue that molded her body down to her waist, then billowed out, and she held in her hand a tiny white silken handkerchief. Her body, too, had ripened, fined out, the curves doing just the

366

right thing at the right places. In the illogical way of a husband, whether from love or jealousy, he grew angry toward the woman, already condemning her in his mind. No telling what had been going on since he left her. The image of her lying with another man had remained in his heart and had embittered all his thoughts of her; and now she stood before him, more lovely than ever before, a sensuous woman, offering herself again to him.

"Bill, aren't you glad to see your children?" she said.

It was only then that he removed his eyes from her. The children had been standing near their mother all the while, very quiet and mystified by the tall, handsome man in the room.

He dropped to his knees and held out his arms to them. First to come was Charles Edward. The boy approached, timidly at first, then when Travis gathered him in tenderly, he smiled and clung to his father, feeling strangely loved by someone alien. Susana Isabella remained close to her mother's side. Rosanna patted the child on the head and urged her toward Travis. She looked up at her mother, then at Travis, who held his arms outstretched. Apprehensively she moved toward him. He kissed her on the forehead and then both cheeks. She smiled and returned the kisses, planting a wet smack on his cheek.

"I named your daughter Susana Isabella, after my grandmother," Rosana said. "I hope you don't mind."

He gazed hard at Rosana. *"My* daughter?"

"Yes, Bill. Your daughter. She is your child." She returned his gaze, levelly, unflinchingly.

He kissed the child again, lifted his face to her mother. "She *is* beautiful, Rosana. She's four now, isn't she?"

"Yes, and in case you've lost track of time, Charles Edward is nearly seven."

"Of course, of course!" he said, smiling now; the children had softened his attitude. He stroked the boy on his auburn head. "He has my hair, hasn't he?"

"And Susana Isabella, she has your stubborn, hot-

367

headedness," Rosana said pleasantly, smiling a little undecipherable smile.

The greetings over, Rosana sent the children out of the room, saying that Mrs. Long would be kind enough to give them some milk and cookies. "I'm happy to see that you still love your children, Bill," she said when the two had gone.

"I do love children. By the way, have you seen my Negro boy, Jared? Mrs. Long keeps him for me. He's eight. I got him as a fee on a law case I handled."

Rosana fixed him with a steady look. "Bill, aren't you going to ask why I'm here?"

"To bring Charles Edward to me—and finalize the divorce, isn't it?"

"Of course," she said, tossing her head slightly. "I've agreed you should have Charles Edward, and so you shall."

"I'll be happy to have him with me, Rosana. I promise you that he will get the best care—the best of everything. I'll send him to the finest schools—"

Somehow the conversation between them died. Rosana sat quietly, toying with the handkerchief in her hands, Travis stood awkwardly in the middle of the floor. Both felt there was still a great deal to be spoken, yet each was constrained to find further words. Finally, Rosana said what was really on both their minds.

"Bill, is there no longer any hope for us? I had to see you—to know if I still love you, and if there is any possibility that you'd want me again."

"No!" he almost shouted. He began pacing back and forth. She had exploded the shell too suddenly. Glancing at her, he saw in her eyes the hurt he had caused her. He calmed himself and spoke more gently. "I mean, no, there's no hope for us. I didn't mean to hurt you. I left you once. I'd only do it again, Rosana."

In a subdued voice she said, "You haven't even asked if I still love you."

"Quite honestly, Rosana, I don't want to know."

"Tell me, Bill," she said, getting up and walking to the window. She did not immediately complete her sentence; she looked outside at the hewn log buildings for a few moments, then turned and faced him with her warmest smile. "Am I no longer desirable?"

Another bombshell. He looked at her, the slanting sun's rays coming in throught the window and playing in her dark hair, her somber face set in a frame of the diffusion of afternoon light. She *was* desirable, he thought. But for how long? It didn't last before; was there any reason to suppose it would now?

He did not answer her and she took up the conversation. "I know, Bill, what women mean to your ego, how important sexual excitation is to you. I know you have had many women since me. And I am glad you have had them. Yes, Bill, I'm glad for you. Because to deny them would take away your drive, there would be no achievement of any kind left for you. But please look at me, Bill, and tell me, honestly, would you like to take me to bed—now?"

Travis had heard far more than he had bargained for. Yes, he told himself, she was desirable, completely and enravishingly desirable. Were she any other woman but his wife he would throw her across the bed, tear off that lovely gown he was sure she had bought just for this occasion, and brutally take her. She made him feel mean and violent, beastlike. Woman was an inexplicable mystery, her doings not to be anticipated in any direction. To deceive, he believed at that moment, was natural in women, even to lie outright was not considered very wrong by them, if it was a means to get what they wanted. They practiced the art of dissembling until there was no telling what their true thought was. A man might believe he was foremost with one of them and find that secretly she desired another, besides him. Isn't that what happened before with Rosana? No creature could be as cruel as a woman. With them cruelty was an object, an art, a part of their enjoyment. In making a man suffer they saw the proof of their power over him. Suddenly he thought of Rebecca and for an instant doubted all her love, all her nobleness, doubted that even she transcended this devious game of womanhood. He faced Rosana, feeling somehow insulted. Anger welled up in him.

"Rosana, stop it! I could answer you a thousand ways but all the answers would come out as you wish them. You should know, having lived with me, having bedded with me, that I am not a man you can fob off with a sugar tit. I remember those many attempts at lovemaking, when I strove desperately to arouse you, tried to bring you back to me. I haven't forgot your mechanical, rather resigned bodily reaction, with your mind completely uninvolved. I have known enough women to understand that the involvement of the mind, even a little bit, as well as the heart, is everything. It is what adds warmth and passion to this kind of union. Was there ever any true warmth in you?"

"Bill, please . . ." There was a cry in her voice, an appeal. She advanced toward him. "Things change. I have changed. Everything will be different. I promise, Bill . . ."

"No!" He backed away from her.

She looked as if she would weep, or flee. He bowed his head before her, struggling not to take her in his arms out of sheer pity.

"Rosana," he said softly. "It is not in my nature to turn back. I shall never look back for anything."

She stood there, within arms reach of him, looking at him with longing in her eyes, her bosom rising and falling rhythmically. A vision of her of long ago flashed in his mind. He saw her, his young pupil, lying on his bed, naked, her young breasts rising and falling as she breathed, her flat smooth stomach, the soft fleece of her girlhood, the curving columns of her alabaster limbs.

"I'm sorry," he said.

She took a step backwards, turned her eyes away from him. "I know, Bill," she said quietly. "You won't look back because you are afraid of what you might see catching up with you."

He turned, opened the door, and was gone.

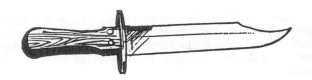

Jim Bowie wanted action. Anything that might help ease the tragedy of Ursula's death. He saddled his horse and rode toward San Felipe.

When he arrived at Austin's capitol he found the town astir. News had reached Austin about Lieutenant Dickinson's victory at Gonzales, and the leader had sent couriers scurrying to other settlements and towns with instructions to gather men and arms and march to Goliad, where Austin would head up a "Volunteer Army of Texas."

Jim found the flamboyant William Barret Travis at Austin's side, urging him to move at once against any Mexican force within the borders of Texas. Jim declared his readiness to serve in Austin's army. Austin knew that Jim Bowie was popular with the settlers, but he also knew that many of the War Party resented him because he had been so closely associated with the Mexicans in San Antonio and Coahuila and through them had become exceedingly rich. Being reluctant to put him in command of regular troops, Austin attached him to his personal staff as a volunteer aide, with the rank of lieutenant colonel.

There was distressing news. Santa Anna was forming a huge army south of the border, at Saltillo, and would march toward San Antonio any day now. Travis and

James Walker Fannin, who had been commissioned by Austin, were urging the leader to press on to San Antonio, overpower General Cos' forces there and then move south to intercept Santa Anna's army. Jim advised a more cautious course of action. Austin agreed that his army was not ready for an operation of such magnitude.

Sam Houston at forty years of age had seen a great deal of life; he had fought, he had loved and lost, he had suffered, and he had experienced much that other men only dreamed of. And he understood what was in the hearts of men. His travels in Texas had caused him to pause and take inventory of himself. In so doing he came face to face with the three images of himself that are basic with all men. He saw the man he believed himself to be as opposed to the man that others saw him to be; and behind these he saw the man he really was. This devastating revelation made him realize the pendulum of time was trembling high above all. He saw restless men dashing about underneath it like disheveled ants. Yet he knew in their hearts they, as rational men like himself, craved a home of some kind for mind and body—for family.

Houston had always been a man of change. Since he had fled his young wife Eliza and turned his back on the governorship of Tennessee and future presidential possibilities, restlessness had been his coachman, driving him ever recklessly into the sunset with a desperate urgency. Whether that restlessness was due to the individual dissatisfaction of what went on before or what the present offered or to what the world beyond the horizon promised, did not matter. He would not, he told himself, behave spasmodically forever. No matter what the vista ahead might promise he had to come to some decision, at some place. He saw in this new country, at last, a rest, an end—a beginning.

Sam Houston put his stake down at Nacogdoches and opened a law office. But when it became inevitable that Texans had to go to war if they were to keep their liberty and gain independence, he closed shop and rode into San Felipe and offered to build an army for Stephen F. Austin such as he had seen his old mentor Andrew Jackson command. Houston, advising Austin to move carefully and discretely until a dependable army could be mustered and trained, went to Washington-on-the-Brazos for the purpose of doing just that, with Austin's blessing and a commission as General of the Army.

Austin moved the volunteers who had ridden to his call toward San Antonio for the purpose of surrounding and isolating the town and bottling up General Cos' sixteen hundred Mexican troops. Austin's "army" numbered less than five hundred untrained farmers, settlers, and volunteers from the States. When the army reached within a day's march of San Antonio he ordered Jim Bowie to proceed with Fannin and a detachment of ninety-two men to select a campground for the army on the river as near the town as possible.

Dressed in fringed buckskin, as were many others in the company, Jim Bowie rode a steady grey mare, his heavy pistols protruding from saddle holsters, his rifle resting in a scabbard under his left leg, his trusted knife, as always, slung in its sheath from his belt. The men followed him confidently. They possessed no standard arms; each man carried his own rifle, jaeger, smoothbore, horse pistol, or shotgun, which had been picked up when he left home.

This was country with which Jim was thoroughly familiar. Austin's orders were specific and yet confusing. Specific in that Jim was to establish the camp at the location of the abandoned Mission Espada; confusing its wording: "You will also reconnoiter, so far as time and circumstances will permit, the situation of the outskirts of the town and the approaches to it. You will make your report with as little delay as possible, so as to give time to the army to march and take up its position before night. Should you be attacked by a large force, send expresses immediately with particulars."

Austin was well aware that he was sadly misplaced

as a general of an army and this order bore out his deficiency.

Jim first led his forces to Mission Capistrano, less than a mile from Mission Espada, thence northeast three and a half miles to Mission San Jose. Finding, however, no suitable military position at any of these points, he advanced to Mission Concepcion, about a mile southeast of Mission San Jose. He liked the two tall towers of the old mission church and the surrounding area. The approaches to the mission consisted of a level plain, roughly the shape of a triangle, the apex of which converged on the mission church. The plain was broken only by scattered clumps of brush. One side of the triangle was formed by a wooded area, and the other by a low bluff, eight to ten feet high, that skirted the bank of the river. The riverbottom itself was heavily wooded and provided good shelter for the horses.

"Settle the men in," Jim told Fannin. "We'll camp here. Post sentries in both of those towers of the old chapel, and throw out pickets in the plain beyond."

Then he set a party of men to cutting a footwalk in the clay bluff which fell to the river bottom. This would allow the men to take cover, ascend to fire, descend to reload without exposure or waste of time.

In case of attack the enemy would have to approach the mission from the base of the triangle across the open plain, ever narrowing into cross-fire from the woods on their right flank and from the bluff on their left flank.

Jim sat down and wrote a report of his position, and dispatched John Hutchings to deliver it to Austin.

Night came, but not Austin with his army. Jim left Fannin in charge and rode alone down the road toward the distant lights of San Antonio. When he reached the lane that led to the great white house he had built for Ursula, he left his horse tethered in a small grove and scrambled partially hidden by the scattered live-oaks across the fields until he reached his house from the rear. Carefully circling it, he saw only one light, and that in the rear by the kitchen. He approached the window, peeked in and saw what he hoped to find. He softly called, "Sam . . ."

Almost instantly Sam's broad, shining face was looking out at him. "Marse Jim!"

"Open the back door, Sam."

Jim learned from Sam that General Cos was aware of Austin's plan of encompassment and had put the town under strict military control. Sam gave Jim full particulars of the new fortifications and much other valuable information. A number of persons suspected of being in sympathy with the colonists, both Mexican and American, had been arrested and jailed. The city was rife with rumors that an army of ten thousand men under President-General Santa Anna's personal command had crossed the frontier at Laredo and was marching toward San Antonio, with the incendiary item that Santa Anna himself had declared he would drive every Anglo-American beyond the Sabine. People were fleeing the city daily with their worldly possessions piled on carts, in wagons, packed on mules and horses when they could find them. An officer from General Cos' staff had inspected Jim's house, preparatory to occupying it when Santa Anna arrived.

"Sam," Jim told his faithful servant, "you just sit tight. It won't be long now before General Houston organizes a large army of Americans to drive General Cos out of San Antonio and deal with any other Mexican soldiers that Santa Anna might bring into Texas."

"Yessuh!" Sam agreed enthusiastically. "Yessuh, Marse Jim. I'se gonna wait right here til you comes back."

When Jim got back in camp at Concepcion no word had been received from Austin. The men had cleared the brush from the plain and about thirty others were in position on the prepared fortifications of the bluff. He ordered Fannin to take a company of thirty men and position them in the wooded area on the left of the approaches. That left about thirty men in the mission itself to handle the assault from the front, in case it came.

Jim did not sleep that night. He felt sure that General Cos' spies had picked up their position by now and that an attack would come. He hoped Austin would arrive before dawn with reinforcements. He was well aware that he had not followed the specifics of Austin's orders. But this did not bother him at the moment. He thought about Fannin, his second in command. He had no particular liking for Fannin. He belonged to Travis' hot-headed crowd, was pushy and anxious for command to compensate for his failure at West Point. Already Austin had commissioned him captain, with a promise of quick advancement. As he lay awake he tried to imagine where Austin's forces were; he hoped they were marching through the night. Ninety-two men, huddled sleeping in their blankets, seemed pathetically few compared to General Cos' forces of sixteen hundred in the town, less than three miles away.

Day broke with a heavy fog obscuring the approaches to Concepcion. Jim sat by the fire in front of the chapel swallowing his breakfast. Austin still had not come. The flat whiplash of a rifle brought him to his feet. It came from one of the chapel towers. A voice from the lookout: "Here they come, boys!"

Jim's eyes searched the mist. He made out shadowy figures approaching. As he peered into the fog the long ragged line of blue uniforms with white crossbelts became vaguely visible. A quick volley from Jim's pickets and the Mexicans opened fire blindly. Bullets thudded around the breakfast fire, zinged through the branches of the trees on the left. The flat dampened reports of rifle and pistol shots filled the air. Henry Karnes, one of the pickets, came running for the camp. "The sonsuvbitches have shot the bottom out of my powder horn!"

"Here, take mine." Jim thrust his own into Karnes' hand and sprinted in the direction from which Karnes had come.

As he ran he saw that his men were all on their feet, getting ready for battle. Up ahead an opening in the fog revealed the blue rank of Mexicans still advancing. "Keep down!" Jim yelled to his men. "Wait till you have a clear shot. Make every bullet count."

Jim crouched, fired both his pistols at the half-obscured blue uniforms. The whiplash of rifles and the explosions of pistol shots rent the fog above the plain. From the blank face of the mist came a volley of bullets that zinged overhead, some pounding into earth around Jim.

The four men who had followed Jim flattened themselves on the ground, raising only to pick off a blue uniform. Gaps appeared in the Mexican ranks. Volleys of shots now began from Fannin's company in the woods to Jim's left, followed by the cracking of rifles from the bluff on his right. The blue line began to retreat into the white bank behind them.

Fannin dashed from the woods, moved in beside Jim. "Reload men," Jim yelled. "They'll come back." To Fannin, "Get back to your men in the woods. Wait till we have them well in the triangle, then open fire." To Karnes, "Take charge of the men at the church. Fire whenever the Mexicans come in range. Kill them in the open. Cut them down before they reach the mission."

Fannin sprinted back to the woods. "You men follow me," Jim called. He led the four, in a run, to the riverbank, where the footwalk had been cut.

By eight o'clock the sun broke through. The fog thinned, lifted. Jim could see the enemy then and estimated their force at about three hundred infantrymen, with several fine companies of cavalry as a reserve— about five hundred in all. And he saw a single brass cannon glinting in the first light of the sun.

"That looks like a double-fortified four-pounder," Jim said to his men.

"It ain't gonna be nice when that field piece begins filling the air with grape and cannister," Richard Andrews on his right said.

377

A drum rolled. The line of Mexican soldiers, stretched out across the plain, began its movement into the triangle toward the mission. They had no choice but to advance across the open plain, exposed to the cross-fire from the woods and the bluff.

"No need of two of you men shooting the same Mexican," Jim called to the men on the footwalk. "See that drummer in the center of the line. You men on my right. Pick off the soldiers in order from the drummer's left. You men on my left take them one by one on the drummer's right. But hold your fire till you're sure of your range. Make every shot count."

The drum rolled, stopped. An order. The line of blue uniforms and white cross-belts knelt, fired. A hum of bullets whizzed overhead. No answer from Jim's men. The Mexicans reloaded. The drummer rolled his drum. The soldiers advanced fifty yards, knelt to fire. A bullet splashed into the bank at Jim's ear but he ignored it. "Now, boys!" he yelled.

Shoulders rose above the bank. Rifles cracked. Mexicans toppled back, leaving blank spaces in the blue ranks. Volleys from the woods rang out, numerous puffs of white smoke appeared among the trees. The Mexican drum rolled and the blue line advanced slowly, firing as rapidly as they could reload. When fire cut them down from the riverbank, they swerved toward the woods only to be decimated by Fannin's company. The ground became littered with blue uniformed bodies. No troops could stand up to such deadliness. They broke and retreated. Their officers whipped them back into line. Raggedly they moved forward again, passing the crest of the first assault marked by the bodies that patched the grass. Karnes' men in front of the Mexicans opened fire. The soldiers charged, shouting, firing their rifles. Again the ranks thinned as the deadly fire from left and right and from the front cut them down. The assault faltered once more and fell back.

The brass cannon gleamed as it was hauled to the fore in the Mexican ranks.

"They're aiming it at Fannin's position," Jim said.

As the men watched, gunmen busied themselves. All at once the *BAA-ROMMM!* of the brass-mouthed cannon filled the air, drowning all lesser sounds. Grapeshot whirled through the branches of the trees over the heads of Fannin's men.

Four men scrambled over the bank.

"Get back down!" Jim yelled.

"Fannin needs help!" someone yelled back. And the four raced for the woods across the open ground.

A volley from the Mexican line. One of the four went down. Impetuous action without an order. A casualty. The others dragged him into the trees, but the effort was useless. Richard Andrews was dead from the bullet that had entered his left side under his ribs.

BAA-ROMMM! This time the grape slashed through the woods at a lower range. No company could withstand such direct blasts for long. Jim worked his way along the ledge and half-crouching made his way to Fannin's position. Just as he got there the brass field piece opened its mouth again, vomiting fire and smoke and shot. A shower of leaves and branches rained down upon Jim. Rifle shots from both sides answered, but they sounded feeble against the mighty throat of the cannon.

"If they lower the range a little more," Fannin said, "they'll drive us from our position."

Jim crept forward, shaded his eyes with his hand as he peered through the bushes. The gunners were reloading the field piece. He called to Fannin. "Give me your rifle."

He aimed, the rifle cracked, the gunner with the lighted match spun to the ground. The others looked stunned. But one reached for the match.

"Another rifle—quick!" Jim said to Fannin.

Jim aimed, fired again. The second gunner fell, smacked in the face by Jim's bullet before he touched the fuse to the vent. A third, crouched low, cast around like a frightened cat. A rifle cracked at Jim's ear and the gunner's body pitched to the ground. Fannin's men had taken up the fire. Bullets thudded all around the brass cannon. The survivors of the gun crew got the idea. Crouching, they ran to the protection of the main body.

"That cannon! We've got to take it!" Jim shouted to the men around him.

He quickly checked his pistols, bounded from the bushes followed by eight stalwarts. As they ran they fired, stopped to reload, fired. On they dashed. The Mexican officers had seen nothing quite like this. Men in buckskin charging, firing with deadly accuracy. Men were falling around them, kicking at the grass. Shots from the Mexicans rang out but they were half-hearted and ill-directed.

Jim and his men reached the cannon. "Swing her around, boys!" he roared.

Eager hands lay to; the big muzzle frowned directly at the blue uniforms, now clustered in the clearing. Jim seized the fuse stick, still burning, and touched it to the cannon's vent. *BAA-ROMMM!* The brazen monster roared and lurched back.

The smoke cleared and Mexicans were writhing on the ground. Some were groping around blindly, others fleeing from the clearing.

As Jim and his men hastily reloaded the cannon, from the woods and the bluff came yelling and cheering and shooting.

The Mexican officers made a frantic attempt to rally their ranks. They cursed, shouted, beat angrily at men with the flats of their swords. With pistols at their temples they threatened to shoot them point blank. But the blue front with white cross-belts was gone. It was each man for himself. Singly and by twos and in groups they fled over the field and through the woods toward San Antonio.

When Austin arrived an hour later the Americans had counted sixty-five dead Mexicans and estimated that a hundred more had been wounded. Austin, irritated and frigid, demanded to know why the detachment, with success already within its grasp, hadn't followed the Mexicans into the town itself. He proposed that the combined forces do so at once, before General Cos would reorganize his demoralized soldiers.

"I would advise against it," Jim said.

"Any good reasons, Bowie?" Austin asked.

"I have reliable information that the city has been greatly fortified recently. Every plaza is strategically covered by artillery, with guns placed to rake every approach. It's no good sending men on a suicide attack."

Austin didn't like the answer he got from Jim. "What's your opinion, Fannin?"

"Sir, I agree with Bowie."

Austin swallowed opposition hard. His eyes stony with antipathy, he turned them on Jim. "You may camp here with such volunteers as wish to remain with you. I will find a more suitable camping place. I think I will take the main army to that old mill north of San Antonio.

Jim knew, then, that there was nothing left to do but wait until General Houston could assemble an army and lead it himself. Austin simply would not do as commander.

So he waited, and after Ben Milam's forces took San Antonio on the ninth of December, he rode into the city with sixty of his volunteers, those who had remained with him.

If the Elegant Gentleman roosting on the Alamo wall had seemed sloth in summoning his puppets, that was all over. Events now would move more rapidly, one on the heels of the other, for the young gallant seeking the road to glory. His *Gotterdammerung* awaited him in the near future—at the old fortress-mission Alamo in San Antonio.

Rosana had departed Texas without again seeing her husband, but she left him his son Charles Edward. The boy was of school age and Travis took him to Washington-on-the-Brazos and boarded him with Mrs. David Ayers, where he would attend Mrs. Lydia McHenry's school with the other children of Mrs. Ayers and the neighbors'.

Upon saying goodbye to his son, Travis knelt, took the boy warmly in his arms and held him thus for a long time. "Son," he said huskily, "I will now speak to you as an equal, as a grown man. Listen carefully, Charles Edward Travis. I must leave you. I have to go away. I may never see you again, never hold you, kiss you; and you adn yours, as free persons, will be able to and study English, mathematics, and the refinements of society. We have to do these things, you and I, so that your children may enjoy the elegance of poetry, painting, music. There's a new dawn blazing forth for you, and you and yours, as free persons, will be able to enjoy all the wonderful things to come in the future, just for the taking."

Charles Edward's mother will hasten the Alabama legislature's finalization of her divorce, and five weeks later will marry wealthy planter Samuel G. Cloud, and never see the boy again.

Committees of Safety sprang up in every town. The hounds of war were yelping throughout the land. Gail Borden's highly influential *Telegraph and Texas Register* hammered away for "liberty" and "freedom." The *Texas Gazette* joined the cry with inspiring editorials and the most heroic of Lord Byron's stanzas. Recruiting posts were opened in all settlements. General Houston was making great progress at Washington-on-the-Brazos organizing an army. The several hundred colonists who had collected in Gonzales was growing daily. They marched on Goliad and captured two cannons and several hundred muskets from a Mexican force stationed there. More celebrating, more volunteers. The little army grew to six hundred, and Stephen F. Austin, with William Barret Travis riding beside him, left San Felipe to take command and march them to San Antonio and throw General Martin de Cos out of Texas.

Caesar had proclaimed it and all conflicts recorded have borne it out. There are always two basic causes of war: the underlying cause and the precipitating cause. The former for the Texans had been there for a long, long time. Had Santa Anna followed a blue print of King George III's oppression of the Thirteen Colonies, he could not have better prepared the Texas settlers for a rebellion. Now he provided the catalyst—the precipitating cause. Rumors were wild and rampant. Word spread among the colonists that Santa Anna was collecting an army in Mexico of fifteen thousand men to invade and clamp his iron-bound dictatorship on the state of *Tejas*. Already his brother-in-law was occupying San Antonio with a force of two thousand or more men; rumor increased the number daily.

Austin had commissioned Travis a captain of artillery, and before leaving San Felipe, Travis went to Dinsmore's and placed an order for two uniforms. There was a house in New York, Dinsmore told him, that would manufacture uniforms to his specifications, but it would take some time. No matter. Travis knew what he wanted and would wait. He ordered two complete uniforms; both of the same design, only the color patterns would be different. The jackets would be frock-type with double rows of silver bullet-buttons, one in blue and the other a light yellow. The blue jacket was to have yellow collar and cuffs, the yellow one blue collar and cuffs. For wear with the blue jacket he ordered yellow breeches with wide blue seam welts, and for the yellow jacket blue breeches with yellow seam welts. With both he wanted black leather belts with red sashes. For headwear, high *kepis* type with black leather visors decorated in red trim and cording. The uniforms arrived at Dinsmore's the same day news of the massacre at the Alamo reached San Felipe.

After the morale-boosting battle of Concepcion, Austin was successful in laying a siege around San Antonio. He would now wait—wait until his army received enough recruits to launch a successful attack upon the town.

The siege was slowly strangling the town and reducing the hopes of General Cos' troops. Austin's men captured war material, supplies, and farm products bound for the town; they attacked and killed Cos' patrols and scouting parties. Travis was everywhere, burning grass, killing Mexicans, capturing horses, acts none of which were of import enough to heroize any man.

The seize dragged on, with little to do. The men waited to attack Cos' forces in San Antonio. What could sixteen hundred or even two thousand Mexicans do against six hundred Americans? Hadn't Jim Bowie proved it at Concepcion. After the battle Bowie had proclaimed that one American with a musket was worth ten Mexican soldiers. Austin restrained the men, but they continued to grow restless. These were frontiersmen, unused to discipline. Each man was his own commander. Take San Antonio, run Cos out of Texas and that would teach the Mexicans a thing or two! Austin had spent a year and a half in Mexico and he knew better.

Austin's presence was demanded in San Felipe. The convention, in assembly, voted to request that Austin go into the United States and rally support for the Texans. The assembly wanted to be sure of support from the States when the big war with Santa Anna came. Before leaving his army, Austin placed Colonel Edward Burlson in command. This was a disappointment to Travis, who thought he should have had the post. Disappointed and feeling unfairly treated, he tendered his resignation but Austin, perhaps understanding the young fire-brand better than most, simply chose to ignore it. Instead he promoted him to lieutenant colonel.

With Austin's departure, inactivity precipitated quarrels and discontent among the ranks. Much of the conflict was due to the scarcity of supplies, medical needs, clothing, ammunition, and, of course, money. All were sadly lacking. Also, too many men, unused to military restrictions and jealous of their officers, tried to dictate to their superiors.

One dreary day a man named Conway killed Sherwood Dover in a quarrel over the ownership of a pistol. Dover's friends hung Conway from a pecan tree, and the incident would have created a rebellion had not the camp been suddenly snapped to life by the appearance of two of San Antonio's American residents, who escaped from the town. They were Sam Maverick and John W. Smith. These men reported that the Mexicans were starving, dispirited, low in ammunition. The newcomers urged an immediate attack and offered a plan, backed by maps, that Maverick had smuggled out.

For two days Colonel Burlson hesitated, unwilling to attack, fearing defeat. The men were itching for a fight. They were impatient—and supremely confident. All that was lacking was a leader brave enough and willing to launch the attack. Another situation tailor-made for Travis. But again he missed his chance for fame and glory. He was away with a detachment of sixty men trying to overtake and capture nine hundred head of horses that were being sent to the Rio Grande by a small escort of Mexicans. The horses were to be used to transport Santa Anna's cannon and other heavy equipment when his army reached the river. The mission was a failure. Travis returned without the horses, and San Antonio had been taken.

Ben Milam, anxious to get the war over and return to San Felipe and Jane Long, led a force of three hundred and fifty men into San Antonio and, after four days of fierce fighting, forced the surrender of General Cos. But the battle cost Milam his life.

The victorious Americans allowed Cos to march his defeated army toward the Rio Grande under pledge that he would never against bear arms against Texas. But the parole was worthless, as Travis warned when he returned and learned of it, for almost at once Cos and his troops were added to the army being assembled by Santa Anna south of the Rio Grande in the city of Saltillo.

After the capture of San Antonio and the expulsion of General Cos' army from Texas, recruitments practically ceased and desertions by the colonists became commonplace. The settlers felt that the danger had passed. It was December and the men wanted to be home with their families for Christmas.

Travis and Jim Bowie, however, did not share the complacency of the others. Travis, because of his innate distrust of Mexicans, fully expected an invasion in force. Bowie, in San Antonio with a group of sixty or more of his volunteers, was at home. He also believed that with the departure of Cos' soldiers Texans had not seen the last Mexican soldier in Texas territory. He was prepared to fight, as always.

Colonel Burlson had retired to San Felipe at the request of the Assembly. James W. Fannin was promoted to colonel and ordered to take the main body of the army, some four hundred and twenty men, ninety-three miles southeast to Goliad and fortify them behind the walls of the old Spanish presidio there. Travis was sent into San Antonio with a detachment of eighty cavalrymen with orders from Sam Houston to dismantle the old Alamo mission-fort and fall back to join Fannin at Goliad. Houston had twice sent similar orders to James Bowie, but that individualist had also chosen to ignore the commanding general's specific orders.

So the stage is almost set. Travis and Bowie, following the threads of their lives, come face to face before the Alamo. David Crockett, pursuing his white thread, has left Nacogdoches and will arrive in San Antonio shortly after the New Year of 1836. Eight hundred miles south of the Alamo, a well-built man of forty-two, with keen black eyes and thick Negroid lips and a flaming hatred for *americanos,* buckles on his $7,500 sword, mounts a saddle heavy with gold trim, and turns his horse northward toward the Rio Grande. The black thread of his life will once more trail straight to San Antonio.

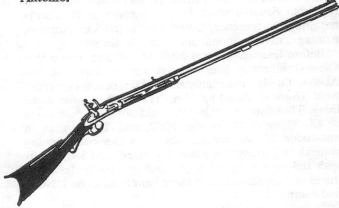

General Houston's orders to James Bowie were specific: "Blow up the Alamo and abandon the place." But Jim Bowie was accustomed to making his own laws; moreover, having been a long-time resident of San Antonio and feeling that he understood the Mexicans better than any of the other Texans, believed his judgment best. Who, after all, knew Texas better than he did? He interpreted Houston's order of January 17, 1836, to destroy the mission fortress as just another test of his independent judgment. Jim Bowie's decision that San Antonio was the "key to Texas" was one of the few decisions upon which he and William Barret Travis agreed.

After the taking of San Antonio by Ben Milam and the expulsion of General Cos and his army, the Texans had fallen into frightful confusion. Austin handed the San Antonio command over to Colonel Edward Burlson, who in turn had conferred it upon Colonel James C. Neill, and the men were daily riding away, going home to be with their families and tend their farms.

When Bowie, in command of the volunteers, decided that he had "rather die in these ditches than give up to the enemy," Colonel Neill was none too enthusiastic about dying in any San Antonio ditch—or anywhere else. So when William Barret Travis arrived with thirty regulars, pleading there was a sickness in his family requiring his presence, Colonel Neill left San Antonio, naming Travis as commander in his absence.

Before leaving, Colonel Neill confided to Travis that General Houston had ordered him to blow up the Alamo. Travis surprisingly showed the colonel an order from Houston directing him, Travis, to do the same thing. Therefore, the Alamo should not have been there at all. Three men—Bowie, Neill, and Travis were in possession of separate orders from the commanding general to destroy the place, fall back, and join forces with the contingent of four hundred men under command of Colonel James Walker Fannin at Goliad. None had complied.

It was about this time that Travis' friend, James Bonham, rode into San Antonio with half a dozen men who had joined him in casting their lots with the Texans' fight for independence. Travis at once dispatched Bonham to Goliad with an urgent appeal for Fannin to move his army posthaste into San Antonio.

A few days later, about the middle of January, David Crockett showed up in San Antonio with twelve Tennesseans. He reported to Travis and asked for Colonel Bowie. Travis told him sourly that Bowie probably was in the Bexar *cantina* near the Military Plaza, where he usually could be found swilling hard liquor. Crockett remarked that a man of Bowie's reputation should not be allowed to drink alone, and asked to be taken to him. Travis, feeling that courtesy demanded it, escorted Crockett and his men to the *cantina*.

It was a singular encounter. Crockett and Bowie struck hands, looked each other up and down. Pleasure was evident at the meeting. David took off his cap, hung it on the muzzle of his long rifle, and leaned the rifle against the end of the bar. Soon Bowie and Crockett were deep into a bottle of whiskey and conversation. Travis felt neglected, left out.

"How many fighting men have you got here?" David asked Jim.

"Counting yourself and your twelve Tennesseans, a total of one hundred and fifty. But we expect reinforcements any day now."

"Who might be in command?"

It was a dangerous question, but David was unaware.

"I'm in command here!" Travis said petulantly, nudging in between the men.

"Not true!" Jim countered.

David gazed at Travis, then at Bowie, saw the two men holding each other with fierce eyes. "Well—who?"

"By Colonel Neill's authority, I'm in command," Travis said.

"Neill had no authority to name you commander, Travis," Jim said succinctly. "I'm in command by General Houston's order."

Travis bristled. "That murder weapon slung from your belt does not give you military authority here," Travis said, insultingly nodding to Jim's sheathed knife.

Jim calmly lifted the knife from its scabbard, laid it

on the bar beside the bottle. "Now, if you care to un-buckle your authority—" he indicated Travis' sword—"we'll settle the matter man to man."

Travis bristled, flushed, seethed. Slowly he unfastened the sword's trappings and placed it on the bar.

Jim's fist shot out viciously, caught Travis squarely on the jaw. The younger man went reeling. It was a powerful blow. A whoop of delight went up from the Tennesseans. Travis picked himself up from the floor slowly, cautiously. He remained on his knees for a moment, rubbing his swelling jaw. Then with the quickness of a cat and the power of a ram he lunged, still in a crouched position, at Jim's middle. His head crashed into Jim's stomach, driving him backward through the door, where he crashed into the dirt outside.

Raging, Jim picked himself up. With a roar he came thundering back into the *cantina*. But Travis was ready for him. A quick one-two from the younger man's fists rocked Jim's head side to side. Jim countered with heavy blows to the belly—powerful, murderous blows. Travis hammered Jim's head. Neither man went down.

David Crocket pushed between them. "Now look here," he said. "This is not fittin' to settle a matter of command. I've a better way."

"And what way is that?" Travis wanted to know.

"Call the men together, let them elect the leader they want."

"Good idea," Jim said, knowing full well that the volunteers outnumbered the regulars.

"Agreed?" David probed Travis.

Reluctantly Travis assented, and gave the order to assemble the men.

To the men gathered in the plaza, David Crockett explained the purpose of the meeting. The men discussed the matter, took a vote. Jim Bowie won easily.

Travis chose to assume that Jim's command was supplementary to his own in the regular army, taking it to mean that Jim was to command only the volunteer group. Jim on the other hand, having no desire to turn command over to a youth in his twenties, a youth who seemed to despise all things Jim valued, chose to regard his as total command.

In the days that followed, Jim Bowie and David Crockett became bosom pals, drinking and cavorting together. Travis, dismayed and disgusted, wrote a letter to Governor Smith:

Dear Sir:
My situation here is truly awkward and delicate. Colonel Neill left me in command, but wishing to give satisfaction to the volunteers here and not wishing to assume command over them, I issued an order for an election of an officer to command them, with the exception of one company that had previously engaged to serve under me.
Bowie was elected, and since his election, has been roaring drunk all the time, and has assumed all command and is proceeding in a most disorderly and irregular manner. If I did not feel my honor and that of my country compromised, I would leave here instantly for some other point with the troops under my immediate command, as I am unwilling to be responsible for the drunken irregularities of any man. I hope you will order immediately some regular troops here as it is more important to occupy this post than I imagined. It is the key to Texas. Without a footing here the enemy can do nothing against us in the colonies . . .

The following day Jim sent Travis further into despair. As Commandant of the Volunteer Forces of San Antonio, he went to the Alamo with a corporal's guard and, with loud huzzas, liberated from military custody D. H. Barrie, who had been tried by Travis' regulars and found guilty of mutiny. Then Jim marched his little contingent to the city jail and ordered the release of a selected number of municipal prisoners.

Another letter went out to Governor Smith, which in part read:

Bowie immediately went to the Alamo for troops and they paraded in the square, under arms, in a tumultuous and disorderly manner; Bowie himself and many of his men being drunk, which has been the case since he has been in command.

A few nights later David Crockett, again acting as a dutiful politician, proposed a sort of reconciliation between the two commanders.

Jim was amenable. "This is no time to quarrel, Travis," he proposed.

Travis showed astonishment, not sure there wasn't a trick somewhere. "I never expected this of you," he said.

"I never expected it of myself, Travis. I think it's time we worked together."

The next day the following letter went out to Governor Smith:

His Excellency Henry Smith
Governor of Texas
Sir:

By an understanding of today Col. James Bowie has the command of the volunteers of the garrison and Col. W. B. Travis of the regular and the volunteer cavalry. All general orders will henceforth be signed by both.

W. Barret Travis
Commd. of Cavalry
James Bowie
Commd. of Volunteers

The differences settled, at least temporarily, the commanders set about strengthening the defense of the old mission fort. Jim labored among the men, building a pallisade of logs and an entrenchment to guard the opening between the church and the wall of the main enclosure. A wooden scaffolding was built inside the walls so that riflemen could fire over the walls. The padres who had built the mission had not provided the place with loopholes.

On the third day of this steady work, when Jim was helping mount the largest cannon in the fort, an eighteen-pounder, on a platform above the chapel, the huge gun began to slip before its wheels were chocked. Jim tried to hold the big field piece in place. No use. It rolled back, careened off the platform, crashing timbers and earth. Jim was thrown ten feet below underneath part of the scaffolding.

The men dug him free and took him to a cot in the old baptistry. Dr. Pollard examined him with a sober face.

"How long, Doc?" Jim asked.

"Ummm . . . Four to six weeks at least. "You've got a fractured hip, lacerated lung, and some crushed nerves."

The next morning, when Jim fully realized the seriousness of his injuries, he summoned Travis and David Crockett to his cot and formally surrendered full command to the twenty-six-year-old lieutenant colonel.

On the twenty-third of February Santa Anna with an army of five thousand soldiers reached the outskirts of San Antonio. Jim Bonham returned to the Alamo with word that in spite of the strongest persuasion he was unable to move Fannin to start his army toward San Antonio. However, thirty-two men under command of Lieutenant Almaron Dickinson from Goliad came through the gates of the Alamo. The garrison now numbered one hundred and eighty-three men, together with a small group of non-combatants which included the wife and child of Lieutenant Dickinson and Sam, Jim Bowie's faithful slave.

Santa Anna sent a courier demanding immediate surrender of the forces and works. Travis answered with a cannon blast of the eighteen-pounder. Santa Anna ran up the red flag of "No Quarter" atop the San Fernando church.

The stage was set for the siege and battle.

Santa Anna by all the rules of performance should not have been in San Antonio at all. It had been a near impossible feat to transport his vast army and its attendant cannon, wagons, and impedimenta across the bleak plain in the month of February. But he was there—with about five thousand troops. And he was determined to destroy the Americans behind the wall of the Alamo.

From Mexico City to San Antonio the route was almost straight north. Santa Anna had chosen Saltillo as the base for the Texas campaign. This town was some three hundred miles from the Rio Grande, while from the Rio Grande it was another one hundred and fifty miles to San Antonio.

At Saltillo, his flair for organization was employed to the full during the month of January. This campaign was to be his greatest triumph. Already his was the foremost name in the southern half of the New World. The glories he anticipated as a result of this northern campaign would awaken Washington and London and Paris to the importance of the name Santa Anna; indeed he would be a man reknown round the world, a man to be reckoned with—like his hero Napoleon Bonaparte was in his day and prime. Secretly in his mind the President-General had determined that this war against the "pirates" in Texas would be of such a horrendous magnitude that it would put his sanguine Zacatecas Campaign and the Medina slaughter in the class of minor skirmishes. Never again would foreigners dare invade sovereign Mexican territory—after he finished with the brazen *norteamericanos*.

A correspondent of *El Mosquiete Mexicano* accompanying the campaign described Santa Anna as "a man about five feet ten inches in height with a slight build, intelligent and expressive countenance, dark hair, and an olive complexion." The report stated he was possessed of excellent manners, read and spoke only his own language; and although he loved luxury and public display, he observed moderation in eating and drinking. He valued money only for what it procured for him. He desired to acquire great estates and vast power. He understood his countrymen and generally supported the causes and interests of the army and church. As a military man he was "not a good general," but as an organizer his talents were "unrivaled." He knew little of strategy and demonstrated neither a diligence for details nor the ability to carry out his intricately constructed plans.

His problem at Saltillo was money. To raise and reorganize the troops was a considerable undertaking in itself. The Mexican army was an appalling sieve. It had already virtually emptied the treasury. But Santa Anna put himself to this task with his usual fine disregard of governmental economy and alert consideration for his own pecuniary betterment. He made the church contribute until the bishops screamed, but this was not sufficient. Thrusting aside the house of Esnaurrisar which had floated other government issues and which offered more advantageous terms, he turned to a firm of notorious *agiotistas*—as the Mexican call loan sharks—Rubio and Erraz, to underwrite the expedition. These accommodating gentlemen supplied four million pesos at a

rate amounting to forty-eight percent a year. The most
favorable contracts for supplies went to the President-
General's family and friends; and bond issues bearing
on the loan were found among Santa Anna's effects after his defeat at the battle of San Jacinto.

Whatever questionable means was employed, it was
a fact that by the end of January the glittering *Generalissimo* watched as six thousand drilled and equipped
men marched in grand review. They passed parade in
good order. The officers in uniforms of dark blue with
scarlet fronts, the dragoons with their shiny breast
plates, the *zapadores* displaying their ladders, crowbars,
and other implements of engineering, and endless rows
of infantry in neat uniforms of blue with white belts
worn in an X across their breasts.

Santa Anna sat his horse and watched with gleaming
eyes. These troops gave him his greatest pride. Of all
the armies he had commanded this was the most Napo-
leonic—if a bit oddly antique. Many of the weapons
were relics from the days of Waterloo. Against the rifles
of the Americans, made principally in Pennsylvania by
transplanted Germans and accurate at a distance of two
hundred yards, the Mexican *escopetas* barely carried
seventy yards. But no matter. The Mexican army by
weight of sheer numbers would win out against the
Texans.

The *Generalissimo* in his speech that day warned the
soldiers that "civil wars are always bloody," and assured them that this one would be a war "without remorse or mercy." So saying, he announced a special
Legion of Honor for those fighting against "invaders of
Mexican territory." In his impressive, deep voice he
stated:

"The insignia of the Legion of Honor shall be a cross
or a star of five radiants. The center shall be surrounded by a crown or laurel; at one side shall be the national arms, on the other the motto, *Honor, Valor, and
Country*. On the reverse side of the medal in the center
shall be the name of the campaign or action for which
this decoration is awarded with the words *Republica*

Mexicana. The cross shall be of silver for the cavalry-men, but of gold for all officers. The grand crosses will wear a band with red border on each edge across the right and left shoulders. This is purely a military order and shall be considered the highest honor the Mexican soldier can merit. None besides soldiers ought to obtain it."

Morale high, the troops began moving out of Saltillo on the day after the review. Winding north into the bare, dry hills of Coahuila, Santa Anna's greatest army presented a glittering display of military ostentation. The *Generalissimo,* surrounded by his splendidly uniformed dragoons, proceeded ahead. After his party, rode the cavalry. To the rear plodded the infantry. Behind all crawled the supply train, strung out along the rocky trail—eighteen hundred pack mules, three hundred two-wheel carts, two dozen cannons, and sixty-two wagons drawn by four oxen each. Compounded among the troops were the *soldaderas,* the women who followed their men to war. Aside from the companionship they offered, they foraged and cooked for the men. Santa Anna had not bothered to provide any formal commissary.

To the rear of all this array of men, vehicles, cannon, women and children, straggled another army of sorts—the sutlers who trailed the army with wagons and carts and barrows loaded with processed foodstuff, whiskey, liquor, wines, tobacco, cooking utensils, pots, and pans, anything that might sell.

Santa Anna, soldiers, *soldaderas,* sutlers—all pushed on, moving ever into the barren and wild northern reaches of Mexico. The countryside itself offered no assistance. In this harsh and arrid land were no food crops, only scattered chaparral and other desert bushes. But on they went, sore feet, parched throats, constantly hungry.

Scarcely on their way, water became a problem. It had been a dry winter and suddenly there was neither sufficient grass nor water for the horses and mules and oxen. Some fell from *mal de lengua,* a swelling of the

397

tongue from thirst and dry fodder; others died from drinking of stagnant pools. Many more died simply for lack of grazing grass, which Travis with his ranging cavalry had burned. The men, too, began falling. Santa Anna himself was seized with an inflammation of the stomach. The troops were put on half ration and the officers were forced to shift for themselves on one *real* a day—about twelve and one-half cents. Hundreds were struck with dysentery. Others succumbed to fever and spotted itch. The ill-clad paramour-*soldaderas,* unable to forage for food in this infertile land, died with their mates. Over three hundred fell from pneumonia and exhaustion.

Early during the march the correspondent of *El Mosquite Mexicano* had conceded "there have been sufferings, but these ills only spur the men to greater efforts." Now the paper printed grim accounts of the campaign: "Many have tried to desert. Many succeeded only to die, lost in the vastness of the desert. More have been caught and returned to the ranks."

The journey to the Rio Grande proved to be a heartbreaking ordeal for man and beast. Some of Santa Anna's officers had protested the use of this route and had urged an attack by sea, to cut off supplies for the rebels. This Santa Anna was utterly opposed to. He had received word of General Cos' defeat at San Antonio and was determined to strike directly for that point.

So on he led his suffering and dwindling army, galloping far in the lead. Around him were his personal bodyguard-dragoons, well-fed and splendid in their shining helmets and bright trappings. Just behind, his ornate carriage rattled and swayed over the rough plain, followed by his baggage train loaded with the luxuries befitting the "Napoleon of the West"—his red and black-striped marquee, his huge royal bed with its feather-lined comfort, his private liquors and wines, salted meat and delicacies, his medicine chest well supplied with bottles of his favorite opiate—sulphate of morphine, his tea caddy and cream pitcher, his monogrammed china, the decanters with little gold stoppers, his silver chamber pot . . .

Behind, the hungry troops broke rank to pick prickly pears from scrubs aspiring to the dignity of trees as they reared themselves on fibrous trunks only to the height of ten or twelve feet. they chewed bitter mesquite and picked reddish berries from writhing and twisted branches that reminded the men of souls in torment.

But the march went on.

At last, on February 12, the Rio Grande. With a cry of delight from the troops, the army raced down the hard, flat plain toward the river and stormed into the old Spanish town of Presidio de Rio Grande. General Ramirez y Sesma was waiting at the military headquarters with one thousand, five hundred and forty-one men, insufficient replacements for those who had fallen or deserted along the way.

When Santa Anna crossed the Rio Grande he was master of a vast country which reached from Yucatan to Oregon, and whose area was greater than that of any other nation in the world, save Russia. This extraordinary man held the future of all the southwest in his hands. Had his mission been a success—beyond San Jacinto—his portrait would today hang in the gallery of governors in seven American states.

After resting his depleted army Santa Anna moved the force on to the Texas border at Laredo, arriving there two days after Christmas. General Cos with the remnant of his expelled troops awaited his arrival there. Santa Anna issued peremptory orders for Cos to violate his word of honor given to Travis and Bowie that he would never again fight against Texans, and to join the expedition. This raised the Mexican force once more to about five thousand. After being the elegant guest of honor at a ball given by Mexican partisans in his honor, the President-General pressed the combined army on toward San Antonio.

The Texas population had changed greatly since the young, raw Lieutenant Santa Anna had learned to despise *norteamericanos* at the battle of Medina twenty-three years earlier. But he still considered them barbarians to be terrorized—and eliminated.

On February 20, the army reached the Medina River, scene of the horrible butcheries of Arredondo's soldiers. A mexican priest met the commander and told him that the Americans in San Antonio—only about a dozen miles distant—were diverting themselves at a *danza* that night and could easily be surprised. Good! He'd slaughter them all by an overwhelming night attack.

But the ammunition train had been left on the other bank and as the troops were making ready to move, the Medina River suddenly rose as a result of a wet norther which had blown over the country on that day. The swollen river was dangerous and it was impossible to make a crossing to get the ammunition. Santa Anna fumed. An opportunity missed.

Six days later, on February 26, Santa Anna's army marched into San Antonio. Most of the inhabitants had fled at the approach of the Mexicans. And the little band of Americans had fortified themselves in the Alamo.

The Texans, outnumbered at least thirty to one, were undisciplined, untrained, divided in command. The Mexicans were united in both organization and habits of a lifetime. Centuries of a master-slave society had made of them stand-by roberts, oiled and ready to bend and dash about to the will of a ruthless master such as Santa Anna. But the handful of Texans inside the walls of the Alamo, each to his own deserts, was above all master of his own soul and the maker of his own destiny. And each man carried in his bosom a dream of "freedom— individual liberty". And they, each to the man, were clearly willing to die fighting for that dream.

THE ALAMO

Two men sit on their haunches at the foot of the wall, inside the Alamo, their muzzle-loaders across their laps. Through the night shadows they can see the outline of each other's face, bewhiskered and unwashed. Both are wearing buckskins and homespun. They are passing the stub of a brown cigarette between them, and as each draws deep of its sweet-scented smoke, the glow casts a red pall over their faces. Thinking the same thought, they both chuckle. "Old Louis Rose shore wuz a-goin' when he got across the river, warn't he, Slim?"

"He shore wuz! A-drippin' wet and high-tailin' it like a scared cat. I declare, I never seen a man so anxious to git to Noo Orlean. Reckon he'll make it, Will?"

"Shore, Slim, I reckon he will, at that. When we let him down the wall on that blanket and the Mex didn't git him right then and thar, I figured he had a chance."

"He shore wuz lucky. They'd shore carve 'im up if'n they'd ketch 'im. But I reckon he got away, all right. Here, gimme puff o' thet loco weed, Will. Reckon this stuff'll blur our aim?"

"Naw. The Mex smoke it all the time. Makes 'em feel kinna lost to the world, that's all."

"Makes me see my wife and kids back home—just like they wuz right here. How's it make you feel?"

"Like everythin's gonna come out just fine."

The two fall silent. From over the wall floats the

sound of clomping sandals and the scraping and creaking of equipment being moved into position, the low rumble of Spanish.

"Say, Will . . . I been thinkin'. Do you ever wisht you wuz back home in Kaintuck?"

Will takes a draw of the weed, looks searchingly at his buddy, then drops his eyes. "My old granddad used to say, 'Wish in one hand and shit in t'other and see which one fills up first."

"Will, we caint beat the Mex this time, can we?"

"Naw, but we shore can kill a passel of 'em."

Lying helpless on his cot in the darkness of the dank little room in the Alamo, Jim Bowie swears silently. The fever sweeping through his racked body stimulates his brain, giving him a false sense of euphoria and brings an urge over him to weep. But Jim Bowie cannot weep. He has never wept in his life. Were he capable of tears he would welcome them now. Not out of self pity. But because of the cold fury that shakes his frame for not being able to stand up and die fighting. James Bowie, the most feared and respected fighter of the century—dying of natural causes!

Propped on an elbow, he gazes for a long time at the door through which Travis had disappeared moments before. "Jim, I'll say goodbye now," the young commandant had said, looking down with compassion upon the felled giant. The two men had clasped hands warmly, each forcing a little smile.

And Travis was gone.

Still gazing at the door through the dimness of the room, his lips barely moving, Jim mutters some dimly remembered lines:

> The boast of heraldry, the pomp of power,
> And all that beauty, all that wealth e'er gave,
> Awaits alike the inevitable hour.
> The paths of glory lead but to the grave.

Sam shuffles to the bedside. "Marse Jim, wuz you prayin'?"

"No, Sam. Just grumbling to myself—thinking of something Rezin used to quote."

Jim thinks of the teen-age mother who has for days sat on a pallet in the sanctuary of his sick quarters. The vision of her young lieutenant-husband kissing her and holding the little girl in his arms comes vividly to his fever-swimming mind. He can hear Susanna Dickinson pleading, "What will happen to us, Al?" And her husband tenderly reassuring her. "You'll be all right. Oh, Sue . . . my darling!" Jim Bowie's mind, pyretically energized, envisions many things. But the wildest of dreams cannot tell him what is to happen to that babe in Lieutenant Almaron Dickinson's arms: that she will be christened by the State of Texas "Babe of the Alamo," that she will be feted, indulged, and heroized; and, before entering a public grave in Oakwood cemetery in Austin, she will become a Civil War camp follower, leaving behind her a trail of wantonness throughout the South and West.

Jim hears other voices. *"Jamie, my darling . . ."* The vision of Ursula, his wife—his life—hovers in his flushed mind, her dark liquid eyes overflowing with love for him. So little time, it seemed, they had been together. *"But Jamie,"* she would say when he was leaving, *"must you go away again?"* The last goodbye was the most painful, when he sent her south to Monclova to escape the danger of the yellow plague, the *vomito* as the Mexicans called it. She had clung to him ever so tenderly. With the strange mysterious forboding of a woman deeply in love she had fought against this parting. *"Jamie, my husband, please! Please come with me."* But he had sent her alone and it was too late. Already the yellow fumes of death were coursing through her veins.

How many times during those days of waiting had he climbed the circular staircase to the bell tower of the mission and, gazing at the white walls of the town, thought of the happy days he had known there. Once more, for a little while, he would have Ursula at his side, hear the musical ring of her laughter, feel the

403

touch of her hand upon his cheek. Then he would put the vision away, climb down the tower, thankful that in the action of the revolutionary movement, whatever its value, he could find some surcease from his loneliness. Ursula was too good for him he now realized, as most men do when it is too late. Jim thought of the two great treasures in his life—Paula and Ursula. Luckier than most men, he had had not one but two headlands. And he had not even known it.

Thinking, thinking of the long trail he has woven behind him, a colorful and fascinating pattern—forty years of wonderful excitement. A surge of deep affection rises in Jim Bowie as he dwells on the brave men who will die with him here. Brave and fearless men. But are not rebels and outlaws always brave and fearless? Here are men from many states and several nations. Bob McKinney of Tennessee, Isaac White of Louisiana, Dan Cloud of Kentucky, Bill Johnson from Philadelphia, Will Lightfoot of Virginia, Robert W. Ballentine from Scotland, James Durkin from England, John Garvin of Missouri, Charley Zanco from Denmark, Chuck Hawkins from Ireland, Charley Nelson from Charleston, and Gregorio Esparza from San Antonio and Jose Marie Guerrero from Laredo. These men, whose faces come clearly to Jim's mind, are personal friends; and there are others, faces, names, men who should live a long and productive life, tilling their land, making love with their wives, raising fine sons and slim, pretty daughters, and, in old age, die peacefully in their own beds, in their own homes, surrounded by their own flesh and blood. These mortal men, who for thirteen days have left their offal on the ground in the cattle pen at the southeast corner of the mission yard or have buried it in shallow holes beside their sleeping pads, will within a few hours meet their last enemy, death, and then, their bodies stilled, will join in stench and decay with their feculence.

For the first time in his life Jim Bowie is sorry he cannot cry. Suddenly there is the sweet taste of life in his nostrils. From deep in his memory come poetic words, heard long ago from the lips of his religious mother, Elve. "Life, like a dome of many-colored glass, stains the white radiance of Eternity, until death tramples it to fragments." Jim pounds his head, trying to dislodge the vision from his mind. The men of the Alamo! The most impelling event motivating the lives of these men was the American Revolution—in so recent a point in time. And the most powerful document influencing them was the Declaration of Independence. Whatever their personal histories and characters and crimes, they are willing to die for what David Crockett's Tennesseans like to call "our rights."

In the yard, Colonel Travis, Jim Bonham, and Lieutenant Dickinson are busy stationing the men, distributing powder, ball, and lighting fuses. Travis is especially attentive to the cannon, since he himself will command the artillery. Save for the two four-pounders guarding the low eight-foot wall and three twelve-pounders put in position on the earthen mound extending to the level of the chapel's east roof, the remainder of the cannon are mounted on the roof of the chapel itself. The little force in the Alamo is numerically insufficient to man the entire wall, but with the cannon thus strategically positioned Travis will be able to rake the enemy upon every area of approach. The main powder supply for all arms, that used for the riflemen as well as that of the cannoneers, he orders brought and stored in the sacristy of the chapel.

Dave Crockett and his twelve loyal Tennesseans have taken position on the eight-foot wall. David, standing, is ramming a charge down the barrel of his rifle. Every day since the beginning of the siege, the figure of this man, his coon cap covering his red head, has been seen on the wall firing his long rifle, and cooly standing there to reload. He has become a familiar tableaux to the Mexicans. They have learned to keep out of range of his deadly far-firing gun. They know his name is Crockett and that he calls his rifle "Betsy." Corrupting and compounding the two, they refer to him as "Kwockety." Travis inspects the little force of Tennesseans, is quite satisfied, gives David a cheery salutation. He has no instructions for these men. Each knows what he is to do: kill Mexicans.

Santa Anna, reading a pamphlet while pacing the fore of his marquee, suddenly trembles with fury, his face reddening. It is a pamphlet labeled: SANTA ANNA'S DICTIONARY, a sample of the surreptitious literature that is being distributed in Mexico by those the general-dictator has suppressed. He reads. ARMY: a collection of automatons which are moved like pieces on a chess board at the will of the player. When they lack bread give them false finery and they are contented. When they become uneasy discipline them and they are silent. PATRIOTISM: The art of deceiving the public by giving them false facts. OATH: A ridiculous formula which I am accustomed to go through with and which I break daily. PATRIA: A large area of land which I am able to dispose of at pleasure as of my own house. MEXICAN: Poor devils whom I have deceived whenever it suits me and whom I control by kicks.

He flings the booklet aside. "Where did you get this seditious nonsense, Colonel Almonte?"

"I found it in the hands of one of your officers, Sir."

"Bring him to me!"

The officer is brought before Santa Anna. He is a cavalry captain and wears the silver cross of the "Legion of Honor," Santa Anna's newest, much coveted metal.

"Captain, have you been circulating this trash among the soldiers?"

"I took it from an infantryman this morning, *Mi General estimado*. I do not know his name, nor can I identify him, Sir."

"Captain, I regret that you shall not be with me when I plant the Mexican flag in Washington. Adios!" To Almonte: "Have this man shot."

The officer is whisked away. Santa Anna addresses his staff. "Gentlemen, the attack shall begin."

"General, may I say something?"

"Speak, Almonte."

"It will cost much."

Santa Anna reaches for his plumed hat. "It is of no importance what the cost may be."

He places the hat on his head, glances at himself in a mirror that has been hung for his convenience on one of the supporting poles of the marquee. He then takes from a drawer underneath his map counter a small bottle, pries the cork stopper from its large mouth with a pen knife, carefully measures a small portion of the snow-white powder on the knife's blade, places it on his tongue and washes it down with a sip of wine. He replaces the stopper in the bottle, which is labeled SULPHATE OF MORPHINE. Beneath this is a skull-and-crossbones poison symbol printed in red. He steps outside, surveys his staff, thrusts his right hand inside his jacket. As he feels the first wave of euphoria, his hand gently squeezes his left mammory and he gives the awaited order for the attack to begin. "Sound the bugles!"

David Crockett is supremely calm, standing tall atop the wall of his Tennessee volunteers on either side of him. He fondles "Betsy" lovingly. His eyes travel over the marvelous weapon, taking in every detail—barrel, bolt, breach, hammer. In the first light he can distinguish the maker of the piece incised into its housing: *N. SHENNFELT—CLARION, PA.* And as he turns the rifle in his hands his finger runs along a line of fine Old English engraving, mute testimony to a man whose marksmanship is legendary: *"Presented By The Young Men of Philadelphia, To The Honorable David Crockett."*

Suddenly the air is filled with the assassin-wild notes of the *deguello*. "Here they come, boys!" David raises his rifle, centers the sight in the middle of the forehead of a charging Mexican. He gently squeezes the trigger. The Mexican stumbles forward, his carbine slipping from his hands.

The man's name will be revealed as Juan Basquez, the first soldier to die in the storming of the Alamo. Beginning on the morrow he would have had nine years more to serve in Santa Anna's army before returning to his home in Durango, where he no doubt would have taken up his trade as shoemaker. A conscripted soldier, he had tried to desert and had first been forced to run a gauntlet of troopers beating him with rifles and iron ramrods, then sentenced to ten years service without pay. Eschewing the opportunity to again desert, as two thousand others had done in the march into Texas, Juan Basquez, in the cold dawn of March 6, found himself hemmed in by a ring of bayonets and tiers of muskets at his back charging an enemy he did not know or care about. He died in the first volley, mounting a common denominator with the one hundred and eighty-three Americans behind the Alamo walls: he died cursing Santa Anna. His only claim to glory will be that he was the first to fall in the assault upon the Alamo, and scriveners will note that he died with a David Crockett musket ball in his brain.

On they come, a human wave of soldiers, a dark mass of men, across the plain, little spurts of red and yellow flame licking out of their carbines. The barbaric no-quarter bugle call mingles with the terrible yells and screams and the deafening *WHAM-WHAM-WHAM* of the muskets, the *BAA—ROMM—BAAA—ROMMM* of the cannon, and the *PONGG-PONGG-BEE-ZZZING* of pistol shots. But they continue to come, wave after wave. The sullen roar of Travis' cannon atop the fort shatters the night, belching grape and cannister and fire, cutting them down. The deadly explosions take their terrible toll.

Los zapadores scurry up their ladders, yelling and firing. "Cut 'em down, men!" The Tennessee stalwarts fire their muskets, discharge their pistols, club and hack them back. Ladders are seized and thrown from the wall. Mexicans drop from the rungs screaming. No time to reload, the Tennesseans smash skulls with the barrels and butts of their guns. They split heads and hack off arms with their knives. David, swinging his rifle by the barrel, lays out Mexicans on top of Mexicans. The enemy fall to the ground below, brained, piling dead on dead. "Knock their goddamn heads off, boys! Roll 'em back!"

Travis, his eyes burning like firebrands, is all over the roof of the chapel at once, catlike, excited, exhilarated. The cannoneers are inspired by his fire and zeal. They work like demons. Brandishing his sword, he spurs them on. *BAA—ROMMM!* Flame, thunder, and lead belch from the cannon. Another fuse is lowered to the firing plate, another cannon lurches, belches flame and ball, rolls back. "At it, men! Fuses!" *BAA—ROMMM!* Again. Again. "Steady with the big one, boys. Aim 'er! Touch 'er off!" *BAA—ROMM!* "More fuses, more powder, more balls!" Thick smoke hangs over everything. The acrid sulphur-based gunpowder fumes smart the eyes and choke the lungs. Travis, notwithstanding, is overtaken with a fine, excited sense of well-being. His cannon and men are doing effective work. The Mexican lines, mercilessly raked, are being blasted back. "Never mind the heat, boys. Reload! Fire!" His cannons are killing, killing, killing! *"Victory or Death!"*

The attack on Crockett's sector having been repulsed, the Mexicans mount an assault upon the sixteen-foot south wall, where a company of cavalry under Lieutenant Dickinson are stationed on a platform. The Mexicans hoist their ladders, scurry up like frenzied rats. The carbines of Dickinson's men turn them back. Santa Anna's cavalry drives the fleeing Mexicans back upon the wall. With the unreasoning fury of madmen they are wild to get over the wall. In desperate confusion they imagine there is safety on the other side. Certainly, behind them is death. Dickinson's men stand like oaks. A head pops up over the rampart, is blasted at close range. A face becomes a bloody, powderburned mass of flesh and blood. A head becomes torn skull bones, scattered brains. Horrible screams pierce the air. Guns empty, the men on the platform slash with swords, knives, and hammer with sword hilts. The

Mexicans drop their carbines in amazement at the Texans' ferocity, screaming, *"Diablos! Diablos!"*

"Where'd he git you, Will?"

"In the neck. I reckon I ain't gonna do no more Mex killin' today."

"I'll git you over to the chapel."

"Naw. Leave me be. I ain't got a chance. But you have. High-tail it, Slim, ole buddy, like old Louie Rose did."

"I ain't leavin' you."

The two men sit there in the dirt, looking helplessly at each other. Blood covers the wounded man's face, flows over his buckskin shirt.

"You got one o' them Mex weeds left?" the blood-covered man asks.

His friend fumbles in his pocket, comes out with a stub, lights it and puts it between the lips of the dying man. "Here, draw on thet real hard, Will. It'll take yore mind off them goddamn Mex."

"You do like I tole you, Slim. Leave me be, and mind out fer yourself."

The friend takes the fiery stub from the lips of the dying man, draws deeply of its contents. "I'll git 'im, pal. I'll git that goddamn Mex thet killed you. I'll git a dozen!"

He puts the stub back between the bloody lips of his buddy, scampers up the wall. He stands there a moment, knife in hand. Then with a ferocious yell, he leaps, spread-eagled down into a mob of milling, stewing Mexicans.

"General! Mi Generaldo! Our *zapadores* are driven back." It is Colonel Almonte, out of breath, on the run.

"Turn them round with the cavalry. Drive them back to the wall."

"But, *Muy estimado Generaldo,* there are none left to turn round."

"None? What are you saying Almonte?"

"Of a thousand *zapadores* over eight hundred are

410

lying in their blood at the foot of the wall. The rest have run, screaming that the *americanos* are devils.

Supreme General Santa Anna paces up and down. His eyes, their brilliance heightened by drug, are glittering beads of onyx. His face is suffused with fury, the frustrating fury that overtakes a man of extreme ego whose ambition is suddenly defeated through the weakness or failure of others. He turns to Almonte.

"Colonel Almonte! Ready all reserves. Every man! We will hit that wall with everything. Devils you say?"

"Yes, *Muy estimado Generaldo!*"

Suddenly Santa Anna looks tired, and a little sad. Almonte goes about the business of organizing the final assault. Over the clash and hustle of his army, the wild, violent notes of the *deguello* rise. Santa Anna's face becomes constrained with anger. Words form on his lips.

An imprecation? A supplication? "I might have spared them. Now? This is where the pavement ends. The *americanos* will see the very Devil himself on that wall!"

While the Mexicans regroup, the little band of Americans inside the battered bastion move their wounded into the barracks and rally the able-bodied men. Surgeon Amos Pollard, working alone—Doctors Edward F. Mitchasson and Jessie G. Thompson are among those killed—moves swiftly among the bleeding and dying, staunching a spurt of blood here, applying a tourniquet there, shaking his head hopelessly over a torn body. Many he sends back to the wall with, "Only a scratch, my boy."

"Fifty-one dead, seventy-eight wounded," Dr. Pollard announces to Lieutenant Dickinson, who is mounting the roof to the cannon.

"Where's Travis?" Dr. Pollard asks.

"Down. Over yonder by the wall. How many of the wounded can still fight, doctor?"

"About half."

His black bag swinging, Dr. Pollard strides in the direction Lieutenant Dickinson has pointed. He finds Travis lying prostrate with his face in the dirt. He gently turns him over and he knows instantly by the leaden inertness of the body that Travis is dead. As he looks into that youthful face whose slitted eyes reveal sickly white lines beneath half-drawn lids, the mouth falls open, making a dark little hole in that fair and hopeful countenance. There is a single, neat bullet hole in Travis' temple. As Pollard lifts the body to place it alongside the other dead nearby, Travis' pistol slips from his dead hand. Later Jim Bowie's slave Sam will tell early day Alamo historians that Colonel Travis was the first American to fall in the battle. Some of those scribblers will write that Travis ended his own life by firing a pistol ball into his brain.

The final assault is launched from all sides. The Mexican cannon *BAA—ROMMM* hard and steady. Musket, pistol, and human noise is close and fierce. Streaks of light, shooting up over the eastern edge of the world cast an eerie pallor upon the remnant of the little American force pitifully scattered along the expanse of the walls, and reveal to the enemy their depleted condition. Ninety-three men to defend nearly three acres of enclosure. The Mexicans charge from every direction, fiercely driven by their determined and threatened officers. Cavalry, cannoneers, *zapadores,* clerks, and cooks are climbing upon the walls.

The cannon, now under the sole command of Lieutenant Dickinson, scatter and halt them until he runs out of cannonballs. He rams nail, scrap iron, rock—whatever comes to hand—down the muzzles of the guns. He cannot fire his cannon too near the wall without running the risk of cutting down his own men. He now directs his fire at Santa Anna's baggage and rear guard. From his vantage point on the roof, he sees, with cold and bitter heart, Mexicans rolling over the walls at every quarter.

Crockett and his men are among the first overrun. "Fall back, boys! But slowly. Keep firing! We'll make a stand inside!" The Tennesseans cover their retreat with pistols, clubs, and knives. Only Crockett and two stalwarts make it. The others lie strewn over the bloody ground between the wall and the barracks.

Sam leaves the opening from where he has been watching, comes to Bowie's cot. "De Mexicans are tryin' to git in, Marse Jim! Dey's comin' over de wall! What we do now?"

"Nothing, Sam. My pistols! Give them to me."

David Crockett and his two remaining Tennesseans have made a stand in a small room at the end of a hallway of the barracks. For the moment they have fought the Mexicans to a standstill. The Mexicans, wary of dead-shot "Kwockety," are loath to rush him. "Three pistols, three muskets," David says. "You men load. Pass 'em to me."

Outside, a Mexican officer is prodding his soldiers. A lethal fire cuts them down as quickly as they enter the hallway. Firing from a narrow doorway from behind a pile of dead Mexicans, David is not an easy target. The Mexican officer realizes he must take a drastic measure if he is to put an end to this terrible slaughter. He orders his soldiers out of the barracks. There is a small conference, a respite while his men remove the bodies from the hallway. David listens, wonders, does the only thing he can do—waits, guns loaded. Silence, save for the yells and screams as the Mexicans roam through the other rooms killing the wounded as they lay bleeding and dying.

Listening, David hears a passage of words from one of the nearby rooms that turns his blood to ice. "Don't kill me! Here—see—I have money. Lots of money. I give you! Here, take it. Spare my life!"

"Si, Señor. You got money! What else you got?"

"My watch! Take it. You won't kill me, will you? Listen! You know who I am? I'm David Crockett. Understand? David Crockett. I'm a congressman of the United States! You are a brave soldier. I'm a brave fighter, too. You don't want to kill me!"

"This is all you got, Señor? Money? . . . Watch?"

"That's all . . ."

BLOOWAM!

Comes the sound of heavy steel on the stone floor. The Mexicans are dragging a small cannon into the hallway. The cannon's muzzle is trained on the room in which David is barricaded. It belches fire, smoke, and a charge of grape, wreaking terrific havoc. David's right arm is blown off, his companions killed instantly. Trailing blood and strings of pulverized flesh and bone, David steps into the clearing of the hallway.

Yelling fiercely, he cries, "I'm still here! Come and get me!"

A hail of gunfire cuts him down.

Mexicans are everywhere, swarming over the yard. They go from body to body, bayoneting, hacking, mutilating the wounded and dead alike. It is barbaric, an incontinent feast of blood. It is the code of the *deguello·*

Lieutenant Dickinson leaps from the roof of the chapel, a lighted fuse in hand, Travis' last order burning in his brain. "When they come blow up the chapel—powder magazines and all!"

Dickinson halts in his tracks, frozen between duty to obey an order from his dead commander and love for his wife and child. He does not have to resolve her terrible dilemna. A dozen Mexicans charge upon him, carbines drawn. He dashes into the chapel. Multiple shots ring out behind him. He falls in the doorway. The fuse in his hand drops to the floor, burns brightly, then blinds out, trailing a little feather of white smoke.

The Mexicans tramp over Lieutenant Dickinson's body, bayoneting, hacking. They crowd into the room where Jim Bowie is propped up on his cot, a pistol in each hand. Jim squeezed both triggers. One arm jerks back with the impact, the other pistol misfires. He throws them at the Mexicans, draws his knife. *"Here, Jim, take Old Bowie. She'll never snap."* His brother Rezin's voice. A dozen bayonets converge upon him, and he hears other voices. "Goddamn you, Bowie, you've killed me!" And still another voice, soft, warm, and musical. *"But Jamie, you're always going away . . ."*

A bright warming Texas sun bathes the Alamo courtyard. A profound quiet lies over everything. Only the drip, drip of blood can be heard. A cock crows mournfully in the distance. Half a mile away at the chapel of San Fernando church several old women are kneeling and offering prayers for the dead, Mexican and American. A maiden with Latin skin and solemn eyes comes into the Alamo, looking among the dead. She finds the American who had become her lover before the siege, folds his arms, soaks her handkerchief in his blood and slips away to Sunday morning mass.

Supreme General Santa Anna, accompanied by his staff, inspects the battleground. The stillness is broken by a group of soldiers, now drunk, rushing out of the barracks carrying the body of a big red-headed man high on their bayonets. "Kwockety! Kwockety!" they are crying.

"Kwockety?" Santa Anna inquires.

"David Crockett," Almonte explains.

"Yes, Crockett. He's the tall one with the long rifle who's been trying to pick me off." He looks around, sweeps the compound with an arm. "Burn them. Make a pyre outside. Burn them all!" Then in a quiet voice. "But gather our own dead and give them a decent burial."

"Very good, Sir." Almonte's voice assumes an apologetic tone. "But *Muy Grado Supreme del Generaldo,* there will be over a thousand graves."

Entering the chapel, Santa Anna finds Susanna Dickinson cowering in a corner of Bowie's cubicle. Sam is beside her, holding the child. Santa Anna uncovers the little girl's face. "Take them to my marquee," he orders. "See that they are not harmed. I will need someone to take the message to Houston. Texans must know how we deal with insurgents!" Pointing to the bloody mass on the cot, "What's that?"

"Colonel James Bowie," Almonte replies.

Santa Anna approaches the cot, gazes silently at the horribly mutilated body of the man who was a legend. Santa Anna removes his hat. "Bowie was too brave a man to be treated like a dog. Bury him with my

415

soldiers." He looks at Almonte, thin thoughtfully at the stone floor. "A thousand dead, you say?"

Replacing his plumed hat, he strides out. At the doorway he pauses, his last fiber of mercy spent. "It is of little consequences. Burn Bowie with the other rebels."

EPILOGUE

It is known to Satanists and admitted by certain pietists that one of the Devil's favorite roosts is the wall of the Alamo. If you are in Texas and if you visit San Antonio, you likely will go to San Fernando church and gaze upon the white marble crypt that is said to contain the bones of Travis, Bowie, and Crockett. And if you are a nocturnal soul and are abroad in the city between the hours of midnight and dawn, and you happen to wander beneath the southeast wall of the old mission-fortress, you might be one who can see him. Believers say he sits there—old Beelzebub himself—elegantly decked out in early nineteenth-century dress coat, bottle-green pantaloons, flaming waistcoat, and rolled-brim, high-crowned top hat, having the time of his life. Guests of the Menger Hotel, cheek-and-jowl with the Alamo, sometimes complain that they can hear him in the early hours just before dawn out there—laughing like hell . . .